3/00

Old
Wounds

Nora Kelly

Poisoned Pen Press

M

3 | 0 0 BT 12 ⁹⁵ ~

Poisoned
Pen
Press

Copyright © 1998 by Nora Kelly.

First U.S. Edition 1999

10 9 8 7 6 5 4 3 2 1

Library of Congress Catalog Card Number: 99-66273

ISBN: 1-890208-25-6

Poisoned Pen Press
6962 E. First Ave. Ste 103
Scottsdale, AZ 85251
www.poisonedpenpress.com
sales@poisonedpenpress.com

Printed in the United States of America

To Sharon

CHAPTER 1

For the last mile or two she'd been alone on the road. Her lights sliced through the misty autumn darkness. Signs gleamed and slid past. Nearly home, now. But where was everybody? There was always traffic on the Post Road.

The car climbed another slope. In the daytime, you could see the light on the Hudson from the top, a brightening beyond the trees. Tonight, Gillian saw a traffic jam. Damn, she muttered. She was already late. At the tail of the line she pulled on to the shoulder and peered ahead. The box of a jackknifed semi-trailer lay across the road. A white blaze of headlights came from the traffic halted on the far side. Car doors were open.

There was no point in waiting. She could take the back road by the ponds. She made a U-turn a few yards behind the last car and started north again. Estelle would be worried, and worry was bad for her heart. Should have bought a car phone, Gillian thought. At least she'd gotten a cordless for Estelle; it would be right next to her on the sofa unless she'd lost it again. The last time, Gillian had found it in the fridge.

A distant white spot enlarged, became a floodlit rectangle: the sign for the Dutch House. There were public phones in the bar. She parked the car and got out. The long white porch and weathered fieldstone walls looked the same as ever. A neon martini glass glowed blue behind a mullioned window.

The tavern had once been a house, built by a Dutch settler. Then in seventeen-something it became an inn, a stop on the post road from New York to Albany. The rooms upstairs had still been rented when Gillian was a child. 'Washington Slept Here', read a sign over the stairwell. It was possible, but if Washington had slept in every bed that claimed him, the British would have won the war. Now the rooms were closed. In other hands, the Dutch House might have been turned into a restaurant, the kind with duck à l'orange on the menu and overpriced French wines from the wrong years. The rooms would have featured four-poster beds and ruffled pillows and bowls of potpourri. But Frankie Sheridan, the present owner, had no truck with wine lists and linens. Frankie ran a bar.

She stepped into smoke and noise. A row of heads and shoulders watched a thunderous basketball game on the television screen above the bar. She recognized Frankie in his green paisley vest; he'd gone completely bald since she'd last seen him, and his mouth was filled with gold. The room was dimly lit by candle bulbs in brass wall sconces. Two men were playing pool, moving in and out of the light over the table. No one took any notice of her. She walked past a row of empty booths to get to the telephone. Jamming the receiver to her ear, she could scarcely hear the dial tone over the electronic hubbub as a foul was called. Then an ad came on. Balls clicked on the pool table; a soft crescendo of chatter rose from the tables.

Estelle answered the phone. Gillian shouted a few words of explanation, then hung up and turned to go. One of the booths wasn't empty after all. A man slumped in his seat by the wall, watching her. He was thin, with narrow hunched-up shoulders and bony wrists. He wore a baseball cap. Under it she saw a lined face frosted with stubble. His eyes were startled.

Gillian's mind darted through a maze of possibilities, hit dead ends. He must be someone she knew. She stood by the telephone, waiting for him to speak. His eyes slid away, and he fumbled for a cigarette in his breast pocket. The sleeves of his checked flannel shirt were frayed. He lit up, squinting at the quaking flame. The ashtray was half full; the two beer glasses in front of him were empty. He sucked on his cigarette, darted a quick glance at her and then exhaled a cloud of smoke, looking down. He wasn't going to say anything.

She could speak to him. For an instant, Gillian considered it. But she was already late. She saw the glowing tip of the cigarette tremble. Better leave it, she concluded, and walked past him to the door. Outside, out of sight, she paused, wondering. Would she have recognized him in a better light? She made her way back across the parking lot crowded with battered sedans and Jeeps on steroids.

She would come back some Sunday afternoon. She used to like to stop in for a hot rum by the fire. The Hudson Valley had a history, and the inn, with its heavy ceiling beams and great stone fireplace, its scarred, wide-planked floor, was part of it. It was one of the oldest buildings in the county. Traders, soldiers, landowners, painters had stopped there, traveling to and from New York. Sailboats and steamships had plied the river, armies had fought in the valley. Painters found a new Eden in its wild grandeur. She liked to sit in the Dutch House when it was quiet and feel its connection to the past.

As she swung the car around towards the exit, her lights glided over two gigantic links of chain laid across a bed of white stones. The metal was mottled and dull, weathered to a blackish brown. According to Frankie, they were relics of the Revolution, links from the great chain across the Hudson that barred the way to British warships. It was possible that he believed it.

At the edge of the highway, she could see the distant flash of a patrol car by the overturned truck. She pulled away, looking for Dykeman's Pond Road. The sign was hard to see.

'We're at Dykeman's,' Maya said. 'I can see the water. How many minutes was that?'

'Sixteen,' Lynn answered, breathless.

'Not bad. Ten more to the Slough.'

It was a clear morning, but the chill of night still hung in the air. The two runners, taller chocolate-brown and shorter freckled redhead, wore identical neon-orange sweatshirts and caps: regulation running gear at Stanton College since 1970, the year a student had been peppered in the thigh by a trigger-happy hunter. They pounded steadily downhill, past Dykeman's Pond and up the next rise. The road was narrow, a winding track half roofed by trees. Here and there, a house stood in a clearing, well back from the road. Driveways made small openings in the palisade of trunks, running away through the woods to hidden houses further in. An occasional bit of shingled roof showed on the ridge above the road.

They topped the rise. Below them was the Slough of Despond, the wooden bridge, and beyond that the longest uphill section of the team's usual run, which explained their name for the water. The slough was not really a slough at all, but a sluggish stream and a pond. On maps, it was known as Dee's Pond.

'Look. Deer,' Maya grunted, slowing her pace.

There were two on the near side of the pond, nervously scenting the air.

'Ten minutes,' Lynn said. 'Keep moving.'

A pheasant rocketed upward from the brush beyond the water, and a sharp crack burst the air. The deer bounded away, white hindquarters flashing as they vanished into the trees. The pheasant dropped, flapped frantically in the grass and lay still.

'Hey!' Maya yelled.

Silence. The two women stopped. They were on the bridge now. They stood still and listened. Their breathing rasped, loud in the quiet. Nothing stirred, only a little murmur of moving water under the bridge.

'That was a gun, wasn't it?' Lynn said. 'But the land's posted. There's no hunting around here.'

'Shit. The idiot could have killed us,' Maya muttered.

'The poor pheasant. Maybe it's only wounded. Should we go see?'

'No way. The guy's over there somewhere, with his stupid gun.'

'He must have heard you. He wouldn't shoot again.'

'Unless he's a nut. He must be hiding in the woods. I wonder if anyone's home around here.' Maya turned slowly, trying to stare through the scrim of branches. Sweat rolled down her bare neck. She took off her cap and rubbed her shaved brown scalp. Below the wooden planks of the bridge, water trickled, a secretive sound. She looked over the edge.

'What?' said Lynn, as Maya backed away, sucking in a deep breath.

'Shut up.' Maya stared around at the woods.

'Are you sick or something? You look weird.'

'Go look.'

Lynn stepped to the rail and looked down. A body lay crumpled in the weeds. A woman, one arm thrust awkwardly behind her. Her face rested at the water's edge, her body sagging into the spongy mat of grass and reeds. Dark strands of hair plastered her cheek. There was something familiar about her coat. Lynn shrank back from the rail. 'Is she dead?'

Maya glanced down again and away. 'Maybe she drowned.'

'She looks dead. Come on, we should find a phone,' Lynn whispered. 'Let's go.' But her feet were welded to the bridge. Her knees wobbled. In the silence she gazed fearfully at the woods across the pond. The air chilled the sweat on her skin.

'We have to see if she's still alive.'

Lynn's instincts said that the woman was dead, but her reason said Maya was right. What if the woman's heart was still beating? They had to check.

'Shouldn't one of us keep a lookout?'

'For the hunter? OK, I'll go down.'

Maya clambered down the slippery bank. Lynn looked up and down the road, hoping for a car. 'Don't fall,' she warned. But Maya, nearly down the bank, didn't hear her. She was looking at the coat, at the dark hair. 'It's Nicole,' she said. She stumbled, her foot slipping in the weeds, the water gurgling into her shoes. She pulled at the body's shoulders, pushed wet hair from the eyes.

'Nicole,' Lynn said blankly. She couldn't see the face. 'It can't be.' She forgot the hunter and lurched down the short slope, grabbing at grasses.

Maya fell sideways into the shallow water. 'Shit.' She was crying. Fearfully, Lynn peered at the face, closed her fingers around Nicole's icy wrist. Her skin was stained with brownish ooze, her open eyes coated with scum. Her arm was stiff. Lynn couldn't lift it. There was no pulse at all. 'Nicole,' she said. 'Nicole, wake up.' She should at least move Nicole's head away from the water. She pulled clumsily. The black raincoat was rucked up around Nicole's neck. Lynn hauled on the collar. It was slimy. She snatched her hand away, but her fingers were brown and slippery. Revolted, she wiped them on the dirty grass. 'Please,' she whispered.

'Christ, what's that?' Maya said. 'Oh Jesus.'

They both saw it, the big bruise on the neck. Dirty water had soaked parts of the white shirt under the coat, wicking from fibre to fibre, but the collar and patches of the shirt front were dyed a darker, rustier colour.

'Come on,' Maya whispered hoarsely. Lynn thrust her hands into the stream, rubbing them together in a frenzy. Brown trickles of water ran off her fingers. She'd seen a wound in Nicole's neck. A vile taste rose in her throat and she retched into the weeds.

Maya shivered in her wet clothes. 'I'm going,' she said, struggling up the bank.

'Wait,' Lynn wailed.

'Hurry up!' Maya was already off the bridge, moving uphill, but she made herself stop and wait. Lynn crawled up the bank to the side of the road and stood up. A movement in the field caught her eye, and she stifled a cry. The wounded pheasant flapped its wings desperately and sank into the grass again. Maya was racing away. Clumsily, Lynn began to run, her feet heavy. Then the adrenaline cut in and she fled up the hill, catching Maya before she reached the summit. Panting, she looked back. Sunlight edged over the treetops, drying the dew. The pond was as flat and opaque as metal, the trees perfectly still. There was nothing to see.

CHAPTER 2

Estelle sipped her tea. She was eighty-four, and her physical energy was failing, but not the energy of her opinions.

'If you want to know who he is, I need some more details, dear. A baseball cap—you might as well tell me that he had two eyes.'

'He smokes.' I wish I could draw, Gillian thought. Describing people was hard. 'He was thin,' she told her mother. 'The lines in his face were deep. He'll look like Auden in twenty years if he lives that long.'

'Does he write poetry?'

'He didn't say. He just stared as if he'd seen a ghost.'

They were having breakfast by the kitchen window. The sun was climbing above the oak trees that hid the road. The garden still bloomed here and there among the seedheads and dry stalks; there had been no killing frost, but the fall air was nippy in the early morning. Close to the window, where Gillian had worked the day before, the earth was raked and clean, but further away the weeds flourished, buttercups embroidering the soil, bindweed threading itself through the rose bushes. Beside the gravel driveway, the dandelion leaves were ragged and dusty, the stalks bare. Next year's crop had floated off, dropping down on lawn and rosebed, or between the pebbles on the drive.

The weeds' health measured her mother's decline. In the past, she would never have let them get started, much less allowed them to run to seed and propagate. Now she watched them muscling their way into the flowerbeds and fretted. It would be Gillian's job to finish clearing them out, when she had time.

Weeds, thought Gillian. Invaders from Europe, stowaways in the settlers' baggage, in the straw they slept on. Weeds, like the settlers, colonized. They staked out territory and moved on, following the frontier, moving west. Indians called white clover 'Englishman's foot'. Or was it a different weed? Maybe it depended on which Englishman. Or which Indian.

'You could ask Frankie,' Estelle said.

'Mmm. I'm not sure I want to. I'd rather people didn't know I'm curious. The guy gave me a pretty strange look.'

'Well, then, give me a little time. Maybe it'll come to me.' Estelle rested her chin on bony knuckles, a puzzled look on her face. It was slightly exaggerated, like many of her expressions, as if she were playing to the back row. 'What brand does he smoke?'

Gillian shrugged. 'I didn't notice.'

'Edward would have.'

Gillian laughed. 'Yes, but that's his job. He's a cop. I'm a historian. I only care what people smoked a hundred years ago.'

In the hillside pasture, she could see Jim Whitlock's sheep. He had a software company; he tried to combine a four-day week at the office with farming on weekends. A lot of the farms in the valley were supported by other income; the farms were small, and hardly anyone could make a living from small farms nowadays. You needed to own half of Kansas. 'I have to run. I'm going to a lecture on Mary Magdalen. I'll do the shopping on the way home.'

'Did you put Jack Daniels on the list? Lewis and Kitty are coming for a drink.'

Her mother's memory was going, Gillian thought. They'd had this conversation yesterday. 'There's an unopened bottle in the back of the cupboard. Shall I get it out?'

'Is there? Oh good. We can fetch it later. They're coming at five. Will you be back by then?'

'I'll try.' Gillian put her jacket on, felt in the pockets. Where the hell had she left her keys? She wandered into the hall, pawed through her bag. Not there. Now whose memory was going? With an audible sigh, a conscious imitation of Estelle, she went upstairs to look for them.

She had set up her office in her mother's old bedroom. It was the nicest of the five, with a fireplace and wide view of the hills to the west, now spattered with gold under the sharp blue sky. Estelle found stairs too exhausting now and had moved down to the main floor, into the study that had once been Gillian's father's. He was dead. It had been over fifteen years since he'd died, so it was a fact Gillian was used to, but at odd moments she was still surprised that it was irrevocable, or that the house had in some ways erased him. She'd been a little chilled when her mother moved downstairs. I've lost one parent already, Gillian thought, and soon I won't have either. The years go so fast. And I forget where I put my keys.

Her own bedroom was the same as ever: the narrow bed with the walnut headboard, the watercolour view of the Hudson from Castle Rock, the cream curtains with faded green silk tassels, the closet door that stuck. Some of the books that used to be on the shelf were missing; she'd given them to her nephew. But the Little House books were still there, and the blue Nancy Drews.

Gillian had come home in August, on leave from her job in the history department at the University of the Pacific Northwest. She'd made the decision after an emergency visit in the spring, when her mother had suffered a stroke, fallen and broken her shoulder. What Gillian saw, abruptly, as if she'd been asleep like Rip van Winkle, was that her self-sufficient, amused, undemanding mother was not, after all, impervious to time. She was old. Shocked, Gillian had made an instant change of plan. She lived alone, she could suit herself. Her sabbatical year had already been arranged, but she would go home instead of going to England. Edward was expecting her to come to London, and when she considered Edward's point of view, she felt guilty. But the chance would never come again, she felt that in her bones. And on the guilt meter, going to England would put her in the red zone.

'I have to do this,' she'd told him. 'You should feel her hand. It's cold. You can practically see through the skin.'

'Couldn't you think about staying through the autumn, and having Christmas there? Then you could come to London in the new year.'

'I don't know. I don't know if she can make it through another winter in the country alone. Why don't you come over for the holidays? You haven't been to the farm for such a long while.'

'I don't usually have time off at Christmas.'

'That's because you always let the "family men" have it. I know you're overworked, but a detective with your years of seniority can get time off if he *wants* to.'

Silence.

'Or come sooner.'

He said he would think about it. Then, rather sulkily, in her opinion, he clammed up. He made no comments about Gillian's arrangements—her house rental, her car, her new laptop.

She should check her e-mail. She dialed in and waited. Nothing from Edward; she hadn't heard from him in days. But there was Laura, popping up on the screen.

'You picked a good season for your sabbatical,' Gillian read. 'The whole west coast is washing out to sea. The news around here is mainly about budget cuts (what else), but a row is brewing over an exhibit at the museum. Drove past your house yesterday; it's still there.'

If Edward had said little about Gillian's plans, her friends, Laura in particular, had said plenty. 'You're going back to the farm?' Laura yelped. 'If I shared a house with my mother, I'd kill her after the first week.'

Some retired schoolteachers never leave the classroom; Laura's mother was an authority on everything. Anybody would kill her after a week, Gillian thought. But she'd probably live to be a hundred. Whereas Estelle wasn't going to.

'What'll you *do* there?' Laura said. 'Sit by the fire and spin?'

'I thought I'd finish the revisions to my book—I was supposed to send them in months ago—and work on a couple of articles. The one on the marriage laws. Caroline Norton, all that. I've done the research, but I haven't written a word. I never have any time. I thought when I finished off my term as department head all sorts of beautiful blank spaces would appear in my schedule, but I'm always busy. I'm still on too many damned committees.'

'Oh, right. Caroline Norton. I read one of her novels.' (Laura was in the English department.) '*She* thought moving to the country was a fate worse than death. I mean, if you're not going to London, at least get out of the house—go give a few lectures at Vassar and see if they can find you an office.'

Laura's advice was sound, and Gillian took it. She contacted her old friend Jo Oliviera, who was teaching at Stanton College. As it happened, there was an opening for a visiting lecturer. Their British historian was on sick leave while undergoing chemotherapy treatments, and the faculty couldn't pick up all of the slack. Stanton offered her a shared office and a stipend (both small) in return for giving a few lectures and teaching a seminar for upper-level students. The college was only ten miles from the farm. She went in two or three days a week, taught her course on British India and planned a short series of lectures on marriage and property in the nineteenth century. She was glad to go, even though this was a sabbatical year and could have been a year free of teaching. She had no administrative work, but she had a place to go and people to talk to, especially Jo. She told herself she wanted to see what women's colleges were like nowadays, but the truth was more complicated. She'd made her decision to go home instantaneously, in a moment of shock, and though, later on, she was still sure the decision was the right one, the prospect of long winter weeks on the farm, during which she would see no one but Estelle unless she invented the occasions herself, began to induce little flutters of panic. She was used to more structure and more varied company. When she tried to put herself in Estelle's shoes, she felt sure that her mother would be relieved to have the house to herself at times.

Gillian found her keys on the table by her bed, under *The Age of Innocence*. Estelle had the complete works, and Gillian had decided to read Wharton again, now that she was back in Wharton country. *Ethan Frome* was the one she'd read at school. Not her favourite. Schools, wanting to introduce the great writers, selected their novels for brevity—how else to account for the awfulness of reading *Silas Marner* when they could have had *Middlemarch* or *Adam Bede*? An absence of sex, perhaps.

The paint on the bedroom walls had faded to a watery yellow, like a baby's sleeper after many launderings. The curtain linings were rotten. The house was old-fashioned in ways that she hadn't thought about until she started living in it again. There was only one telephone, for a start. She'd bought a cordless for her office upstairs and another one for Estelle as soon as she'd seen how long it took her to get to the phone in the hall. The storm windows still came down in the spring and went up again in the fall, and needed to be painted. There was one bathroom upstairs, and no shower, only a deep, clawfoot tub. The new bathroom was downstairs, next to Estelle's bedroom. It had once been a back parlour, but all through Gillian's childhood it was known as the ironing room. There was a sewing machine on the table under the window, and sometimes Estelle's other projects, her dried flowers and the scraps of fabric saved for a quilt she was going to make someday, took up extended residence. The ironing board presided, giraffe-legged, over baskets of stiff, wrinkled clothes that came in from the line. They lay heaped there until needed; Estelle had always hated ironing. It was funny that she'd called it the ironing room, when she used it for so many other things, things she liked. Maybe it was because women didn't have their own rooms in their houses. In theory, the whole house was the woman's domain, so she needed no private space in it. 'Ironing room' could have been camouflage, a front to disguise illicit activity. Like laundromats that were fronts for the drug trade, Gillian thought now, amused. She remembered playing in the ironing room when the living room was out of bounds and the bedrooms were icy. The central heating had been too feeble to warm the rooms upstairs in the coldest weeks of winter, or her parents had been too Spartan to turn it up.

Things had changed. The house had blown-in insulation now, and there was a good heater in the car, too. Thank God for that, she thought fervently, remembering long, cold trips in the school bus. She was no longer accustomed to the rigours of eastern winters. She was using her father's car, a Buick only two years old when he died and up on blocks in the shed since. It was big enough for a pair of sumo wrestlers and it was an automatic, but, like Everest, it was there. And her father had loved it. Jim Whitlock's son Brian, who tinkered with engines, put in a new battery and replaced the points and plugs, plus some other things which he explained to Gillian. She'd nodded, pleased and grateful, if still vague about the details. He'd revived it without much trouble, that much she understood. It was almost a new car, except where the owl turds had eaten through the paint.

Outside, she stopped beside the garden to admire her handiwork. The part she had already weeded and raked looked very tidy, like a child whose wet hair still holds the toothmarks of the comb. Except, she now noticed, there were footprints in the dirt.

Gillian was irritated. They spoilt her hard won perfection. She was tempted to get out the rake, but she was dressed for work, not gardening, and anyway, it would be awfully anal. Like ironing underwear. She didn't want to be that sort of person.

But who had been in the garden? Estelle hadn't mentioned any visitors. The feet that had made the prints were bigger than hers or Estelle's, and the prints looked fresh, like the ones Nancy Drew always found. If she were Nancy, then the footprints would have to be a robber's, and he'd be after jewels hidden in a secret cupboard in the house, or a treasure map. He'd be disappointed. No cupboard, and no jewels. Only her mother's pearls, which she always wore. She said it was because pearls needed to be worn, but Gillian thought it was because her father had given them to her on their twenty-fifth anniversary. He hadn't made it as far as their fiftieth.

On the way to Beekman Corners, she continued to puzzle over the footprints. They went straight into the garden and stopped; someone had stood in one place for a bit, leaving deeper prints. Then the footprints came back out, at a slight angle to the line that went in. It looked very much as if someone had stood there, looking into the house through the window. For no logical reason, she imagined the thin man who had looked at her in the Dutch House standing in her garden and staring at her inside the house. Once, she'd known everyone for miles around. If he knew her, why couldn't she place him? Her memory was going to hell.

CHAPTER 3

At Beekman Corners, the grocery store was open. She could stop and ask Jean about the thin man, but too many people were there now. Three or four cars were parked outside the store; the regulars would be drinking coffee and carping about the news. Among them, they would certainly solve her conundrum, but she didn't want to turn her private curiosity into a public enquiry. She knew Jean, always saw her when she came back, but Jean had customers now who were strangers to Gillian. Perhaps Estelle had met them, but Gillian doubted it. So many new people had moved to the county in the past ten years. She turned on to the Post Road. How long had it taken to clear up the accident? Probably hours.

Stanton College stood on the banks of the Hudson. It had been built as a country house, an elegant retreat on a high point looking down on a great bend in the river. It had once belonged to Eva Vanderplaat, whose father owned steamships and whose brother lost them in the Wall Street crash of 1873. Miss Vanderplaat died, and the house, furniture and all, was auctioned. Henry Delamar, the Hudson River School painter, bought it, lock, stock and grandfather clock, and christened it Delamar House. His daughter Olympe, a poet and ardent suffragist, inherited the estate when her father died. She promptly sold most of the furniture and paintings and used the money to open a women's college.

The house still stood, and so did some enormous trees, planted by Miss Vanderplaat and now serving as a graceful backdrop and a screen between historic grandeur and the functional architecture of classrooms and dormitories. These, and the library and the assembly hall, were grouped behind the house, away from the riverbank. Only the dining hall and Delamar House commanded a view of the river: of lawn sloping down to clifftops, rocky and wild, and the ever-changing water wearing its way beneath the tall palisades of the opposite bank. Old woods, oak and maple logged and grown again, framed the opening, stretching from the clifftops all the way back to the road, enfolding the campus. The dorms were tucked under the eaves of the forest.

Gillian parked in the faculty lot and hurried along the walkway past the new classroom building. It was oddly quiet. On other mornings she'd heard snatches of laughter or argument, lines of poetry or French phrases coming through the open windows. Today, she heard nothing at all.

She crossed a corner of the wide lawn behind the house. It was empty. No students were gathered under the big trees, no bicycles wheeled along the network of paths. But parked beside the pristine facade of Delamar House, like a beetle on a white tablecloth, was a police car. Something was amiss.

Gillian used the side entrance of the house and went straight to the faculty lounge, upstairs in the south end. There she could expect to find a cup of coffee and the news. The room was deserted. Only the red eye of the coffee machine returned her stare. If it hadn't been for the police car, she would have thought she'd forgotten some national holiday. Columbus Day, maybe. She hurried down the steps again and out to the lawn. The empty stretch of grass looked like a science-fiction scene: aliens had taken everyone away. She decided to try the dining hall. The vestibule, where important notices were posted, might give her a clue.

There was nothing new on the board. She stepped through the heavy swinging doors into the dining room. The floor was swept, the big room quiet. Light from the river glistened in the air. She heard a murmur of voices and went through to the kitchen. The three cooks, large, broad, muscled women, with arms that could lift ten-gallon pots of hot soup, were preparing lunch. Whatever was wrong, people must be fed. They looked at her. She thought she read suspicion in their faces.

'Where is everybody?' Gillian asked. 'What's going on?'

'Who are you?' the nearest woman demanded, a frown creasing her bright pink face.

'I've seen her in the dining hall, Vi,' said a second, a big black woman. She laid her knife down and came towards Gillian, breasting the thick, steamy air of the kitchen like an oil tanker. 'What's your name, honey?' she said to Gillian. 'You teach something here, don't you?'

'I'm Gillian Adams; I teach a history course. I live on Salt Hill Road,' she added, as if a part-time position required some additional credentials.

The black woman nodded. 'I'm Annette, this here is Vi, and the redhead back there is Torchie.'

Torchie, who was squarely built, with powerful shoulders and densely freckled skin, looked faintly familiar, though not very flammable; only a hint of red lurked in her almost colourless hair.

'You just get here?' Annette continued. 'They're all up in the assembly hall.'

'You haven't heard about Nicole?' Torchie broke in. 'Nicole Bishop's dead. They think a hunter shot her.'

'Jesus,' Gillian gasped.

Annette asserted herself. 'It's a terrible thing. Maya and Lynn found her this morning.'

'Where?'

'Up by Dee's Pond.'

'And they saw someone shooting up there,' Torchie put in.

'They found her in the water.' Annette shook her head. 'Terrible thing.'

'The guy was probably drunk,' Torchie said. 'I've seen them weaving all over the highway.'

'Maya and Lynn. What did they do?'

'Ran back here,' Annette said. 'They don't know anybody on that road.'

'Jesus,' Gillian said again.

Vi pinched her thin lips together. 'Instead of taking His name in vain, we should be praying for that poor child and her family.'

'Gillian's just shocked,' Annette said, 'like we all are.'

Gillian turned to go. The heat in the kitchen and the smell of frying onions was making her feel a little sick. Then something clicked in her mind. 'Torchie?' she said. 'Torch Regan? Roosevelt School?'

'I wondered if you'd remember,' Torchie said.

'You live around here?'

'Used to be on this side of the river, when Milt was employed. He's my husband. We're in Newburgh now. Are you back home?'

'For now.'

'How's your mother?'

'Getting on. You have children, don't you?'

'Two. Boy and girl. Sean's still in school. Lily's working.'

Annette interrupted. 'You know each other?'

'Torch was famous at our school,' Gillian said. 'She beat up Ricky Sands when he pulled her pants down. After that, he left girls alone.'

Torchie flushed pink under her freckles. 'You remember that?'

'They should have put up a plaque,' Gillian said.

When she left the kitchen, her thoughts were confused. She was shocked by the news about Nicole, but seeing Torch Regan had opened her mind to a rush of memories. She wanted to go away and think about them, let the details of the half-forgotten past rise like springwater and run over the surface of her mind. But Nicole Bishop, a student at Stanton, had been killed. It wasn't possible to contemplate old times. Nicole had been in her class.

Gillian's friend Jo was walking across the lawn. Gillian cut across the path to meet her.

'You've heard about Nicole?' Jo asked, stopping. As usual, she wore a hat with a brim to protect her eyes from glare; under it, her face was pale and drawn. Gillian could hardly hear her words.

'Just now. She's really dead?'

'I can't believe it.'

'What have the police told you?'

'Nothing. It was Maya and Lynn who found her. They heard a shot. The police told Margaret to keep the students off the back roads. I guess they're looking for the guy, and some of them are up at the bridge by Dee's Pond. Collecting the body.' Jo shivered.

Gillian touched her shoulder, then let her hand drop. Jo was far inside herself. 'It was a hunting accident?'

'It must have been. Some asshole shooting on posted land.'

'This morning?'

'We don't know. Nicole wasn't in her dorm last night. But that's not unusual these days.' Jo put a hand up to her face, pressing the fingers to her temple. 'I've got to go. I've got a killer headache and I don't have my pills in my bag. Everybody's still in the assembly hall. Margaret called an emergency college meeting and canceled classes for the day. They're all in there talking. I couldn't stand it any more.'

'What can I do?' Gillian asked.

Jo shook her head and then winced with pain. She took a couple of steps along the pathway, moving cautiously as if each step jarred the pain loose. 'You can go to the assembly hall, but you don't have to. It doesn't have to be your problem.'

'I'd like to help.'

'I don't know what anybody can do. But I'll tell Margaret you offered. I'd ask you to stay and hold my hand, but when

I've got this kind of headache, all I can do is lie down in a dark room and be quiet.'

Gillian wasn't sure where to go next. The lecture she'd come for would not be given today, and she felt like an outsider. It didn't have to be her problem. Jo had said it. Nicole's death was a catastrophe for Stanton, but Gillian knew few people here and had only a partial and temporary connection to the college. There wasn't anything she could do for anyone. Yet it seemed callous to leave.

She didn't want to go to the assembly hall; she could see students coming out, clinging together, moving erratically towards the dorms. She wandered aimlessly back to Delamar House and checked the faculty lounge. It was still empty. She loitered in the corridor, leaning on the balustrade above the central hall. It was a high airy space, where twin staircases descended to a landing under a Palladian window, and broad, shallow steps linked the landing to the reception area on the main floor. She looked over the shining mahogany rail, straight down, and saw the top of a man's head. The head tilted up, and the eyes met hers.

Cop eyes, thought Gillian, though she might have been influenced by the uniform and the gun. He looked her over. Then his beeper went off and he strolled away. Gillian sidled into an empty meeting room and looked out of the windows. There were two police cars now. One door was wide open, and she could see the driver talking into his radio. Too bad Edward was in London; she wanted to know what the police were doing. Students drifted around the corner of the building, stopped, whispered and stared. The meeting in the assembly hall must be breaking up. The president's office was directly below where Gillian was standing. When Margaret Bristol returned, she'd have to face the phone call to the parents, if she hadn't spoken to them already. And more talks with the police. And then the local TV stations and newspapers would hover and swoop, like buzzards.

Gillian was glad she wasn't a college president. 'Not for all the tea in China,' she muttered, quoting her grandmother.

Nicole Bishop. The media would say she was a beautiful brunette. They'd call her willowy. She was tall, a lanky, athletic young woman, with dark, thick hair pulled straight back to a clip at the nape of her neck, clear-cut features and skin as bare and clean as a nun's. She was beautiful, Gillian conceded, the media would not be wrong. But a 'beautiful brunette' was a piece of boilerplate, not a person.

There were fifteen women in Gillian's class, all in their early twenties. Their age was what she had noticed first. (She didn't count the absence of men; that had been a given.) At her own university, many of the students were older. Some had children, and many were working slowly towards their degrees, studying part time, always broke, or working at night, or coping with a crisis: a crazy babysitter, a parent or child in hospital, a car that wouldn't start. Most lived off campus. Here, nearly all the students were young, attended full time and lived in college residences. She hadn't asked them about their finances, but she thought that most of them were supported by their parents. They were vigorous, sleek, shining with youth and high expectations, just back from the summer vacation, backpacking in Europe or waiting tables on Martha's Vineyard. They looked carefree, with no worries other than their own education. So they seemed, but in fact she knew nothing about their real lives, which were bound to be more complicated than what could be seen on the surface. Human lives always were.

The police officer got out of his car and went inside. He came out again, with the first cop. Gillian watched, but without making any sense of what she saw; her mind was flapping like a broken fanbelt. She'd been on Dykeman's Pond Road last evening, she was thinking. Jo said Nicole wasn't in her dorm. But surely she hadn't been shot at night?

Poor Jo. She would take this very hard. The emotional connections here were closer, more intense than was common at Gillian's larger, urban campus, and Jo was a natural den mother. Phones were ringing below. Abruptly, Gillian headed for the back stairs. She didn't want to wait in the lounge for whoever showed up, most likely someone she'd never talked to before. She would go to her office and try to work. It would be lunchtime soon, she could go to the dining hall and perhaps find people she knew.

Jo didn't come to lunch. Gillian took an empty place by Carla Muller and asked her about Maya and Lynn.

'They're still in the infirmary, I think.'

'They weren't in the assembly hall,' said the man on Carla's other side. He was an American historian Gillian had once met in the coffee room. Martin something-or-other; she'd forgotten his surname.

'They must be in shock,' Carla said. 'Margaret told us they'd found Nicole when they were out running, and they thought she'd been shot. That was about all anybody seemed to know.'

They talked about guns. Gillian could remember when the hunting regulations hadn't been as strict; she'd heard shots near the farm every autumn, despite all the land being posted. Dairy farmers upstate lost their cows.

'At least there's no deer hunting in the county now, or we'd have more accidents.'

'But any idiot can still buy a gun,' said Martin. 'And they all do. "The right to bear arms" is the mantra of the maladapted.'

'I wonder if anyone at Stanton has a gun,' Carla said. 'I hope not.'

Guns at Stanton. How ridiculous, Gillian thought. But it was true that they were everywhere. Even some of Estelle's friends kept a gun in the house.

'What was Nicole like?' she asked, knowing that Nicole had been one of Carla's students the previous year, and had also taken courses in American history. Carla's field was the Italian Renaissance; Gillian had asked her a few questions at previous lunches and found her disappointingly dry. The most wonderful material could be ground to dust by scholars with no eye for the enlivening human detail. Still, she was bound to know more about Nicole than Gillian did.

'She has a Blackwell Scholarship, you know that?' Martin said.

'She wasn't your typical Stanton student,' Carla added.

'How do you mean?'

'I don't really know. It was just a feeling.'

'She had a good mind,' Martin remarked. 'A great pair of legs, too. What a waste.'

'Don't be crude,' Carla said sharply.

'Can't we mourn a body as well as mind?'

'Maybe, but we don't mourn body parts.'

Carla wasn't so dry after all.

'Sorry,' Martin said, with an edge of sarcasm. He turned to Gillian. 'Nicole had a different perspective. Who knows why? These kids at Stanton, they're all smart, but you can usually predict what they'll say in class. It's like tennis—they play a baseline game. Nicole surprised you. Questioned what she read. She wasn't afraid to challenge the party line.'

Carla nodded. 'She's intense. Jo sometimes thought she was overdoing it. And Judy—have you met the track coach, Gillian?—was worried about her, too. Judy thought she was too thin, especially this term. Not eating enough, running on adrenaline.' Carla craned her neck to look up and down the dining room. 'Poor Jo, she's been hit really hard; she was close to Nicole. Judy's not here, either. She's probably at the infirmary with Lynn and Maya.'

The noise level in the room was well below normal, Gillian noticed, in part because lots of people weren't there. Many tables were empty. Margaret Bristol wasn't at lunch; Gillian supposed she had too much to do. Roberta wasn't present, either, and most of the senior class—Nicole's class—was missing. Gillian wondered if her parents had arrived; it would depend on how quickly they'd been reached and where they lived. New York, maybe. Nicole was a city girl, she was pretty sure.

When lunch was over and the tables were cleared, those who had chosen to come in the first place seemed disinclined to leave. They sat there like the shipwrecked. A few of the missing wandered in, looking forlorn, and then another straggling group, more agitated. Maya and Lynn had made some kind of mistake, but no one was sure what it was. People clustered around the new arrivals, eager for news. Someone had heard that Nicole might still be alive. Someone else said maybe the body wasn't Nicole's, it was someone who looked like her. Rumours raged, whirling from table to table like dust devils. Nicole hadn't been shot, she had drowned. Someone had tried to kill Maya and Lynn, too. A stalker was loose, and he could be prowling the woods near the college. Voices rose, people were arguing and crying. Carla went to deal with a new student who was weeping hysterically and wanted to go home.

Martin and the other male faculty member present, Russian literature, as Gillian recalled, were at either end of the room, calling for quiet. No one listened.

'This is dreadful,' Carla said, coming back. 'No one knows what's true and what isn't.'

'A few facts would help,' Gillian agreed.

'Someone should get Margaret and the police over here.'

By that time, someone had. Margaret came in, her blonde bun askew. Two police officers came in with her and stood to one side. She waited for a moment, standing still, while the noise in the room died away. Her control had a calming effect.

'I can't give you many details yet; I don't have them,' she said, her voice steady and rather formal. 'Nicole is dead, as we were informed this morning. She died sometime last night, before Maya and Lynn found her. What I'm afraid I have to tell you is that it was *not* a hunting accident. Maya and Lynn heard a shot and drew a natural conclusion under the circumstances. However, the police have informed me that Nicole was not shot. They have concluded this as a result of examining her body.' (Here Margaret's voice faltered.) 'I can't tell you how she was killed. We have to wait for the results of a more thorough investigation. But there is something you need to know now. Nicole's death wasn't an accident. It was a, a purposeful act. The police have advised that no one walk or bicycle anywhere alone, on or off the campus.'

The hush was profound. Margaret took a breath. 'I will tell you more as soon as I can. I'm still making efforts to reach her family. There will be another meeting later today, at five o'clock. In the meantime, I ask all of you to remain calm.' She left the room again.

The two officers stayed behind, answering questions and observing the crowd. Anyone who had seen Nicole on the previous day was asked to identify herself. A large number of hands rose. Most of these, Gillian supposed, would have seen her in the dining hall or the dorm, and would have little information of any use.

Not an accident, not a stupid error, not a negligent homicide. A murder. Everything would be different. Probably no one here knew how different.

Gillian left an hour later. They were diverting their feelings to arguments about campus security. There was nothing she could do to help. Her mother was waiting, dinner must be cooked.

CHAPTER 4

Jean's, in Beekman Corners, was all right for basics, but Gillian wasn't resigned to iceberg lettuce. Since she'd returned, she'd put miles on the Buick exploring the back roads, visiting farmers' markets, stopping at roadside tables where she left a dollar in a box and took away a bag of apples or a squash, or a pound of ripe tomatoes. What was the point of buying store tomatoes? You might as well cut up tennis balls and eat them. She found a wine shop. She bought greens from a couple of New York graphic designers who'd left the city to start an organic garden. Estelle, who had slipped into the habit of boiling an egg for her dinner, told Gillian she fussed too much. But Gillian liked prowling the old roads.

This valley was her own country. She was imprinted with this landscape; it looked the way it was supposed to look. The rocks were the right colour and shape, the hills were the right size, the trees were the right kind of trees. She'd loved other places since, England most easily, because literature had taught her how to see it. But here in this valley her childhood's eye opened and could see again. What that eye saw was home. Bedrock.

Yet it was not the valley she used to know. Nothing stayed the same. Once, it had seemed to stand outside of time, but that had been a child's view.

In the nineteenth century, the Hudson River School had painted it as sublime wilderness: river, rock, tree and sky radiant with divine light. The purity of the wilderness stood for America as a new beginning, where 'man' was still a mere brushstroke on a huge canvas. But already, as the artists worked, peoples had been displaced, whole forests felled, farmlands exhausted and abandoned. Roads wound through the valley, captains of industry built pillared mansions along the riverbank. The new Eden the artists painted was already a myth.

Olympe Delamar, painter's daughter, had looked out of her windows at copper beeches and honey locusts planted there by Eva Vanderplaat: no wilderness, but part of a garden Eva had designed. Now the garden was gone, too. Only fragments remained. The specimen trees still shaded the lawn, and two classical urns ornamented the stone steps set into the grass, but the rest was lost, destroyed by roads and classrooms. The beautiful rosebeds had been too expensive to maintain. They existed only in photographs, and in Eva Vanderplaat's landscape drawings. A few of the rarer specimens had been moved by Dr. Lewis Grogan, to augment his collection. The avenue of elms arching over the drive had been killed by blight: an import, like the roses, like the weeds.

Gillian had admired her own modest patch of raked earth that morning. She had spent many an hour on her knees under the peonies, besieged by bandit hordes of dandelions. And she knew of many lost gardens up and down the river, some as fine as Eva Vanderplaat's. It was tempting to think of the garden as enclosed and pure, of evil as imported. But if, like the painters, you saw purity in wilderness, then Eva's garden itself was an invader: Dutchwoman's foot. 'Nature' had been rearranged. But then who were the painters to lay claim to nature? They had painted their own designs: thoughtfully moving tree or crag to improve on God's. They, too, had gardened. And gardening, to judge by her own labours, amounted to a process of relentless meddling to produce an illusion of artless serenity. 'Serenity'—that was what Huckleberry Finn would call 'soul-butter and hogwash'. Gardeners were always in a fuss about something.

Nothing stayed the same, no matter how hard one fought. All victories were provisional, Gillian thought, everything is fragile. 'My name is Ozymandias, king of kings.' Poor Nicole. She drove past a new development, houses on one-acre lots with two-car garages and blue-black swathes of fresh asphalt driveway. The old houses, the old gardens and farms and wild woods were on the ebb. Every inch of the world was someone's back yard, complete with mower, weed-eater, and satanic leaf-blower.

She drove home slowly, dawdling over her shopping until darkness gathered under the trees. She didn't want to discuss the day's headline event with Estelle and her guests. The Grogans made her uncomfortable. Lewis was like a prize bull: massive and well tended. He used all the oxygen of any room he was in. Kitty, complementary, was thin, melted into corners, breathed Lewis's exhalations. She didn't seem to mind, but Gillian minded for her. 'What sort of example are you setting for your daughter?' she wanted to say. But one didn't. Lewis's favourite subjects were horses and roses, local politics and hi-tech medicine. He was well informed on all four. But today, inevitably, they would talk about murder. Nicole Bishop was dead in a swampy little ditch only a few miles away. The news would be all over the county by now.

Estelle sat alone.

'Kitty called,' she said as soon as Gillian walked in. 'Lewis had to go to an emergency meeting at the college. There's been a dreadful accident.' She'd been polishing her reading glasses, and now she let them dangle, waiting for Gillian's reply.

Of course, thought Gillian. Lewis was on Stanton's board of trustees. She'd forgotten that. Kitty must have canceled hours ago.

'Accident?' she asked, temporizing. Estelle seldom resorted to euphemism.

'I thought you would know all about it. Kitty said one of their students has been killed. They found her on Dykeman's Pond Road. Was she hit by a car?'

'No.' So Kitty hadn't told her. Or perhaps Estelle hadn't heard her. She was deafer than she used to be. Get it over with, Gillian thought. 'It's worse than that.' She raised her voice slightly, not wanting to say it twice. 'Somebody murdered her.'

'Mercy.' Estelle's hand went to her heart. Her glasses fell into the folds of her skirt. 'My pills,' she said, with difficulty, scrabbling at the little table beside the sofa.

Gillian darted to the table, snatched up the bottle. Nitroglycerine. Estelle had told her. She prised the lid open. Estelle was sweating, her skin had gone greenish-grey. She took a pill, popped it under her tongue and shut her eyes. Gillian stared at her anxiously, waiting, listening to her laboured breathing. Estelle had told her not to worry, people lived with angina, the pills took care of the pain. But she felt her own heart pounding with fear. She couldn't speak. Her mind was stuck. Estelle opened her eyes, fumbled at her glasses. The colour came back to her face. 'That's better.'

'Thank God.' Gillian brushed the *Times* crossword puzzle aside and sat down on the sofa. 'Should I call Dr. Brinker?'

Estelle's young ginger tomcat mewed enquiringly in the arched doorway. Estelle turned her head towards the sound. He bounded across the room and jumped up on the sofa, dislodging her pencil, which fell noiselessly between the cushions.

'Rumpole,' she croaked.

He thumped downward on to her lap. Her hand, quivering a little, reached to stroke his round, blunt head, and, like a warm engine, he instantly produced a purr.

'The pills are wonderful,' she said. 'So quick. The pain's almost gone already.'

'I didn't mean to shock you. I'm so sorry.'

'I don't know why it hit me like that. I know these things happen; I read the papers.'

'It's too close to home, I guess.'

'But I haven't even met the girl. Who is she?'

'Her name's Nicole Bishop. She's a senior; she's in my class. *Was* in my class. An A student. Serious, more aware of the world than a lot of people her age. She asked me a question about dowries and female infanticide in India—most of the class had never heard about the issue. But I only met her a few weeks ago; I don't know much about her.' Or anyone else on campus except Jo, she thought.

Estelle stroked Rumpole from nape to tail, as he lay across her bony lap, the tip of his fat tail twitching with pleasure. She looked all right.

'Your angina—is it getting worse?' Gillian asked.

'Worse?' Estelle said vaguely. 'Maybe a little. I'm all right if I don't overdo it. Now, I want to know more about what happened. What was this girl doing on Dykeman's Pond Road? How was she killed?'

'The police aren't saying. At first people thought it was a hunting accident, because the two students who found her heard shooting, and they saw some kind of wound when they touched her. But the police told the college it wasn't an accident. I'm sure that if she'd been shot or drowned, they wouldn't have ruled out an accidental death so quickly. Nobody knows what she was doing on Dykeman's Pond Road. She wasn't in her dorm last night. I don't know when she died, but the police want to talk to anyone who drove or walked along the road in the past two days. Who lives over there?'

'A lot of those people are only here on weekends,' Estelle said. 'We don't know them.'

We, thought Gillian. Estelle's generation, she probably meant. Her parents had bought this house before she was born. Cousins of various degrees of removal were scattered up the valley, one branch of the family having stayed after the Revolution, the other—having fought for Britain—hightailing it to Canada. The two sides hadn't spoken for several generations, but now the cousins savoured their old conflict as a spicy ingredient in the family story.

Gillian hadn't stayed in the valley, but the ties to land and family were still strong. 'How could you have left?' Jo had once asked. Well, she had. She'd gone away to seek her fortune in the wide world, like the children in fairy tales. She'd failed to marry the prince, however, though she'd met plenty of talking frogs.

'They don't come into Jean's very often,' Estelle added.

'The shopping is much better in the city. Think of Balducci's.'

'That's all very well, but if they don't buy from Jean, the store will close, and then we'll be in a fine pickle. I don't want to have to drive to town every time I want a carton of milk.'

'No indeed,' Gillian said. 'Especially not in the winter.' And the way you drive now, she added, in her head.

'The Nelsons are still up there,' Estelle said, following the road in her mind, picturing the houses she knew.

Gillian had thought of them, too. Peggy Nelson had been her best friend when they were children. Her parents still lived in the same house, not far from the college. They were high up and could see the Hudson from their porch. Peggy, like Gillian, had moved away, but now she was married and lived just over the border in Fairfield County. Her husband practised law in the same firm as Gillian's brother.

'Who else?'

'The Hornbecks, Carrie Pilgrim, she's ninety now. They're not on Dykeman's Pond Road, though, they're on Beacon…. There's the writer, Simon Steele. He lives on Beacon, too.'

'Oh yeah, that guy who writes the Studley Royal thrillers.'

'Oh, he's not writing those now. He wrote a book about his awful drinking problem. He's famous.'

'Simon Steele is famous?'

'He is around here. Everybody's read it.'

'Doesn't sound like bestseller material.'

'Neither did *Jonathan Livingston Seagull*.'

'You've got me there.'

Estelle sat silent, stroking the cat. His eyes were closed, his white paws dangled. The tendons on the back of her hand moved under the freckled skin like taut strings. She was thin, stiff, frail, like a dried flower.

'But who could have killed this poor girl? Nicole?' she said, persisting. 'It doesn't make sense.'

'No.'

'I thought the girls didn't run alone.'

'She may not have been running. She might not have been killed where they found her. Her body could have been dumped there. I'll bet it was.'

'Oh.' Estelle digested this. 'So she could have been killed somewhere else, like New York.'

'That's about the size of it. The police lab tests will probably give some indication. But why would anyone kill her in New York and then drag the body all the way up here?'

'How should I know? But lots of people are murdered there, and they aren't around here. I wish you and Edward would get married.'

Gillian had no difficulty following this train of thought. 'I'm not going to be murdered in my bed because I live alone. Statistically,' she added with a touch of malice, 'marriage is more dangerous.'

Estelle didn't rise to the bait. 'I wish he were here right now. I'd feel better.'

'Yes, me too. But I'm afraid the local talent will have to do.'

Neither of them wanted much dinner. Gillian heated some soup, and they ate it in silence. Gillian stared morosely at the *Times*. Crime rates were down, it said.

Afterwards, she put the bowls in the sink and poured a hefty Scotch for herself and a smaller one for her mother.

She'd witnessed a few of Estelle's attacks, but they'd had obvious physical causes, like climbing the stairs. They hadn't come out of the blue. Was she stupid to be pouring her a drink? Estelle's doctor had told her that it would be beneficial if she gave up alcohol. But Estelle, who had banished butter and cream on command, who gave up red meat with hardly a sigh, drew the line at Scotch.

'Your angina scares me,' Gillian said.

'Scares *you*?' It was an attempt at humour.

'Isn't there anything else that can be done?'

'The pills work pretty well, though I used to be able to do more than I can now. I take drugs for my blood pressure. They tried angioplasty last year, you know that. I didn't really want it, but I thought I might be able to garden again. So, I let them try.'

Gillian remembered. Estelle hadn't told her about the operation until the last minute, and they'd said not to fly east, it was a minor procedure. She'd looked it up in a medical dictionary. They made an incision in the arm or leg, inserted a catheter into a major blood vessel and threaded it into the coronary artery. Then they blew up a little plastic balloon that compressed the fatty deposits blocking the artery. When it worked, the blood flow was restored. In Estelle's case, the artery wall, too old and brittle, had torn. Gillian heard about it from Franklin, her brother, who'd rushed up from the city. The surgeon had proposed a coronary bypass, but Estelle said no.

'What about surgery?' Gillian asked now. 'If the drugs can't do the job as well as they used to—'

'Don't *you* start. I've made up my mind. I'm eighty-four, and I don't want major surgery. It's *my* choice.'

Two pink spots glowed on Estelle's cheekbones. She was angry. Gillian decided to shut up.

❧

'I've been thinking,' Estelle said after a while. 'I've been trying to remember who used to know you. People who still live around here. So many of your generation moved away.'

Gillian slipped a bookmark into *The Age of Innocence*.

'And I did remember somebody,' Estelle said triumphantly. 'I think he's your man in the Dutch House.' She paused, relishing Gillian's suspense. 'It took me a while because I hardly ever see him.'

'Who is he?'

'You said a lined face and he was thin, didn't you? Well, I know who that is. It's the Mitchell boy.'

'Arnold!' said Gillian. 'Yes. Arnold, God, of course. You're absolutely right. Mother, you're a genius.'

Estelle laughed and looked pleased.

'But he's really changed,' Gillian added. 'He looks ill.'

'Does he? He's almost a hermit, you know. He doesn't talk to people much. At least that's what I hear.'

'Where does he live?'

'In his parents' house. They're both dead now; I think I probably wrote you when his mother died. And then his father—do you remember Booter?'

'Not really.'

'A thoroughly unpleasant character. They moved here a few years after the war. Booter had the Reds-under-the-bed mania. He used to get drunk and start accusing people. And he thought McCarthy was a shining hero. He and Virginia had two boys, Arnold and the younger one, Tommy. Tommy died in a hunting accident when he was only twelve or fourteen. We heard about it a few days later when we came down for Thanksgiving.'

'I remember.'

'Booter got worse after that. Tommy was his favourite.'

'What does Arnold do?'

'Goodness knows. I don't think he's ever had a job.'

'I wonder what his life has been like, all these years.'

'Carrie Pilgrim might tell you. She's ninety this year, did I tell you? She knows everybody's stories, and she never forgets a thing.'

'Really?' The historian in Gillian suddenly surfaced. 'Has she kept journals? Has anyone talked to her about her life or recorded her memories? She was a pretty famous painter, even if she's not in fashion now.'

'Some would-be biographers have pestered her. She said they weren't people she wanted to talk to. That's all I know. You'd better ask her.'

'I will. Memories like that shouldn't be lost.' Gillian looked at her watch and decided to clean up the kitchen while the Sherlock Holmes rerun began. Sometimes she watched them with Estelle, but tonight she didn't want to.

'Carrie will be in bed now,' Estelle said. 'She goes to bed when it gets dark and gets up at dawn. You could call her tomorrow.'

'Arnold's house is up near hers, isn't it?'

'Not far. It's on Dykeman's Pond Road.'

Arnold Mitchell. Maybe he'd been miffed when she didn't recognize him. Or, as an almost-hermit, he'd been too shy to say hello. She hadn't thought about him for a long time. Would she have known him in daylight, without the cap? What was a hermit doing in the Dutch House, anyhow?

Arnold wasn't someone she'd forget, not after Tommy's death. She'd seen him only a day after she'd heard the news. It was a year or so after her father changed jobs and they'd moved away, only coming back to the farm in the summers and for long holiday weekends. This time, they'd come down for Thanksgiving. Everyone had been full of the story. They heard it from all their neighbours, almost before they said hello. The next day she'd taken her bike to Warren's Knob, a high, bald rock on a hill a few miles from the farm. The trail up the back side was an easy scramble, and she'd gone by herself. Girls roamed on their own; nobody worried about them, not in those days. The Knob was on private land, close to the Hudson, but no one lived there. An empty house, abandoned when the owners ran out of money, stood marooned on the hillside; warped boards were nailed over the window openings. The No Trespassing signs posted at the old gateway were renewed now and then, but no caretaker came around to enforce them. The view from the summit, nearly eight hundred feet above the river, was part of local lore, and the trail was well used.

It had been a cold, bright November afternoon, with dry leaves thick on the path. She hadn't met a soul on the way up, but when she got to the top, Arnold was there. She wanted to turn right around and go down again. She had no idea what to say. Back then, she'd never known anyone who died, not even an aged relative, let alone anyone who'd died like Tommy—young and suddenly, in a stupid accident.

When children died, back then, they died of polio. Even now, the word recalled the fear, as the scent of rubbing alcohol recalled the ache of fever. Polio had haunted her childhood summers, in dreadful, pathetic newspaper photographs of children trapped in iron lungs, the terror in their eyes visible even through the smudgy ink. The big machines, tended by crew-cut men in white coats, looked cruel, like equipment for mad scientists. Adults murmured their fears in private; children passed rumours around the swimming pool, which was where you got it, they said. But none of her friends died, nobody at her school. Polio menaced from a distance.

Then Tommy was killed, with Booter's gun. That was her first encounter with rude mortality. It was also her first experience of the need to respond to other people's tragedies, and the embarrassment of feeling one had nothing to offer. What relief or comfort could she give to Arnold? She had rarely spoken to him at school. He'd been a skinny, friendless boy, bullied and shunned.

To leave was impossible. She stepped on to the bare rock where the view opened wide. Miles of river wound below, blue under blue sky. The leafless trees bristled on the opposite bank. Tiny boats moved over the water, trailed by chevrons of white foam.

'It's beautiful,' she said.

Arnold, standing near the edge, where the rock plunged down into scrub and trees, glanced sideways at her.

'Cold, though.' She was wearing a thick sweater, but the wind at the top sucked the warmth from her body. Did he know how nervous she was?

He shrugged, as if to indicate an indifference to temperature. She could see the baronial walls of West Point in the distance, frowning over the river. And there was Bannerman's Island.

'I'm home for Thanksgiving,' she offered.

'I figured.'

It was like talking to a stump. She cast about, unable to mention Tommy. 'Have you ever been to the island?'

'Bannerman's? Nah.'

The crenellated walls of the castle were plainly visible in the clear light. When she was a child, she'd dreamed of living there. What child wouldn't? 'Didn't you want to go when you were little? I did. I was going to live there like a queen. The Queen of the Island.'

Arnold looked at her. 'Yeah, I did. I was going to be a pirate.'

'With a cutlass and an eyepatch and bags of gold buried under the castle floor?'

Arnold's voice came to life. 'In the walls. Secret compartments.' He kicked at a pebble. It rolled over the edge. 'Bannerman must have been cracked.'

Gillian knew the story; they all did. Francis Bannerman was an arms merchant. He'd started when he was only fourteen, buying up Civil War surplus. He'd made piles of money in the Spanish American War and spent some of it to build the turreted keep on the island. It was his summer residence, but he hoarded live ammunition in it, too. A couple of years after it was finished, a huge explosion blew one of the walls away.

'My mother told me about Tommy. That's terrible.'

Arnold hunched his shoulders. 'Yeah.'

'I'm sorry,' she faltered. 'I don't know what to say.'

'It doesn't matter.'

She looked at him, perplexed.

'Nobody ever talked to me when Tommy was alive.'

It was like a slap, hearing it said out loud.

'I'm sorry,' she said again.

'Sorry,' Arnold mocked.

She was stung. 'Well, I am. I am sorry. I'm ashamed.'

He was silent.

'It was mean and stupid, how some people behaved. And the rest of us were cowards. Including me. Jesus, Arnold, what more can I say?'

He shrugged. 'Not much, I guess.'

Gillian shifted position, looking down the river. There was a pause.

'Should I go?'

'If you want to.'

She was shivering. 'I'm cold.'

He looked into the distance. 'I used to wish Tommy was dead.'

'You did?'

'Do you remember my brother?'

'Sure.'

'One thing was, he liked guns. He used to play with Dad's and pretend he was going to shoot me. When I told my Dad, he just laughed.'

She'd never said a word about that conversation to anybody. She'd seen Arnold a few times, when she'd been home in the summers, and she'd said hello, but they hadn't talked about anything personal. Then she hadn't seen him any more. He'd gone into the army, she heard, and after that she didn't know what happened to him. Once in a while, she thought about that day. He wouldn't have forgotten it either. She was sure he hadn't.

❧

A pale light still hung above the western horizon, a line of hills above the great river which wound into night in its deep channel. Estelle was asleep, her book face down in her lap. Gillian went out. Around the old house lay the silence she remembered. An owl called, small creatures rustled in the grass, but these sounds only ruffled the edge of the stillness, an ocean that rose, submerging house and hill.

There was no silence in the city, not ever, even in the darkest hours of the coldest nights of winter. The machinery never stopped. Here, down an old road that went nowhere in particular, no trucks whined and ground their way uphill, no radios played, no car alarms startled sleepers from their dreams.

Gillian shivered a little in the cool. The grass was soaked with dew. The moon came up. A harvest moon, spilling light like honey. The pasture was still, the hills like bronze. The upper windows of the house were blank and black between their shutters.

She had not lived in this house since she was twenty, since those distant college summers before she left for Cambridge. Now she was back. For a year, she guessed. It wasn't a simple life, though it might look as easy as an old shoe. To share a house with her mother, when both of them were used to living alone, was an exercise in diplomacy. She and her mother were ambassadors from two solitudes. And from two ages. Their customs and habits differed: their hours of rising and retiring, their preferences in eating and drinking and arranging their possessions. It was Estelle's house, so Gillian might rearrange a room for herself, but the public spaces remained her mother's domain. The tables, the chairs, the sofas, were where her mother had always had them, and were available for Gillian's use only if she moved things: Estelle's books, her newspaper, her glasses, her mail, a discarded sweater. Sometimes Gillian thought that these items were Estelle's way of marking her territory. She'd said so to Jo, adding, 'It's better than pissing on the furniture.'

'That comes next,' Jo replied. It was only half a joke.

Estelle lived in a magpie's clutter, her history assembled in objects kept where she could see them: letters, candlesticks, a glass case of stuffed birds, photographs of children and grand-children in silver frames, the portrait of her mother, who'd been a belle, the little jade elephant Gillian's father had brought home after the war. The drawers and the closets were crammed, too, with spools of thread and linen napkins and ancient winter coats. Gillian's house was neat; there were bare surfaces and empty hangers dangled in the closets. But then, Gillian had not married; her house was not a storehouse for the generations. She knew this, yet it was hard to live in the clutter.

And there were other revelations. Living with her mother, sleeping in her old room, she found herself not only inhabiting the present, but the past. Gillian's long-forgotten teenaged self materialized at random like an irate ghost, uttering sharp retorts that galled her conscience afterwards; she was seized by impatience and then remorse, astonished that she could still react like a child, just because she was living with her mother. Did one never disconnect the wires from those old buttons?

If she was going to, she'd better do it right now. There was no time to waste. Estelle might talk of living with angina, but if the array of pills on her table failed, and she didn't want surgery, then…And they couldn't even talk about it. Not after what had happened this afternoon. Shock and anger were dangerous.

What had she provoked with her question about surgery, Gillian wondered. Estelle had bristled like Rumpole when he saw Jim Whitlock's dogs. 'Don't *you* start.' Who had been pressing the issue? Franklin? Gillian would ask him—her brother had his patriarchal moments. She could respect what she imagined were the reasons for her mother's decision; she'd no doubt weighed the risks against the potential benefits and had decided to play the cards she held. If she survived the surgery, what then? She'd have a repaired heart, but the rest of her body was failing. Gillian knew that she was often in pain.

It was hard to face. For so long, time had seemed to stand still, one year like another, and now, suddenly, like the end of Shangri-la, it turned out that time had passed. Now, Estelle couldn't walk to the top of the meadow. She couldn't work in the garden—her knees hurt too much. The heat suffocated her, she gasped for breath if she lifted anything heavier than a small watering can. Her bones were brittle. She tired easily. Estelle was old.

The moon floated, shrinking and silvering as it rose. Out here in the dark it might be any year: 1938, when her parents first came and saw the house standing empty on the hill above the road; or some year in the fifties, when Gillian rode the bus to school, and Booter Mitchell drank and damned the Commies in the tavern, and Carrie Pilgrim had a one-woman show at the Andre Emmerich Gallery in New York and Gillian's parents went to the opening; or the year she came home because her father died, and Estelle stopped closing the farm in winter and settled permanently in the valley.

Or it might be now, a night when a young woman lay dead in the morgue, and her killer could be anywhere, watching the same moon.

CHAPTER 5

'Any word from the police?'

Gillian was sitting in Jo's office, a squat, square room in one of the older new buildings: barracks covered in white clapboard that had been added when the original college became too crowded. The casement windows and old oak chairs had a certain battered charm, but the rooms were cold, the chairs weren't ergonomic, and the electricity supply fainted away when asked to meet modern demands: two kettles going at once blew the circuit. Then computer data fell into the void, and faculty raged impotently in the corridors. Jo had made tea in the photocopier cubicle, where the rules ordained that a single kettle could reside. In her office were three chairs, a heavy oak desk, two metal filing cabinets and a wall of books. The furniture, like the building, was worn with use. Spending priorities lay elsewhere.

'They can't locate Nicole's aunt. Her parents are dead— you probably didn't know that.' Jo's expression was distant, clouded with pain. Even in the dim light behind the half-drawn blind, Gillian could see her pallor, the puffiness around her eyes. 'I've still got a headache. Nothing's working,' Jo explained. 'I shouldn't have let myself cry.' Her voice was hoarse. 'But I was Nicole's advisor, I knew her better than most of the faculty and admin people. Her parents died in a fire when she was thirteen, and her Aunt Charlotte took her in.'

'Where does she live?'

'New York. Nicole told me they're very close. But Margaret couldn't reach her at the number in Nicole's file.'

'She's away?'

'That's what we thought, but Margaret finally got an answer at the number last night, and it's not Nicole's aunt's. Whoever has the number doesn't speak very good English, so everything was very confused, but it turned out they've never heard of Nicole or Charlotte Bishop.'

'There could be an error in the file.'

Jo shook her head. 'Roberta dug out the original form Nicole filled in, just in case there'd been an error in transcribing, but there wasn't. Then we thought the number must have changed and Nicole forgot to inform us. We checked with information, but there's no new listing. The police went to the address we have for her. It's in Manhattan. Riverside Drive. There's an apartment building there, but there's no apartment rented to a Charlotte Bishop. Her apartment number belongs to Leslie somebody. So we still don't know where her aunt is. I don't understand it. I'm sure Nicole never said anything about anybody named Leslie.'

'Did the police talk to her?'

'She wasn't home. But the neighbours said she's young. So she can't be Nicole's aunt. They'll keep trying, I guess.'

'Her aunt pays her fees?'

'Her Blackwell Scholarship covers her tuition.'

'Room and board still cost plenty.'

'We charge less than Vassar or Sarah Lawrence,' Jo said, automatically defending the college.

'I was only asking whether her aunt paid the fees, however paltry they may be.'

'Yes, though Nicole told me she'd earned some of the money herself. She worked as a model, and her aunt invested most of what she made for her education.'

'The power of compound interest,' Gillian said. She was thinking about Nicole's clothes. They were drab. A little sloppy, even, but not in-your-face sloppy. They were some kind of negation. A reaction to her modeling experience?

'I heard that the track coach was worried that she was too thin.'

'Who told you that?'

'Carla, I think. She said you were worried that Nicole was doing too much, and that Judy thought she was too thin.'

'We did talk about that. She was bony. But models are skinny.'

'Do you think she could have been anorexic?'

Jo looked distraught. 'It's so hard to tell. They're all hypersensitive about their bodies. They all diet. Some of them have been dieting almost since they were babies. It's frightening.'

'What's her aunt like? Have you seen her? Is she in the fashion business?'

'I've never met her. So far as I know, she hasn't been up here. Nicole said she had her own business, but she sold it. She's retired now. And a widow. Her husband was an importer—he traveled a lot. I don't think Nicole was too clear about what exactly he did, just that he was away most of the time.'

'The admissions committee must know. People bare their financial souls to apply to these places. It's like filling out entrance forms for St Peter.'

'Only if you want financial aid. The Blackwells are merit scholarships, and Nicole pays her tuition and board in full, so her family assets are none of our business.'

'How do you apply for a Blackwell?'

'You're invited to, on the basis of your grades and recommendations and exam results.' Jo twiddled a pencil, making lumpy circles on an envelope. 'Then you fill out the mother of all application forms. I've been on the committee that reads them.'

Absently, Gillian helped herself to more tea from the pot on Jo's desk. It was cold and it lay on her tongue, revolting.

Gillian took the pot away and poured it down the sink. She put the kettle on and drank a little water. While she waited, she stood in the hall listening to the quiet. She knew the usual sounds of this building. The silence was abnormal. She had passed several open doors, people in their offices, but the background chatter, the orchestral accompaniment of echoes and vibrations through the wooden walls, was missing. No one was laughing or slamming drawers, or rushing along the hall, late for a class. No one was talking in tones above a whisper. It's like crossing an avalanche slope, she thought; we're afraid a sudden noise or movement will bury us.

'Do you still like living on campus, Jo?' she asked when she got back with the tea.

Jo reacted with irritation. 'You don't understand it, do you? Most people don't. They think it's strange, as if I'd joined a sect like Brook Farm.' She pointed her pencil at Gillian. 'You know what I think? Privacy is a vice, but our civilization doesn't realize it. We're getting worse and worse at living with each other. We're all going to end up in separate cells, communicating only by fax and e-mail. A nation of only children.'

'I wasn't criticizing your choice.'

'No, but don't you see, you question it in a way you don't question other choices. You don't say to people, "Do you still like living alone?"'

'That's often because you know they don't, but they have no other option.'

Jo was not to be mollified. 'Yes, they do. They don't even think about the possibilities. It's hard to find anyone who's willing to live on campus now. Why? It's so easy to live alone. Privacy is becoming a pathology. Look at you and Edward.'

Gillian laughed. 'I can't see us supervising a dorm in our declining years.'

'You've known him for what, fourteen years?'

'Longer.'

'But you don't live together.'

'I'd have had to quit my job. I haven't wanted to do that; I've scared myself just thinking about who I'd be without it. I wouldn't find a good position in London, and he wouldn't be happy if he left the Yard. That's his habitat—he has to live there, like the spotted owl in old-growth forests. Like a cottonmouth in a swamp.'

'Or maybe the relationship has lasted because you both want to be alone most of the time. If you didn't want to, you would have found a way around it.'

'I've thought about that. It was probably true at one time, but it isn't any more. We're just in the two-career trap, like lots of people. I don't think it's pathological.'

'Of course you don't, because living alone is a demographic trend. But so is loneliness.'

'When I've been at meetings all day, I'm not lonely—I'm often relieved to come home to an empty house—not to have to deal with the pressure of another personality. But what I'm discovering, living with my mother and coming here to Stanton a couple of days a week, is that life feels much more balanced. I don't want to work all the time.'

'It's harder to be a monomaniac when you live with someone else.'

'True, but the adjustment's tricky.'

'It's like losing energy from not exercising. You need to exercise your tolerance for human reality.'

'Then I'm on a Stairmaster to reality these days. There's nothing like living with your own parent to give those muscles a work-out. My mother's getting her exercise, too.' Gillian thought she recognized the sort of state Jo was in: communal living had always been one of her hobbyhorses, and now, in the aftermath of violence, her anger flared at every manifestation of the atomized society she held responsible.

Jo, perhaps realizing something of the kind herself, dropped the argument. 'Anyway, I don't like isolation. I like this. The fuss and muss of living in a crowd. I saw a documentary last year, about the Inuit. In the summer, they cook and sleep in big tents, all together. They pile their bedding on a platform and everybody sleeps in a big, warm huddle. Living in college is a bit like that. I feel at home with the noise and the jokes and even the bitchery. Besides, I get to know the students on a whole other level. I learn something, being part of their lives; it's too easy to forget what it's like to be young.'

'Funny, isn't it? If I'd grown up like you, in a New York apartment with five siblings, I think I'd have fled to a desert island. But then I'm just imagining me as I am. I'd be different.'

'I'll say. You in my family? I can't picture it.'

'I'm scared I'm going to lose my mother, Jo. She had an angina attack yesterday when I told her about Nicole. She's getting worse, and she doesn't want surgery.'

'Would *you*?'

'How can I know? But we can't talk about it because she gets angry.'

'She's probably scared.'

'Yes, but I think that's not all there is to it,' Gillian said, dissatisfied.

'Give it time. You just got here in August.'

'How much time is there?'

Jo didn't answer. There wasn't an answer. But Gillian could read her thought like a bumper sticker. It said, 'Your mother is eighty-four. Nicole was twenty-two.' Gillian knew it wasn't reasonable to expect Jo to listen to her troubles today.

'Why was Nicole on Dykeman's Pond Road? It's a regular route for the running team, isn't it?' she asked.

'Yes. And she was on the team—one of the strongest runners, in fact. She could have been captain, but she didn't want it. Too much social work, she told me. She just liked to run. But that doesn't mean she was running on Dykeman's Pond Road on Thursday morning.' Jo sounded ready to argue the point.

'I didn't say she was.'

'But that's what some people *are* saying—that she went out on her own. The team are supposed to use a buddy system.'

'And everybody "knew" she was shot. Jo, you're a social historian, and you've got money in the stock market. You know what rumours are all about. When people don't know, they invent. Any explanation is better than none at all.'

'We'd know more if the police would tell us what they're doing. Maya and Lynn say they've seen a guy near the pond a couple of times when they were out running. They thought he might have been watching them.'

'What kind of guy?'

'Scruffy, skinny. "Older," Maya said, which means forty, maybe? Fifty? Even thirty looks "older" to somebody who's nineteen. He had a camera, she thinks. Lynn told the police about him, but who knows if they're paying attention? They were here for hours and hours yesterday, pawing through things in Nicole's room, asking questions about her. They asked if she took drugs. You'd think *she* was the criminal.'

'Know any of the cops?'

'I've seen the highway patrol at work. I don't know any detectives. Why?'

'Just wondering who would be on the case. It can make a difference.' Gillian sipped her tea.

'It just seems like everybody's questioning who she is. Looking for dirt.'

'As any homicide cop will tell you, people are seldom killed by strangers. They're murdered by their nearest and dearest. That's why the investigation starts where it does: with the victim.'

'OK, OK.' Jo still looked angry. 'But where does it end?'

Poor Jo. She mothered her students, worried about them, delighted in them, missed them when they'd gone. She doled out advice and comfort. Gillian, used to the impersonal structures of a university, and by nature more detached, thought Jo's approach was risky. But Jo was well equipped for the risks; she came from a large family that had never heard of the word dysfunctional. They even had fun at Christmas.

She'd met Jo at NYU where they'd both been hired, back in the heady days of academic expansion. Josefina Oliviera, then known as Josie. The first one in her family to go to graduate school, as her father had been the first to finish high school, she had once wished to be a nun. But the offer of a scholarship diverted her to another path. A course on Voltaire changed her world, she told Gillian, and right then she'd known she wanted to teach. She'd moved from NYU to U of Texas, before realizing that a liberal arts college was where she wanted to be, preferably near New York. She fished around and eventually landed the job at Stanton. Now she'd been happily settled there for fifteen years. She remained close to all of her brothers and sisters and a legion of nieces and nephews, none of whom had strayed from the greater metropolitan area.

'They *are* a greater metropolitan area,' Gillian said once, after accompanying Jo to a family celebration. 'They should have their own zip code.' Whenever she went home to see Estelle, she always had a visit with Jo, and, seeing her so well suited, wondered what her own life would have been if she hadn't moved west.

Jo was a solid woman built low to the ground. She wore her hair very short, showing three diamond studs in each of her neat little ears. There was a graceful economy to Jo's compact energetic roundness that Gillian admired. By comparison, she felt gangly: tall and thin, like a plant struggling for light. There was nothing she could do to tidy herself up except cut her hair, but very short hair meant more frequent haircuts, so she couldn't be bothered.

They had been immensely pleased with themselves when Gillian's appointment at Stanton was arranged. A perfect fit, they'd crowed. Right now, however, Gillian wished she'd gone to England instead. Only a few years before, one of her own grad students at UPNW had been killed. When she was with Edward, in London, his murder investigations felt like powerful vortexes which sucked him out of the flat and into a whirling darkness like the prairie blizzards people got lost in only a few feet from their own front doors. Sometimes the horror was a palpable presence. She hadn't expected it here.

'What was Nicole like?' she asked Jo. 'Was she popular?'

'No, I don't think she was popular. But she wasn't unpopular, either. She didn't strive for position. The students live cheek by jowl here; there are pecking orders and cliques, to some extent, but Nicole kept more distance than most.'

'She must have had some kind of social life here.'

'Oh sure. She had people she'd sit with at dinner, friends to go to the movies with, that kind of thing. She wasn't isolated. Some of the younger students were intimidated by her, and some admired her. Janice Grogan followed her around like a puppy. But she seemed older than most of the students, even the seniors, maybe because of losing her parents. And she was very focused. Whatever she got involved in, she was intense about it. I think she may have looked on dorm life as a bit of a joke.'

Gillian thought about the students in her class. Fifteen unknown quantities who had barely begun to reveal themselves. Visually, they fell into two camps—classic and pop. Smooth hair, no make-up and natural fibres, or flat-tops dyed green and rings in their eyebrows. The weather had been pretty warm when term started, and shorts and tank tops had revealed the amazing popularity of tattoos. Female symbols, roses, a broken chain—personal logos stamped into the skin. At least they didn't label themselves 'Guess' and 'DKNY'. Calvin Klein was probably working on an ad campaign using tattooed buttocks. What would be next? Cicatrices? Ubangi lip plugs? And what would they think about their tattoos when they were thirty or forty? But of course they didn't know how fast the time went. A year was still an epoch at twenty.

Classic or pop, most students looked as if they thought about what they wore. They dressed to draw the eye and announce a persona. But Nicole, Gillian realized, thinking about it, had a kind of anti-style. Gillian couldn't recollect any particular garment. Nicole wore no jewellery, displayed no tattoos, and confined her hair in a clip. If all clothing is costume, Gillian thought, then Nicole was playing the invisible woman. Melanie Wilkes, not Scarlett. She could think of a few reasons why Nicole might have chosen that role, but she had no idea which, if any, was the right one.

Already, the students had sorted themselves into tortoises and hares in class discussion, but Gillian had learned over the years that some of the quiet ones simply took longer to open up and often had the most incisive comments to make in the second half of the term. An early paper was usually a better indicator of what the student might produce later, and Gillian could usually tell by the end of the first page what the quality of the whole was likely to be. Her class were to hand in their first papers on Tuesday. She wondered, fleetingly, what Nicole would have written about.

As she had told Estelle, she didn't know much about Nicole. But soon she would know more, and so would everyone else. How much more would depend partly on who had killed Nicole and how quickly the police could close the file. Nicole might soon be filed in the world's short memory under 'tragic victim'. On the other hand, a murder investigation was a kind of archaeology. The victim's past was carefully excavated, and all sorts of odd finds might be made. The dead, she had learned, have no privacy but that donated by lack of interest.

CHAPTER 6

'Have you told Edward about what's happened?' Estelle asked on Saturday.

'Yes. We had a long telephone call yesterday, after I came back from Stanton.'

'What did he say?'

Gillian hadn't told her mother that Edward had been rather distant for the past few months, since her decision not to go to England. She suspected that Estelle knew but was too reticent to ask. What a complex weave there was between parent and child, even now. What to reveal, what to conceal, what to ask, what not to ask?

'He thinks that it would be better if he were here.'

'Amen to that.'

Gillian snorted.

'Don't you want him to come?' Estelle demanded.

'Naturally, but that's not the same as thinking he's the cavalry, which is what you mean.'

'At my age,' Estelle said with dignity, 'I can be rescued by a man if I want to.'

'It's one of your golden age privileges, is it?' Gillian said. 'Like seats on the bus?'

One good thing had happened as a result of Nicole's death. She'd sent Edward an e-mail about it, and he'd been on the telephone the same day, not distant, not silent, but full of questions and anxious affection. The pack ice had broken up, and the pieces were floating away. She was glad, but she wished the reason had been a different one. For Nicole's sake, of course, but also because now he would worry about her—Gillian—being alone with her mother in a house in the country. He thought of himself as the cavalry just as Estelle did. He couldn't help it.

The bright weather lingered through the weekend, and Gillian was rooting out buttercups when Kitty Grogan dropped in on Sunday afternoon. Estelle sat in a wicker chair, wrapped in an ancient paisley shawl. A pair of fingerless gloves warmed her hands as she read the *Times* book reviews and kept a vigilant eye on Gillian's progress. Rumpole was asleep in her lap.

'That's Kitty's car,' she observed. 'How nice.'

'Is her husband with her?' Gillian asked, her view blocked by a clump of dahlias.

'No, I don't see Lewis.'

Good, Gillian thought. Kitty on her own was easy company.

Kitty parked her spotless white BMW and stepped daintily on to the lawn. 'I thought I'd stop, because we had to cancel our drink with you the other day. Lewis's still caught up in this awful business at the college. But if you're busy, I'll run on home.'

'Do stay, Kitty. I don't see enough of you.' Estelle pointed to the garden chair nearest her own. 'Sit there. Gillian was just going to make tea.'

Oh, was I? Gillian thought. She was making slow headway with the buttercups. But her knees were tired. She went in and washed her hands and made a pot of Earl Grey tea. Rumpole abandoned Estelle, following Gillian to the kitchen. He sniffed at his empty dish, then leapt to the counter where Estelle kept her vitamins and an assortment of small items she often used: pens and pencils, notepads, teabags, scissors, a magnifying glass for reading labels, a flashlight, and some cough drops. Each time Gillian had come home in recent years, the open counter space had shrunk, and the objects had spread and multiplied, rather like the new houses springing up beside the old roads. Her own habit was to put everything away, but she realized that Estelle had evolved an energy-conservation system in which the things she needed were in plain sight and within her reach. If she'd thrown away the things she never used, the cupboards would now be empty. But Estelle threw nothing away, and the lower cupboards still held the heavy pots, while the upper shelves contained spare place settings of the everyday china, an assortment of heavily tarnished silver trays and bowls, old jars of powdered spices and condiments with their lids gummed shut.

Gillian hunted for the light lacquer tray Estelle used. It was under a heap of cups and saucers. Rumpole patted a small plastic bottle of pills and then swiped at it with a broad paw. He watched with pleasure as it hit the floor and rolled towards the fridge.

Gillian scoured the cupboards for cookies. 'Cookie' was a Dutch word; so was 'kill', meaning stream, a term which lingered in place names in the valley. Estelle liked cookies; she must have finished off the gingersnaps, and Gillian had neglected to lay in a fresh supply. The cupboards were bare of substitutes, but Kitty probably didn't eat cookies, she looked too thin to be a between-meals snacker. Estelle would think that there ought to be a plate of cookies. And I think so too, she admitted. What's more, they shouldn't be from a supermarket package. If I could now produce an offering of cookies I had made myself, they would prove that the richness of my private life hasn't been sacrificed to my profession. I would deserve a gold star, from whoever it is I think hands them out.

Gillian carried the tray to the garden.

'Darling,' Estelle said. 'Aren't there any cookies?'

Gillian wished Laura were there, or Edward. Someone whose eye she would have to avoid so as not to laugh.

'I'm sorry, madam. The scullery maid's run away with the gardener's boy, and cook is having hysterics.'

'Please don't bother. I never eat them,' said Kitty.

'Don't you? You should, then. You're way too thin,' Estelle replied. She waited for Gillian to pour.

Kitty pulled at a long swaying tendril of bindweed. It had wound itself through the arbor behind Estelle's chair, choking the grapes. 'Horrible stuff. I hate bindweed, the way it strangles everything.' She dropped a broken piece on Gillian's weed pile and took off her sunglasses.

Kitty was very tanned and almost gaunt. Her wrist and collarbones stood out under the skin. Her hips were narrow, her breasts small, and her waist fitted neatly in between. She reminded Gillian of an Egyptian mummy—fleshless, a parchment stretched over bare bones. Yet Kitty had two grown sons, and a daughter in college. She went to a spa a couple of times a year, Estelle said.

Gillian handed her a cup. 'Is there any news?'

'Have they found that poor girl's aunt?' Estelle put in.

'No. It's the strangest thing. Margaret told Lewis they've only found someone named Leslie Lang. And she's never heard of Nicole or her aunt. I believe they're tracing Charlotte Bishop through her bank, now. Lewis says the whole thing's very fishy.'

'It's odd, certainly. People don't evaporate, even in New York City.'

'Lewis says they think she's never visited Stanton. That's funny, if she lives in New York. I mean, people usually do like to see where their children are. Lewis thinks she must be an alcoholic or something like that—so Nicole didn't want her to come.'

Always parroting Lewis, Gillian thought. I should have offered her crackers.

'If they can't find her it's probably a computer error,' Estelle said. 'Those silly machines won't admit it when they're wrong; you can complain until you're blue in the face.'

Gillian gave Estelle half a cup of tea. Sometimes her hands shook, and things spilt, which upset her. Kitty sat on the edge of her chair and crossed her legs. Her pretty gold watch glittered in the sun as she raised her cup. Her wrists were as tiny as a child's. Rumpole could bat her off the chair, Gillian thought. Her bone-china looks were deceiving, however; she was an excellent rider. Kitty was what, in her late fifties? She seemed to Gillian to be more like a member of Estelle's generation than someone who was younger than Gloria Steinem. In England, she would have been county all the way—sensible shoes, pearls, horses. Here, the shoes were a little less sensible and golf competed with the horses. There was something immovable about her. You would never guess that her body had borne three children. An image of Kitty and Lewis in bed formed in Gillian's mind, and she tried to eject it.

'How's Janice?' Estelle asked, aware that Kitty and Lewis's daughter also attended Stanton.

'Awfully upset. We all are. It's such a terrible thing. But she *knew* Nicole. We didn't. So it's worse for her. She keeps bursting into tears.'

· 'Maybe you should bring her home for a day or two.'

'She wants to stay at Stanton. Some notion of solidarity in the crisis. I'd pull her out anyway, but she'd raise such a fuss. I'll have to see.'

'What about the criminal investigation?' Gillian said. 'Have you and Lewis heard anything?'

'That's actually what I wanted to tell you,' Kitty said. 'I ran into Marsh at the club this morning.'

'Do you remember Judge Marshall?' Estelle interrupted, before Gillian could ask who 'Marsh' was. 'He was a state supreme court judge. He used to come to those big Fourth-of-July parties the Brewsters had. You went to those parties.'

'Yes.' She remembered the din and the smoke and hundreds of empty glasses. 'Annie Brewster and I sneaked cigarettes and smoked them down by the pond.' Annie's parents used to fill bowls with cigarettes and leave them lying around like potato chips. Times change.

'He's retired now,' Estelle finished. 'Go on, Kitty.'

'Marsh says the police already have a suspect.'

'Who?'

'The Mitchell boy. Arnold Mitchell.'

'Oh, dear,' Estelle said. 'That's just awful.' She looked at Gillian.

Gillian quickly set down her teacup, watchful. How bad a shock would this be? The pills were in the house. Estelle's hands trembled a little, but her colour was good. She was going to be all right.

'Why do they suspect him?' Gillian asked. Her own heart thumped.

'Gillian just saw him the other night,' Estelle interjected. 'In the Dutch House.'

'I haven't been there for years,' Kitty said. 'There were beetles in the ladies' room.'

'Why do they suspect Arnold?' Gillian repeated.

'Have you met Lynn Hatch—one of the girls who found Nicole? Her parents came up to see her yesterday—she'd phoned them, of course. They took her out, and on the way back, she recognized a man who's been watching the running team. She saw him, I don't know where, but he was getting into an old pick-up truck. She wrote the licence number down, and then they told the police. Not that the police would have needed the number. Everyone who lives here knows Arnold's truck.'

'I see. So the police have to check him out.'

'I hope they lock him up. I've made Janice promise not to go anywhere alone, but I won't believe any of those girls are safe until they put him in jail. It *is* probably him, isn't it? Watching's so creepy.' Kitty's nostrils flared with distaste.

'So they went to his house? To the Mitchell place?' Gillian pictured the police car bumping down an overgrown driveway. She'd never been there.

'They must have—that's where he usually is, isn't it?' Kitty said. 'He was always strange, wasn't he, Estelle? Not normal.'

'He was never a happy child. But oh, dear, I don't want to think...' she trailed off.

'We thought he was a recluse. But now you have to wonder what he's been up to, hiding in that house all these years. And why does he always have a camera? What's he been taking pictures of?' She turned to Gillian. 'Did you talk to him?'

'No.'

'I always thought it was too bad that Virginia died first. She and Arnold might have gotten on all right with Booter gone,' Estelle observed.

'Maybe,' Kitty said dubiously. 'When did you see him?'

'The night of the accident,' Gillian said reluctantly. 'I stopped to make a phone call because the road was blocked.'

Kitty was excited. 'But they found Nicole the next morning! You should tell the police when you saw him. It might be important.'

CHAPTER 7

Monday was not one of Gillian's usual days on campus. But in the crisis much had been left undone, and she'd forgotten to take home a folder of bibliographies and some page references she needed. Forgetting things was a continual irritant. She couldn't even remember when it had started to be a problem. At least she had a crisis to blame this time, and she would have made the extra trip anyhow, just to see how the college was doing.

She hunted for the folder. She'd left things in a mess. Where had she set it down? The corridor was busy—college life resuming its rhythm—and she didn't look up when she heard footsteps stop outside her door. A notice board hung opposite, and people often stopped to post notes or read them. She'd learned not to pay attention.

There was a brisk knock: someone for her after all.

'Come in,' she called and looked up as the door opened. A man came through, a short, wry-nosed man, balding and pear-shaped. He stopped just inside the door and looked at her quizzically.

'"What, my dear Lady Disdain! Are you yet living?"'

'Eli! My God! Eli Pink! Mr. Cardero's drama class.' She laughed with surprise, stood up. She was just taller than he was. She looked him over again. She remembered the nose all right, and the voice. But he'd been a skinny kid, a pencil in loose jeans, a sharp-eyed restless fidgeter with a briar patch of brown curls. She'd never seen him out of Levis. Now he wore a jacket and tie, and his belly hung over his belt buckle.

He looked back. 'You haven't changed a bit.'

'You mean my hair was turning grey in junior high? You never told me.'

'I was a nice boy.'

'You were a smart-alec. Remember your imitation of Miss Bork? I do.'

Eli crossed his arms over a large imaginary bosom. 'That one?'

'Yes, that one. "I want your *un*divided attention." But you know what, Eli, you're not the first person from our class I've seen recently. Guess who else I saw here on campus.'

'Who?'

Eli asked it casually, but his eyes stopped roaming around the room and stayed on Gillian.

'Torch Regan. She works here as a cook.'

'Oh.'

He relaxed again.

'Do you remember when she beat up Ricky Sands?' Gillian said.

'No, I don't think so. But she was terrible in Mr. Cardero's class. My dog could have read the lines better.'

Mr. Cardero had been a tiny man of titanic energies. In front of the class, he went off like a string of Chinese firecrackers. He read lines aloud that stayed in their memories for weeks. He made them laugh.

'He made us do a scene from Wilde, didn't he? Christ, we massacred it. I did. Students shouldn't be let loose on Wilde. You were good, though.'

'The next Olivier.'

It was meant as a joke, but the bitterness in Eli's voice was audible. She changed the subject. 'How did you find me here?'

He pulled out his wallet, flipped it open and handed it to her.

'Eli Pink,' she read. 'You're a cop! A detective! Jesus—you're on the case here at Stanton, aren't you?'

'I'm the man.' He waited a moment, letting her absorb it.

'I don't know why I'm so dumbfounded,' she said.

'Because my name was going to be in Broadway lights.'

Another prickly joke. Maybe seeing her brought back memories. Eli had had big dreams.

'Is there any coffee around here?' he asked.

'Sure. We can go to the faculty lounge, or get some down the hall.'

'Whatever's easier.'

He followed her to the cubicle where the coffee machine sat. The pot was two-thirds empty, and the coffee smelled stale, so she started a fresh batch. Not that it would be very good; the premeasured packets didn't have much flavour. Eli nosed around the hallway and read the bulletin board. When the coffee was ready, he loaded his up with cream and sugar.

'I'm supposed to cut back on coffee. I get heartburn. I figure if it's the acid, the cream will cut it.'

'Did you come to see me because of the Nicole Bishop case?' Gillian asked when they got back to her office and shut the door.

'It's how I heard you were here. If I'd heard it some other way, I'd have dropped in sooner or later. Sooner.'

'Are you going to ask me questions?'

'It's my job.'

'Then let's get it over with.'

'Right.' Eli snapped open a little brown notebook. 'You're staying with your mother on Salt Hill Road?'

'Since August fifteenth.'

'How long are you planning to stay?'

'Probably through the spring. She's not very well.'

'She must be pretty old by now.'

'Eighty-four.'

'Not bad. Better than my parents did. They've been gone over ten years now. Heart trouble, both sides. So I'm supposed to be on a diet, but doctors change their minds twice a week. Don't eat this, don't eat that. To hell with them. I figure genetics'll get me anyway, so I eat what I want. You're teaching here part time?'

'One course. I'm on sabbatical leave from my regular job.'

'A year off? Good scam. Beats free doughnuts.' He shifted restlessly in his chair. 'Is your regular job at a girls' school, too?'

'No. At a university. The students are boys and girls; the faculty is still mostly boys.'

'So is Stanton different? The atmosphere?'

'More inbred. More personal. But that's because it's much smaller and it's residential. College isn't a joyride these days; most of the students are too tense about the future. They compete hard to get in, and it costs a lot to go.'

'Nicole Bishop had a good record. She worked hard, never got into trouble. A model student, I'm told. Is that your impression?'

'She was good. There's pleasure in teaching students like her.'

'What else do you know about her?'

'Nothing. You'd be better off asking the students, or any of the permanent faculty. It's an intimate place; everybody knows everybody. But I just got here.'

'She was in your class. No unusual behaviour? Signs of distress?'

'Not that I noticed.'

'She didn't miss any classes?'

'No, but it's early in the term.'

'Any ideas about who might have killed her?'

'None at all.'

'OK.' He tasted his coffee. 'A good bean is hard to find.'

'It used to be impossible, outside the city.'

Eli took another sip. 'So what do you think of the old neighbourhood? It hasn't changed too much.'

'It seems different to me. Houses used to be built one at a time. Now they come in packages of twenty, like cigarettes.'

'OK, I grant you. But most of your road looks the same as it did thirty years ago.'

'For how long? The whole pattern is changing—who lives here and what they do. Out go the barns and in come the two-car garages and the shopping malls.'

'What do you want? Brigadoon? Christ, the towns along the river are half dead anyway. You been up the valley? Been to Hudson?'

'It's a beautiful town. The heart hasn't been ripped out of it.'

'Yeah, because there's no money. Not a dime.'

'It could pay off later, when they have something other towns have thrown away.'

'Later's later. Now's now. Mr. Cardero lives in Hudson, you know that? I went to see him once.'

'Really? I'd like to see him. He was a treat.' This was a funny sort of interview, she thought. She supposed the questions about Nicole were an excuse—after all, she didn't know anything that could help him solve the case. They'd been close friends once, for a year or so, and now he was curious. She was, too.

'Whatever happened to Joey Florio?' she asked. 'Every girl in the class used to dream about him.'

Eli grinned. 'He sells cars. He's bald. And he's already had a heart bypass.'

Gillian's amusement faded. Joey had been a high school prince; she didn't want to hear that he had a bad heart.

Eli flicked a glance at her, a quick sidelong look she remembered. 'You remember Arnold Mitchell?'

'Lynn Hatch told you he's been watching the running team.'

'Yeah. Sharp-eyed kid. You remember Arnold?'

'Of course.'

'What do you remember?'

'Nobody ever talked to him.'

'And his little brother Tommy got himself killed.'

'Yes. You've talked to Arnold?'

'I've been to see him. He claims he didn't know about Nicole. Hadn't even heard she was dead. Do you believe that?'

'My mother says he hardly ever talks to anybody.'

'Mm. Same old Arnold. That's what I hear.'

'So then what makes you think he had anything to do with Nicole?'

'He had a picture of the victim. A photograph.'

Gillian swallowed. 'Of the victim. Of her body?'

'Not the way you mean. Not her dead body.'

'What kind of picture?'

'You wouldn't want him to have this picture of you.'

'Not pornography?'

'Maybe, maybe not. I'm just a simple cop.'

Gillian was at sea. What was he getting at? She looked at him, uncertain. He studied her, then said:

'It's a lousy photo. Blurry and a lot of grain—a long exposure. But it's her, OK, no doubt about it. And she's wearing nothing but her panties.'

Gillian felt sick. 'Where did he get it?'

'Took it himself. He's got quite the telephoto lens.'

'Where?'

'Here. She's in her dorm room. It's on the first floor. He was in the woods. She's standing at the window with a lamp shining on her like she's Mary in a Christmas pageant.'

'Then she had no idea he was there?'

'That's a fair assumption. Have you ever walked past the back side of that dorm at night?'

Gillian shook her head. The dorm stood at the edge of the woods. There was a path behind it, but it led only to the fire exit and a trail through the woods to the riverbank.

Eli snorted. 'It's a regular peep show. I've told Madam la President she'd better do something about it. Who knows what will come crawling around the campus if this case gets any real play in the media?'

Gillian thought of Kitty. She'd wondered what Arnold was doing with his camera. Perhaps she'd been worrying about her own daughter. In the first weeks of term, when the weather was warm, he might have photographed half the campus in a state of semi-nudity.

'Does he have pictures of any other students?'

'Nothing recognizable. Not that we've found. But he's got Nicole all right. A pin-up on his wall.'

'And you're sure she didn't know?'

'It's happened before. Even people with bodyguards are snapped on the sly. Think of Princess Di and the other one, with the toes. It happens.'

'To celebrities. People chase them. Their images are for sale.'

'It's not always about money. There's obsession.'

'Arnold Mitchell was obsessed with Nicole?'

'How do I know?' Eli said sourly. 'The experts will testify for the defence and the prosecution. One will say yes and one will say no. It's all crap.' He propped his notebook on his knee. 'Maybe he did know her. He could be lying. But ask yourself, what would she be doing with a guy like Arnold?'

It was true, Gillian thought. It was far easier to imagine Arnold obsessed from afar than to picture Nicole on intimate terms with him.

'Nicole was last seen at dinner on Wednesday. She was found Thursday morning. When did you last see her?' Eli asked, leaning back, returning to routine.

'In class Wednesday morning. And she didn't do anything unusual. I left Stanton in the middle of the afternoon to go into Poughkeepsie to see an old friend who has a daughter at Vassar. I stayed longer than I meant to, and when I drove back there'd been an accident on the road, and the highway was blocked.'

'The semi?'

'That's right.'

'That poor SOB is still unconscious.'

'Is he going to be OK?'

'Nobody knows. How'd you get home?'

'I turned around. But I went to the Dutch House to phone, because I was late. Arnold was there.'

Eli sat up. 'You saw him? What time?'

'A little after eight. A quarter past, at the latest.'

'That's helpful. Frankie couldn't be very specific about times. Did he have a drink already?'

'There were two glasses; both were empty, or nearly empty.'

'So he was there before eight, unless he was guzzling. Was anybody with him?'

'No. Didn't he tell you he saw me?'

'Didn't mention you. He didn't talk to you, did he?'

'He was just sitting by himself in a booth.'

'Frankie says he comes in once in a while. Never says boo. Just nurses a few beers, goes away. Do you remember anyone else?'

'A few students. The people at the bar were mostly strangers—to me. They were watching TV. I was only there for a couple of minutes. Arnold seemed pretty surprised to see me. He stared.'

'Did you think he was acting strange?'

'I was a little bit spooked. Normally, people don't stare at you like that. Maybe if I'd known right away that it was Arnold, I wouldn't have worried about it. I know he's not used to talking to people.'

'You didn't know him right away? How long since you'd last seen him?'

Gillian frowned, thinking back. 'I don't know. It must be twenty years.'

'But you recognized him?'

'No, actually. My mother figured out who he was, and I knew she was right.'

'Did you recognize me?'

'Sure. You haven't changed a bit. Look, when was Nicole killed? You're asking me all these questions about Arnold in the Dutch House Wednesday evening. Was she lying in that ditch all night?'

'How much do you know about dead bodies?'

'More than you'd think,' she said, then wished she hadn't. It sounded foolish. 'Have you got anything from the postmortem yet?'

'You watch cop shows?'

'Not often. My partner is a detective. He works on murder cases.'

'Your partner is a cop? Come on. That's bullshit.'

'At Scotland Yard.'

'A cop,' Eli repeated. 'I would have lost that bet. You sure he isn't a lawyer?'

Gillian was irritated by his tone. 'He's never mentioned billable hours.'

'Scotland Yard. Murder cases.' Eli laughed.

'What's funny?' If Edward's hours *were* billable, she thought, he'd be as rich as Rockefeller.

'The murder rate in England is nothing. What's he do all day?'

'Paperwork. He says.' She was tempted to mention the Yard's high clearance rate for murder cases, but forbore; the conversation was edgy enough already.

Eli chuckled, relenting. 'OK, I believe you. He's a cop. What's his name?'

'Edward Gisborne.'

'Partner, you said?'

'We're not married.'

'Good choice.'

He hadn't answered her question about when Nicole had been killed.

'OK. How did you get home from the Dutch House?' he asked.

'I looped around the accident. Back up the Post Road to the northern end of Dykeman's Pond Road, then down it to Croft, and along Croft to where it comes out on the Post Road, below the accident.'

'What time?'

'It must have been twenty past at the earliest. Maybe a few minutes later. I was only doing thirty—it was dark, and I don't know Dykeman's that well—it would have taken me five or six minutes to drive from the top end to the bottom and along Croft.'

'Did you see anything?'

'You mean people on the road?'

'Nobody walking? No cars? Nothing on the bridge?'

'No.'

'You could have been the first driver to use that detour. The accident happened at about eight. Try and think about whether you saw anything. Anything at all.'

Gillian thought, with no results. Eli clicked his ballpoint in and out. She wondered if Nicole had been lying under the bridge when she drove over it. How many people had driven down the back road before the highway had been cleared? How long had Nicole been dead? She was sure she hadn't seen any other cars driving along Dykeman's that evening. Eli stood up, putting his notebook away. 'Let me know if you think of anything. And I might have some more questions about Arnold.' He gave her a card with his pager number on it.

'What does Arnold say?' Gillian ventured.

'That he's innocent. What else?'

'What about the photograph of Nicole?'

'She just happened to be there, he says. What he really wanted was pictures of an owl. A jury would love that.' He looked at his watch. 'I'll be in touch.'

She wanted to ask him about his job. He'd longed to be an actor. How had he ended up as a detective? Had he ever handled a murder case before? It didn't seem to be the right moment to ask that. Who was still around that they used to know—who would know about him?

'Eli,' she said. 'Do you ever see anyone from our school?'

'Who would I see?'

'Whoever's around. I don't know who's still in the area, except Torchie and Peggy Nelson. I see Peggy sometimes. Her parents still live on Beacon. She was incredibly pretty. You had a huge crush on her.' Gillian began to smile. 'I haven't forgotten that.'

Eli flushed. 'Yeah? And have you seen her recently? How much does she weigh these days? Two hundred pounds?'

He was angry. Startled, Gillian made no attempt to answer him, looking for safer ground.

'We were told Nicole wasn't shot. What did happen to her? The students who found her saw a wound.'

'A stab wound, near the base of the throat.' He kept his eyes on her face, watching her reactions. 'It would have bled plenty. Doesn't look much like a bullet hole, but I've seen a few. Those girls had never seen a corpse before. They saw a body and some blood, heard a shot, and they stuck it together. People do that all the time. They say they saw things they didn't see. Half of them have been abducted by aliens.'

'Stabbed.' She shuddered a little at the thought.

'In the throat. Body temperature indicates she was there less than twenty-four hours, which is good, since she was seen Wednesday after six p.m. She had dinner. Curried chicken. Was it on the college menu Wednesday evening? Your college president couldn't remember. What else do you want to know? The body was stiff when we got there—rigid as a Jehovah's Witness. I'm sure your mastermind at the Yard has told you all about rigor mortis.'

'Dead at least eight hours, probably longer.'

'Longer. It was cold that night. Be seeing you.'

He left without closing the door. She could hear his footsteps going away. She stared at the doorway. What had gotten into him? First that crack about Peggy, and then answering her question about the wound like a guy on a cop show—a pretty brutal form of mockery. He probably thought she should mind her own business, which was fair enough. But that wasn't why he'd suddenly turned nasty. He'd always been moody. And he had a temper. She remembered it flashing out, like a switchblade. It wasn't a good qualification for his job.

CHAPTER 8

'What am I doing here, anyhow?' Gillian asked the unresponsive air. She walked around the library building, hands stuck in her pockets, and contemplated the wasteland where the rose garden had been. The breeze was chilly, but her office felt like a prison cell. Something was wrong with this picture. The interview with Eli had unsettled her, and now she was annoyed. She'd been so pleased to see Eli after all these years, and then he'd turned on her for no reason. She wished she were in London, with Edward. At moments like this, she felt like an alien in her own country. 'You can't go home again.' It wasn't home any more, it had changed. Or you had. Or else you'd made it different in your mind as you drifted away, improving it, the way the painters improved nature. Then when you went back, the original looked all wrong.

The year before she'd moved away, she and Eli had been in nearly all the same classes. In the drama group, which they'd both loved, they'd done *The Crucible* and talked about McCarthy and the Red Scare—rather brave of Mr. Cardero with the likes of Booter Mitchell in the neighbourhood. They'd read *Much Ado* and *The Merchant of Venice*; they'd had Sheridan and Molière and Wilde. They'd read some scenes aloud. Eli had been remarkably good—stunning compared to everyone else. He was already determined to go to acting school in New York.

Eli had been in Mrs. Fisher's English class, too, the advanced class, along with Gillian and Peggy Nelson, but she couldn't remember much about it, except that they'd read Hemingway stories and *Silas Marner*, and they'd had to write descriptions of their classmates. She'd described Eli and got an A+ on her paper; he'd wanted to see but she'd never let him. He was too easily offended.

Then there was the biology lab, with fierce, bosomy Miss Bork, whose breath smelled like butterscotch. Gillian shared a foetal pig with Eli. She'd liked dissecting; discovering the marvellous intricacy of the body. She hadn't asked where the piglets came from; no one asked. They stank of formaldehyde and felt stiff and slimy, like old, wet linoleum. They weren't like anything that had ever been alive. She remembered girls recoiling from the slithery cold skin, boys joshing. She thought the pigs were like plastic models, like the bits of reproductive system that stood on the teacher's desk in health class. Inside, the veins and arteries were injected with blue and red dye. You could be curious about such a body, knowing its systems were like your own, but not feeling any kinship. How did pathologists develop that same distanced curiosity about dead humans, with their soft skin and hair, their veins leaking real blood?

The year of the foetal pig was her last in the local school. By the next year, when she and Estelle went back to the farm for six weeks in the summer, the crowd at the local high school was already part of a life she'd left behind. The tyrants and toadies, like Alice's kings and queens, had shrunk and flattened, receding into dim grey snapshots in school albums. Gillian had once been friends with Annie Brewster, who lived on Salt Hill Road and whose parents gave the biggest parties in the county. But then Annie made it into the ruling clique and lost interest in anyone outside it. Annie lived in Santa Fe now, Estelle said. Of all Gillian's old crowd, only Peggy Nelson, her friend since kindergarten, remained close. They had never lost touch, except when Peggy had dropped out of

college to go to Katmandu and vanished for nearly two years.
When she came back from Nepal, she was full of parasites
and was nearly a skeleton. Gillian rushed down from college
on the train and stayed with the Nelsons. She sat by Peggy's
bed and cried to see her sunken eyes and her bones sticking
out, and they joked about death, not believing in it. But
Peggy hadn't had a period in eight months and was terrified
she'd never be able to have children. Now she had three and
fervently hoped they would stay away from drugs. She'd put
on weight since her third child, but two hundred pounds!
Eli was being childish.

What was eating him? Eli had been around all through
elementary school, but they'd only become friends in Mr.
Cardero's class, the year before Gillian moved. It had been
one of those brief, intense friendships that flares up at the
discovery of a mutual taste scorned by the majority. No one
else at school thought Cassavetes's *Shadows* was incredible;
no one else even went to New York to see it. The herd went
to the drive-in to see Sandra Dee in *Gidget*. While their
friendship lasted, Gillian and Eli went into the city together—
to Washington Square, the Bleecker Street Cinema, the Cafe
Borgia. They saw *Breathless* twice and rolled their eyes at Doris
Day in *Pillow Talk*. Even then, Gillian remembered, there
were disconcerting moments, when Eli's mood suddenly
turned hostile. She'd been careful about what she told him,
for he was liable to use it against her. Later, after she left the
farm, the friendship wilted. When she came back for holidays
and talked about her new school, Eli started humming or
put on a record. He made snide remarks about her
appearance, or her changing tastes. He still wanted to act
and could talk forever about movies he'd seen and parts he'd
like to play, but when Gillian had had enough of that topic
they seemed to have nothing else to say. Gillian stopped
calling him.

Why had he stayed, or come back, she wondered. Was he
married? She hadn't gotten around to asking, in part because

she'd felt uncomfortable and on the defensive. He hadn't any reason for animosity, so far as she could see, so perhaps he was just soured on life in general. At least he'd found something to do, some kind of place in the scheme of things, unlike Arnold, who lived in his parents' house, apparently without work or friends.

It troubled her to think about Arnold. An outcast, and now, maybe, a murderer. What had happened in between? He'd gone into the army, and his parents had died. And then? Nothing. No marriages, no children, no jobs, no moves out west, no fame or fortune. A biographer would have a terrible time writing about Arnold.

Yet Arnold had a history, however devoid of the usual chapter headings. When she was a student at Cambridge, the famous historian Alistair Greenwood dismissed Africa as a continent without a history—history according to his definition, which was the definition that counted, since he'd occupied the Regius Chair. He was dead now, and 'history' had been redefined. Scholars considered new kinds of evidence. Empires, trade routes, vast migrations, all unrecorded on paper, had nonetheless left their marks, and they could be deciphered. Now that Arnold was under scrutiny, the blank that stood for his life would be filled in.

Where to start? He'd always been funny looking, with a bulgy forehead and big ears. She might have recognized the ears if he hadn't been wearing a cap in the bar. Perhaps he wore it to hide them. The movie *Dumbo*, about an elephant whose ears were so big he could fly, had given Arnold his nickname. He was always at the bottom of the pecking order—the child other children avoided, because low status was contagious. The teasing had been sporadic but merciless. Gillian could remember no occasion when the school authorities had intervened. Back then, teachers ignored cruelty unless it threatened to break bones. Schools were Darwinian training grounds, where children learned to survive the savagery of their peers. Arnold, lacking other skills, attempted invisibility. It was an unreliable defence, depending more on the caprices of would-be tormentors than on the evasive manoeuvres of the victim. No one had helped him, had even tried. No one had faced down the bullies or told the teachers or parents. She hadn't, though she knew someone should. She'd lacked the courage to leave the herd.

And Arnold, she'd later understood, had had no refuge at home, where he'd been subjected to the same bullying by his overbearing father and favoured younger brother. He'd bitten his nails, she remembered. The ends of his fingers were scabby and raw. In the schoolyard, he'd been a passive bundle of misery. That was Arnold from the outside. But inside, who? Someone else, certainly, she'd seen that on the Knob.

<hr />

Estelle was out when Gillian returned home. She came back several hours later, having driven herself in her old Saab, despite the offer of a lift from the Hornbecks. Gillian saw her drive up, extricate herself from the confined space behind the wheel. It wasn't easy; even shutting the car door was an effort. But Estelle said she wanted to keep her hand in. Gillian hoped to God she wouldn't hit anything. Her eyesight wasn't good, and her reactions were delayed, like the slow-motion replays on the sports news. But if she stopped driving, she would have to move out of her house. It was the last thing she wanted. The subject of driving was closed; Gillian could only wait, knowing that something would change, hoping to escape catastrophe.

Estelle's bimonthly game of bridge, played with the same three friends, had been a fixture for a dozen years, ever since Beau Brewster died, leaving TZ without a partner. It was a floating game, each household taking it in turns to provide lunch. Estelle had been at TZ's, just down the road.

'How was your game?'

'Fine, dear. Clam chowder for lunch, very nice. And we won. But I don't know how. TZ can never remember trump—not from one trick to the next. It's unnerving. "What's trump?" she says, and then she plays her card. We go around the table, and then there she goes again: "What's trump?"'

Estelle was full of pep, Gillian saw. She should get out more often.

'I don't know what's the matter with her,' Estelle continued. 'She's only seventy-four—ten years younger than I am. I can remember if it's three spades or four hearts. "What's trump?" She must have asked me twenty times.'

'But you still won.'

'Yes.' Estelle laughed. 'I can't account for it. Oh well, it doesn't matter.'

'How are the Hornbecks?'

'The same as always. Did you know they saw that girl—Nicole Bishop—biking up Dykeman's the night she was killed? Or someone like her. They think it was her. They passed her in their car.'

'When?'

'Before seven, I think they said. They were home by seven, because there was a show about bird migrations Gordon wanted to tape.'

'Have they told the police?'

'Oh yes, they knew it was important, if it really was her. They'd seen her on the road before. Martha said Alice Nelson thought she'd once seen someone who looked like her going down Simon Steele's driveway.'

The focus was narrowing. Nicole was alive and on the road shortly before seven. Gillian thought about what Eli had told her. He'd only mentioned Nicole being seen at dinner. He certainly wasn't telling her everything. But then, he wouldn't.

Estelle sat down, looking less lively. 'I'm tired. Dammit. Just when I've been feeling better than I have in months, the perk suddenly goes out of me, and I feel like a balloon losing air.'

CHAPTER 9

Gillian had already had breakfast and read the *Times* when Estelle made her appearance the next morning.

'I told Kitty you'd return her scarf,' she reminded Gillian, who was writing a list of errands. Groceries, two prescription refills for Estelle, oil change, cat food, bank.

'That's right,' she said, writing it down.

'I thought you might as well, it won't be much out of your way.' Estelle sounded guilty.

'I don't mind.'

'Handsome, isn't it? Hermès scarfs all have the same look, but they're all nice.' She wrapped it loosely about her neck, tilting her head to rub her cheek against the silk.

Gillian smiled. 'It suits you. Maybe you should keep it.'

'*Pourquoi pas?*' Estelle put on a Gallic pout. 'She probably has a dozen like it.'

❧

It was still early when Gillian drove to Beekman Corners with her shopping list. Only one car in the parking lot— Jean's old station wagon. A cold front was drifting south from Canada; her breath plumed in the still air. By midday, the sun would vanquish the chill, but the light and warmth no longer lingered through the afternoons.

The door to Jean's, propped open all summer, was now closed. Inside, a steamy warmth and the smell of coffee ageing on the burner. Jean was making up sandwiches for the cooler. The work counter was laid end to end with slices of bread. She was working her way along the row, laying on a slither of mayonnaise. The stools at the customer counter and the booths at the far end, varnished pine and red Naugahyde, were empty.

The grocery store was a fixture at Beekman Corners when Gillian's parents bought their house, and the same owners had still been behind the counter when Gillian left for college. The next summer the big news in the neighbourhood was that the grocery store had changed hands. A stranger appeared and got the the *Wall Street Journal* and *Times* orders mixed up.

Now Jean's had been Jean's for almost thirty years, purveyor of newspapers, coffee, groceries and gossip. The same sycamore shaded the dusty parking lot. The Christmas lights framing the window shone summer and winter on the same faded postcards, the same baskets wrapped in dusty cellophane. The cash register did not read barcodes. The rolls of lifesavers and flat boxes of Chiclets on slanted racks, the columns of cigarette packs in their wooden slots on the wall, were where they had always been. In the tall coolers, behind glass doors streaked with mist, the shelves were stocked with Coke and Seven Up, milk and orange juice, packets of weiners, blocks of Philadelphia cream cheese in silvery wrapping and eggs in grey pulpy cartons. You could still buy Velveeta.

Nevertheless, Jean's had been tempered by time and urban expectations. There were no chocolate babies on the candy rack now. Quart bottles of olive oil jostled the Mazola, and feta cheese, tortillas and balsamic vinegar were staples. In the freezer, the domain of the hamburger patty had been conquered by the microwaveable burrito. Jean, who was nearing sixty, dyed her brush cut purple and wore a fringe of gold hoops around one ear. She came from Ossining, down the Hudson. 'We could see Sing Sing on our way to school,' she said. 'My dad used to tell my brother he'd take him down there and hand him over if he didn't behave. Worked every time.'

She nodded when Gillian came in, and went on working at the sandwiches. Gillian picked up a basket, cruised along the shelves. Her list diagrammed two diets: Estelle's skimmed milk, margarine and camomile tea; her own two per cent, butter and coffee beans. Estelle had raised Gillian on roast beef; now she scolded when Gillian ate a mouthful of steak or buttered her toast. Gillian fought back with articles about fatty-acid chains which confused them both.

'So did you hear the police are talking to Arnold Mitchell?' Jean said, her back turned, dealing ham slices.

'Yes, I heard.'

'You ask me, he's always been a bit off.'

'Does he come in often?'

'Sometimes. He's not a regular. Had to make a living off Arnold Mitchell, I'd've starved. But he comes in. Buys matches, peanut butter, baked beans. Things like that. Bought an old freezer off me once—Jesus knows what for. Dead bodies.'

Gillian dropped a bunch of bananas in her basket, looked at Jean. 'You think he did it?'

Jean paused in her sandwich construction. 'Stands to reason. Had that photo, didn't he? He could be a stalker. Police are searching the woods around the house today. Heard it from highway patrol. Scottie was in.' Jean dipped her knife in the relish. 'Maybe his back yard is full of bones.'

The door wheezed, thudded shut. Roberta, the president's assistant at Stanton College, hurried in. She smiled at Gillian, miming a shiver. 'Nippy this morning.'

Jean picked up a *Times* with 'Morgenstern' scribbled across the corner in blue ink and handed it to her. 'Coffee's hot.'

Roberta looked at her watch. 'I just have time for a cup, and I can use one. Gillian, coffee? It's on me.' She had a narrow face with a full-lipped mouth, smooth, heavy dark hair and vivid blue eyes. Gillian, who knew almost no one at Stanton, had responded gratefully to her extroverted friendliness.

They sat on the padded chrome stools at the counter. Jean poured three cups, proffered packets of sugar and light cream from a pint carton.

'How are you?' Roberta said cheerfully. 'I'm ready to keel over and the day's hardly begun. Josh was up half the night, being sick. He's fine this morning—kids are amazing—throw up all night and then they're Mr. Sunshine at seven a.m. I feel like driving off a cliff, just to get some sleep at the bottom.'

Roberta didn't look tired. She brimmed with vitality, as usual. A few years earlier, she'd been earning twice what Stanton paid her, applying her brains and talent for organization in the corporate world, but two years after Josh was born she was looking for a way out of commuting and twelve-hour workdays. The Stanton job met her requirements. She got through double the workload handled by her predecessor. Jo had introduced her to Gillian as the only truly indispensable person on campus. Even her recent shift to single-mother status hadn't slowed her down.

'You took Josh to daycare?' Jean asked.

'Yup. He seemed OK. I hope he is.'

'Doesn't Simon want to look after him?'

'Why, Jean, he'd just jump at the chance, if he wasn't so busy with his new agent. If he wasn't pickled, or on Oprah talking about his *problem*.' She smiled, icily sweet. 'If he wasn't such a putz.'

Jean stared. 'On Oprah? You're joking!'

'Yes, thank God. It was bad enough when he went on local TV. I wish he'd just go to AA, but of course the last thing Simon Steele wants to be is anonymous.'

Gillian knew that Roberta and Simon had broken up at the beginning of the summer, but they'd never discussed Simon's new book, and Gillian had never heard Roberta speak of him with such open hostility. He must have done something to rile her.

'I take it you don't like the book.'

'Like it? I guess you haven't read it. I'm glad there's somebody in the valley who hasn't. You know how crazy it can make you when the whole world hears his side of the story, and nobody knows yours?'

Jean ripped open a packet of cheese slices. 'Everybody takes his with a grain of salt.'

'Thanks, Jean, but I know some people think it's the real me in there, just because it's in print. I know I lose my temper, but Simon's so irresponsible. Josh was supposed to visit him on Saturday. It's not much to ask of a father—to see his son for a few hours a week. But I couldn't leave Josh there. If you'd seen the shape Simon was in…He's probably fine now, but he was so hung over then he was practically comatose. I didn't even want Josh to get a look at him. My parents were against it, you know,' Roberta added ruefully to Gillian. 'They said it was a mistake to marry him. So on top of everything else, I have to hear about how I should've listened to them.'

'How old were you when you got married?'

'Twenty-four. A young twenty-four. Now I'm an ancient thirty-two. And Simon's over forty.'

'Is your divorce coming through soon?' Gillian asked.

'ASAP. But—major but—I want money for Josh. Simon's going to be Mr. Deadbeat Dad, I just know it. So I'm trying to get some of the cash upfront. He's got an advance on his next book, I've sniffed that out. My lawyer's working on it. And I want a cut of the royalties he's getting now. It's the least he can do. I supported him for years. I'm *in* the book, like it or not, why should he get all the dough? Besides, I'm not asking for the moon. I'm letting Simon keep the house, and it's worth a bundle.' Roberta's voice sharpened. 'But if he isn't reasonable, I'll claim half of it. He wouldn't like that at all. Not one tiny bit.'

Roberta was an unstoppable force, Gillian thought; she'd get her money; no doubt about it. 'Where are you living now?'

'A condo. Kind of a comedown after the "historic house on the Hudson" bit, but it's OK. It's new, so it's easy to keep it clean; that old house was impossible. I've set up a little office in my bedroom. It's kind of cramped, but honestly, I wouldn't want to be in Simon's house. It's too isolated for a single woman. And now it would feel creepy. I haven't talked to Carrie Pilgrim, but in her shoes I'd be wishing there were bars on all the doors. And I'd hate to drive over that bridge every day.'

Gillian thought, yes, she was glad Nicole's body hadn't been found on her own road.

'Did you ever see Arnold when you were still living there?' Jean asked.

'Hardly ever. He was a hermit, just like people said. I used to go past his place when I took Josh for walks. I wonder if he was watching. He wasn't someone you thought about— nobody ever said he was dangerous.'

'Nobody knew.'

'Does he buy his cigarettes here?' Gillian asked.

'Tobacco, mostly. He rolls his own, it's cheaper. But he buys a pack now and then.'

'What brand?' Gillian asked.

'Um, Marlboros, I think.' Jean glanced at the stacks of cigarette packs. 'Yeah. Why?'

'Estelle wants to know.'

Jean grinned. 'Is she playing Miss Marple?'

'She's not a Christie fan. She prefers to be addressed as Sherlock Holmes.'

Gillian and Roberta walked out to the parking lot together. Roberta tucked her scarf around her pretty neck.

'It's not nice to think you've been living down the street from a murderer.'

'It makes you wonder about the rest of the neighbours, doesn't it? Who are they, really, all those people you thought were normal? Who beats his wife, and who goes to Thailand to bugger little boys?'

'Exactly. And now there's a mystery about Nicole, too. You know about her aunt? The police can't find any trace of her. They went to her bank, and it turns out that the account—the one the college gets the cheques from—is Nicole's! They think there may be no such aunt—that Nicole made her up.'

'No aunt?' Gillian was surprised. Hadn't Jo told her how close they were? 'No aunt named Charlotte?'

'Charlotte is Nicole's middle name.'

'Where's her family, then?'

'The police don't have a clue. Why would she do a thing like that? And where did she get the money to pay her fees? There was plenty in her account.'

'Jo says she worked as a model.'

'I see. They make piles of money, don't they? But why tell fibs about her aunt? We all feel so bad for her, but I must say we're wondering who we're feeling bad for.'

'You're bound to find out soon. The police have to locate her next of kin.'

'They're not working fast enough. The situation is impossible for the college; Margaret and I are spending most of our time trying to keep a lid on the crisis, and the trustees are having conniptions because we haven't contacted the family yet. Meanwhile, all our other work is falling behind.'

Roberta didn't look as if anything in her life would be allowed to fall behind, or get out of control. She got into her car. A large, handsome briefcase lay on the passenger seat. She was pressed, coiffed and her shoes were shined. If she could look like that on a morning when her child had been up half the night, Gillian thought, she could handle anything at the college, even a whole herd of wild trustees.

'Oh well. At least they found the killer right away,' Roberta said, starting her engine. 'That's the main thing.'

CHAPTER 10

In town, Gillian left the car at the garage where she'd booked
a lube and oil change and went to the bank and then the
drugstore. She waited for Estelle's pills, looking absent-
mindedly at the vitamins and nutrition supplements. Vitamin
E in golden bubbles, multivitamins for a race of giants,
ginseng extract, calcium, chelated minerals, vitamin B stress
formula, carbo-load. She preferred her own stress formula,
from Scotland.

'How are you, dear?'

It was Alice Nelson, Peggy's mother. She was wearing an
ancient Persian lamb coat and a little black hat perched on
top of her thin white curls. 'And how's Estelle? I hope she's
not too nervous, when she's alone in the house. This is just
awful. Tragic. And that Arnold Mitchell being mixed up in
it. You and Peggy went to school with him! I called and told
her, she just couldn't believe it. But he's always been peculiar.
She remembered that. She said you hadn't been over to see
her for a couple of weeks. She'll be here next weekend, do
come up.'

Alice raced on, as she always had. Peggy talked just as
fast, but she remembered to stop occasionally.

'You know his brother was killed years ago. That was
supposed to be a hunting accident, but now you have to
wonder, don't you?'

'There must have been an inquest.'

'Well, of course, dear. They have to have them. But nobody seriously thought it could be anything but an accident. So it might not have been a thorough enquiry. I felt so bad for Virginia. She was never the same, afterwards. Died a few years later. Of a broken heart, I always said.'

'Virginia was Arnold's mother's name, wasn't it? Do you remember his father, too?'

'Oh Lord, yes. Booter. Awful man. Pawed my knee under the table once at dinner.' Alice sniffed. 'I tipped my water glass into his lap. Pretended it was an accident. Virginia was there, of course. Poor thing. If she hadn't been, I'd have stuck him with my fork.'

When the car was ready, Gillian had checked off most of her list. There was only Kitty's scarf to deliver.

The drive was lovely, winding northeast through diminishing hills turning red and gold as the days grew shorter. In a mile or so the choppy suburban lots gave way to woods, then the woods turned to fields. A farmhouse. Pumpkins. A crossroads, where a stand of maples blazed against the sky. Then sloping pastures ran down to painted rail fences bordering the road. The Grogans' house, pillared and porticoed, was as white and formal as a bridal gown, as immaculate as Kitty's car.

No BMW was visible, nor any other car, so she couldn't tell whether anyone was at home. The garage was somewhere behind the house, by the stables. She left her car on the gravel drive and walked towards a front door flanked by neatly clipped shrubs in tubs. She should ask Kitty who did the gardening, but probably Estelle couldn't afford anyone Kitty used. Kitty's family had once, long ago, owned enormous tracts of land further up the river. Her brothers and uncles were lawyers and stockbrokers in the firms of their forefathers. Now, Gillian thought, the daughters and nieces probably joined the firms, too.

Before she reached the steps, a man and a young woman came around the corner of the house. They were both on horseback, the man in proper riding attire, the young woman in jeans and a sweater. They both wore helmets, so it took a moment for Gillian to be sure the man was Lewis. The two horses shone, smooth and glossy with health, though not as glossy as Lewis's boots. He dismounted and held out his hand.

'Gillian! Saw you drive up. You know my daughter, Janice?'

Gillian had only met her once, when Janice was still a child. She was stubby and muscular, with heavy features like her father's. Gillian couldn't see anything of Kitty's parched delicacy. Janice's hello was nearly inaudible. Her eyes flicked to Gillian's, made the briefest possible contact and then stayed on her horse. Lewis handed her his reins.

'Give them both a good rub,' he said, as she turned back towards the stables.

Lewis walked the other way, towards the front steps. 'Brought her out here for a morning with the horses. Take her mind off things,' he rumbled, lowering his voice, but not enough. Gillian could see Janice's shoulders stiffen.

'I'm just returning Kitty's scarf.' She was carrying it, neatly folded in her hand. She held it out.

'Scarf?' He turned his head, scrutinized it. 'Oh, Kitty. She leaves a trail. Nice of you to bring it over.' He held his hand out for it, thrust it into a pocket. 'I'll give it to her when she comes in.'

Gillian turned to go.

'Stay and have something. I've got—' he looked at his watch—'let's see, half an hour. I wanted to ask you about Estelle. I didn't see her the other day, of course. How is she?'

'All right, I think.' Gillian wasn't sure how much she wanted to say. Lewis was a doctor—a heart surgeon, in fact—although he didn't practise any more. He might have good advice. But Estelle had her own doctor and a strong instinct for privacy; Gillian had to tread carefully.

She followed him down the hall into a pretty little conservatory furnished with wicker and chintz. Miniature orange trees scented the air.

'I'll see if there's any coffee,' he said, and left her. In a couple of minutes, he was back, carrying a bottle and two glasses. 'Sorry, I thought Kitty might have made a pot for me. I never know where things are.' He set down the bottle and glasses and chafed his hands together. 'Nippy today. How about a little sherry to take the chill off the bones? This is a nice Oloroso.'

He loomed over the table, a keg-shaped, short-limbed man, with heavy shoulders, large hands and a hard bulge of belly like a horse's rump—a belly of the kind that was said to threaten the heart, but he of all people had to know that. His clothes must be tailored, Gillian realized; nothing gaped or pinched. He had a big round head, the hairline high on the skull and the sooty grey hair cut as short as a colonel's. No comb-overs for Dr. Grogan. He'd been one of the top men in his field when he was in practice, one of the first to perform successful coronary bypasses when they still operated on beating hearts. Now, of course, there were heart-lung machines, and the living organ lay inert under the knife. Heart surgery was less heroic and more routine, and bypasses were done by the hundreds of thousands every year, as Gillian knew in rather more detail than she wished, having asked around when Estelle started having trouble.

Lewis hadn't practised for years. He'd quit after a car accident maimed his right hand. Despite the best efforts of the best hand surgeons, and relentless physiotherapy, the thumb had never regained its full power or dexterity. Lewis had hung up his scalpel.

He'd found other things to do. He sat on hospital boards and government committees. He raised money for Stanton College and the Republican politicians the county always elected. In his spare time he schooled his horses and grew roses. He was a fiercely competitive horseman and had the trophies to prove it; his roses had been photographed for magazines. He had two sons—one on Wall Street and one sweating out his early years in corporate law—and a daughter in college. Altogether, Gillian thought, he had made himself a success despite the accident that had wrecked his career. He deserved credit for that.

His eyes were grey and shrewd. A second, soft chin was beginning to form below the bone. He had wonderful skin, Gillian noticed: tanned, almost unlined, with the pearly glisten of youth. The luck of the gene pool, she supposed, remembering Eli's dour comments on dieting. Kitty looked older, despite the facelifts and the spa and the fifty-dollar-an-ounce moisturizers.

He pushed a thick thumb against the top of the bottle and then twisted it off with a slightly awkward motion. It was a cold day and he'd been riding without gloves.

'Not the best term you could have picked to visit Stanton,' he said sympathetically, handing her a glass. 'This sort of thing doesn't happen here. We're all shocked. It's a very unpleasant mess.'

'Horrible.'

'Did you know the Bishop girl?'

'She was in my class.'

'A gifted student, with a scholarship. A credit to the school. Not quite who we thought she was, though. I've read the file. Fine letter of application, good grades, top test scores. She looks like our ideal applicant. I can't blame the admissions committee for being taken in.'

'She's done well; her ability must be real.'

'Nothing wrong with her brains. But a school like Stanton has to take character into account. She fooled us there. Your typical Stanton girl, like Janice, wouldn't be capable of such a deception. Financed by a fake aunt. Where did she get the money?'

'Does it matter now, if it had nothing to do with her death?'

'It might, if the media dig up something that could embarrass the college. A college reputation is a precious commodity.' He smiled grimly. 'I like to know what's coming. As a member of the board of trustees, I don't want to find out the real story when someone thrusts a headline under my nose.'

'Are the police working on it?'

'They're trying to trace her family. I'm sure they're doing their job.' It sounded as if he meant the opposite. He tossed off the rest of his sherry, waited for the warmth to hit. 'What did you think of Nicole Bishop?'

'She was intelligent and more reserved than most. I didn't know her long enough to get further than that. I don't know any of the students well.'

'Are you surprised about Arnold Mitchell? You grew up here; Kitty says you know him.'

'Knew. That was years ago.' Gillian twirled her glass. 'Of course I'm surprised. But I'm not convinced he's guilty.'

Lewis considered this with interest. 'Why?'

'No good reason. Or the best reason—there isn't enough evidence. Not yet.'

Lewis unstoppered the sherry bottle again. She waited for him to contradict her. Kitty had seemed quite prepared to believe that Arnold was a murderer. But Lewis merely raised his brows. 'Not a very popular opinion,' he said, refilling her glass.

'No. Everyone's sure he's guilty. I just hope Eli Pink can find some rock-solid evidence.'

'The detective. You know him, too?'

'I went to school with him—at the same time as Arnold. All three of us. It's like old home week,' Gillian said.

He caught the sardonic note. 'I see. And what do you think of your old schoolmate?'

'I thought he was going to be an actor, not a cop. But he's no dummy.'

Lewis frowned. 'He's probably bright enough. Smart. But smart only gets you so far. This isn't the city. The police know all about highway accidents and bar fights, but life in our county doesn't produce a crop of homicide experts.'

She nodded. She'd had a feeling that Eli was on new territory.

'Normally, we view that as a fortunate circumstance,' Lewis went on, 'but let me put it this way: you want a surgeon who's done a few hundred bypasses before he operates on you. Everything will go faster. Speed counts. The smoother the investigation, the faster it's wrapped up, the less attention it will attract. The less publicity about this, the better for the college.'

'I think Eli is as anxious as you are to close the case. If he's right about Arnold, it shouldn't take much longer.'

'Then let's hope he is. Have you heard anything that suggests otherwise?'

Gillian shook her head. To mention Simon Steele now would be malicious. Lewis had his own sources of information. 'I'd like it to be over, too. Apart from everything else, I'm worried about my mother. Nicole's death was a shock for her, and the "unpleasant mess", as you put it, is making her anxious, which can't be doing her any good.'

Lewis pushed his glass aside. 'I'm glad you're worried. Someone damn well ought to be. Your mother should have had a bypass done last year. Earlier. I told her precisely what to expect, and what the benefits would be. I've talked to her more than once. But she won't face reality.'

'She—' Gillian began, stuttering a little.

Lewis hadn't finished. 'What you need to understand is that her condition is precarious. If she doesn't have surgery pronto, she's probably not going to live very long.'

'I think she knows that,' Gillian said.

He waved this aside. 'People say they know, but they don't. She's just denying the facts because she doesn't like them. Have you witnessed one of her angina attacks lately? You must have.'

Gillian nodded. 'It scared the hell out of me.'

'It should.' He leaned towards her, his face coming closer, the fleshy pad under his chin almost, but not quite vanishing. His voice was gentle. 'Listen. I've known your mother for a long time, and Kitty's damn fond of her. Let me explain something to you. There are new techniques now. If you know anything about bypass surgery, you probably think they'll make a cut a foot long and saw her sternum in half. Major surgery, pretty hard on a frail eighty-four-year-old lady, I admit, though if it were the only option she should take it anyway. But she might not need that. She's probably a candidate for the new procedures that are coming in now. It's brilliant work,' he said urgently. 'A whole new field.' His conviction stirred her. It was the force that had driven his professional life. 'Minimally invasive bypass surgery,' he said impressively. 'Ring any bells? Has she mentioned it? Or has her doctor?'

Gillian shook her head.

'It's pretty new. You know about laparoscopic surgery? It's an analogous type of procedure. Little incisions, using a camera and fibre optics. I could use my contacts; I know who can do it. A three-inch cut here—' He drew a line with his finger across his shirt from the area of his left nipple to his breastbone. 'A couple of one-inch incisions for the camera and the instruments, and it's all over in two hours. Think about it.'

'If it's that new, it must still be experimental. Isn't that a risk, especially for someone her age? What if she would rather risk letting nature take its course?'

Lewis was suddenly impatient. 'You're an intelligent woman, don't be obtuse. She needs the surgery. If she were my patient, she'd have had it already. Get your brother up here. If you both talk to her, she'll see sense.' He glanced at his watch and stood up, putting a friendly hand on her shoulder as if to soften his words. 'This isn't the time to pussyfoot. You and your brother should take charge of the situation if she's not competent to decide. Sorry to cut this short; I've got to change. Meeting this afternoon. I'll tell Kitty you were here.'

He saw her out. Janice was nowhere in sight.

Oh hell, Gillian thought, sitting still at the wheel of the Buick, I bet I know why Estelle won't let me say a word about surgery. 'Don't *you* start,' Estelle had said. Lewis must have been offering her his brand of wisdom. Gillian became aware of a pain throbbing in her left temple, as if she'd drunk cheap sherry on an empty stomach. But Lewis's sherry wasn't cheap.

CHAPTER 11

A couple of miles down the road Gillian passed a car coming the other way. The driver tooted, but not until after they passed did she recognize Jim Whitlock's Cherokee. She'd had to swerve to avoid a collision. She slowed down, realizing that she'd been going too fast and hogging the centre of the road. A wave of anger broke. Lewis Grogan could be the world's greatest heart surgeon, but she wouldn't let him bandage a cut finger. Why did Estelle put up with him? Because of Kitty, Gillian supposed. And, damn his autocratic bones, he was probably right that the new surgery would help. But Estelle had her defences up, and, right or not, Gillian didn't see any way of approaching the subject.

Back at the Post Road, she went north. Stanton was close, but she didn't want to go to the college. She turned into Dykeman's Pond Road without a clear purpose in mind. She could go on up to Beacon and talk to Carrie Pilgrim, but it might be better just to drive to some spot where she could look at the river. Its immensity had a calming effect. Henry the Eighth would have had a better bedside manner than Lewis.

She drove slowly downhill and past Dykeman's Pond. The water was smooth, reflecting the trees beyond. Two ducks swam at the far edge. A new house stood in the meadow, its foundations barely screened by spindly young shrubs. The curtains were closed downstairs. A weekend house, with no sign of life. She didn't like Lewis's manner, but she had to admit that part of the reason she was so furious was because she felt guilty. He could be right. Maybe Estelle would be glad she'd had the surgery afterwards, maybe Gillian was failing her by not taking a firmer line.

Gillian drove on through the trees, up the next rise and towards Dee's Pond. She was going to pass Arnold's house at any moment. Not that she would see anything; it wasn't even visible from the road. She wondered if the police would be there.

They were.

A car came out of Arnold's driveway and turned towards her as she slowly approached. The road was narrow, and she edged over to let the car pass. Arnold sat in the back, with another man beside him. A cop. Arnold's head turned to look at her as they went by. He wasn't wearing his hat. His hair was pulled back in a greying ponytail, exposing a high, pale forehead. The tips of his big ears poked through the hair. His eyes caught hers. He twisted his neck, staring over his shoulder as the two cars moved apart. She stepped on the brake, shocked. But the police car kept going. Arnold's white face receded, became a blur.

She stopped the car and sat still, her hands in her lap. Those eyes, she thought, shaken. She took several deep breaths, then got out of the car. She stood at the edge of the narrow road, listening to the silence. The trees had already swallowed the sound of the police car. The Mitchells' driveway hadn't seen a load of gravel in a long time. The dirt was packed hard now, but it looked rough and was probably potholed and mucky whenever it rained. She walked across the road and tried to see the house. What kind of place did Arnold live in? It was none of her business, really. She turned her back to the driveway and looked up and down the road. Dykeman's Pond was out of sight, in a dip to the south, and Dee's Pond and the bridge were in a shallower depression to the north, before the road climbed and bent back towards the highway. Arnold's house stood on a short, stony rise between. How strong was he? Nicole might be skinny, but there was muscle under the skin and she'd been five foot nine or ten. She would have weighed at least one hundred and twenty pounds. Could he have carried her to the bridge and tipped her over the edge?

A scraping step.

'Looking for something?'

'Christ!' she said, her heart leaping under her ribs. She spun around. It was Eli.

'Thought I heard a car stop. We don't want any more trouble than we've got. Highway patrol had to boot a couple of sightseers off the bridge this morning.'

'I stopped because I saw Arnold in the car that just left,' Gillian said. 'He looked awfully pale. And his eyes ...' She stopped. He looked like *The Scream*, she thought.

'Ever been to the house?' Eli asked. He sounded friendly again.

'Never.'

'My car's there.' He turned, motioning to her to follow.

'I don't know,' she began, but he wasn't listening.

She walked with him along the drive. Her heart was still drumming. In a few steps, the house came into view. Tall and gloomy, it stood in the deep shade of large maple trees. The mansard roof suggested a French country house, but the decorative details, if they had ever been consistent, were so no longer. A thin lawn spread out in front like chewed carpet. An ancient hand mower, its blades caked with clippings, rested beside the porch steps. The paintwork didn't look too bad, Gillian saw, but the shingles on the roof were curling, and the moss was thick, like frosting. Old blinds, cracked and yellowed, covered the upstairs windows. Downstairs, someone had attempted to let more light in by adding a picture window. The front steps showed signs of recent repair. Rotten boards had been pulled up and fresh ones nailed in. Galvanized nails. Arnold knew a thing or two about building. And the porch was clean, nothing on it but an ancient wicker rocking chair. Interested, she went closer. The faded blue canvas cushion had been mended with clumsy stitches in white thread. Her surprise told her that she'd expected something different: an old wringer washing machine, maybe, rusty cans, tyres in the front yard. Anyhow, not these dogged efforts to hold things together with nails and string. Poor old Arnold, she thought.

'What does he live on?' she asked Eli.

'Not much. There's a little money from his mother. He doesn't work. Can't, he says. He got kicked in the head when he was in the army. Fractured his skull. He has memory losses. Constant headaches. That's his story, anyway.'

'I can't imagine him in the army.'

'Wanted to leave home. Should've known better than to pick the army—a dickhead's way out. I get a migraine once in a while. If I had them all the time, I'd have killed somebody by now—probably myself.'

'He should have a disability pension.'

'He got kicked in a bar. The army says it's nothing to do with them.'

'Has he been arrested?'

'Not yet.'

Gillian glanced around uneasily. 'Was she here? In the house?'

Eli shrugged. 'We haven't finished searching.'

The image of Bluebeard's chamber receded. They obviously hadn't found any pools of blood.

'Does he have a lawyer?'

'Says he doesn't want one.'

'Why?'

'Who knows?' He's an oddball. Always was. He kept a diary in code when he was in school. Did you know that? I saw it once, when he dropped it.

'He needs a lawyer.'

'What am I supposed to do, according to you—beg him to get legal advice?'

Gillian looked back down the long driveway. Arnold didn't look strong enough to carry Nicole very far. But he did have a truck.

'You think Arnold's pathetic, don't you?' Eli said, his voice dripping scorn the same way it had in the old days when she disagreed with him about a movie. 'Remember, he watched Nicole Bishop. He took a nudie picture of her without her knowledge and hung it on his wall. And we found her body on the road where he lives, less than half a mile from his house. In high school, he used to stare at girls when he thought no one was looking.

'So did you, I bet.'

'Not like he did.'

'Why would he leave her under the bridge? Why not bury the body, or move her much further away?'

'Move her? In that old truck? It's way too conspicuous. And how fast do you think you could dig a hole in these woods big enough to hid a body? There's nothing but rocks and roots. I don't know why he would dump her under the bridge, but it could have been the quickest solution.'

'Depending on where she was killed,' Gillian said.

'Have you remembered anything else about the night you saw him?'

'His hands were shaking. I saw that when he lit a cigarette.'

'He was nervous? Jumpy?'

What would she say in court, Gillian thought. 'I thought he was surprised to see me.'

'And that was why his hands shook?'

'I don't know,' Gillian said firmly.

'It's possible.' Eli eyed her speculatively. 'He has some kind of attitude to you.'

'Attitude?'

'Yeah. I told him you'd seen him. He didn't want to talk about you. Do you know why?'

'No.' She was damned if she'd tell Eli about the day she'd met Arnold on the Knob. It was private, it couldn't have anything to do with the murder investigation. Eli wanted to know if there was a connection between her and Arnold, because she'd said Arnold ought to have a lawyer. He was probably nervous about the case, that was all that was going on.

'You're sure?' he pushed. 'You and Arnold didn't have something going? Back when we were in school, maybe?'

Gillian recoiled. 'For God's sake, Eli. Don't be ridiculous. What's this all about?'

'It's about what makes Arnold tick.'

'But that was a long, long time ago.'

'Time is strange, isn't it? What's long to you can feel like no time at all to someone else.'

'You mean Arnold?' Gillian tried to think of herself at fourteen. Her memories from that time were fragmentary, like single pages—isolated moments of feeling, incidents stripped of context.

'Could be.' Eli slipped a three-by-five-inch photograph out of his notebook and handed it to her. 'Courtesy of Stanton College.'

It was a picture of Nicole, her head and shoulders.

'What about it?'

He took the picture back, snapped his notebook shut. 'She looks kind of like you used to. Same type.'

'Same type,' she thought. A contemptuous phrase, at least in his tone of voice. 'You told me Arnold has a photograph of her. Are you sure he didn't take pictures of other women at the college?'

'I told you we haven't found any. Why?'

'Every woman in that dorm will be worried sick that he's got pictures of her, too. You should know that.'

'Photos like that aren't so easy to get.'

'Why not?'

'Technical reasons.'

'*What* technical reasons?'

'Light problems. It's not like taking a snapshot at the beach, or using a flash when somebody's a few feet from you. You need someone to stand still in a good light for a long time. People don't normally do that.'

'Then why did Nicole?'

'Why do women leave windows unlocked? Why do they walk down dark streets at night?'

'Eli, are you mad at me, or at women?'

'Mad? I'm just doing my job. Why do women think everything's personal? She smoked dope—maybe she got lost in dreamland. Did Arnold ever say anything to you about his brother?'

'About Tommy? Why would you think that?'

'Just curious.'

'No. He didn't,' she heard herself say.

Eli opened the door of his car. 'There's no proof Arnold was at home when Tommy was shot, you know.' He got in and slammed it. Then he rolled down the window. 'A word of advice. He may be back here in a few hours, if he keeps his mouth shut. This isn't a main road. Not much traffic goes by. Don't come up here alone.'

12

Gillian sat upstairs at her desk. In front of her, stored in files in the computer, were the words she had already written about Caroline Norton. She'd opened one of the files and looked at what she had written. Her own words, but they might as well have been Sanskrit. She couldn't take them in, or recall her line of thought. She'd done nothing. The screen was dark, waiting.

She'd driven home from Arnold's hours ago, but she was still too unsettled by the day's events to think about anything else. She hadn't gone to see Carrie, or said a word to Estelle about either Lewis or Eli. She'd phoned a photographer friend in New York, who had listened to her tale about the photographs of Nicole and had confirmed Eli's explanation—with rather more clarity and patience. She'd also tried to call Peggy Nelson, to see if she had any insights about Eli, but Peggy wasn't home. What Gillian really wanted was to talk everything over with Edward, to replay the scenes for him; he would pick them apart like a good theatre director.

Damn Lewis, she thought. He was so sure, so absolute in his opinions. She wasn't, and she didn't like the pressure. That shouldn't influence her, but it was hard to think clearly about whether he was right. Should she try to make Estelle reconsider? Tell her about 'minimally invasive' surgery? Should she call Franklin? Share the burden? She wished

Edward would drop out of the sky in a parachute. Not that he would have all the answers to her questions, but he was a deft separator of fact and feeling. It was one of the skills detectives had to acquire, if they were going to be any good at interrogation.

Then there was Eli. His behaviour puzzled her. He'd sounded friendly enough, and he'd seemed to want to talk about Arnold, but then he'd gotten pissed off again. Why had he shown her that picture of Nicole and said that it looked like her? Coming after his remarks about Arnold's attitude, it sounded like a threat, or a warning. He had certainly warned her about going up there alone. She was hardly likely to go to Arnold's house by herself, but Eli seemed to think she shouldn't even walk on the road alone. Not much traffic goes by, he'd said. And why was he dwelling on Arnold's past?

Stars swam in the deep space of the darkened monitor. It was all so long ago. Tommy's death, meeting Arnold on the Knob, Eli's ambition to be a star, their prickly friendship. Could any of it really matter now? She didn't know; she just knew that for some reason she didn't trust Eli. She knew because she'd lied to him. She got up and walked to the window. The sheep were grazing near the road; a hawk was circling the meadow. Every year when she was small, she'd played in that meadow, building dams in the brook. She could remember the feel of the cool, slippery stones under her bare feet. She could remember the heat of summer nights, smells of hot grass and tar, fragments of conversation, the sound of her parents laughing, moments spiked with triumph or humiliation. A handful of tiny, glittering tiles from a lost mosaic.

Later memories, of her teens, were more layered and complex, but seemed too much like old stories not to be suspect. The agonizing self-scrutiny of those years turned everyday events to melodrama, and many scenes were obsessively analysed and replayed and rewritten in private. She didn't trust what she retained in her memory now to resemble what she experienced then. She could use her historian's tools: dig out her old albums and letters and whatever documents Estelle had kept—probably cartons full of letters and drawings, school reports, old swimming cards, and God-knows-what, all unsorted—she could go through everything and reconstruct herself as if she were Caroline Norton. But to what end? It would be an embarrassing exercise, and it would yield no secrets about Arnold Mitchell.

The photographs of Gillian and Franklin that had once been in this room were downstairs, now, in her mother's bedroom and on the piano. She'd seen them so often through the years that she knew exactly how she looked in them. If she turned, she could see herself in the oval mirror that hung on the opposite wall, but she had no need to check. Compared to her pictures, she thought, she looked like Arnold's house: not enough money spent on upkeep. It wasn't just her bushy hair, which she put off cutting because haircuts bored her; it wasn't just the streaks of grey. It was her clothes. New clothes looked fresh; her own were mostly old favourites, good to start with, but wilting. Estelle, who cruised the catalogues, had more new clothes than she did. Maybe it was time to go into New York and look around.

But even if she spent half her salary on new clothes and colour rinses, they wouldn't stop time—wouldn't stop the thinning of flesh over bone, the fading of light from the skin. She was still lanky and grey-eyed, like the girl in the photographs downstairs. She weighed about the same. But she didn't look like that girl. Even if she were to go to a spa as often as Kitty Grogan, she'd never look like that again. It hurt to think about it.

Nicole Bishop was more beautiful than Gillian had ever been. Her flawless skin and fluid athletic movements were especially memorable. Gillian hadn't noticed any striking resemblance between herself and Nicole; Nicole was tall and had dark hair and grey eyes. So had Gillian. So what? What had Eli mentioned it for? He'd been trying to stir her up. She shouldn't let him get to her. But the photograph of Nicole reminded her of one of her own portraits downstairs. Something about the carriage of the head. Under the circumstances, it was a disagreeable observation.

Gillian paced up and down in front of the window, then looked into the mirror and sighed. She had to pull herself together before going downstairs to see about dinner. She missed Edward. When she'd talked to Jo, she'd told her how much she enjoyed not working as hard as she did at UPNW. It was true, but there was a downside. Her job at UPNW kept her so busy she didn't have any time to miss Edward, whereas here, with hours to call her own, she thought about him more and more. It was frustrating, especially when she lay awake at night, or dreamed about him and then woke up in an empty bed. When she was working, she was more apt to dream about losing her briefcase. Part of her wanted to shove her feelings back into the cramped little corner they usually occupied. It was easier that way.

She sat down again at the computer and ignored Caroline Norton. She wrote an e-mail to Edward instead.

This has been a horrible day. I've been bullied by a doctor and picked on by a police officer. Both men, of course. If the doctor were in England he'd be the chairman of some Tory constituency in the Home Counties, a Euroskeptic and ready to napalm the National Health. His wife is a friend of my mother's. She always looks as if she's about to break into pieces, but she must be shatterproof to have survived marriage to him. He doesn't practise medicine any more, but he's even more opinionated than those who do. He's told my mother to have surgery; he thinks she's got her head in the sand about dying and should be made to face facts. One fact is that there's some new kind of surgery now—little cuts instead of huge ones—like the gall bladder ops that came in a while back. I'm up a tree; Estelle gets into a state if the topic is even mentioned.

Then there's this bloody detective. I told you about him. Eli Pink. He marched me up Arnold Mitchell's driveway today, and bit my head off when I asked if Arnold had a lawyer. He seems to think that Arnold harbours feelings about me that could be dangerous. He's cynical (Eli, I mean, not Arnold), but not in the detached way you coppers usually are. There's some personal grudge in it. And he questioned me as if I were guilty of something. Well, we're all guilty of something, but I thought homicide investigations were supposed to be specific.

I feel pummelled. I'm going downstairs now to drown my sorrows in a couple of inches of Scotch. I wish you were here. I could weep and you could offer me your handkerchief the way men always do in novels of the pre-Kleenex era.

love G

That evening, Gillian built a fire, the first of the autumn. There was plenty of wood. Jim Whitlock, the weekend shepherd, had split the logs and stacked them in the shed. When winter came, he would shovel the walk and plough the driveway when it was blocked with snow. Estelle would have hired people to do these things if he hadn't wanted to, but he did. In return for the use of the pasture, he said. A refugee from the city, he'd read books on the sociology of rural life, and he helped his neighbours with the methodical passion of a scientist validating a pet theory. They were lucky to have him.

Estelle wanted to hear about her day. 'What did you do this morning? Did you give Kitty her scarf?'

'Kitty wasn't there. I gave it to Lewis. He doesn't know where the coffee is in his own kitchen.'

'He's that kind of man. There's no use getting worked up about it.'

Gillian opened her mouth to argue, then shut it. Her aversion to Lewis had nothing to do with the coffee, but she hadn't decided what to say to Estelle about the real reason.

'The usual?' she asked. Estelle didn't share her interest in single malts, and generally stuck to her Johnnie Walker. Gillian poured herself a generous slug of Laphroaig. No one she knew touched the hard stuff these days. People seemed to think of whisky what the Victorians thought of gin. Her friends drank wine, sometimes beer, an occasional brandy or marc, which, though highly alcoholic, apparently didn't count as 'hard' because they were made from grapes. Estelle might lecture her on the hazards of buttered toast, but at least she regarded Scotch consumption as a normal human pleasure, not as the next thing to glue sniffing. It really had been a horrible day, and Gillian was glad that no one would be looking at her glass with a critical eye.

'I ran into Alice Nelson in the drugstore. She said Booter Mitchell tried to feel her leg under the dinner table.'

'Did she?' Estelle snorted. 'Your father saw him in the city once, with a floozie. But Alice! What a ninny! He should have known she wouldn't put up with that sort of thing.'

'What happened to them—the Mitchells?'

'Oh, that's a sad story. After the hunting accident, when Tommy died, Virginia just collapsed. She pretty well stopped eating, and lived on tranquillizers. Booter had always been a heavy drinker, but he got worse after that. Much worse. He spent all his time at the Dutch House. And Virginia never got out of bed. She died early, and Booter didn't last much longer. His liver gave out. Some of us tried to help at the beginning—we'd take Virginia out to lunch, that sort of thing. But it wasn't any use.'

'And Arnold?'

'I guess Arnold had to fend for himself. You know, I can't criticize Virginia; how could I? But it was too bad for Arnold that she couldn't cope at all. It was as if Tommy had been her only child. Arnold didn't exist.'

'He was drafted, I think you told me?'

'Was he? Yes, that's right. It was after Virginia stopped getting up in the morning. He was glad to go, in a way. That's what we thought. Anything to get out of there. I don't know it for a fact, but I believe that Booter could be quite brutal. Especially right after they lost Tommy. Later on, he wasn't so strong. Not when he was putting away a quart of bourbon a day.'

'And then?'

'Then Arnold came back. It was a couple of years afterwards. He'd got a medical discharge, as I remember. He took care of Virginia before she died. I used to see him sometimes, shopping, but he hardly ever said a word. After she was gone, he went off somewhere for a year or two. I think she must have left him a little money. Then when Booter died, Arnold came home to bury him. He moved into the house and stayed there. He's been there—goodness— for twenty years.'

'Alone.'

Estelle nodded. 'We never heard about anyone else living in the house.'

'Alice is wondering whether Tommy was really shot by accident.'

'Oh, dear. Is all that going to be raked up again? We went to the inquest, you know. They said there was no evidence that it was anything but an accident. He was carrying the gun cocked; he tripped and fell, and the gun went off. I remember that.'

'Was he hunting legally?'

'No, I believe he was trespassing. That's right. The Fitzwilliams owned the land, and Tommy was trespassing. Going to look for ducks, I think.'

'Where was Arnold at the time?'

'Oh Lord, I don't remember. At home, I think. But no one else was, something like that. Booter would have been at work. There were rumours, because everyone knew that Tommy was the favourite. Somebody was idiotic enough to tell Booter about them. And he couldn't keep his mouth shut—he told Virginia. It didn't help. But he did say Arnold didn't know how to use a gun.'

'Sounds like Tommy didn't know how to use a gun either.' Gillian drank some Scotch. It tasted even better than usual. 'I saw Roberta when I went to Jean's this morning. She was really glad I hadn't read Simon's book. What did he say about her?'

'It's around here somewhere,' Estelle said, waving in the general direction of the large bookshelves. 'It's called *Juicer*. I told you that when it came out. Her portrait's certainly not a flattering one. A termagant. You can imagine her as a prohibitionist—preaching and smashing bottles. I don't remember many details, but it sounds like a dreadful marriage. You wonder how people can go on like that.'

'He probably drove her crazy. She gets along with everyone at work. Is the book any good?'

'I don't much care for confessional literature. Saint Augustine put me off.'

'But you read Simon's book anyhow?'

'Most of it. He lives here, dear. Everybody was talking about it, and a lot of people thought it was brave—searingly honest, that sort of thing.' Estelle shifted stiffly in her seat, and the little muscles around her eyes and mouth contracted. She was feeling pain somewhere, Gillian could tell, but she went on talking. 'I was curious, but I thought it was a rather nasty and self-pitying book. I'm out of touch with the times, though, I know that. I don't like those tell-all TV shows, either.' She paused. 'It was one-sided. There's always more than one side to these stories—as you would know if you'd been married.'

Gillian overlooked this sally. 'Roberta's certainly bitter. They're fighting over money.'

'Not the child?'

'She didn't say. But she said Simon's too unstable to look after him. He was practically comatose on Saturday when Josh was supposed to visit.'

'Poor little boy. You know, your father used to put away a bit too much now and then. At parties. Then he told stories—funny stories he never told me at home. I used to enjoy those evenings so much, when he'd stop being such a banker. But if he'd ever done the sort of thing Simon Steele writes about, it would have been unbearable to me. I would have divorced him.'

Gillian felt slightly disoriented, as if picked up and set down at a different angle. She'd seen a painting recently, by a Japanese artist, a reworking of *Las Meninas*. Velázquez's painting of the Spanish Infanta with her maids-in-waiting and her favourite dwarf was still recognizable, but the point of view had been moved, closer in, off to the side and lower; a maid's view, the title said. The painting hadn't been very good, but the shift had done its job, reminding her that those pictured had their own perspectives, different from the viewer's. What if her parents had divorced? She'd never imagined it; they had seemed happy together; she'd assumed they were.

'Did you ever think about divorce?'

'No, but Nat did once.'

'Why?'

'The old story. He met a young woman. She was pretty and smart and admiring, and she made him feel youthful. You children were nearly grown up; he was turning grey.'

'What happened?'

'They went to a bar, after work. Not one of the places where they would run into people from the office. They were there when Booter Mitchell walked in with his floozie. And Booter saw Nat, and winked at him. Nat said he saw himself from the outside, suddenly, and he didn't like what he was looking at. Not that his young woman was the same kind as Booter's, but he felt that he was being the same kind of man. So he bought her a drink and caught the next train.'

'And told you all about it?'

'Not that night.'

So, her father's picture of himself had shifted when Booter winked. He'd seen the tableau from another angle: Booter's, and maybe Estelle's. Gillian had a passing thought for Booter's floozie, remembering how her father detested bleached hair and scarlet fingernails. He would have looked no further. The tarty look was in, now; half the students at Stanton wore tight clothes and dyed their hair. They would all look like floozies to her father.

Gillian leaned her chin on her palm and regarded Estelle. 'It's awfully hard to see your parents as human beings. You could have told me that story about anybody else in the world and I would have said, "So what's new?" But because you're my parents, I'm jolted.'

'No doubt that's why I've never told you before,' Estelle said drily. She put her hand up to her eyes and brushed them, as if they felt dusty. 'I'm afraid I have to go to bed. I'm terribly tired.'

Gillian could see her fatigue; it was like water filling a boat; in a few minutes she would sink. 'All right. I just wanted to tell you, I've got an answer to your question about cigarette brands. Arnold Mitchell is a Marlboro man, when he doesn't roll his own.'

'Oh. How did you find out?'

'I have my methods, Watson.'

Estelle sat up, indignant. 'Now that is downright unfair. *I* was the one who figured out who he was. Then I send you out for a trivial piece of information, and you bring it back like Rumpole bringing in a mouse. That's the Watson role. You can't suddenly start stealing Sherlock Holmes's lines.'

Gillian began to laugh. 'You're absolutely right. I can't think what came over me.'

Estelle grasped at the sofa arm and heaved herself up. Then she fell back again with a gasp.

'What's wrong?'

'Nothing much. I just don't have any feeling in my feet. I knew I'd fall over if I took a step.'

Gillian knelt on the rug. Her mother's long, thin feet were thrust deep into fleece-lined slippers. Gillian touched her bony ankles. 'Are you cold?'

'No. Maybe a little. I just can't feel anything.'

'Shall I rub them? It might help.'

Estelle fluttered her hands. 'Oh, don't fuss, dear.'

'Why not?'

'Because it makes me feel helpless,' Estelle said crossly.

'But if you don't let me do anything, then *I* feel helpless.'

They were at an impasse. Gillian didn't move. Estelle was silent. At last she sighed. 'You're the child, you see. You're the one who's supposed to be helpless, not me.'

Gillian felt tears pricking her eyes. 'Oh, Mother. I know. But I'm a big girl now.'

Estelle gave a little croak, some kind of laugh. 'Fiddle. You just won't settle for playing Watson.' She wiggled a foot. 'Ouch! Pins and needles. I should be grateful, I suppose.'

CHAPTER 13

The next morning, Estelle was distressed. She called Gillian into her bedroom, where she stood holding a pretty, handknit cardigan Gillian had given her the previous Christmas.

'Look at this! Moths have been at it.' She held it up, a lilac-blue mesh against the morning light. Gillian could see the holes. Estelle brought it close to her glasses, peering at the damage. 'I should have put everything in the cedar chest, I meant to in the spring, but it's so deep, I have trouble getting things out again. I never got around to it, and now look.' Her lips quivered. 'I can't manage anything! Not even taking care of my sweaters.'

'Maybe we can mend it.'

'I don't have any wool now, and anyway, everything in the drawers is probably ruined. The damn moths never eat just one sweater; they go around and try everything, like people at a buffet.'

Gillian emptied the drawers and they searched through Estelle's sweaters. She had fifteen, including three pullovers. 'Might as well chuck those,' she said morosely. 'They're old, and anyhow I can't get them on over my head any more. And we'd better have all the others cleaned, or I may wake up next month with nothing to wear.'

'I could try darning this,' Gillian said doubtfully, looking at the broken strands of lilac wool.

'No,' Estelle said, rallying. 'You're already taking on so much. And anyhow you'd do a lousy job.'

'Yes, I would.'

'Ask Paula at the cleaners. She sews. She's done zippers and hems for me. I don't know what else to do.'

'I'll go on my way to Stanton.'

Gillian hadn't planned on a trip to the dry cleaners, but she was resigned. Chores sprouted like weeds in spring. The sabbatical effect, perhaps. At home, where she worked too hard, like everybody she knew, her job forced her to compress her errands into a few frantic hours a week. On Saturday mornings, she would make a list of essentials, plan a strategic route, and then join the harried throng, grim-faced and simmering with resentment as the precious minutes peeled away from the day.

Now that she had more time, errands took on a social character of their own. The quick, anonymous exchanges of urban life gave way to the personal, whether you liked it or not. By and large, she liked it. Besides, if something needed doing, Estelle fretted until it was done. It was easier to go to the cleaners now than to be asked several times a day when she was going to go.

When Gillian arrived at the cleaners, only a block from the pharmacy where she'd been the previous morning, she saw Kitty's BMW in one of the two parking spaces. She pulled alongside, thinking she would ask Kitty about mending. Not that a moth would live for more than a nanosecond in Kitty's house. The bells above the door jingled and Janice came out with a load of clothes in filmy plastic shrouds.

Gillian had found Simon Steele's *Juicer* on the bookshelves at home and tossed it into the front seat of the car with the pile of sweaters, thinking she might peek at it in an idle moment in her office. As she opened the passenger door to collect the sweaters for Paula, it slid out and landed on the ground.

'Damn.' Gillian bent down to rescue the book. 'Hello, Janice. Have you read this? I'm just starting it.'

Janice looked down at the big black letters on the Christmasred cover. 'Yeah. Lots of people have.' She sounded tense.

'What do you think?' Gillian turned the book over and read from the blurb. '"Brutally frank." Is it?'

Janice dumped the clothes in the back seat of Kitty's car and stuck her hands in her pockets. 'He admits he did dumb things. But, I don't know, he goes on and on about it. It's boring. Why is he such a hero for writing about it? If he thinks he's so disgusting, why doesn't he go to a clinic and dry out? And he makes his wife sound like a total bitch. She can't be. She works at the college, and she's always nice to everybody.'

'My mother said the book was one-sided.'

'Nicole didn't think so. She loved the book. She thought it was honest. She said he was showing how his drinking had wrecked everything. Like, his wife was OK until she married him, and then she became this other person.'

'Very different readings.'

'Nicole said I probably didn't have any alcoholics in my family. The book was like a big confession, that was her idea. She thought it meant he could turn his life around. Start over. She said people should be allowed to start over. We met him—Simon Steele—one time. He was at a store signing books and Nicole talked to him. He signed her book.'

'Really? When was that?'

'Last spring. April. She was excited to meet him in person.'

'It sounds as if you and Nicole were pretty close friends.'

Janice's eyes brimmed with sudden tears. She looked away. 'I can't talk about it.'

Gillian chucked Simon's book into the back seat of the Buick. Had Nicole found him attractive? The jacket photograph was quite sexy, with a vulnerable, slightly over-the-edge look in the eyes. Like Peter O'Toole, or Hamlet with a substance-abuse problem.

'I wish they'd hurry up and arrest Arnold Mitchell,' Janice said.

'If they haven't, it's because they don't have enough evidence.'

'That's what Daddy says. But what about the photograph he had? Everybody in the dorm is totally freaked. We have the blinds down all the time. What if he took photos of all of us?'

'I understand how you feel. But I don't think you need to worry about that. He's not likely to have other pictures. Certainly not pictures of everybody.'

'Why not? Because he was after Nicole?'

'Apart from that. I mentioned the photo yesterday to a friend of mine—a photographer. There's no question of using a flash—a flash is no use at that distance. So for Arnold to get that picture, there must have been a lamp right beside her. He would need a long exposure, because there wouldn't be a lot of light. Nicole had to stand still for long enough. That wouldn't happen often. If she'd moved sooner, he would just have gotten a blur. He was lucky, you could say.'

Janice thought. 'I see. Her desk lamp is next to the window, she always sat there when she worked. But did she have to be right by the window?'

'Have you stood at the edge of the woods and looked up at the windows? I have. The angle's steep—if she'd been in the middle of the room, he couldn't have seen much of her.'

'So if I was just walking around my room he couldn't have gotten a picture?' Some of the tension went out of her shoulders.

The bell jingled again, and Kitty came towards them, holding another load of clothes high to keep the plastic from trailing on the ground. The light wind fluttered the ends.

'Your white blouse is just fine,' she said to Janice. 'They got all the coffee out.' She glanced at Gillian's bundle of sweaters.

'Moths,' Gillian said.

'What a shame. Estelle must be upset. That's the trouble with living in the country. The critters are always trying to move in. If it's not moths, it's ants. How bad are they?' She handed her load to Janice. 'Just put those in the car for me, dear.' She glanced at her daughter critically. 'And don't slouch.'

'Little holes,' Gillian said, 'but in some of her favourite things.'

'It always is. Like toast falling buttered-side down. Get Paula to look at them. She's a magician at repairs. Wait.' Kitty leaned into the car and riffled through the plastic layers, pushing up the bottom of one bag. A fine brown tweed jacket lay inside. 'See the sleeve? There was a little tear a few months ago, and she mended it perfectly. She sewed on a button for me, this time— one of these nice horn ones, I always have a few spares. Of course, anyone can sew on a button, I could do it myself if I had time, but Paula can mend and do alterations.' She straightened up and closed the door. 'I'm exacting, if I do say so myself, and I've got no complaints about her work. She'll fix the sweaters, I'm sure. Tell Estelle not to worry.'

'I will,' Gillian said, reassured. She smiled at Janice, who hadn't said a word in Kitty's presence. She'd been silent around her father too, Gillian reflected. Both parents seemed to treat her like a child, but she must be over twenty.

'Thanks for bringing my scarf back,' Kitty said, sliding gracefully into the car. 'I found it in Lewis's pocket this morning—he'd forgotten where he'd put it. I love my little collection. Couldn't do without them.'

Janice banged her knee getting into the car.

'She's a wonderful rider,' Kitty said, laughing, 'but she can't manage on her own two feet.'

Janice turned her head away, towards the window. Gillian couldn't see her face.

Gillian found Jo in the dining hall at lunch. It was a long room lit by rows of uncurtained casement windows. The wainscoting was slathered with cream enamel, the oak floor and round wooden tables preserved beneath thick sheets of varathane. Outside, the river ran grey and opaque under a whitish sky. High, thin cloud had drifted in since the early morning, when frost had been thick on the grass. Surely it was too early for snow, Gillian thought. The voices of several hundred women ricocheted off the hard surfaces and competed with the banging and clanging of china and metal. She squeezed in beside Jo just as a crowd of students rose like a flock of sparrows and swooped off, carrying their trays. The noise level dropped a little.

Jo looked drawn and weary.

Gillian spooned pea soup from an indestructible bowl. She gazed at the tabletop, at the dark shining wood distantly alive under the plastic, like pondwater under ice. Painted goldfish would have been a nice touch.

Jo also seemed to be staring into the tabletop.

'Any old boots down there?' Gillian asked, to break the gloomy silence.

Jo didn't smile. 'Margaret talked to the police this morning. They've been to the address on Nicole's high school transcripts, the place where she lived before Riverside Drive. The building had been renovated and turned into condos. There used to be rental apartments there. The people in the building are all new, and nobody in the neighbourhood remembers Nicole's aunt. They hardly found anybody who remembers Nicole. There's a guy who runs a corner store— he recognized her picture. She used to come in all the time, then she disappeared. He remembered that she started wearing nicer clothes suddenly, and then she disappeared. He figured she'd found a rich boyfriend and moved uptown.'

'What about her school?'

'Their records list her aunt as Charlotte Bishop, but she never had any contact with the school.'

'So the police are getting nowhere with the family search. Where was she born?'

'We still don't know,' Jo said.

'But don't you have that information on her registration form?'

'We have what she wrote down. But there was no Nicole Bishop born in New York City on that date.'

'Could she have a criminal record?'

'The police told Margaret they ran her fingerprints. Nothing turned up.'

'What do they think?'

'That she was hiding something. Brilliant deduction.'

'A fictive aunt and a false name or birth record. It sounds as though she's trying to hide her parents. What could the secret possibly be?'

'She told us they were dead. Maybe they're in a witness protection programme.'

'Nah, the trail would be covered better. You wouldn't find these obvious gaps as soon as you started looking. Maybe her father's a Catholic priest.'

'And "Aunt Charlotte" is her mother? Then where is she?'

'Maybe she's not hiding her parents—maybe she's hiding *from* them.'

'Then who's putting money in the bank account that pays her room and board?'

Gillian shrugged. 'The rich boyfriend uptown?'

Jo gave a derisive snort.

'OK, scratch that. I don't have any ideas. The police will have to go back to Leslie Lang. There's the mail connection to that apartment. It must mean something.'

'But Leslie Lang didn't know Nicole.'

'That's what she said. But she may have lied.'

'What for?'

'She's scared? That would explain a few things. Suppose Nicole was hiding from someone dangerous. Her parents aren't dead. They're paying her college fees, but they're also hiding her identity from the person who's threatened her. No one is supposed to know her real name.'

'That would seem totally crazy, except that somebody killed her. But the police suspect Arnold. She can't have been hiding from him. So your theory doesn't fit.'

'Or Arnold doesn't.'

Jo picked at her salad. 'You know, Nicole told me that she went on a Buddhist retreat just before she applied to Stanton. She wanted some peace, she said, somewhere to think. It was in a house out in the Berkshires. She loved it, it seemed so pure and clean and quiet. She wanted to stay forever and to quit modeling completely. But when she got back to the city she realized that being a Buddhist was too extreme. Instead, she decided to go to college. Start a new life. I'd told her about wanting to be a nun, and I understood her feelings very well. It made me feel very close to her. Now I wonder if the story was even true.'

'Why shouldn't it be?'

'I don't know. So much of what she told us wasn't.' Jo sighed. 'How was your class this morning?'

'Rocky. Their minds are not on race and gender under the Raj. Half of them hadn't done this week's reading, and the rest didn't know what they'd read. Only two handed in the essay that was due. I can't blame them. It's only been six days since Nicole was found. So we had a little seminar about homicide.'

'Did you tell them any of your personal experiences?'

'Some. I told them about Wendy—the chemist who was killed at Cambridge when I was there a couple of years ago. And I talked about Edward and his work. If any of them decides to be a detective, it won't be my fault. I told them they'd be up to their necks in human stupidity for seventy hours a week.'

'Hah. Aren't most jobs like that these days?'

'You're just getting tired and cranky, Jo. Like me. I must say, sabbaticals are supposed to be restorative, but maybe they're like drugs—you have to keep taking bigger doses to get the same high. I think I need five years this time.'

CHAPTER 14

Late in the afternoon, Gillian found a note from Roberta in her pigeonhole. Another form required her signature. She must have signed thousands in her life, and so had everyone else. When we were one with Ninevah and Tyre, who would study our history? Only lunatics. To remain sane, scholars would have to opt for the pre-Xerox era. Librarians thought our problem was shelf space, but that wasn't it. She hadn't forgotten the agonies of collecting material for her thesis. Every document referred to others that might have some relevance; every article bristled with footnotes to further sources; every attempt to find a starting point suggested new directions. She had nearly drowned in the shoreless sea of material. The records left by the British Empire were vast indeed, but they were a slim volume of poetry compared to the archival tonnage being churned out now. It wouldn't surprise her if the British government produced as much paper in one day as it had in a whole year in those bygone decades when it had ruled half the world. No, the problem wasn't shelf space. And putting everything on disk wouldn't be the answer. The people who thought it would be didn't understand that historians thrived on the gaps in their material. They made their narratives from scarcity; a collection of documents was like a group of stars: pinpoints of light in a vast darkness. Histories were like constellations—

shapes imposed on the darkness by lines drawn between points of light.

How long would this tiresome form lie in a file somewhere after she had signed it? Where were all the thousands she had signed in her life? The requirements for form-filling and duplicating amounted to a mania. Maybe the people of the twenty-first century would use our archives for building material, like the Italians burning the marble pillars of Rome to make lime.

Roberta was cramming papers into her briefcase when Gillian tapped on her open door.

'I'm here. Where's the dotted line?'

'Oh, Gillian, thanks. I'll just find it in the file.' Roberta opened a drawer and pulled out a sheet of paper. 'Here, go ahead and read it, I'm still packing up work to take home.'

Gillian looked at the form. It was something to do with the college's insurance. She'd seen it before. She'd already signed one like it.

'Are you sure there isn't a signed one in the file? I remember this.'

Roberta looked taken aback, but she picked up the file and leafed through it. 'I must be losing my mind,' she said. 'You're right. It's here. I just didn't see it.' Mechanically, she returned the file to the drawer and closed it. 'Sorry, I don't usually lose track of these details. This morning I lost my keys. I *never* do things like that.'

'What's wrong?' Gillian asked.

'Everything's been out of control around here. Because of Nicole. But it isn't just that. I'm letting the damned divorce get to me, I'm afraid. I shouldn't. I can't afford to. But Simon is so unpredictable. He's been Scrooge in person since we separated, and now all of a sudden my lawyer phones and says Simon's caving in, and then Simon calls out of the blue and says he's got a cheque for me. "When can I come and pick it up?".'

'Isn't that good news?'

'It should be. But something's fishy. He wouldn't shift ground so suddenly without a reason.'

'Maybe his lawyer told him to.'

'That barracuda? I doubt it. Simon's softening me up, I think, but I don't know why.' Roberta stuffed a few more papers into her briefcase and snapped it shut. 'Have you ever seen the house?'

'Not up close, only glimpses from the top of the driveway.'

'It's worth a look. Why don't you come up with me and see it?' Roberta looked appealingly at Gillian. Under her immaculate exterior, she suddenly seemed vulnerable. 'I know it's a big favour, but I don't want to go alone, and whatever Simon's up to I want to get the money before he changes his mind again.'

'Now?'

'While he's feeling conciliatory. Not to mention sober.'

It was the pastel hour, when the colours of the day blurred and faded. The roadway swung around the pilastered corner of the house, past the spot, empty now, where a week earlier Gillian had seen the police car. The verandah was lit by lamps hung high under the roof, the pillars casting an indistinct lattice of shadow across the steps. A scrub game of field hockey raged over the lawn behind the dining hall. Two students wheeled by on bicycles. Ordinary life was beginning to reclaim the college, filling the moments between thoughts of Nicole.

The wrought-iron gates at the end of the drive, ornamented with gilded fleur-de-lis—a Delamar touch—stood open, as always.

'There's been talk of shutting the gates at night,' Roberta said. 'A stupid idea. Any psychopath could just park his car and walk in.'

The Vanderplaat estate, now the Stanton College grounds, occupied a long rectangle between the Hudson and the road that ran parallel to the river on its eastern bank. The stone wall that edged the road was only four feet high, while the boundaries between the college grounds and the adjacent properties were unfenced. The woods ran along the river in a continuous ribbon, divided among their owners only by lines on paper and old survey markers buried in leaf mould. Locking the gate would prevent vehicles from entering, but not their occupants.

Roberta took the main road north. 'I don't want to drive over the bridge,' she said. 'We'll go in at the other end.'

They made the left turn on to Dykeman's Pond Road, and then a right on Beacon. She hadn't been up to see Carrie Pilgrim yet, Gillian remembered. Had Eli talked to the Hornbecks? Their house was on the left, before Simon's. The Nelsons lived across the road, and Carrie's place was at the end. Some other people owned the property at the corner; the entrance was on Dykeman's. They were only around in the summers. She'd seen the house once, with Peggy. It was tiny, like a treehouse, and built on stilts high above the rock. The view of the river was fabulous.

'My kids think it would make a great fort,' Peggy said. 'But I miss the old cottage. An enormous wisteria grew all over the front. They bulldozed it.'

'Do you know the people with the treehouse?' Gillian asked Roberta.

'They invited us over for drinks once, but Simon was rude, and that was that.'

'Rude? Why?'

'Their house. Simon's house belonged to his grandfather, and he thinks the valley's being ruined by commuters and summer people from the city with too much money and no taste.' Roberta stopped the car halfway down the drive and pointed at the view of her former house against the darkening hills. 'Simon used to visit when he was a boy, and he remembers this part of the valley before there were new developments like the one I've moved to. His house is a Calvert Vaux, as Simon will be happy to explain. He'll tell you the story of each brick if you let him. I must have heard it a million times.' She switched to the nasal monotone of a tour-bus driver. 'It's a simple picturesque country house; the design's in *Villas and Cottages*. Vaux worked with Frederick Law Olmsted on Central Park, and he designed the Metropolitan Museum of Art.'

'It's awfully pretty,' Gillian said, gazing at the balcony over the double front doors, the little dormers and the finials sprouting from every peak.

'And awfully cold in the winter.'

They walked down the drive towards the entrance.

'I see he's fixed the pane he broke.' Roberta pointed at the glass-paned front doors. Her voice tightened with anger. 'One of those was smashed when I came on Saturday. I asked Simon about it, but he wouldn't tell me. He probably can't remember what he did.' She knocked. 'I wonder if he's here. He usually leaves the car in the driveway. If he's not home, it'll be the last straw.'

Gillian had been looking with pleasure at the whitewashed brick and the delicate arched brackets along the verandah. Now she glanced at Roberta and saw that her hands were clenched. She looked ready for a fight.

Simon Steele opened the door.

'I've come for the cheque,' Roberta said in a firm but positive tone, as if giving a demonstration for a self-assertiveness training session.

He'd shaved recently. A nick on his chin gleamed red. His hair was damp. He wore jeans and a loose white shirt with the sleeves rolled halfway to his elbows. He was worth looking at, nicked chin and all. Black hair, nervous blue eyes, a pallor, the skin a little bruised in the eye sockets. He was older than the photograph on his book jacket, and he looked half wrecked, but a lot of women would love to bid on the repair job.

He didn't seem pleased to see Gillian.

'I didn't know you were bringing anyone,' he said to Roberta. Then, turning to Gillian, 'You her lawyer?' It was almost a snarl.

'Er, no, UN observer.'

'Roberta, listen. I just wanted to talk to you. But not with you and all your friends.'

'After Saturday, what makes you think *I* want to talk to *you*?'

'I'm sorry about that.'

'Sorry? You bastard. You never change, do you?'

'What do you expect?'

'I expect you to make an effort for your son. Poor Josh— how do you think he felt?'

'I meant to see him.'

'Meant to. You make me sick.' Her eye fell on the open door. 'What did you do to the windowpane, anyway? Try to walk through it? You're slipping, Simon,' she added mockingly. 'You haven't even used old glass to replace it. That's ordinary glass; even I can see the difference.'

'Shut up, Roberta.'

'Shut up? I will not shut up, you asshole.' She was shouting. 'You knew Josh was supposed to visit, and you got plastered anyway. You're not really sorry. You can't keep a promise—you can't be a father for two lousy hours, you're a drunk but you think because you wrote that book you're something special. You're a liar and your writing is shit. It's just shit.'

'Yeah, I've heard your opinion before,' Simon said.

Well, thought Gillian, I walked into this one. At work, Roberta was always calm and controlled, her fund of patience inexhaustible. Here, she'd gone from zero to scream in about sixty seconds.

'You don't give a damn for anything except your precious house, and you can't even mend a window without doing a half-assed job.'

Simon's eyes blazed. 'Shut up about the house, you bitch.' He turned around and walked down the hall. 'Forget about talking,' he flung over his shoulder. 'I'll get your goddam cheque.'

'Fuck you,' Roberta muttered. 'I should break all your windows.'

Simon came back. 'Here's a cheque for seven thousand. It's all there is right now. I've told my lawyer to work out a deal. Let's not turn this into Desert Storm, OK?'

'I'll let you know when I see the deal.' Roberta inspected the cheque. 'This better not bounce.' She opened her bag. 'What did you want to talk about?'

Gillian edged away.

'Should have brought your blue helmet,' Simon sneered.

'And my rules of engagement. May I look at your house?'

'Feel free.'

She walked along the drive to see the house from the far end. The windows were low to the ground and she could see right through the room to the view on the other side. She gave Simon and Roberta a few minutes of privacy and then returned. The atmosphere seemed less stormy.

'Calvert Vaux did a lot of good work in the valley,' she said to Simon. 'Too bad we've lost some.'

He visibly reassessed her. 'This one won't be lost if I can help it. It's quite an early one, built in eighteen fifty-two, two years after he came over from London. My grandfather bought it in nineteen twenty-four. Are you an architect?'

'No. I grew up around here. On Salt Hill Road. The Federalist house across from the sheep meadow.'

'The Adams place?'

'I'm Gillian Adams.'

'Simon Steele. Sorry I was rude. Divorce doesn't bring out the best in me.'

'Neither did marriage,' Roberta remarked distantly.

'Nothing does. I told you that before we got married, but you refused to believe me. I believed you, instead. Look, I want to see Josh. I'll come pick him up on Saturday. I'll take him to the zoo, OK? He likes the zoo.'

'All right. But if you disappoint him again, I'll make you pay for it. And I mean pay. I can be a twenty-four-carat bitch if I need to.'

'How true. I'll be there.'

'You're going to drive him?'

'I'll pick him up at one.'

'And you'll be stone-cold sober.' Roberta looked around. 'Where's the car, anyway? How come it's not in the drive?'

Simon exploded. 'Christ, what is this, the Spanish Inquisition?'

'So where is it?'

She certainly knew his sensitive spots, Gillian observed. One thing people learned when they got married was where to hit when they wanted to hurt. But it seemed a bit tactless to hammer on him with his cheque for seven thousand dollars in her pocket. She could at least wait until she'd cashed it. People are nuts, Gillian concluded.

'In the garage.'

'How come? Did you damage it, too?'

'I don't drink and drive,' he said between his teeth.

'You used to.'

'Not for twenty-five years.' He looked angry enough to hit her, but he didn't. 'Roberta, go away. Get off my case. I don't want to fight. I just want to get things settled. I'm sorry about everything.'

'BS,' Roberta said, but without heat. She'd discharged her rage, for the moment. Now she sounded weary.

The afternoon was fading into evening. Wind rattled the leaves overhead. Back in the car, Gillian wondered whether Simon cared about the child. Was he just placating Roberta because he was afraid of losing the house? He hadn't done a very competent job of soothing her, but then she'd arrived primed for battle. She seemed to be the sort of person who lacks a middle register; once she let herself get angry at all, she went nuclear. Her rage at Simon seemed boundless. She had excellent reasons for being furious with him, but his broken faith with his little boy had almost been crowded out by accusations about his writing and driving.

'Sorry about the scene,' Roberta said. 'I thought I was going to keep my temper, but I couldn't. He does that to me.' She drove in silence for a moment. 'He drives me to it. He's like a stone. He doesn't feel anything.'

'I doubt that,' Gillian said.

'Then why doesn't he change?' She gave an exasperated sigh. 'Oh well, he gave me the cheque. That's something. Maybe I'll take Josh to Disneyworld this winter.'

CHAPTER 15

Roberta dropped Gillian back at Stanton so she could collect her car. The lights were on in the dorms. The hockey players had gone to bathe before dinner, and the parking lot was deserted. At this hour, anyone could walk through the campus unnoticed.

Most of the blinds were lowered over the dormitory windows; a few were raised, the rooms dark, or lamplit but unoccupied. Gillian walked around to the back of Nicole's building. She hadn't been down this path since her explorations of the campus earlier in the term. Then the weather had been warm and the windows open; she'd heard voices and music and seen people at their desks, studying. Four floors of windows faced the lacy curtain of leaves. Now, nearly all the blinds were down. Eli Pink's warning had had its effect. She walked a few steps into the forest, following a narrow dirt path that wound its way through the woods to the riverbank. Eli hadn't believed Arnold when Arnold said he was looking for owls. It did sound absurd: a man with a camera lurking in the dark behind a women's dormitory was very probably looking at women, not birds. Were there owls living in this stretch of woods? It was quite possible; barn owls had been nesting in the shed at the farm for years and years. But at this hour it was too dark under the trees to hunt for roosts. What was that line from *Macbeth*? 'When blood is nipp'd and ways be foul, Then nightly sings the staring owl . . .' The nights were getting nippy, but she couldn't stand around waiting for the owls, if any, to sing. She should ask Janice Grogan if people in the dorm ever heard owls hooting when they were awake at night. She turned back towards the dorm. A light went on in one of the second-floor windows. Gillian saw a female figure move towards the window. She stood still, backlit, looking out; then arched, raising her arms above her head in a luxurious stretch. Gillian could see the silhouette of her arms and breasts, the halo of her hair. Then the blind rattled down and her shadow moved across it. The sequence was simple and ordinary, the woman anonymous, yet Gillian, standing unseen in the shelter of the trees, was aware of an accidental intimacy, the invasion of a private moment.

The students had been told not to go out alone; belatedly she realized that she should probably be more careful herself. She was unlikely to be in danger, and it was all too easy for the police to tell women to stay indoors, but still, wandering behind Nicole's dorm when it was getting dark was perhaps not the smartest thing to do. She walked briskly away from the woods and angled across the lawn towards the main entrance to Delamar House. The shortest way to her car was through the building and out the side door at the rear. She made a mental note to contact Eli; he should know that Nicole and Simon Steele had met. It gave the Hornbecks' story about Alice Nelson seeing her on his driveway some credibility; Gillian had been inclined to think that Alice's imagination had been overactive, but now Janice had proved that there was a connection. She didn't much want to talk to Eli; she decided it was a chore that could wait until she got home. With luck, he wouldn't be there, and she could leave a message.

She walked past the door to the president's office. It was open. Margaret Bristol was at her desk, looking fatigued. She glanced up.

'Gillian! Jo just went to see if you were still in your office. Can you spare a few minutes?'

Gillian hadn't been in Margaret's room since the beginning of the term. It was elegant, dusty sage and cream, a room like one of Robert Adam's in England. The windows looked out on the river, but at the moment, only a dim outline of the opposite bank could be seen, under a pink stripe of sky.

Margaret got up and closed the door. 'Do sit down.' She placed herself opposite Gillian, but didn't speak for a moment. She looked ill at ease. 'It's about Nicole, of course.' She stopped.

'Of course,' Gillian said. 'What can I do?'

Margaret relaxed a little. 'I hope you don't mind being roped in. I know our problems aren't your responsibility, and I won't blame you if you decide to keep your distance, but I do hope you won't. I understand from Jo that you've had some experience with, er, situations of a similar nature.'

'With murdered students?' Gillian said.

'Exactly. There was a student in your department at UPNW who was killed, isn't that the case? And a research fellow at Cambridge, someone you knew?'

'I didn't know her; my friends did. Look, I'm not a professional investigator.'

'I know; I'm not sure what I'd do with one. But I'm desperate for knowledgeable advice. You're an academic, like us, and you've been through investigations like this one before. You know a lot more about the police and the way they proceed than we do. We have to support the police in every way we can, but this murder could do serious damage to Stanton. We're small, and we're always in competition with other colleges for the best students. And of course we're in great need of increased endowment funds. I'm sure you understand without a great long speech from me. It's a quagmire, and, frankly, I feel we need whatever help we can get from someone with more experience.'

'I'll do what I can,' Gillian said, 'but it may not be much.'

'Thank you. That makes me feel a little better.'

They were sitting in two armchairs by the fireplace. Wood was laid in the grate, but the stones were swept clean. A little blaze would have been a comfort, but Gillian surmised that the fire was lit when parents or benefactors or trustees were entertained, and not for the pleasure of the president.

'I must ask you to keep whatever I tell you confidential,' Margaret said, apologetically. 'I have an obligation to keep the trustees informed, but otherwise, Roberta Morgenstern— my assistant—and Jo Oliviera, who was Nicole's advisor, are the only two people on campus who have access to whatever information I receive. Everything will be public sooner or later, but, at present, the less exposure the better. This is what I feel. I'd value your opinion.'

There was a knock at the door.

'That will be Jo,' Margaret said.

'Oh. You're here,' Jo said to Gillian. 'I looked in your office and in the library. I knew you were somewhere because I saw your car.'

'It's hard to miss it.'

'Let me fill you both in,' Margaret said. She had a deep, resonant voice, a good voice for authority, Gillian thought. Her hair was a faded blonde, drawn back in a fearlessly severe and out-of-date French twist. She moved slowly, carrying her corseted weight with dignity. Before coming to Stanton, she'd been an art historian at Yale.

Jo shut the door and dropped wearily on to the sofa. 'What's the latest?'

'I had some news from the police this afternoon. The young woman who was registered here as Nicole Bishop wasn't born Nicole Bishop. She changed her name.'

'Why?' Jo demanded.

'She changed it when she moved in with her aunt, after her parents died. Her aunt's last name is Bishop. Nicole's file is accurate on that point.'

'There is an aunt, then. Where is she?'

'She hasn't been located.'

'Then where did they get the information about her name?' Gillian asked.

'Leslie Lang told them.'

'So she does know Nicole.'

'Oh yes, very well, I'm afraid.'

'Afraid?'

'What about the bank account?' Jo interrupted.

'That's Nicole's.'

'Did her aunt give her the money?'

'No. Unfortunately.'

'Good Lord, Nicole didn't steal it?'

'No, she earned it. When the police talked to Leslie Lang, they found out that she works for an escort service. And so did Nicole.'

Jo sat upright. 'No, she didn't. She was a model.'

'That's only what she told us.'

'She was a model,' Jo cried. 'She showed me photos!'

'Maybe she modeled, too. But she worked for an escort service in New York.'

'My God,' Jo groaned. 'Is *that* where the money for her fees came from?'

'I'm afraid so.'

'I don't believe it! She was so modest. She dressed like a missionary. She never talked about men. When she talked about modeling, she told me she was tired of it. Could this Leslie Lang person be lying?'

'No, she's clearly what she says she is; Mr. Pink has no doubt about that. She works for "Ecstasy Escorts". A top-of-the-line business. She told him that herself. And the New York police confirmed it.'

'You mean the vice squad has a rating system? Ecstasy Escorts.' Jo was disgusted. 'That's just great. Fantastic. "Murdered College Girl Used Sex to Finance Education". The media will go ape.'

'It's not good news for Stanton.' Margaret looked rather despairing. 'The tabloids haven't taken any notice of us so far; we're not high profile enough, but they might latch on to this. What do you think, Gillian?'

'Can the police keep it quiet for now?' Gillian asked. 'Leslie Lang won't want publicity. If evidence turns up linking Nicole's death to the escort business, then there won't be any way to suppress it, but if someone else killed her for reasons that have nothing to do with that side of her life, then the police could try to keep it out of the press.' The defence would probably bring it up at the trial, she thought, but that was a problem for another day. 'What you most want to avoid,' she added, 'is a story that dribbles out bit by bit—develops over days and weeks, with new details. Then the news runs and runs; you're like a dog with a tin can tied to your tail.'

'I did ask Detective Pink whether he planned to release any information about the escort agency; he said not at this time.'

'I can't believe she told us such a pack of lies,' Jo burst out.

'She was an accomplished actress,' Margaret said drily. 'She'd have to be, to do that kind of work.'

'How much money did she make?' Gillian asked.

'Three to five hundred a night, after the agency took its share.'

'Jesus!' Jo did some arithmetic. 'If she worked five nights a week, she'd make ten thousand dollars a month! A hundred and twenty thousand in one year!' She went on calculating. 'If she did it for two years and then quit to go to school -'

'If she'd quit, things might not be quite so sticky for us. But she was still working for the agency this year.'

'But she's been at school here, in residence, for three years, she can't have been working much. Summers, maybe,' Gillian pointed out.

'Leslie told the police Nicole just did "specials" during term.'

'Specials?' Jo demanded.

'I couldn't bring myself to ask.'

'Shit,' said Jo. 'How can a blow job be special enough to cost five hundred dollars?'

Margaret grimaced. 'People pay two hundred for a haircut.'

'Do the police think one of her clients might have killed her?' Gillian asked. 'It's an obvious line of enquiry.' That would get Arnold off the hook, she thought, but at a greater cost to the college.

'I don't know.'

'What about Arnold Mitchell?'

'He certainly hasn't been ruled out. But he hasn't been arrested—Detective Pink told me they've let him go, for the time being.'

'They might have focused on the agency first, if they'd found out about it sooner.'

'They didn't because they were looking for Nicole's aunt— they didn't explain to Leslie Lang that Nicole was dead. She knew Nicole hadn't seen her aunt for years, and she didn't know what the police wanted, so she played dumb. They've been sharing the apartment on Riverside Drive for several years. Nicole used another name when she was working, by the way. Nicola Stone.'

Little galaxies of lights began to twinkle on the opposite riverbank.

'Most women who are into that life and that kind of money don't leave it, not while they're still young and gorgeous,' Gillian said. 'I wonder why Nicole came to Stanton.'

'I had her in an art history course,' Margaret said. 'She wrote a terrific paper on Byzantine mosaics, of all things. Most people aren't interested; the images are too stiff, too flat. But Nicole got all fired up about them, went down to the Met to look at theirs, and did extra research. She once asked me about graduate school at Yale. Whatever she did with her body, she had brains, and she liked using them.'

'She must have gotten good grades in high school, or she wouldn't have been accepted here,' Gillian said, considering. 'Then she seems to have worked as a model and an escort for a while—a couple of years, I suppose. Then she came here. She could easily have gone to school in the city, so she must have wanted to leave that life behind.' She remembered what Janice had told her. Nicole thought that people should be allowed to start over. 'She could have had her nice apartment, her city friends. Instead, she chooses Stanton and lives in a dorm, like a retired courtesan taking up residence in a convent.'

'Still doing a few "specials" between the Hail Marys,' Jo said sourly.

'She probably needed the money. She was paying her fees here plus rent on a New York apartment. And women in that line of work pay an awful lot for clothes.'

'I still don't understand why she told us all those lies about her aunt,' Jo said. 'Why did she tell me they were close?'

'It's not hard to see why she would want to present us with some sort of relative, on paper at least. We would have asked too many questions if she seemed to have no family at all.' Margaret looked at Jo. 'And we would never have accepted her if she'd told the truth. You know that.'

'I suppose you've got to tell the trustees about this,' Gillian said. She was thinking about Lewis Grogan. He didn't want to find out the real story when he picked up a newspaper. Now Margaret would have to tell him about Ecstasy Escorts. Again, she was glad she wasn't a college president. What did Margaret earn? Probably less than Nicole Bishop a.k.a. Nicola Stone.

Margaret winced. 'Yes, I can't wait very long. It wouldn't do if the story leaked out and they hadn't been informed.'

'What do you think the police will do now?' Jo asked Gillian.

'They'll try to pry the client list out of the escort agency. But they won't drop their leads here. They'll just have more to do. They've got to trace Nicole back to her family. Find out who she is. She had to have parents. Who were they?'

Jo's mouth twisted. 'Why do you say "were"? We only have her word for it that they're dead.'

CHAPTER 16

As Gillian manoeuvred the Buick out of the parking lot and around Delamar House, her mind jerked in badly edited cross-cuts from Nicole to the scene at Simon's house and back. Then she remembered Arnold's face at the window of the police car. He'd looked like someone driven to the very edge, but by what? Suspicion, accusations, the violent breach of the walls he'd built around himself? Or by a terrible act of his own? As everyone said, he'd always been odd; had he, in his loneliness, made some dream of Nicole that then turned into a nightmare? Her lights swept past the edge of the drive, catching a flash of red reflectors at the bicycle rack. A wisp of memory floated up near the surface of her mind, then sank before she could catch hold of it.

The car was low on gas again. The engine drank like a fish. She pulled into the station that had once been Taylor's Garage, filled the greedy tank, squeegeed the windows and went inside to pay. The Taylors had fixed cars; the new proprietors sold automotive products. The shop floor was heaped with supplies for the coming winter: anti-freeze, motor oil, plastic scrapers. A row of snow tyres festooned with red ribbons caught her eye, and she remembered that she should check the right front wheel. It was looking a little soft. The steering felt the same as usual, but the car drove like a mattress, so the steering was never going to feel different unless she lost a wheel. She moved the car to a space by the air hose. The rubber was old, maybe there was a slow leak. The gauge said it needed air. As she squatted by the wheel, Jim Whitlock drove in and rolled to a stop beside her.

'How's she running? No trouble, I hope?'

'The car's fine. Brian did a great job.'

'He's good at cars—likes them. The older the better. He's got a Studebaker in the shed now. It'll be worth some money when he's fixed it up.'

'Has he seen Arnold's truck? It's pretty old, isn't it?'

'Seen it? Four or five years ago, when he was around twelve, he used to bike past Arnold's house hoping for a glimpse of it, like a boy riding past a girl's house in case he could see her through the window. He talked to Arnold a couple of times and even got to ride in the truck once. He's pretty upset about what's going on.'

'I'm kind of queasy myself.'

'Yeah.'

Jim Whitlock was brawny, blond, balding, with pale eyes and lashes and the scared hands of an amateur builder. In the cold weather, he wore baggy jeans, flannel shirts and big Norwegian sweaters with snowflake and reindeer designs. In the summer, he changed into shorts, revealing legs like bollards covered with blond fuzz. 'You busy?' he asked. 'How about a coffee at Jean's?'

'As soon as I'm done here.' She patted the whale-sized flank of the Buick. 'This car is absurd. I feel as if I'm driving the Starship Enterprise.'

'"To boldly go where no one has gone before"?' Jim chuckled. 'That's pretty hard to do in New York.'

At Jean's, they settled into a booth at the back. Gillian asked Jean for rosehip tea. It was a sign of the times that she could get it; herb tea used to be something you bought in health-food stores. Now it was everywhere, except on airplanes. Even airplanes probably stocked it in first class. If she drank coffee at the end of the day, she told Jim, she didn't sleep at night.

'Coffee never bothers me,' Jim said. 'What I can't do is drink alcohol at lunch. Not that anyone does these days. Show me a glass of beer at noon, and by two o'clock I'm snoring. How did the businessmen of my father's generation do it? They used to drink two or three martinis at lunch and go back to work.'

'"There were giants in the earth in those days."'

'Genesis six, verse four. I didn't know you were a Bible reader.'

'Um,' said Gillian, feeling trapped. She hoped he wasn't going to ask her if she'd been born again. Oh help, she thought. And I like him so much. 'I'm not religious.'

He held up two crossed fingers. 'God and me, we're like this,' he said solemnly. Then he started laughing. 'You should see your face. Relax. I'm no preacher. Not my style. I go to church sometimes. And I read the Bible pretty often. It gets me out of computer-geek mode.'

'What does going to church give you?'

'Community and some peace of mind.'

'Peace of mind,' Gillian repeated. 'That's a precious commodity.'

'Where do you find it?'

'Listening to Haydn, preferably with a glass of Scotch.'

Jean brought the coffee and tea.

'Couple of guys broke into the package store last night. Took a bottle of champagne and two cases of whisky.'

'How'd they get in?' Jim said.

'Drove a truck right through the front window. Ray lives across the road; he called the police and ran out with his gun, but they were already driving out of the parking lot. He was in here this morning; he was mad. I asked what they took, and he said they cleaned him out of Wild Turkey. That's Simon Steele's brand, so I said they must have been reading *Juicer*. Ray didn't laugh, and he usually sees the funny side, so he had to be pretty upset. I guess his insurance will go up again.'

'The police didn't catch them?' Gillian asked.

'Nope.' Jean shrugged. 'But if they're dumb enough to drive through a window to steal two cases of booze, they'll be caught for something pretty soon. You want anything else, just holler.'

'Things like that never used to happen around here,' Gillian said. 'Or so I fondly imagine. It's very confusing to be told that the crime rate is going down when experience tells you the exact opposite.'

'Lots of things are confusing. That's why I go to church. I'm still just as confused, but I feel better about it.'

Gillian laughed. 'A glass of good Scotch has the identical effect.'

'I hope you have plenty in stock then, in case they steal all the single malts next time.'

'I find myself wondering whether Arnold ever found any peace of mind,' Gillian said.

'Because of the murder?'

'Not just that. It's a question that goes way back. I saw him yesterday, in a police car. He looked like a soul in torment.'

'Do you think he did it?'

'I don't know. I have a bad conscience about Arnold. I was in school with him when we were kids. Everyone was mean to him.'

'Why?'

'I wish I knew. He was one of those kids who are rejected by the pack. He was funny looking and clumsy. Other kids teased him. Once that kind of thing starts, it has its own momentum.'

'Unless someone stops it.'

'Nobody did. I don't know what he's done, but I'm sure he would have led a different life if he'd had some friends.

There was one boy who used to kick him in the bottom. Wasn't that a laugh riot?'

Jim stirred his coffee. 'I bumped into Arnold a couple of years ago. An accident. I was on my way to Millbrook, and I went through Freedom Plains, just to go by the church. You know it? It's a gem. Well, Arnold was there; I recognized his truck, so I stopped and got out, and sure enough, he was wandering around, taking pictures of the church. I'd heard he took a lot of photos—people had seen him with a camera—and I like old buildings, so I talked to him about what he was doing. It turned out he had a whole collection of church photos, from up and down the valley. He'd been at it for years. He had pictures of other things, too—barns, houses, bridges, even old fences. It seems amazing now, but he actually let me come to his house to see them. Because of Brian, I think. Ever been there?'

'I saw the outside yesterday.'

'It's a funny place. Grim looking. You know, Arnold has a kind of bug about this area. The Hudson Valley. Sort of like Eric Sloane with a camera. Maybe a little bit, anyway.'

'*Our Vanishing Landscape*?'

Jim lit up. 'You know the books? I'm a huge fan.'

'They're wonderful, but they make me sad about what we've lost—are still losing every day.'

'They were part of what brought me here—all those drawings of little old mills and fields and different kinds of bridges and barns. Remember the sketch of the early mailbox? A boot nailed to a post. I told Arnold about Eric Sloane when he showed me his photographs; he'd never heard of the books. But they have a lot in common. The landscape around here is changing fast, now.'

'I've noticed.'

'And Arnold records things. Especially things from the past, things that are disappearing. That's what he talked about, anyway. He has a kind of archive in the house. The negatives are all labeled, and the prints are too, but he got frustrated when I was there because he wanted to show me things and he couldn't find them. He talked about his filing system, but I could tell that he keeps changing his mind about the categories, starting one classifying system and then dropping it and starting a different one. The prints were in cardboard boxes in the living room. I don't know how he finds anything, or even if he tries. Taking the pictures is more important to him. He built his own dark-room. Did you know that? When I was there, he told me about some kind of foldaway shelf he wanted to make. I had a couple of ideas. The darkroom was immaculate—no dust, and in perfect order, with things fitted in, like being in a sailboat.'

'The Freedom Plains church, that's the little church that looks as if it's wearing a crown.'

'That's right. The photos of that church were really good— some of the best I saw. I happened to know some people up in Ancramdale who were putting out a Hudson Valley calendar, and I took some of Arnold's shots to show them. They chose one, and they sent him fifty dollars. He was glad to get the money, but I think it meant a lot more to him to have one of his pictures in a calendar people would buy.' Jim scratched his head. 'I thought after that he might not be so shy. I invited him over, Brian was going to be home. But Arnold got scared, I guess. He didn't come, and I've hardly talked to him since.'

'Eli Pink told me Arnold said he was in the woods at Stanton because he wanted to take pictures of owls. Do you think it could be true?'

'Owls. Well, I don't know about wildlife, I don't think I saw any photos of birds when I was there, but he could have gotten interested since. Especially if the owls are endangered. If he got the idea that they were going to disappear, he'd probably want to take pictures of them.'

'We've had barn owls in our shed forever. They seem to be doing all right. But the woods are shrinking, there are more and more people around. Sometimes I'm afraid I'll come back one year and the owls will be gone.'

'That's the way Arnold feels about a lot of things around here. I'll tell you something, though: if he was out there looking for owls, and he happened to see girls in their windows instead, photographing them would have been hard for him to resist. He's a shutterbug.'

Gillian felt her anxiety rising as they talked about Arnold. As she finished her tea, she considered telling Jim about the time she'd met Arnold on the Knob. He was the only person she knew who might understand. But if she hadn't told Eli, she probably shouldn't tell anyone. It would get her no closer to the truth about Arnold and Nicole. Instead, she said, 'Would you go with me to Arnold's house? Now?'

Jim looked doubtful. 'Why?'

'Because I'm worried about him. And you've been there before; it wouldn't be so strange for him to see you.' Gillian looked Jim in the eye. She knew that would make it harder for him to say no, because Roberta had done it to her. 'And I'm afraid to go alone.'

Jim rubbed the side of his head as if it hurt. 'I don't like to interfere.' He sighed. 'But if you think you have to go, I'll come with you.'

'Thanks. You're a peach. I'll just call Estelle, tell her I'll be later than I planned.'

Gillian didn't mention Arnold to Estelle. The phone at Jean's wasn't private, and she didn't want to worry her mother, either. They took the Buick.

'You know,' Jim said, as they drove west on Salt Hill Road, 'even if there weren't any owls, even if he went there to watch the girls in the dorm, it doesn't mean he's a murderer. There aren't many men in the world who wouldn't watch a crowd of girls undressing. We're all voyeurs.'

Gillian thought of the figure in the window of Nicole's dorm. She remembered an apartment she'd had once, high up in a tall building facing another across the street. There was a bank of windows, big windows, six or seven floors of apartments she could see into. It was like looking at a wall of television screens, each with its own channel. She saw people talking on the phone, eating take-out food from cartons, ironing, flipping through magazines, lifting weights. Even in the dark, she could see the blue flicker of a hundred little TVs through the drawn curtains. During the day, everybody opened the curtains. Yet people paraded in their underwear, or even naked. Once or twice, she saw someone with binoculars studying the show in her own building.

Closing the curtains in daylight made her claustrophobic. It was like being locked in. Obviously, that was why everyone left them open. She was gone most of the day, but when she was at home, having breakfast on Sunday, for example, she felt exposed, almost like a person on stage. She'd moved after a year, but she was fascinated by the way other people adapted to their visibility. They ceased to care, as indifferent as people filmed at cash machines. She had watched, periodically struck with amazement that each figure in its Warhol documentary was conscious, had thoughts, a whole world. If she dwelt on this idea for long, she got an almost panicky feverish feeling, as if she were hemmed in by a crowd.

'Not only men,' she said now. 'Everyone likes a cutaway view of other lives; we all like privileged access, the power to be the seer, not the seen.' That was what she had felt in the woods behind the dormitory.

Arnold stayed away from people, she thought. Women probably scared him. And there he suddenly was, safe in the dark, peering in at their secret lives. He shouldn't have looked, but looking wasn't deviant behaviour—quite the opposite. He absolutely should not have photographed Nicole, but he'd had the opportunity, and he took pictures all the time. Perhaps as a photographer who'd focused on things, not people, he'd never thought about how Nicole would feel. He probably didn't know much about other people's feelings.

'Do you think Arnold was interested in pornography—in turning young women into body parts?' she asked Jim.

'You mean with the camera? Not if you go by the thousands of pictures he's taken. Arnold was obsessed with recording, not with women. That's my guess. But people have sides they keep hidden. He could have a room stacked to the ceiling with porn magazines.'

'The police would have found them.'

They were passing Dykeman's Pond. It winked dully at Gillian's lights, like a coin lost among the grasses. A minute later they had reached Arnold's driveway. She drove up to the front of the house, realizing that he might think it was the police coming back, but not wanting him to be startled by people arriving soundlessly on foot. He might have a gun, she thought suddenly. Lots of people did. His father's gun could still be here, in the house. The front windows were dark.

'Looks like the door's open,' Jim said. 'Maybe he's outside. Could be getting some wood in.'

'Hello!' Gillian called when they got out. 'Arnold!'

There was no reply. The mower still stood where she'd seen it on Tuesday.

'It's Jim Whitlock!' Jim bellowed. 'Don't want him coming out on the porch with a shotgun,' he added, his thoughts running on the same track as Gillian's.

Arnold didn't come out. They couldn't hear a sound.

'We'd better have a look,' Jim said reluctantly, when they had shouted once more.

They walked up the steps and called through the open door. The hall was as dark as a closet.

'Do you want to go in?' Jim asked.

'Not much,' Gillian said. 'But I can't walk away, now.'

'He could be in the darkroom.'

Gillian groped her way forward. She felt something soft and rough and stopped dead. 'Jesus! What is it?'

Jim's voice came from right beside her. 'Blanket. Arnold tacked it over the stairs. He said it kept the heat from rising.

He lives downstairs.' He pulled a corner of the blanket aside, let it drop. A current of air stirred, and she glimpsed a dim rectangle—a tall window on the landing above.

'I'll feel around for the switches,' Jim said, bumping past her. As her eyes adjusted, she could make out paneled walls and the heavy blanket hanging a few feet in front of her. She found a switch and pressed it. A light came on behind the blanket, pricking through the moth holes like stars. She lifted the edge, and they could see their way in the hall. Jim turned more lights on.

'That's the darkroom,' he said, pointing towards a door at the rear. 'The kitchen's through that doorway back there; the dining room and the living room are here at the front. I don't know exactly where Arnold sleeps.' He raised his voice and hallooed, then looked uneasily at Gillian. 'He can't be in there and not hear us. Maybe he's out, and the front door just blew open.'

'Or someone broke in. We'd better take a quick look around, just on the main floor.'

They turned to the right, into the living room. There was another door at the far end. The living room was large and bleak and ugly. Enough bulbs in the twin electric chandeliers were working to reveal old stains on the beige carpet and a film of dust on the tabletops. Part of the room was crammed with Danish modern furniture, shoved into a jumble, as if the Mitchells had bought spindly-armed chairs and teak coffee tables like doughnuts, by the dozen. Above the unused fireplace hung a single Currier and Ives print, a cosy, colonial inn with uncolonial Tudor windows.

In the space made by pushing the furniture to one side, stood brown cardboard cartons in short rows, extending from the wall like library shelves. The boxes had big white labels taped to one side, while on the other sides the printed advertisements for cereals and juice and soaps had faded to dim blues and reds. Gillian eyed some labels as she passed, caught Dutchess County, then Saratoga, then two rows of boxes marked with years.

They moved swiftly down the centre of the room, along a strip of carpet flattened like a forest path, where the nap had been worn away by repeated migrations. At the other end was the door. It stood half open. Glancing at Gillian for confirmation, Jim pushed it. They saw a much smaller room with built-in shelves. A library when the house was built, Gillian thought. Then a 'den' for Booter, where he could crouch, a glass between his paws. And now it was Arnold's nest.

It was a mess, like a room that had been vandalized. Gillian wondered whether Arnold or the police search had strewn the books and clothes about, or whether someone else had been here. The smell must be Arnold's. Caves probably smelled this way when people lived in them, she thought. Arnold slept on the big leather sofa; there were blankets heaped on it. He had a few pairs of jeans and a couple of sweaters, and several holey and dingy golf shirts. There was a patch in the seat of one pair of jeans. Books and old *National Geographics* lay in heaps on the floor beside a reclining chair with a footstool. A field guide to birds, heavily thumbed, *The World Encyclopaedia*. Some basic photography books were on the shelves, and a few battered coffee-table books on the valley. No pornographic magazines, she was glad to see.

A calendar hung on the wall, open at May. The picture showed a simple white church with a delicate octagonal cupola like a crown. She recognized it. 'Freedom Plains,' she read in small script at the bottom. 'Arnold Mitchell.' She lifted the page. A village hall, photographed by someone else.

'That's the photograph,' Jim said. 'But where the hell is Arnold?'

They turned around to go back across the living room, and Gillian made a sound of surprise. A niche in the far wall, that they'd had their backs to when they came in, was covered with photographs.

'That's new since I was here,' Jim said.

There were snapshots, and 5 x 7s and a few 8 x 10s, all in black and white and attached to the wall with tacks, unframed. Another copy of the calendar hung there; Arnold must be proud of it. She recognized a derelict barn in one of the bigger prints. It had been gone for ages, so the print must be an old one. It had turned slightly yellowish, she noticed, but some of the other prints hadn't faded. They would be newer, she supposed, though she couldn't be sure. Different chemistry and papers reacted differently to time. In any event, it was logical to assume that this was where Eli had discovered the photograph of Nicole. He'd said it was a pin-up. She scanned the wall for pictures of people and found none.

Jim stuck his nose into the dining room across the hall and then moved towards the back of the house. 'Nothing in there; I'll check the darkroom.'

Gillian headed into the kitchen, switching on the light. A low-wattage bulb went on in the middle of the ceiling, pinged faintly and went out. The light from the hall left half the room in darkness. It was a period kitchen, Gillian saw, from the awful avocado period. A wood stove had been added, and a shabby wing chair, probably dragged in from an unused room, had been set beside it. Its high back faced the doorway. Someone was there, sitting in the chair.

'Arnold?' she said softly. 'Arnold?'

She walked forward, afraid. A hand hung limply over the arm of the chair, the shape of the fingers and the ragged cuff of the shirtsleeve visible in the light from the hallway. Her own shadow loomed over the chairback, and she was only a yard away when she saw Arnold. What was left of him was slumped to one side. A piece of his face was gone, leaving a gouged hollow, as if his right eye had been scooped out with a trowel. A shard of bone poked out from the pulpy mess. His mouth hung open, his head leaned against the wing of the chair. The chair was soaked with blood, and she saw blotches of dark blood on Arnold's shirt and pants and shoes, and on the floor. There was a disgusting smell in the air.

'Oh, my God,' she said, swallowing. She stepped sideways, away, and her toe hit something. A gun. It spun around on the linoleum. She moved one foot, cautiously, then the other. One of her shoes was sticking to the floor. She lifted her heel, peeling it up like tape.

Jim was at the door. 'What's wrong? It stinks in here.'

'Don't come in.'

He stopped, a step inside the door. 'Is Arnold there?'

'He's dead. Is there a phone? We've got to call the police.'

'A phone? I've got a phone. What happened?' Jim reached into a pocket of his windbreaker.

'I think he shot himself. Let's get the hell out of here.'

They went outside to wait. Gillian sat down in the rocking chair, on the mended cushion. Her skin felt clammy, her breath came in shallow gasps. Her heart beat like a bird's.

'How did you know?' Jim said, sounding stunned.

'I didn't. I didn't. I was worried.'

'You were right,' Jim said. 'Thank God I came with you.'

Gillian was feeling sick.

'Thank God,' Jim said again. 'I would have felt like a prize turkey if you'd found him by yourself.'

Gillian reached out a hand, but it was shaking so badly she pulled it back. Jim took it and held it between his large, warm, calloused palms. She shut her eyes and breathed until she stopped shaking.

'Did you see him?' she asked Jim after a little while. She wanted to take off her sticky shoe and throw it into the woods.

'Not really. I saw his hand hanging down. Just a glance. I think I saw the gun on the floor. A big old pistol, wasn't it? I know absolutely nothing about guns.'

'Arnold told me his brother used to point a gun at him and laugh. I'd always thought it was the rifle Tommy shot himself with. But maybe it wasn't. Booter could have had more than one gun. Jesus. Two sons dead.'

'How long do you think Arnold's been there?'

'He was alive yesterday, I saw him. He must have done it last night or sometime today. A few hours ago, at least. The blood wasn't fresh. Where are the police, anyhow? They're taking forever.'

Jim looked at his watch. 'It's only been a few minutes.'

'It feels like months.'

The lights from the house threw harsh shadows on the steps. The Buick made little clicking sounds as it cooled. All around the yard, the trees formed a black wall, impenetrable to the eye. There was no wind, but Gillian heard rustling noises. She listened intently, waiting for the sound of a car on the road.

A squeak, shrill and frantic, made them both jump.

'Shoot,' said Jim, staring into the blackness. 'It's almost as bad waiting out here as it is inside.'

'Did you see anything in the darkroom? Negatives or prints that might be new?'

'I didn't look for any. I was checking the bathroom.'

'I can't stand sitting here. Let's go look in the darkroom now.'

'Shouldn't we leave that to the police?'

'Maybe we should,' Gillian said, getting to her feet, 'but I'd rather not. It would make a difference to me if I found photographs of owls in there, or any birds. It would make it more likely that Arnold was telling the truth. Some of the truth, at least. Eli's so sure he's been lying. He's got the photo of Nicole, the police have heard that Arnold spied on her, and Eli claims Arnold used to "watch" girls at school; they've got her placed on his road between half past six and seven the night she was killed.' She marched down the hall towards the darkroom, trying not to look at the doorway to the kitchen. 'There's no concrete evidence, but Arnold was in the Dutch House that night, with his hands shaking so badly he could hardly light a cigarette. I saw him, and I told Eli about it. Arnold has no alibi, and now he's dead. Eli won't care about owls; he isn't interested in anything except a chain of evidence that will clear up the case as fast as possible.'

Jim followed her back into the house. 'I've seen Arnold's hands shake,' he said mildly. 'That doesn't prove anything.'

'You mean it was normal for his hands to shake?'

'Depends on what you mean. His hands don't shake when he's taking pictures. But they do sometimes when he's around other people. He gets nervous. Or maybe it's some medical condition. I never asked him.'

'No, of course not.'

Gillian stood in the doorway of the darkroom. It looked orderly and clean, just as Jim had said, and it was very small.

'It used to be a powder room, he told me,' Jim said.

It smelt of chemicals. The space below the sink was crowded with bottles; shallow plastic trays were stacked against the wall. A string with little plastic clips attached made a miniature clothesline for drying negatives. The rack for drying prints was homemade: mosquito netting tacked to strips of wood, but there was an expensive-looking enlarger on the counter. Whatever money Arnold had, this was where he spent it.

Jim pointed to the wall above the counter. 'There's the shelf we talked about. See, he did make it. It has hinged brackets underneath, so it can hang flat against the wall when it's not in use.'

Gillian barely noticed it. 'Where would he keep his negatives?'

'Most of them aren't in here—there isn't any room. He's got them in three-ring binders in the living room. Where the prints are. There might be a few recent ones here. I saw some that other time I came.'

Gillian looked around. No strips of negatives hanging to dry, nothing in the enlarger. She switched on the light table. Nothing.

'Here's a binder on the shelf,' Jim said, reaching for it. Gillian was at the large, rectangular sink. A plastic tray rested on the bottom; it was full of clear liquid. Water, she thought, though it was hard to be sure in this chemical reek. A white

8 x 10 rectangle floated face down. She grabbed a pair of tongs hanging on the wall behind the sink and gripped a corner of the paper. She lifted it. Water sheeted downward over the smooth surface and dribbled into the sink.

'Car coming,' Jim said.

Gillian's head snapped around. 'The police.'

Her grip on the tongs loosened and she dropped the print in the tray.

'Wait a sec.'

It fell backward and sank. Looking up through the water, white and lost and drowned, was Arnold's face.

'Look, Jim,' she whispered.

'Let's get out of here.' He shut the binder and reached over Gillian to put it back in its place on the shelf. A door slammed. Feet thudded up the front steps. A strip of negatives slid from the binder to the floor. 'Rats.' He bent down.

Gillian walked into the hall.

'What the hell are you doing here?' Eli said.

'Arnold's in the kitchen. He's dead.'

'I said, what are you doing here?'

Jim came out of the darkroom and stood behind her.

'I was worried about Arnold,' she said. 'I asked Jim to come because I didn't want to come alone. You warned me not to, didn't you?'

Eli wasn't listening. 'Worried about Arnold! Jesus Christ. Where is he?'

'In the kitchen. I said that.'

'How'd you get in?'

'The door was open.'

'And you just walked right in.'

'That's right. We walked in. We looked around; we found Arnold; we called you. We called the police like good citizens.' She was shouting at him.

Jim shifted uncomfortably. 'We thought vandals might have gotten in,' he said.

A second police officer came through the front door, eyed Gillian and Jim. 'They the ones who called in?' he asked Eli.

'Arnold's in the kitchen,' she said again. 'He shot himself.'

'How do you know?' Eli said.

'I saw the gun. It's on the floor.'

'You went into the kitchen? Oh, great. Did you touch anything? Where's the gun?'

'Still on the floor. My toe touched it, but it didn't move much.'

'You'd better show me exactly where you went and exactly what you did,' Eli said grimly. He gripped her shoulder and frogmarched her towards the kitchen door.

'Hey,' Jim said. Eli ignored him. The other cop moved between them.

'Jesus,' Eli said. They were just inside the kitchen door, about ten feet from Arnold's corpse. 'It stinks.' He was still gripping her shoulder. 'What did you do?'

'I walked a few steps towards him. I couldn't see him until I got close.'

'Did you touch the body?'

Gillian shook her head.

'You sure?'

'I didn't touch him.'

'Where was the gun?'

'Right there. Maybe a couple of inches away. I stepped back and my foot knocked it. I stepped in some blood, I think. The floor was sticky.'

'Then what?'

'Jim came to the door; I told him not to come in, I went out as quickly as I could, and we called you.'

Eli let go of her shoulder. It hurt where he'd grabbed it. He moved a couple of paces forward and stared at Arnold. 'It looks like suicide, but we'll have to wait for the report. You're sure you didn't pick up the gun?'

'I only fired it a couple of times to see if it was working,' Gillian said.

Eli tensed, then let his breath hiss out between his teeth. 'No funny stuff.'

Gillian gazed at Arnold's shattered face. His big ear stuck out of a matted clump of hair. The smell was suffocating. 'What have you been doing to him?' she said.

'Doing to him? For Chrissake. Get real. Arnold Mitchell was a headcase. Always was.'

'Is that why you think he's guilty? Because he's an easy target, the way he always was? You haven't spent two minutes on anyone else.'

'What makes you think you know everything I've been doing?'

'What about Simon Steele? Why haven't you checked him out? He knew Nicole. That's more than you can say about Arnold.'

'Where did you get hold of that? Who've you been talking to?'

'Janice Grogan. She was a friend of Nicole's.'

She heard more feet on the steps. A medical examiner or the scene-of-crime technicians, she guessed.

'Sit on the porch. Don't go anywhere,' Eli said. 'I'll get back to you.' He herded her into the hall. The other cop pulled out a big flashlight, stepped into the doorway they'd vacated and shone it into the kitchen. He grunted, stepped backward. More men were coming through the front door, crowding the hall.

'What were you doing in Arnold's darkroom? What were you looking for?' Eli demanded.

'Pictures of owls.'

Eli rolled his eyes. 'Find anything?'

'A self-portrait.'

Eli considered that for a moment, then shrugged. 'Wait. Outside.'

The night, Gillian noticed when they were on the porch again, had turned cold. She and Jim went to the car instead, and waited with the engine running. She turned the fan all the way up and felt the heat rising around her feet.

'He was pretty pissed,' Jim said. 'But I guess he was right to be. We had no business poking around.'

'He would have been pissed whatever we did. He's pissed at me. And don't ask me why. I don't know.'

'What was all that about Simon Steele?'

'Oh, you heard that?'

'I won't pass it around.'

'I couldn't tell whether Eli already knew.'

'He didn't like you kibitzing.'

'I know. He's the detective on the case. But I'll tell you something—I knew him a long time ago. He had a nasty streak then, and it hasn't gone away. Anyhow, about Simon. I heard from Janice Grogan that Nicole had met him. She liked his book. *Juicer*.'

'Then she had lousy taste.'

'Maybe quality didn't matter. Something in it connected.'

'You think he might have killed her?'

'I don't know. My point was really that Eli wasn't looking anywhere except at Arnold. Arnold's easy meat. He always was. Eli was the one at school who started calling him Dumbo.'

An hour had gone by since they'd left Jean's. Gillian shifted restlessly in her seat. 'I'd better phone home again if Eli doesn't tell us we can leave soon. Estelle will be wondering where I am.'

'Estelle is such a pretty name. Where's it from?'

'Her Huguenot forebears. They ran away from Louis the Fourteenth.'

'My Whitlock grandfather ran away from sheep. Tried to make his fortune in the Klondike goldfields. Never found a nugget, but he turned himself into a businessman, and he swore he'd never set foot in a sheepfold again. He'd think I'm a fool. Shepherd to shepherd in three generations.'

'But he didn't have a solar-powered notebook computer to count the sheep.'

'He didn't need one. His dog could count.'

A car came up the drive, swung around and braked hard. Another police car. As it turned, its headlights raked the house front and came to a stop beyond, where Arnold's truck stood suddenly revealed in the harsh glare. Gillian hadn't spotted it in the dark, or even thought of it. The truck looked small and almost frail compared to present-day pick-ups on the road; it tilted crazily to one side. Gillian saw that two of the tyres were flat. Red paint had been splashed over the windows and doors like blood in a gangster movie. It dripped down the windshield, over the hood and bumpers. The dirt was splotched with red.

'Aw hell,' said Jim. 'Look at that.'

CHAPTER 17

Eli might have kept them waiting for hours, but he hadn't; they'd made brief statements and been allowed to leave. There was more than enough for him to do, and he knew where to find them. As they left, the photographers were setting up in the yard. Driving home, Gillian tried not to think about how Arnold had looked. She watched the road, her lights shearing along the faded centre line, following the pattern pinned to the dark, folded land. She observed the moon. She pushed one of her tapes into the deck. *Tosca*. She almost couldn't listen.

Who had attacked Arnold's truck? Jim had been really upset, and he didn't want to tell Brian about it. She felt a prick of guilt. He was a nice man, and she'd dragged him along. It was true that she hadn't known what they were going to find, but she'd been anxious, and she'd taken advantage of his good nature, his pleasure in being helpful. He could have gone home from Jean's and heard about Arnold's death from a chirpy morning newscaster. She told her conscience to get stuffed. She wouldn't have wanted to find Arnold by herself, or confront Eli, either. Jim had been a stalwart companion, and it made her feel marginally better about poking around in Arnold's private domain that she'd brought the only person who had made any kind of connection with Arnold in recent years.

Gillian liked Jim enormously, she realized, and even now she was grateful for the glow of his headlights following her down Salt Hill Road. Still, she was glad to be alone for a few minutes. She needed to think about how to tell Estelle.

As she neared the farm, she concentrated on this next step. How could she break the news? She would have to be more careful, more delicate. But how? By the time she opened the back door, she was taut with anxiety. She called out a greeting, shed her coat and walked quietly into the living room. Estelle lay on her back on the sofa. Rumpole was coiled at her feet, his chin resting on the white bib of his chest. He opened his eyes at Gillian but didn't move. Estelle didn't either. Gillian hurried across and looked down. Her mother's mouth was open and she was snoring softly in little gasps. Gillian tiptoed away towards the kitchen. She heard a thump, and Rumpole streaked past her, headed for his dinner bowl. Estelle had scrounged some supper for herself. A small pot stood on the counter by the stove. One of the burners was still on, though nothing was cooking. Gillian turned it off.

'Is that you, dear?' Estelle said dozily.

Gillian returned to the living room. She wasn't going to say anything; she couldn't face it, not tonight. She heard Rumpole yowling in the kitchen. 'That dratted cat thinks of nothing but his stomach.'

'You're awfully late. I had an egg,' her mother said, reproof in her voice. 'I waited, but you didn't come.'

'I know. I'm sorry.'

'What are you going to eat?'

'I'm not hungry.'

'You should have something.'

Gillian didn't answer. There were several single malts in the cupboard. She opened a bottle at random and poured a generous inch into a glass. She tilted the glass and let a mouthful slide down her throat. It burned, like a good fire on a winter night.

'Franklin called,' Estelle announced. 'They're coming up this weekend.'

'Good.'

'I'm going to bed. I had to take more painkillers, and they've knocked me out.'

Gillian slewed around. 'Is it anything new?'

Estelle shook her head. 'Just the same, only worse. I'll sleep.' She gripped the sofa and hauled herself up very slowly, then dragged across the carpet, leaning heavily on her cane.

Gillian waited, standing silent with her glass in her hand. The journey seemed to take minutes. When her mother disappeared, she went upstairs. If Estelle needed help, she would call. She wouldn't want it unless she had to have it.

Franklin was coming, with Audrey and Jasper. Her brother, complete with wife and lively seven-year-old son. She was glad. She needed them. Estelle did, too. Jasper would lift their spirits. He'd build forts with the sofa cushions and shift their attention to the dessert menu. She fired up the laptop to check her e-mail. There was a message from Edward, typically terse.

'The usual bungling has landed me with a DNA conference in Washington next week. Arriving New York Friday if convenient.'

Friday! That was the day after tomorrow. She let out a whoop and hit reply.

'It wasn't bungling, I bribed the Home Secretary,' she wrote. She paused for a moment. Bungling indeed. He'd decided to come, and someone had done some fast footwork. Then Franklin would drive up on Saturday. It was going to be a houseful. And Edward would call her tomorrow. She clicked the mouse on send and waited while the message went out, listening to the small scratching sounds inside the machine, like insects chewing. She thought how wonderful technology sometimes was, how wonderful that she could send a letter that would arrive almost as she sat there imagining it. She leaned her head on the table and cried.

Gillian had a sleepless night. Once or twice she drifted off; the second time she woke up from a dream in which she stepped on Arnold's eye. It stuck to her sole like gum. After that, she didn't sleep at all. She thought, repetitively, about Arnold. His ruined face, the face that had stared at her in the bar, from the window of the police car, from the water in the tray. She tried to distract herself with thoughts of other parts of the day. She could hardly believe that she'd driven to Simon Steele's house with Roberta that same evening; it seemed like a week ago. And then there was the news about Leslie Lang and Nicole. Stanton was worried about bad publicity.

Gillian wasn't going to tell her mother about Ecstasy Escorts. Margaret had insisted that no one be told but Roberta and the trustees. Already, by the end of the meeting with Margaret, Gillian had sensed a shift of feeling and direction— towards defending the college and away from concern about Nicole. Whatever their beliefs—and they would say and believe that women who sold their bodies had to have the same rights as other women—they were unable to feel the same about Nicole as they had before.

As she tossed miserably in her blankets, she thought about the shift. Jo had even been sarcastic about Nicole. She hadn't liked being lied to; she saw herself as someone close to the students, someone in whom they confided. But that wasn't the whole story. Another factor was the money. 'Over a hundred thousand dollars a year,' Jo had muttered. 'That's twice as much as I make.' The sex trade was risky, even at the high end. They knew that; they read the newspapers, they'd all seen *Klute*. It was easy to pity the desperately poor, as long as they weren't using your own street as a bedroom, but women who pulled in Nicole's kind of cash were hard to feel sorry for. They had choices, or looked as if they had. They were rather like skiers who left the trail. If they got killed, people who read about it thought it was too bad, but also thought they should have stayed where they belonged. There were plenty of warning signs.

When someone got killed, on a ski hill, in a car crash, even by a heart attack, the natural reaction was to find reasons why it couldn't happen to you. 'I never go that way during rush hour', 'I don't leave the trail', 'He eats junk food all the time, and I only have chips once in a while': little mantras to keep death away. The murder of Nicole-the-student was terrifying because it might happen to others at Stanton, but Nicole-the-escort became someone whose death could be distanced. She was in a different category: one of them, not us. There was relief in that. No one wants to identify too closely with a murder victim.

And then, Nicole had become an embarrassment. Her connection to Ecstasy Escorts could cost Stanton in money and reputation, though it shouldn't. The faculty, and even more, the trustees, who wouldn't have known Nicole personally, might deplore her death, but they would resent her for putting the college in a bad light. She certainly had fooled everyone: not Melanie Wilkes at all, but Scarlett in disguise.

Gillian got up soon after five and made coffee. Rumpole appeared and sat motionless by the door, staring at her as if she'd gone insane. She threw a coat on over her dressing gown and pattered down to the mailbox to collect the *Times*. The heavy autumn dew seeped in through the fleece lining of her slippers and soaked her feet. It was still dark; the light from the kitchen cast a dim glow over the driveway and the lawn, but everything beyond the road was indiscernible, black against black. Somewhere far away, a dog barked. Back inside, she turned on the oven and sat in front of the open door. The radiators were stone cold, and the house wouldn't be warm for an hour. When she settled with her coffee and the paper, Rumpole trotted up and climbed into her lap, something he did only when Estelle wasn't around. The heat of his body against her belly was comforting.

Estelle had a bad night, too. Pains in her legs had kept her awake despite the drugs, and in the morning she was too tired to struggle with the difficulties of bathing and dressing. Gillian brought her some tea and toast on a tray and told her that Arnold was dead. She took the news calmly; the exhaustion and the painkillers wrapped her in fog. Gillian went off to teach her class and planned to be home early. She didn't want to leave Estelle alone for long.

Gillian, too, was worn out and didn't feel like thinking. Driving was useful; following the curves of the road gave her something simple to do. Arnold was dead. She seemed to have to absorb it over and over again. It had been on the local news, so now everyone knew. But the police hadn't released any details, they'd merely said it was a probable suicide. They'd also mentioned the truck.

On campus, Arnold was the sole topic of conversation. Gillian's students were wound tight, in a state of jittery near-elation. He'd killed Nicole, and now he'd paid for it. And he was no longer a threat. The face leering at the window, the threat waiting in the shadows, was gone. They were riding a wave of relief, after the shock and the fear. No one was concentrating on Pandita Ramabai and her rebuttals of conservative interpretations of Hindu law.

If they had final exams this week, Gillian thought, most would take them; that kind of pressure can discipline raw feeling. But a class is just a class. Next week, she told them, they'd have to get back to work, whatever else was happening. She made little comment on their presumption of Arnold's guilt; Leslie Lang could not be mentioned, and arguments about due process weren't destined to make much headway that day. Emotions were running too high.

Teaching gave her a jolt of nervous energy, but by the time she was finished and on her way back to the parking lot via the library, she felt herself sinking again, into anaesthetized depression. She didn't want to hear another word about Arnold Mitchell. She would go home and get into old clothes and divide some perennials. The digging would tire her muscles so she could sleep, and Estelle would be pleased.

As she approached Delamar House, she saw someone on the lawn she'd never seen before. The woman looked young enough to be a student, but no student wore clothes so emphatically elegant, so finished, from heels to handbag. Her blonde hair was cut with surgical precision. She stood still, looking at Delamar House through her sunglasses like a tourist inspecting a minor and rather disappointing temple. She was very striking, Gillian thought, not with the eye-popping lusciousness of a starlet, but with the poise and high polish of a woman whose appearance is a well-managed asset. Gillian had a hunch about who she was but was less certain of why she had come. Well. Margaret Bristol had wanted help; here was an opportunity.

She changed direction slightly to intercept the young woman, acknowledging a pang of envy as she admired her clothes. I would like to look perfected, Gillian thought, but I don't want to do the work. Besides, I don't have anywhere to go in clothes like that. I'd have to shop for a different life. The young woman was looking at her now; she felt slightly nervous. A Parisian life, she thought, that would do, as long as I didn't have to have one of those peevish little dogs. She'd covered the distance; it was time to stop and say something.

'Hello, are you looking for someone?' she asked.

'Not really. I just wanted to see the college.'

'It's pretty, isn't it? But I hope you didn't come to see the gardens. I'm afraid they're gone.'

The young woman turned towards Gillian, her eyes invisible behind her sunglasses.

'Do you teach here?'

'Temporarily.'

'Did you know Nicole Bishop?'

'She was in one of my classes.'

'I'm a friend of Nicole's, from New York.'

'I see,' said Gillian. 'I'm sorry. She had friends here, too, and they're all very sad.' Further explanation seemed necessary. 'I just started teaching here this fall, so I didn't know her very well.'

'Nicole was my *best* friend,' the young woman said. She turned back to the facade of the house, studying the carved swags and tassels glistening white in the sunshine. 'She loved it here.' She pushed her sunglasses up and let them rest on her smooth blonde hair, as if to see the college in its natural colours. Her eyes were carefully made up and slightly puffy. 'She was always telling me that this was her real life. She said she could be herself at Stanton.'

Gillian tried not to show her surprise. Be herself? When Nicole had kept so much hidden? 'She must have been herself with you, if you were best friends.'

'That's different. She was doing what she wanted to do when she was here, and it charged her up. She was brainy. Not like me, I'm not the student type. This is like another planet. But Nicole was into it. Totally.'

'She had the right gifts for it.'

'No kidding. She even won a big scholarship. That was probably the happiest day of her life. Now I wish she'd never won it.' She pulled her sunglasses back down over her eyes. 'I'm Leslie, by the way, Leslie Lang.' She held out a manicured hand, with rosy painted nails and two diamond rings.

Gillian shook it.

'That's a nice ring,' Leslie said, seeing Gillian's little square-cut emerald, the only ring she ever wore.

'It was my great-grandmother's. My mother gave it to me when she couldn't wear it any more.'

Leslie touched one of her own rings. 'Nicole gave me this one for my birthday. I love jewellery. Especially rings. Nicole used to shop with me, she liked to help me choose, even though she never bought anything herself.'

'If you want to look at Stanton, would you prefer to walk around by yourself, or would you like company? I can tell you where things are, if it would be helpful.'

'Which was her dormitory?'

Gillian pointed it out. 'Her room's at the back, but I don't think you can see it; the police have it locked up.'

'I couldn't face it. Not right now.'

They toured briefly around the campus, looking into the library, a couple of empty classrooms, the dining room and the common room in Nicole's dorm. A few students glanced at Leslie curiously, reacting to her clothes. Nicole had dressed to deflect exactly those curious glances, Gillian thought.

'Not many men around, are there?' Leslie said eventually.

'Just a few faculty members.'

'That's what Nicole told me. She said it was relaxing.'

If Nicole had looked as striking as Leslie in her other life, men would have been looking at her all the time. Women, too. Stanton had been a refuge from that, at least. Had Leslie guessed that Gillian knew what she did for a living? Her last remark had skated close to the subject. But now they were passing a class full of students. Voices could be heard through the windows. On the grass under the trees, a gardener rode back and forth, noisily shredding the fallen leaves.

'People look as if nothing's happened,' Leslie muttered. 'Don't they care?'

'There were no classes for two days after she was found. The whole campus mourned. But life goes on, that's the awful thing about it. The leaves fall, the grass grows, courses are taught.'

'Life goes on, but it's like, what's the point?' Leslie said.

They walked towards the riverbank.

'I came up here partly because I want to make arrangements for her,' Leslie said. 'I've contacted a funeral home, but the police won't let me do anything. They told me they're looking for the next of kin.'

'Do you know anything about her family?'

'Hardly anything. She wouldn't tell me where she lived when she was little. Upstate, was all she told me. She said her parents died, and she moved away, and she'd locked up that part of her life and never wanted to think about it again. She didn't have any photographs of herself, even.'

They came to the cliff above the river. The rock dropped away; it was like standing on the roof of a skyscraper, with only a painted metal railing between them and the middle of the sky. The river rolled below, reflecting the heavens, huge and calm and slow.

'Do you mind if I smoke?' Leslie asked. She reached into her bag and fished out a silver case, flipped it open and extracted a black cigarette tipped with gold.

'Balkan Sobranies!' said Gillian. 'They still exist!'

'Would you like one?' Leslie asked politely.

'No, thanks. I was just remembering the first time I saw somebody smoking one. In the Village, way back when. I thought it was the last word in glamour.'

'I was going to quit this fall.' Leslie lit up, and the smoke wafted out over the river.

Gillian watched it drift away. Nicole hadn't even told her closest friend about her childhood. She'd cut it off, started over. Something must have gone badly wrong. 'What did Nicole do after her parents died?' she asked Leslie.

'I told the police what Nicole told me,' she answered. 'Nicole had an aunt she moved in with when she came to the city, but that didn't last. Her aunt wasn't used to having a kid around. She went off with some dorky guy. That's what Nicole said. Anyway, it didn't work out. After that Nicole was on her own.'

'That's not what she told Stanton.'

'So what?' Leslie shrugged. 'Why was her family anybody's business if she was paying her fees? But she figured it would look better to have somebody like a parent. She told me she'd had a lot of fantasies about what her aunt could have been like, so when people asked her questions, she had answers.'

Gillian remembered what Jo had said about Aunt Charlotte—how close Nicole told her they were, how she had put money away for Nicole. Warmth and security.

'She described this path to the river,' Leslie said. 'She used to come here and smoke a joint and look at the water. I can almost feel her; it's so hard to believe she's gone. It drives me crazy that she survived as a kid alone in New York City, but not here. She didn't take chances in the city, so what was she doing out alone on an empty road at night?'

'She must have believed it was safe. I would have, too. Is there any chance that someone she knew in the city could have come up here and killed her?'

Leslie looked at her strangely. 'I don't know what you mean. The taxi driver told me the guy who killed her shot himself last night. Arnold Mitchell. He lived around here.'

'It's true that he shot himself. But the evidence that he killed Nicole is pretty thin.'

'How do you know?'

'The college gets some information about the case; there's no murder weapon, no concrete evidence that he did anything except take her photograph.'

'Why did he kill himself, then?'

'If he wasn't guilty? He was being persecuted, and he was always an unhappy person.'

'How do you know so much about him?'

'We grew up together.'

'Was he a friend of yours?'

'No, I just knew him.'

'Then why do you want to drag New York into it? She was killed here.'

'I'd just like to be sure that her real killer is caught, whoever it is. I expect you want that, too.'

Leslie smoked her cigarette, staring out at the river. It smelled sweeter than American cigarettes. 'Nicole knew a lot of people,' she said finally. 'But I don't think any of them would kill her.'

'No jealous, er, boyfriends?'

'Fuck, no,' Leslie said. 'If I thought so, I'd kill the bastard myself.' She frowned. 'Besides, who would be crazy enough to come all the way up here to stab her in the woods? It doesn't make sense.'

'It might if he were jealous.'

'But she hasn't got a boyfriend in the city. I'd know.'

'Not a boyfriend, then. Anyone who felt sexually possessive.'

'There was no one she was worried about,' Leslie said evenly.

She moved a little, and Gillian thought she might bring the conversation to a close, but she didn't. 'Did the police say it might be someone from the city?' she asked.

Gillian thought for a moment before answering. She admired Leslie's adroitness. She had answered Gillian's questions but had given nothing away, and she'd now asked a question of her own which Gillian could use or not, depending on what she knew. Leslie would be a successful boardroom tactician.

Gillian chose to be candid. 'The police didn't say that in so many words. But they've explained that Nicole worked for an escort agency.'

'Oh. So of course one of her dates murdered her.'

'Not of course.' But it was true they'd all thought of it automatically. 'It does happen, though.'

'She doesn't see many clients any more. The ones she sees, she's known for a couple of years. The police don't think anybody from the city did it. They're just using Nicole as an excuse to lean on the agency. They don't really care about her. About Nicole.'

Gillian didn't contradict her. She didn't know what Eli cared about. He could hardly have much interest in harassing Ecstasy Escorts, but the NYPD, or, more likely, the IRS, just might. And she herself thought Eli was too eager to assign the role of murderer to Arnold, rather than investigating alternatives. She and Leslie had different angles of view, but there was a similarity, too.

'How did you meet Nicole? Did you know her in high school?'

Leslie watched the smoke spiral up to the sky and fade to nothing. 'She was in high school; I wasn't. We met when we were both trying to break into modeling. Sitting around and waiting, watching other girls get the jobs.'

'But she did do some modeling?'

'A little. She never got much work. She looked great, she got a small portfolio together, but nothing happened. I don't know, they want a certain look, and either you have the look they want, or you don't. I'm not thin enough, but that wasn't her problem.'

'No. She was bony enough to be a model. Her running coach was worried that she was dieting too much, or was even anorexic.'

'You mean recently? She used to diet and binge when she lived in the city, but she told me she'd stopped when she came up here.'

'Is that why she started the escort work,' Gillian said hesitantly, 'because modeling wasn't a success?'

'Men like to go out with "models",' Leslie said. 'They like showing off somebody beautiful. And Nicole had class. She could go anywhere. But you need money to be a model—for clothes, for your hair, for your portfolio—it's not like in the movies where you work in some sleazy restaurant and the next day you're a star.'

She dropped the gold stub of her cigarette on the ground and stepped on it. 'I've got to get going,' she said. 'Thanks for the tour.'

'You never visited Nicole here?'

'She used to come down to the city to see me—she said there was no place to go around here. But I was going to come to her graduation.'

They were walking back through the woods. When they reached the open lawn, Gillian said, 'How did you get here?'

'I came on the train. The taxi driver said I could phone when I wanted to leave, and it wouldn't take long for a taxi to get here.'

'I'll give you a ride to the station.'

In the car, Leslie said, 'The police keep looking for her family, but *I* was her family. I was a lot closer to her than her aunt. Her aunt hasn't been near her for years. It doesn't make any difference,' she added bitterly. 'The police won't treat me like I have any rights.'

'Even if they find Nicole's aunt, she may not want to get involved. If her aunt doesn't care about her, she may be relieved to turn over the arrangements to you.'

'Not if there's any money she can get,' Leslie said.

'Will there be?'

'Enough to finish paying the fees here. That's why Nicole never splurged the way I do. She saved her money for the college fees. It was her dream ever since I met her to come to a place like this.'

'Where did she get the idea?'

'I don't know. But the phrase "Ivy League" was like a magic spell for her. This isn't Ivy League, but it was close enough to make her happy. That's why she wanted to model—for the money. She knew she needed money to go to a good college, so she went for it.' Leslie ran a fingertip along the edge of an oval nail, testing for snags. 'The escort thing—it was the fastest way, that's all.'

'Did Nicole ever mention a man named Simon Steele?' Gillian asked, as they drew up near the ticket office.

'Oh, that writer guy. She gave me a copy of his book. *Juicer.* She said she'd met him.'

'That's all? She didn't tell you she was seeing him?'

'Dating? Nicole said when she came up here that she wasn't going to date anybody. Sooner or later the relationship would go rotten, like they always do, and she didn't want it to happen at Stanton and spoil it for her. Why are you asking about him?'

'Just wondering out loud. She had an intense response to his book—different from other people who've read it. Something in it touched her. She wanted to meet him. He's twice her age, but he's very attractive.'

'Is he married?'

'His wife left him last spring. One of his neighbours believes she saw Nicole going to his house, and she was on the road that she would use to get there the night she was killed.'

'Are you saying he could have been the one who killed her?'

'All I'm saying is that if she was seeing him, he's a likelier suspect than Arnold Mitchell.'

'We used to tell each other everything like that. But, I don't know, she lived in two places—here, and New York. She kept them separate, like two personalities. And she swore on a stack of bibles she wasn't going to date anybody.' Leslie turned Nicole's ring around on her finger and closed her palm on the stone. 'She was going to give up the escort thing when she finished college. Start a new life, and then maybe find a guy. He'd never have to know. That was the plan. We were going to take a trip first, her and me, next summer, after she graduated. So if she met this guy up here—'

Leslie bit her lip.

'She might have kept it a secret, even from you?'

'I'd say it was bullshit, but I don't know. I'm not the romantic type. I used to tell her, you know, you can make a good living, you can have fun. Take what you can get. But Nicole would talk about soul. She wanted a guy who had one. I said I didn't have one myself, so what would I do with a guy who wanted to give me his, like a wet fish? And she argued with me. She said I wouldn't be her best friend if I didn't have a soul, and I said, "OK, it's yours."' Leslie turned the ring around again and it winked in the light. 'And she had this made for my birthday. If she was losing weight, it sounds like she was seeing him. She always had trouble eating when she got emotional about a man.'

CHAPTER 18

When Gillian got home, Peggy Nelson was standing in the garden, deadheading the last of the dahlias. She was wearing a denim skirt, a long quilted jacket and Gillian's rubber boots. Gillian greeted her with a sense of relief. An old friend was exactly what she needed, and she'd known Peggy since kindergarten. Besides, she wanted to know what Peggy thought about Eli.

'Peggy! I thought you weren't coming until the weekend.'

'I wasn't. But I had an appointment with my allergist in Poughkeepsie, so I thought I'd stop by. My mother was burning up the wires first thing this morning.'

'So you know Arnold's dead.'

'Yup. What a horror show.' Peggy clipped a final wilted flower and clumped through the garden towards the shed. 'When I got here I saw Estelle's car, so I knocked, even though the Buick was gone. I don't think she heard me, but she saw me through the window.'

'So she's up. She was still in bed when I left.'

'She's up, but she said she wasn't up to conversation—she wasn't very well—and that you'd be home soon. She invited me to wait inside, of course, but I asked her if there was something I could do in the garden. It's a lovely day, and I was afraid she'd feel obliged to entertain me if I stayed indoors. She's looking sort of wobbly. I didn't quite want to leave, in case.'

'Peggy, you *are* wonderful. You can wear my boots any old time.'

'They're too tight. I can barely squeeze into them. I didn't want to ruin my pumps, though, and those seven-league boots in the shed fell off my feet.'

'Boots in the shed? Oh, my father's old galoshes. I don't know why they're still hanging around. Well, Goldilocks, I'm sorry you didn't find any that were just right. How was the porridge?'

Peggy laughed. 'I haven't had any.'

'Then stay for lunch. There must be something in the fridge, God knows I'm always shopping.'

They went in, and Peggy took off her jacket. She certainly didn't weigh two hundred pounds. She was heavy; in her teens she had been a beauty of the soft-fruit type—all roundnesses and a pale skin that flushed easily and didn't take a tan, with chestnut curls and a matching dot of colour on her left cheek, acclaimed as a beauty mark, though if she'd been unattractive it would have been called a mole. She had sagged and thickened since then, but Gillian, remembering her shrunken body in the hospital bed after Nepal, was happy to see her getting stout. No one would imagine now that this busy, humorous Connecticut matron with three children and a collie had once been a starry-eyed hippie who traveled overland in a VW van from Amsterdam to Calcutta, wearing peasant skirts and sandals and her hair in braids to her waist. Who would suspect that she'd lived in a dirt-floored hut with twenty other parasite-ridden Western travellers smoking hashish all day? That she'd nearly died before she got home? Not her daughters, certainly. They hadn't been told these stories. 'I'll tell them when they're old enough to vote,' Peggy said. 'Not now. Nell's so puritanical and critical, and Sarah would start smoking dope just to do the opposite from Nell.

Neither of them has an ounce of common sense, but neither did I at their age.'

Gillian peeked into Estelle's room. She was asleep again. In the kitchen, where they ate lunch, they talked in low voices, though Estelle was deaf enough without her hearing aid to sleep through a shouting match.

'When did you last see Arnold?' Gillian asked after a while.

'Ages ago. It was right after Booter died. There wasn't a funeral, but his ashes were buried next to Virginia's. A few people went, including my mother, for Virginia's sake. It was raining, and nobody knew what to say, so they just huddled under their umbrellas; she told me it was awful. Then she sent me to the house, with a casserole for Arnold. He just stood there; I practically had to shove it at him. He didn't even say thank you. And of course the dish never came back.'

'He never learned anything about greasing social wheels. He could barely say hello and goodbye.'

'Anyway, that was the last time—unless you count seeing him driving his old truck. I've passed him on the road once in a while.'

'I talked to him once after his brother died.'

'I guess a few people did. Everyone at school was so shocked. It was weird, how different Arnold and Tommy were. Tommy was popular; lots of girls thought he was cute, but no one wanted to go out with Arnold. I don't think he ever asked a girl for a date. Tommy was so different, you couldn't believe it. You'd think, "These guys are brothers?"'

'Eli told me Arnold used to watch girls, back when we were in school.'

'Arnold? Huh. I used to feel like every boy in the school was watching me—trying to stare through my sweater. It was gross. The ones I hated the most were the guys who snapped my bra strap or whispered dirty things at me in the cafeteria line. Arnold was somebody I hardly ever thought about.' Peggy paused, remembering. 'When Tommy was killed, my parents said Booter was an idiot to leave guns around with two teenage boys in the house. My father had an argument with Beau Brewster about it and they didn't speak for weeks. When my mother called this morning she talked about it. She never could stand Booter.'

'He groped her.'

'What?! She never told *me* that.'

Gillian chuckled. 'She's waiting until you're old enough.'

'I've got to ask her about it. What'd he do?'

'Felt her knee under the dinner table. She spilled her glass of water on his crotch.'

'She never said that.'

'She said "lap".'

Gillian got up to put the kettle on for tea. Peggy took their dishes to the sink and got the milk and sugar. She was silent for longer than usual. Then she said, 'It doesn't surprise me that Arnold killed himself; if you'd asked me to name somebody who might, I'd have said Arnold Mitchell. But I don't understand why he killed a student at Stanton. I can hardly believe it.'

'Why not? Everybody else does.'

'Just instinct. He was gentle with animals; I guess I think it's the puppy-kickers who kill people when they grow up.'

'I'm sure that's a statistically sound correlation compared to theories about XYY chromosomes or broken homes. I don't see Arnold as a homicidal maniac, either. Eli Pink pounced on him first because a girl on the running team saw Arnold hanging around with his camera and thought he was stalking them. And then of course Eli found that photograph of Nicole on Arnold's wall, but—I keep thinking—if Arnold did kill Nicole, would he really be stupid enough to have a sexy photograph of her pinned up where anybody who walked in would see it?'

'But nobody ever went to his house.'

'He'd have to know that the police would come after the body was found. It was close to his house.'

'Then you think Eli is wrong?'

'I don't know exactly what his ideas are; I just don't like the way he's acting, or how he's handling the case. I can't figure him out. He used to have that touchy pride and moodiness; it made him mean, even to his friends. You'd think it was an adolescent problem that would be gone by now. Maybe he's just hypersensitive because he's never had a case like this before. But listen: he came to see me about Nicole, because she was in one of my classes, and he was really friendly at first, but then later he suddenly got offended at something I said—I don't even know what—and he turned nasty, just the way he used to.'

'What did you talk about?'

'Arnold, of course. How much things have changed around here; people we used to know who are still around. I mentioned Torch Regan—she's working at Stanton, in the kitchen. Did you know?'

'I heard. She's had a hard time. Her husband used to work at IBM, as a technician, but he got laid off when they downsized, and he hasn't been able to find a job since. I heard they couldn't keep up their mortgage payments and lost their house. So Torchie had to start looking for work after years at home with the children. She was always an ace cook, and she got the job at Stanton through contacts, but it doesn't pay much.'

'I see. I thought she looked worn down. And she was such a ball of fire at school. Too bad. Though her kids sound OK, she didn't seem worried about them.'

'Her daughter's interesting—Lily. She lives up on Beacon now, at Carrie's. She's Carrie's gofer, did you know that? Looks after everything. Carrie's teaching her to paint.'

'I reminded Torchie about Ricky Sands—I think she was pleased I remembered.'

'You mean the time she punched him?' Peggy laughed. 'She was tough. I think Lily is, too. She's big and extroverted, anyway. Who else did you and Eli talk about?'

'I said something about him having a big crush on you. It was supposed to be a joke, but he didn't think it was funny.'

'Oh God.'

'Uh oh. What did I do?'

Peggy groaned. 'This is embarrassing. I never told you, because you were away when it happened, and afterwards I wanted to forget about it, and anyway I knew Eli wouldn't have wanted you to know.'

'Wouldn't have wanted me to know what?'

'What happened.'

'Peg! Do I have to use thumb screws?'

'Eli proposed to me in senior year.'

'He did? You're right. I didn't know that. But why is that such a big deal?'

'Just listen. It was crazy. He asked me to this dance, and I went, and then afterwards in the car he told me he wanted to marry me. I said no, but I tried to be nice, so he didn't listen to me. He started pressuring me and then begging. He kept on and on and on, I didn't know what to do. He kept saying he loved me, but we'd hardly ever talked to each other, except at parties. It was excruciating.'

'It sounds awful.'

'Yeah, it was. But I haven't told you the worst part. I was mad afterwards, because he'd made me so uncomfortable and wouldn't stop. And at the end he sneered at me. I should have felt sorry for him. It wasn't as if he tried to rape me. He just sort of grabbed at me and tried to kiss me. But, you know, I always felt like such a target—for boys, I mean. I didn't *like* his icky kiss. He made me feel trapped, and I hate that. And calling it love, when he didn't know a thing about *me*—I despised him. Anyway, I was a bitch. I told two of my friends at school, I practically acted it out for them. So in about five seconds *everybody* knew. And of course it got back to him. Plus people who didn't like him made fun of him. You remember what it's like, kids get hold of something like that and they don't let go. For weeks, they'd see him and start humming the wedding march—*Dum dum* di dum dum dum dum. I heard it in the cafeteria.'

Gillian laughed out loud. 'Oh dear. It's just so absurd.'

Peggy snorted. 'I know. And it was a million years ago. But I shouldn't have made fun of him.'

'No, but -'

'Seriously. It was a cruel thing to do. I still feel bad about it.'

'And Eli's still sore. Well, I put my foot in it, didn't I? He must have thought I knew the whole story. But goodness, he's touchy after all these years. That was kid stuff. I wonder if he could see your side of it now?'

'I doubt it. Anyway, I behaved worse than he did.'

'Did he ever get married?'

'Yes, but they split up. His wife left him. They had a baby first. I think his wife remarried and lives in California.'

'But he's alone?'

'He might have a girlfriend. I would have heard if he'd married again.'

Gillian laughed again. 'You would have been Peggy Pink.'

'I would not. Not in a thousand years.'

Gillian was grateful for Peggy's company. Peggy had no stake in the solution to Nicole's murder, no personal misery about it, only pity for someone young and pretty, as she had been. Peggy was sane and happy and as ready to give as to receive. There was precious little Gillian could do for Jo, or for Nicole's friends Janice Grogan and Leslie Lang; what comfort was there to offer? She hadn't even been able to help Margaret Bristol and the college very much. Nevertheless she felt weighed down by the need to respond, to do *something*. And it was the same at home: she couldn't give Estelle what she wished to—strength, health, a magical draught from the fountain of youth. All she could do was be there. And her own fear and sadness had to be dammed up, because Estelle had enough to cope with already. But Peggy, bless her, didn't have any troubles right now that required outlays of concern and comfort from Gillian's depleted stock.

'That's why I became a hippie,' Peggy said. 'Hippie men didn't grab.'

Gillian chuckled. 'No, they'd look deep in your eyes and talk about brown rice.' She poured fresh tea into Peggy's cup. 'Peg, would you be worried about your daughters if they were at Stanton now?'

'Of course. You don't want anything horrible to come near your children's lives. I'd be worried about how shocked and frightened they felt.'

'Not about their safety?'

'If the police are wrong about Arnold, and they didn't find the real killer, I'd be very worried. I'd wonder if he was a nut who'd kill again if he got a chance. Why?'

'Some of the parents have taken their daughters home.'

'I might do that, depending on how upset they were. I don't think I know anyone with a daughter currently at Stanton, except Lewis and Kitty Grogan.'

'I met Janice Grogan recently.'

'My mother says Kitty's had a hard time with her. She used to bite people when she was little, and she always had problems with controlling her anger. She went to counseling for years. My mother told me they suspect she tried to set fire to the house once, but Kitty wouldn't talk about it. I guess she's grown out of it by now.'

'That's interesting. I thought her parents were a bit heavy-handed with her.'

Peggy shrugged. 'They were strict with all their kids. But the boys went to boarding school. They got away.'

'What happened to Eli? Did he actually try to follow his dream of being an actor? He moved to New York, I remember that.'

Peggy thought. 'Oh, he went. He left when I was in Nepal, and he stayed in the city for, what would it have been? Almost ten years. He got some parts in minor productions, the sort you don't hear about unless you pore over the Off Off Broadway listings. Then he got married, and then his wife had a baby. So he came back here to get a job. My mother told me some friend of his was a cop; that's how he got involved with the police. And you know what I think? He wasn't going to make it as an actor, anyway—hardly anyone does—but he blamed it on the baby.'

'He made a couple of sour jokes about acting, when I saw him a few days ago. I wasn't sure how to take them. When I said he was good in Mr. Cardero's drama class, Eli said, "the next Olivier," in a sarcastic voice. And he said something about his name in Broadway lights. I think that's his real sore point—he wanted to be a star. An actor, sure, but a star, so he could look down on everybody.'

Arnold's ugly death, the sight of his corpse, kept surfacing in Gillian's mind, and she kept pushing it down again. She could tell Peggy, but she knew Peggy would be appalled if she described it truthfully. Besides, she heard sounds from the other end of the house. Estelle was up.

'Have you told Edward about Eli?' Peggy asked.

'A little. He'll be here tomorrow.'

'About time! He hasn't been here for aeons. I've even forgotten what he looks like.'

An image flashed into Gillian's mind, Edward's face in a moment of concentration: dark brows frowning a little, brown eyes narrowed in their deep sockets. Only twenty-four hours. Her heart skipped a beat.

She knew Peggy's heart-throbs, had heard about them since the first crushes. 'Forget? How could you? He looks exactly like Robert Redford.'

'Ho ho. In your dreams.' Peggy grinned. 'I remember his voice—the accent. The wry comments he made went right past some people. But he wasn't blond. Show me a photo.'

Gillian fetched one from upstairs. She studied it with Peggy, trying to see it as a stranger would. He had a thin, bony, slightly beaked nose, dark straight brows and hair. High cheekbones. Something harsh in the set of the jaw, softened by the lines of humour etched at the corners of the mouth and eyes. It was a good photograph, but it didn't quite catch the look of concentration or the gleam of sudden amusement, the two expressions she thought were most characteristic.

'Yeah,' Peggy said. 'That's the guy. If you can't have Robert Redford, he'll do. Will he be interested in the case? I suppose he'll have to be, since you know Nicole and Arnold.'

'It'll be an enormous relief to talk to him.' Gillian began to smile. 'But I'm not sure what part he'll play. Estelle claims she's Sherlock, and she's assigned me the Watson role, so who can Edward be?'

Peggy laughed. 'The landlady. She cooks their dinners.'

'I guess he'll have a choice between the landlady or Watson's wife.' Gillian giggled, some cable of tension snapping, the wild ends swinging around her brain. She was helpless with laughter when Estelle appeared in the doorway, her hair standing up like downy feathers. She blinked at them.

'What's so funny?'

'An outstanding disguise, Sherlock,' said Peggy, winking.

Later that afternoon, Gillian trudged upstairs and tried to take a nap. When that failed, she made an effort to outline a chapter of her Caroline Norton manuscript, but she couldn't concentrate. She looked at the stack of books and journals on the shelf next to her desk. Vrinda Nabar's *Caste as Woman*, a fascinating window on feminism in India; she'd thought of lending it to Nicole. She also had a new book about Western feminists and revolutionaries in India: the women from England, Austria, America, and especially Ireland, who hacked away at the British Empire and fought for women's rights. They sometimes married Indian men, but what had their relations with Indian women been like? That was a murky, complex issue, and one that interested Gillian; she opened the book, tried the introduction, and put it down again. She couldn't read any better than she was able to write or sleep. After checking her e-mail and finding nothing but a message about a meeting she had no intention of going to, she changed tack and decided to work outdoors. She pulled on an old sweater and her boots and went out to pick apples.

The tree was ancient, gnarled and cankered, with spotty leaves, but it still blossomed in the spring and yielded a bushel or two of apples in most years. No one in the family knew which variety of apple they were, though doubtless there was someone in the valley who could tell them. Jim Whitlock would know where to ask. She picked a bowlful and then heard Estelle tapping on the window. She went back to the house.

'Don't you think Jasper would like to do that?' Estelle said.

'Oh.' Gillian shut the door and grumpily kicked her boots off. Estelle was right, but Gillian felt as if she'd found the one thing she was capable of doing that afternoon and had been told not to do it. She marched off to the kitchen in her stockinged feet and tripped over Rumpole.

'Goddammit!' she shouted at him, as the apples bounded over the floor.

He took refuge with Estelle, who tsked and made soothing noises and retreated to the sofa.

At five-thirty, the phone rang. It was Roberta. She sounded beside herself.

'Simon's disappeared,' she said.

'What?'

'Disappeared. He's not at the house and the car's gone. The police came to Stanton and asked me if I knew where he was!'

'They're looking for him? Why?'

'I don't know, but they asked me if I was aware that he knew Nicole.'

'They did? My God! What did you say?'

'That I wasn't. How would he know her? I don't understand what the police are doing. I thought they were going to arrest Arnold.'

'They didn't tell you why they're looking for Simon?'

'They just said they wanted to ask him some questions. They wanted to know if I knew of any plans he had for going away, and when I said no, that he was supposed to pick Josh up on Saturday, they wanted to know what time. Then they asked me if I had any idea where he would go if he decided to leave for a while. I don't know what it's about. Do you?'

'Could he be away just for the day—for some normal reason?'

'I asked them if they'd looked for the car at the train station, and they hadn't. So he might have gone to New York on business. He doesn't tell *me* where he's going.'

'Did you cash that cheque?'

'I took it to the bank this morning.'

'Good.'

'I didn't think I should wait around. Money slips through Simon's fingers. But what do you think the police want? I wish I knew what's going on. And there's Josh. He thinks he's going to see his father this weekend.'

'The police would want to talk to anybody who knew Nicole and lives on Beacon. Even if he only met her once.'

'But they've already been up and down Beacon and Dykeman's.'

'It wouldn't be abnormal for them to go twice, and they've probably got some new questions by now.'

'That's true. They can't think Simon had anything to do with what happened to Nicole.' She paused. 'I wonder where he met her. Some do for that lousy book, I bet.'

Bull's-eye, Gillian thought.

'This is causing an awful lot of stress,' Roberta fretted. 'I thought when Arnold died that the investigation would be over quickly, and we could all try to get back to normal.'

'Well,' said Gillian, 'the police must not be satisfied with their case.' She didn't add that if Arnold hadn't murdered Nicole, then the killer was still at large. Roberta sounded anxious enough already. 'Just sit tight,' she said. 'If they want to ask Simon a few questions, it's probably just routine.' She wasn't being honest, but what choice did she have? To offer up her own speculations, suggesting to Roberta that her husband might have been Nicole's lover, would be outrageous.

She was about to recommend that Roberta pour herself a drink, but considering Simon's habits, she supposed that would be tactless. Roberta probably never touched alcohol. However, she would have something; most people did, even if it was only tea. 'Have you got anything to help you sleep?'

'A few Valium. My doctor gave me some when I moved out.'

'Maybe it would be a good idea to take one.'

CHAPTER 19

In the morning, Gillian went to Jean's for supplies. Rain had fallen during the night, and the dirt parking lot was full of puddles, stirred to a milkshake froth by the comings and goings of many cars. The store was always busy on Fridays, but Gillian had never seen it so crowded. She'd listened to the news again; more details about Arnold's death had been released. She paid close attention, fearing that her own name would be included, and was relieved not to hear it. Jean's would be packed with people avid for the latest news, and having to tell Estelle about finding the body had been grisly enough. She wanted to talk to Edward about it, and no one else. He was the only one who would know from his own experience how horrible it had been.

The gun—vaguely described as an 'older model' revolver—was mentioned in the news report, and so was the damage to Arnold's truck. The flat tyres, she learned, had been shot out. The police were looking for those responsible and asked for information from anyone who had heard shots or seen anyone suspicious in the area on Wednesday. Had Jim heard the report, she wondered. Had he told Brian anything yet? She should phone him later, if she had time.

The girl who usually came in on Saturdays was working the booths, taking orders, while Jean stayed behind the counter. Arnold had died Wednesday night; Jean, a practical woman, had probably booked her help in for the extra day as soon as she heard about it.

There were over a dozen people snugged into the booths, and it wasn't even the busiest hour of the day. Other people stood about talking, holding their shopping baskets like fig leaves to cover their curiosity. Gillian knew most of the faces but only a few names. She picked up two cartons of orange juice, bananas, grapefruits, butter, cheese, extra milk and a box of Honey Nut Cheerios, currently her nephew's favourite cereal. She nodded to the nearest familiar faces but kept moving, seeing with the corner of her eye that there was a lull at the cash register. As she put her groceries on the counter, Jean was filling the coffee machine with water.

'Franklin's coming up tomorrow,' Gillian said. 'With the family.'

'Good. That'll please your mother.'

'Yes, she's getting her hair done this afternoon in honour of the visit.'

'How's she feeling? I know her arthritis kicks up this time of year, when the weather turns chilly.'

'It hurts. It tires her out.'

Jean clucked, then said, 'She's still sharp as a tack. TZ says she plays a mean game of bridge.'

Gillian laughed. 'She remembers what's trump.'

'Good for her. I wouldn't have a prayer. Never got past crazy eights.' Jean swept a professional glance over the chattering throng of customers and began to tally up Gillian's groceries. 'Did you hear they found the hunter?'

'What hunter? You mean the one who was shooting up at Dykeman's?'

'Yeah, they got him. The McElroy kid. You know the McElroys, a couple of miles down 9D? His parents knew he was hunting on posted land, but they didn't say anything. Didn't want their precious Pat to get into trouble. But he's been seen hanging around Dykeman's recently, and everybody knows he's been caught trespassing before, only the people didn't want to lay charges.'

'He's actually admitted that he was there when Maya and Lynn found Nicole under the bridge?'

'That's what I hear.'

'Someone must have seen him.'

'Or the police have got something else on him. They've been investigating a couple of B & Es that happened up there in the last month. Pat's no angel. He was sentenced to community service last year for damaging school property,' Jean said.

'Community service? What a joke,' a voice said behind Gillian. A big black man in a baseball cap and jeans slapped two sandwiches from the cooler on the counter as Jean rang up the total for Gillian's purchases. Jean reached up without having to look and slid a pack of Winstons from the rack.

'Two today,' the man said. 'You know what they do in community service? Pick a couple of Coke cans off the highway and put them in a bag. Just what the hell does that accomplish?'

Gillian had her wallet out and was about to hand Jean a twenty. The man swept up his sandwiches and cigarettes with one large hand. 'Go ahead if you're in a rush,' she said.

'Put them on the tab, OK, Jean? Kids like Pat McElroy need to be hit hard the first time they get caught. Anything else, they're laughing. See you Monday.' He nodded to Gillian. 'Thanks,' he added, already on his way to the door.

'Who's that?' she asked Jean. 'I've seen him around a few times.'

'Oh, that's Toby. He's in here nearly every day, always in a hurry. Owns a little trucking outfit. He knows the guy who crashed last week—went to see him in the hospital. He's going to live.'

'Good. Well, Pat McElroy certainly has a reputation,' said Gillian. 'I don't remember that family.'

'They moved here ten years ago. Trashy people. I don't usually say things like that,' Jean added. 'I'm all for live and let live. But not when people let their kids steal from my store. I had to get Scottie to talk to him, and tell him not to come in here. I tried telling his parents, and they just hollered at me that their precious son wouldn't steal from anybody. And after Scottie went to see him, my tyres were slashed.' Jean shrugged. 'They don't come in here, and that's all right by me.'

'I don't suppose Pat could have seen anything. Nicole must have been there for hours.'

'If he did, he'll find out it isn't smart to keep quiet about things like that.'

Jean glanced around. No one was approaching the counter. She lowered her voice. 'It's a shame about Arnold. But if he killed that girl, maybe it's for the best. You found him, didn't you? Must have been a shock.'

Gillian was dismayed. 'I thought that hadn't gotten out yet.'

'It was pretty bad, huh?'

Gillian nodded. 'I don't want to talk about it.'

'I sometimes hear things first, but I don't have to pass them on,' Jean said. 'That's it?' she continued in her normal voice, as she snapped open a bag for Gillian's groceries. Two customers had finished their conversation and one was making a beeline for the cash register.

Gillian took the bag. 'Thanks, Jean. I'll remember you in my prayers.'

'That's OK,' said Jean, her eyes twinkling, 'I think Jim Whitlock's got the praying all sewn up.'

❦

When Gillian got back, having stocked up for the weekend, Estelle's car wasn't in the driveway. Laden with bags, Gillian kept an eye open for Rumpole, who might be outside and had a habit of streaking for the kitchen door right under her feet. She'd come home in order to give Estelle a lift to the salon where she had an appointment for a haircut and a pedicure, and she was in plenty of time. She set her groceries down and looked for a note. There was a pad of paper on the kitchen counter. Estelle had shifted from writing to printing a while back; her hand shook too much to write in script. In any case, she wrote very little these days. Her note said, in staggering capitals, 'HAIR'. Gillian could have sworn that the appointment was for 1:30. She went to the calendar by the phone. It said 1:30, but then Estelle sometimes became over-anxious about the time. Gillian had driven her to Dr. Brinker's office, only to settle in the waiting room thirty or forty minutes early.

Estelle's little black leather bag lay on a chair. Gillian picked it up, and the catch gaped open, revealing the quilted satin lining and Estelle's wallet and her change purse. Her keys would have been in the ignition. Gillian, with her city habits, had been alarmed by this careless ease until she found out that lots of people still did it. Some of the old ways hadn't changed. Estelle didn't always bother to lock the house when she went out, either. Perhaps she ought to know about the break-ins Jean had mentioned.

Gillian called the salon. Yes, Estelle's appointment was for 1:30; she hadn't arrived yet. They would be happy to let Gillian know when she appeared. No, it wouldn't be a problem if she had no money, she could send them a cheque, or Gillian could come in and pay next week. Gillian hung up. Estelle might be browsing; the garden shop near the hairdresser's had some new shrubs in this week. Gillian wanted to take a bath, wash her hair, change the sheets and fix something for dinner so there would be no cooking to do later. Edward was supposed to arrive at about four, but his plane might be late, and the traffic would be heavy on a Friday night. A limo service was picking him up at Kennedy.

She went to the pantry and looked over the cases of wine she'd laid in when she found the wine shop across the river.

She'd made some inroads, but most of the bottles were still there. She chose a California wine, a big fat Zinfandel. The Englishman should know what country he was in. There would be soup, bread and salad. In her experience, people didn't want much food after long flights.

As she was stowing the groceries, the phone rang. The salon. Estelle had arrived. Gillian relaxed. Estelle's appointment would take an hour and a half. She put bones in water for the soup broth and decided to have a bath while they simmered. Now that the day had come, now that she knew she would see Edward in a few hours, she let herself feel how badly she'd wanted him to come. She sniffed the freesias she'd bought for Estelle at the train station. Their apricot scent pleased her, so she'd bought them. It wasn't the sort of thing she did very often; her life was too austere, it had been too austere for too long. She'd been so much in the habit of denying herself, of ploughing her single-minded furrow, that she'd half forgotten what it was like to want. To desire. She took a deep breath, stopped bracing herself and went upstairs to wallow in the big clawfoot tub.

By a quarter to three, she had bathed, dressed, changed the beds, chopped the onions and cleaned the spinach. She put on Estelle's old record of *Guys and Dolls* and was warbling along with 'I'll Know When My Love Comes Along' when she heard a car in the drive. 'And you'll know at a glance by the two pair of pants,' she sang. Estelle, she supposed. Maybe the salon appointment had finished a little early, since she'd arrived early.

There was a knock at the door. Not Estelle. Wiping her hands, Gillian hurried into the hall. It couldn't be Edward unless he'd changed flights without telling her. It wasn't. Roberta stood in the doorway, distraught.

'Simon's in the hospital,' she said in a high, rapid voice. 'He got beaten up. He's been phoning me. I tried to call my lawyer but she's in court, and I can't talk to her. I *had* to talk to somebody.'

Gillian steered her into the living room and sat her on the sofa. 'Tell me what happened.'

'He called last night from a pay phone. He woke me up. I don't know where he was, he'd been driving for hours, half out of his mind, he said. He was going to drive as far away as he could, but then he realized that was stupid—a panic reaction—and started back. This was before he got beaten up. He said he called because he was afraid he wouldn't be able to pick up Josh tomorrow.' Roberta looked blankly at Gillian. 'He's afraid the police think he murdered Nicole, because he lied about knowing her. She's been to his house, but he didn't tell them that. He said whatever they said to me he wanted me to know he hadn't done it.'

'What a shock. Jesus. Had he been drinking?'

'Yes, maybe. I don't know. I was confused—it was hard to wake up because of the Valium.'

'Have you told the police he called you?'

'No. I didn't know what to do. I took Josh to daycare and went to the office this morning, but I didn't stay—I was too upset. Then I was going to drive over to Beacon, to see if Simon had come home, but I was afraid the police would be there. So I went back to my place. He phoned again a little while ago. He sounded awful.'

'Is he all right?'

'He's got a couple of broken ribs and a lot of bruises. He was unconscious, so they're keeping him for observation until tomorrow. He went to a bar around four in the morning and got jumped in the parking lot.'

'Did he tell you why he lied to the police?'

'He didn't want to get involved.'

'When was Nicole at his house?'

'I think he said she was there a few times.'

'What about the night she was killed?'

'That's why he didn't want to get involved. He said she might have come to the house that night, but he was so drunk he can't remember. Somebody broke into the house—that's why the glass was smashed. Remember, I showed you where he'd fixed it?'

'Broke in? When he was there? Why on earth?'

'I don't *know*,' Roberta wailed. 'He said she phoned him Tuesday night, so she knew what condition he'd be in on Wednesday. He's telling me she knows the way he drinks, and I didn't even know he'd met her. I'm going crazy just trying to guess when he's telling me the truth.'

'OK. So, according to Simon, somebody broke in Wednesday evening.'

'Yeah. He woke up after dark and saw the front door was open and the glass was shattered.'

'He doesn't know what time it was, I suppose.'

'Time? He's lucky he knows what day it was. He said he bought his bottles on Tuesday. Wild Turkey—it's what he drinks. So he was drunk by Tuesday night. That's his pattern—he goes to the package store and buys quarts of the stuff and drinks them over a couple of days. He goes into a kind of zombie state, where he doesn't move or talk, but he just sits and every little while pours another drink. Sometimes it's hard to tell if he's conscious or not. It takes an amazing amount to make him pass out, but he might as well be in a coma, for all the sense you can get out of him. Then the hangover takes a couple of days to get through, and he stops for a while. Then he goes and buys some more—he won't keep it in the house.'

'He could have broken the glass himself, and left the door open.'

'But he's sure someone was there. He says they went through his things.'

'Just a minute. He's telling you that he panicked because he may have had a break-in the night Nicole was killed? And that's going to make the police think he's the murderer? It doesn't add up.'

'But he thinks it was her. *She* was there.' Roberta's voice grew operatic.

'Why?'

'She was mad at him about something. He wouldn't say what.'

'We could both use a cup of tea,' Gillian said. 'Or would sherry be better?'

'Tea.'

Gillian nipped into the kitchen to put the kettle on. She hoped Estelle wouldn't come home in the middle of this; she'd need all her energy to enjoy the family invasion over the weekend. Nearly three-thirty, she should have been back already. Eli must have found some evidence at Simon Steele's. Some proof that Nicole had been there. That's why the police were looking for him. And Simon probably knew there was something to find. He was holding out on Roberta, not a smart move if he wanted her trust. Or maybe he was genuinely confused—alcohol and panic weren't a prescription for lucidity. Funny, in that kind of trouble, to turn to the former wife you'd trashed in your book, the wife who'd left you and had just made you fork over some of your royalties. But Simon, she thought, was probably used to having Roberta handle any crisis he was in. He hadn't gotten out of the habit just because they'd been separated for a few months. And he didn't seem the type to be rich in friends. There was Josh, too. It was possible that he cared about his son, even if he was a lousy father. And he knew Roberta was still crazy about him—he'd have to be an idiot not to. It was interesting that he'd suddenly become cooperative about money after Nicole was killed. One explanation that came to mind was that he wanted Roberta on his side because he suddenly had a problem that made $7000 look unimportant. If he believed Nicole was in his house the night she died, when he was home alone and drinking heavily, he'd be scared. He'd know he was in a bucket of trouble whether he'd killed her or not.

Roberta came into the kitchen, too restless to sit.

'You know what Nicole was doing to make money, right? Margaret said she told you.'

'The escort service.'

'I keep wondering if Simon knew. If that's why she was visiting him.'

'You mean was he a client?'

'I mean, was he paying to lay her? It makes me gag.'

'I don't think so. I think she kept that part of her life as far from Stanton as possible. She tried very hard to keep things in two separate compartments.'

Gillian poured the tea and persuaded Roberta to have extra sugar as a remedy for shock. Where was Estelle? She was really late, now. Excusing herself, Gillian called the salon again. Estelle had left a few minutes before three. She'd seemed fine. Gillian looked at the clock. It was nearly four.

'I don't know what to think,' Roberta said, sipping her tea in a stunned sort of way. 'Simon is a prick, but he's Josh's father.'

Gillian didn't know what to think either. A snow flurry of questions swirled, chasing each other. Had Simon killed Nicole? If so, was he now engaged in an elaborate pretence? A prelude to a plea in court that he'd been too drunk to know what he was doing? If he wasn't the killer, and he was as drunk as he claimed, why was he so sure she'd broken in? Why not someone else, like the McElroy kid who was suspected of the other neighbourhood B & Es? Because of what was taken? The police would find out; he was the kind to go to pieces fast under questioning.

Gillian heard wheels in the driveway again. Estelle, at last.

'I'll just see if Estelle needs help.' She rushed to the front door in time to see Edward getting out of the airport limousine. It felt like a dream, the kind that the dreamer knows at the time doesn't make sense. She always saw Edward in England. What was he doing here? He smiled at her, and she felt her face smiling back, though for a fraction of a moment she still doubted that he was there. Then he really was there, solid and real. He wrapped both his arms around her, and she pressed hard against him, squeezing the time and distance between them into nothing. Roberta's in the kitchen, she thought. What a farce.

'There's someone here,' she muttered. 'Everything's in an uproar.'

Reluctantly, he let go. 'I must be in America.'

The limousine rolled away down the drive. Edward picked up his suitcase and they went in. He followed Gillian to the kitchen. Roberta was still at the table, sobbing into her tea. She looked up, tear-stained and startled to see a stranger. Gillian introduced Edward. 'Roberta's upset because she's just found out that her estranged husband, Simon Steele, is in the hospital. He was beaten up.'

'Is he badly hurt?' Edward enquired.

Roberta was blowing her nose.

'Fractured ribs,' said Gillian. 'Bruises. He's staying overnight, because he was knocked unconscious.'

'I'm supposed to go pick him up tomorrow afternoon,' Roberta explained, sniffing. She turned to Edward. She knew he worked at Scotland Yard, because Gillian had told her when they were becoming acquainted. 'The police want to ask him questions about Nicole. I feel like I'm going crazy. You know, I woke up at five in the morning and thought the whole thing was a nightmare. Then I thought it could be a lie—that Simon just said he was in the hospital because he wasn't going to pick up Josh. But he never would have told me that little slut was there if she wasn't.' She looked at Edward with big wet eyes. 'The police won't think he's the murderer just because he lied about Nicole being there, will they?' she asked him.

Edward's eyes met Gillian's for a brief moment. I have to get rid of her, Gillian thought. I don't care. I can't let her spoil this.

'Lots of people lie for all sorts of reasons,' Edward said, the voice of reason.

'I'm going to the hospital tomorrow,' Roberta said. 'The police won't question him when he's just had a concussion, will they?'

'Not if they don't have to.'

'My nephew is only a little older than your son,' Gillian said. 'He'll be visiting tomorrow; if you need a place to leave Josh, they could play together.' She hoped she wouldn't regret this offer, but she was going to turn Roberta out, and she was feeling guilty.

'That would be wonderful. I certainly can't have Josh with me if I'm going to get the truth out of Simon.'

The clock in the hall struck the quarter hour. Roberta started. She stood up abruptly. 'I'd better go. I've got to pick up Josh right now.'

They saw her out, and then they were alone.

'Sorry,' Gillian said.

'Raise the drawbridge,' Edward murmured. 'Boil the oil.'

'Well, I would,' said Gillian, 'but I don't know where my mother is.'

He was creased with tiredness after the long flight.

'You've lost weight,' she said. His face was thinner, the nose sharper, the eyes deeper in their cave under the dark brows.

'Have I? I hadn't noticed. How are you?'

'Frayed. You know, it feels funny to see you here.'

'Not nearly as funny as being here. How many years has it been?'

'Too many. We should have done this ages ago. God, I've missed you.'

'What was that you said about your mother?' he said into her hair a few minutes later.

'Oh, damn. I forgot for a moment. She's beetled off somewhere. I'm going to have to start phoning people. She's not well, not at all. But she still goes off in the car as if nothing could happen. How can I stop her—she'd feel as if I'd taken her prisoner. Do you want some tea? I made some just before you got here.'

'I'd rather have a drink.'

'I don't blame you. But if Estelle's in trouble we might have to go and fetch her. And her car.'

'Drive? Now? On the wrong side of the road?' He laughed. 'Give me a small whisky and a large tea. Just promise me that we're alone now. You haven't anyone else hidden on the premises, have you?'

'No one.' She felt a rush of happiness hitting her, like a wave catching a wader behind the knees. 'Come to the kitchen while I get our tea. I don't want to let you out of my sight.'

The phone rang. Gillian pounced on it. Estelle's voice came faintly down the wire, as if she were very far away. She wasn't, however. She was at the Hornbecks'. 'Sorry, dear, I ran into Martha and she offered me some day lilies she's been dividing. There's a little problem, I can't drive home. It's the stupidest thing, but I've turned my ankle and it's all swelled up. I don't think I could brake properly.'

'Shall I come and get you?'

'Is Edward there yet?'

'Yes, he just got here.'

'Oh, then you should stay. You can't leave him alone the minute he's arrived.'

'We could both come.'

'Oh, no. Don't fuss. Martha will drive me home in her car.'

'All right, tell her we'll come and get your car tomorrow or Sunday.' She hung up and went to the cupboard where she kept the Scotch. She was flooded with relief. She'd been afraid of something worse than a swollen ankle. 'Love of my life,' she said to Edward. 'Have any size whisky you like.'

CHAPTER 20

Afterwards, Gillian thought that it had been a miracle that she hadn't burned the dinner. If it hadn't been soup, she would have. The bread, warming in the oven, had been rescued by Edward. Estelle arrived, obviously in more pain than she'd let on over the phone. She could wiggle her foot, however, and was adamant that she hadn't broken any bones. She refused to go to the emergency ward for an x-ray. Half the evening was spent wrapping her ankle in ice packs and taking them off again. She was wryly apologetic.

'Vanity,' she said to Edward. 'I was determined to have my hair done before you got here; I wanted to look my best— as good as I can at my terrifically advanced age. And now look at me—an invalid with a big black eye.'

She had fallen in the Hornbecks' driveway. Her knee had given way without warning, and she'd collapsed on the gravel, twisting her ankle and bruising her nose and cheek. She had a beautiful shiner.

Edward said, 'My mother fell backwards last year on the ice. She acquired such a splendid bruise on her posterior that she threatened to send a photograph to *The Guinness Book of Records*.'

Estelle laughed. Edward always made her laugh. It was such a pity, Gillian thought, that he hadn't come to the farm more often. And she thought, again, a refrain of the past weeks, why do we realize these things when it's too late?

Estelle had news from Martha Hornbeck. The police had been all over Simon Steele's property that morning, searching the woods and the house. The Hornbecks had seen the cars in the drive, and the police had asked them if they'd seen Simon leave, if they knew where he'd gone. They'd asked everyone on Beacon Road.

Gillian could see that her mother was rather thrilled to be the bringer of tidings, despite her shock and distress at the two deaths. Her world had shrunk, and it was rare for her to have a piping-hot story and an audience. She didn't care for Simon Steele, or feel sorry for him in the way she had for Arnold, and she was excited by having Edward there. He was an expert—a professional. It was better than watching Morse. There was a pink flush on her cheekbones; they were all drinking whisky after the Zinfandel, the fire was blazing cheerily, and they were feeling quite good, despite the effects of a swollen ankle, jet lag, and the grotesque events of the past ten days.

'I imagine they were looking for the weapon,' Estelle said, cocking her head at Edward.

'Certainly, if they haven't got it. Juries like to see the weapon.'

Gillian had e-mailed Edward parts of the story in bits and pieces. Now he asked questions to fill in some of the details she'd left out. Others, like the connection with the escort agency and her vague mistrust of Eli, she kept to herself, not wanting to discuss them with Estelle. She would tell Edward later, after Estelle had gone to bed. Meanwhile, Gillian told her that Roberta had been there when Edward arrived, and then had to go back and explain about Roberta's request for her company when she went to pick up the cheque.

'I didn't tell you before, because I was thinking about poor Arnold. I went to Simon's the same night that Arnold died.'

Oh, yes, I was in that house years ago,' Estelle said. 'It's perfectly lovely. More upkeep than this house, but not nearly as much as the really big places on the river. I remember Simon's grandfather; he was a cut or two above Simon. You must have met Simon before, Gillian. Don't you remember?'

'When?'

'At the Brewsters'. He was at one or two of their parties when he was visiting Ben—his grandfather.'

'I don't remember him at all. He didn't show any sign of remembering me, either.'

'Well, that wouldn't be surprising. He used to drink too much, even then. He passed out in the garden once. I suppose you might not have met; the Brewsters gave a lot of parties. He was in a serious car accident when he was young—several college kids were badly hurt. We weren't here at the time, but I heard something about it from Ben, later. He was very upset. Simon always loved the house, though, that's why Ben left it to him. Maybe Ben thought it would make him learn to be more responsible. Isn't it likely,' she said to Edward, 'that if Nicole did break the windowpane, she would have cut herself? The police might have found some blood at Simon's house and matched it to hers.'

'Or some glass fragments in her clothing,' suggested Edward. 'A lab might be able to match the pane to the fragments.'

'But he'd cleaned it up,' Gillian objected. 'Wait. No, he hadn't, not by Saturday afternoon. If Eli saw the door before it was repaired…He would have—some officer would have, because they would have gone up and down Dykeman's and Beacon asking the neighbours whether they'd seen anything. I wonder whether they're searching Simon's house because they've got some lab results that prove she was there.'

'How far apart are Arnold's house and Simon's?' Edward asked. 'I don't have a map of the country in my head the way you do.'

'I'll take you past the strategic locations tomorrow when we pick up the Saab,' Gillian said. 'They're about a mile apart, I suppose.'

'And Nicole was seen on the road with her bicycle at seven o'clock? What happened to it?'

'I've never thought about it,' Gillian said. 'Maya and Lynn didn't say anything about a bicycle.'

'Maybe *that's* what they were looking for in the woods at Simon's!' Estelle said.

'If she went to Simon's house, Arnold could have killed her after she broke in, couldn't he?' Edward said. 'He could have seen her on the road and followed her.'

'But why?' Gillian said. 'There's no real reason.'

'Nobody's suggested a reason for Simon, either.'

'But he knew her; she went to his house more than once, and we know she was attracted to him. They were having an affair; at least, that seems probable.'

'Perhaps Arnold was jealous.'

'Simon was fighting with his wife over money. There's a child, too. So there are custody and access issues. He could have been afraid that Roberta would find out and be furious.'

'Would she be jealous?' Estelle asked.

'Oh yes, she doesn't know whether to kiss him or kill him,' Gillian said. 'They haven't been separated long.' She looked at Edward. 'And Simon lied to the police about knowing Nicole, remember that.'

'All right, he lied,' Edward said with maddening composure. 'We take a dim view of liars; they cost us so much extra work. But what I said to Roberta wasn't just for effect.' He darted an amused glance at Gillian. 'Though I didn't care what I said so long as she went away. You have to factor it into your thinking: people lie all the time. There are so many reasons, or excuses, for lying, fear being the most common. And Arnold did have the photograph.'

'You seem to be arguing the case against him.'

'Just perching on the other side of the scales of justice. You seem to have decided that Arnold didn't commit murder. You may be right. But if the police don't have the evidence to convict him, you don't have enough to exonerate him, either.'

'Hmph. I'm not sure your professional expertise is getting us anywhere.'

'Edward thought of the bicycle,' said Estelle. 'We didn't.'

'Oh, all right. He gets an A for the bicycle. But remember, Sherlock, you and I are supposed to solve the case. The landlady isn't supposed to start getting uppity ideas about bicycles.'

Edward laughed. 'The class system isn't what it was.'

Late Saturday morning, Franklin arrived with Audrey and their son Jasper, a load of goodies from Balducci's, a box of Estelle's favourite chocolates, and three bicycles on the roof. Franklin and Audrey had only met Edward twice, and Jasper hadn't seen him at all. Gillian had expected Jasper to take a serious interest in Edward because he was a police detective, but Jasper, for reasons of his own, had expected Edward to drive a police cruiser with a siren and flashing lights. After checking the shed, where the Buick had previously resided, he asked where the police car was. When he was told that there wasn't one, he looked at Edward with annihilating pity, and said, 'You should make them give you one.' Then he ran off to inspect the treehouse and the booby traps he had set for robbers.

'What can I do to restore my credit?' Edward asked Gillian, stifling a laugh.

'Go dust the treehouse for fingerprints.'

Estelle's ankle hurt more than it had the previous evening, and much to her chagrin, she was immobilized on the sofa. She'd needed Gillian's help getting up and hobbling to the bathroom, and she was tired and fuzzy with painkillers.

Franklin and Audrey sat with her for a while and then Audrey took their things upstairs and Franklin came into the kitchen where Gillian and Edward were assembling lunch.

Edward looked at them. 'You two are so alike,' he marveled. Franklin was three years younger than Gillian. Like her, he was long and thin, with the same cheekbones and eyes and flyaway hair. He had begun to go grey at the temples, Gillian saw, with a sigh, and there were deeper lines at the corners of his mouth. He seemed burdened with worries.

'You look like Gregory Peck in *To Kill a Mockingbird*,' she remarked.

'Mother looks awful,' he said. 'Much worse than the last time I was up.'

'I know. She's had a rough week.'

'She can't stay in this house much longer.'

'It's all right while I'm here.'

'Maybe, but then what? We should be looking into places for her to go. I've got a couple of names.'

'She doesn't want to look. She wants to stay here.'

'It isn't realistic.'

'We might hire someone to live in.'

'Who would come and live out here? Besides, she'll need more than a housekeeper pretty soon, she'll need a nurse. We can't afford a team of professional nurses on shift. And she should be much nearer medical help. How long would it take an ambulance to get to Salt Hill Road?'

'Franklin, I know you're worried. Couldn't we talk about this later, after you've been here for more than twenty minutes?'

He fidgeted with the ball of string Estelle kept on the counter, winding up the loose end. 'We can't stick our heads in the sand. We know the problem's coming, we should put some plans in place.'

'All right, but let's discuss it tomorrow, OK? Do you think Jasper would like someone to play with for a couple of hours this afternoon, or Sunday?'

'Sounds like a good idea. If it's Sunday, don't make it too late—I have to get back to the city by six.'

'That's a short weekend.'

'They don't pay me lots of money to take long ones.' He went back to Estelle.

'Talk about heads in the sand,' she muttered, when he'd left the room. 'He doesn't realize that moving out of this house might kill her.'

'But he has a point. You've already given away your sabbatical. What are you going to do next? Take a leave of absence?'

'I don't think so; I'm on sabbatical until next summer.'

'And then?'

'I can't plan that far ahead. You haven't lived here for the past two months. Neither has Franklin. It's different from day to day.'

Edward finished slicing the bread. 'Are you going to talk to him about the new heart surgery?'

'I must, I suppose.'

The phone rang. It was Jo. 'Are you busy? I thought you'd want to know. The police have finally found out who Nicole is. Her real name's Nicole Pierre. She comes from a little place called Malone, way upstate. And it's true that her mother died when she was thirteen, but her father may still be alive. Eli Pink told Margaret last night that the police up there were checking on that.'

'How did he find out her real name?'

'He didn't explain. He just said they'd got the information and had verified the birth record.'

'Pierre. I wonder if that's where she got the idea for Stone.'

'What?'

'Pierre is French for stone.'

'Oh, yes. I wasn't thinking. You mean it was one of those tricks the subconscious plays?'

'Or a conscious play on words. Maybe she liked a name that was her real name and wasn't.'

Roberta had talked to Margaret, so Jo already knew that the police were taking a sudden interest in Simon. 'We're not making any announcements about the case, or updating the student body on the information we get. I don't know whether that's right or not, but they're just beginning to calm down. We don't want to keep reminding them about Nicole, or encouraging speculation. What do you think?'

'You live on campus, Jo. You're in the best position to decide whether more news bulletins would help. If you get in touch with Nicole's father, I'd certainly tell them that.'

'I'm not sure if any of the students have heard about Simon yet, but I hope they haven't. They'll go right up the wall. This case has got to get solved soon, or the term's going to be a write-off. None of us is getting much sleep, and half the students have been in for counseling and sedatives. I'm especially worried about Janice Grogan. She hasn't been attending classes at all.'

Lunch was not a relaxed occasion. Estelle wanted to come to the table, but couldn't put any weight on her foot and had to be helped by Franklin and Edward. Franklin gave Gillian a now-do-you-see-what-I-mean? sort of look. Jasper was fascinated by Estelle's black eye, but he wanted to have his lunch in a dish on the floor with Rumpole, and, when that was overruled, threatened solidarity with the oppressed cats of the world until Audrey put her foot down.

Audrey, Gillian reflected, was in the best shape by far of any of them. She looked rested, fit and happy. She'd gone back to her job eight months after Jasper was born, and after a year of the guilt-a-thon, as she'd termed it, had said the hell with it and quit. Now she looked after Jasper, swam three mornings a week, and worked six days a month doing the books for several of the art galleries that had recently begun to cluster in her neighbourhood. Franklin had been dubious, worried about money, but he'd confessed to Gillian after the change that he liked the new arrangement. 'Thank God we can afford it,' he said. 'It's so much easier, and it's better for Jasper.'

Gillian asked Audrey whether they'd ever discussed which of them would quit. 'Not on your life,' said Audrey. 'This was what I wanted. Besides, Franklin wouldn't do that. He's not a new-age guy, you know.' She laughed.

He certainly wasn't, Gillian thought now. His wife had him pegged. Audrey was a buoyant spirit who naturally made the best of things; Franklin, like the rest of his family, was less flexible. What was Audrey's opinion of Estelle's future, Gillian wondered. She managed to appear cheerfully oblivious of Franklin's tension; she and Edward were discussing the epidemiology of crime and whether a rash of drive-by shootings could be usefully compared to an outbreak of flu.

After lunch, Roberta brought Josh, as arranged. The two little boys eyed each other with wary interest. Their colouring—dark hair, pale skin—was similar, but Jasper was thin and had slanting eyebrows that lent him a look of mischief in all weathers, while Josh, shorter and younger, was also thicker through the body, with blunter features and his mother's bright blue eyes.

'Why don't you show Josh your treehouse?' Audrey suggested to her son.

'Would you like that?' Roberta asked, still holding Josh's hand.

He nodded. 'Let's go,' Jasper said, always a quick starter. Josh followed him across the lawn.

'That was easy,' Audrey said, smiling at Roberta. 'I'll get them a snack.'

'I'm going to pick up Simon,' Roberta said when Audrey had gone inside. 'They're going to let him out today.' She was carefully made up, she smelt of perfume, and she was wearing a pretty suit in soft wool. Armed to the teeth, thought Gillian. I hope her mascara doesn't run.

'How far away is he?'

'Over an hour.'

Roberta hung around for a few minutes until she was sure that Josh was contented, and then she left, promising to be back by the end of the day.

Gillian took Edward for a spin in the Buick. They were to fetch Estelle's car, but she chose a roundabout route, just to be alone with him for a while and to show him the valley on this bright, unseasonably warm afternoon, the squash in baskets by the roadside and the leaves gold and scarlet like the royal coach rolling down the Mall.

'The Hudson River's so big,' he said, as an immense, muscular curve of water came into view. 'Utterly out of scale, like something in an adventure story. I remembered it differently.'

She turned eastward, towards the gently rolling farm country.

'It's Saturday, isn't it?' Edward said.

'Yes, why?'

'Nothing. I'm not used to being on holiday.'

'Are you thinking about work?'

'Now and then. It's hard to disconnect. Give me a few days.'

Gillian snipped the air with scissor fingers. 'A few days is all we've got.'

The road that ran past Lewis and Kitty Grogan's was particularly charming. They passed the house, which she pointed out, and dawdled along, with a vague intention of visiting the church in Freedom Plains. In a few moments, they saw a horse trotting along the verge—a chestnut mare, with a stubby rider in blue jeans and a helmet. 'That looks like Janice Grogan,' Gillian said. She slowed down, not wanting to startle the horse. Janice's body lifted and sank easily with the horse's motion, her knees had a firm grip, she looked both supple and controlled, entirely different from the stiff, awkward person she seemed to be on the ground.

Jo said Janice had been skipping classes. Gillian came alongside the horse and rolled down the window. 'Hello, Janice. How are you?'

Janice turned her head, murmuring a faint greeting. She looked deeply unhappy. When she saw Edward on the other side of the car, her shoulders tensed. She barely slackened her horse's pace.

'That's a lovely horse,' Gillian said. 'You're lucky. I wanted a horse, but I never had one.' She introduced Edward. 'He's here from London for a few days. We're out admiring the valley.'

Janice said something inaudible. She stared ahead, between her horse's ears. Gillian was finding it difficult to maintain the one-sided conversation, but she wanted to talk to Janice. Jo was worried about her, and looking at her bleak, glowering face, Gillian was, too. What had happened to upset her so much since the last time they'd met? Janice hadn't been at ease then, but at least she'd been willing to talk. Now the barriers were up.

'I've been wondering, do you ever hear owls hooting near the dorm at night?'

Janice looked at her with hostility. 'Why?'

'Because Arnold Mitchell might have been trying to photograph them. He told the police that's why he was in the woods there.'

'Oh.' She paused. 'Yeah, we hear owls,' she muttered reluctantly.

'What's wrong?' Gillian said.

'Nothing.'

Janice suddenly jerked on the reins and the horse stopped. Gillian braked.

'My father says they're searching Simon Steele's house,' she burst out, as if against her will. 'Is that true?'

'The police were there yesterday,' Gillian said.

'Daddy says they're looking for Simon. Are they?'

'They were asking the neighbours about him.'

'That detective came to see me. He asked me about Nicole meeting Simon. Did you tell him what I said?'

'I thought he should know.'

'Why didn't you tell me?'

'You're right—I should have.'

'It wasn't your business, it was mine.'

'I'm sorry. I know Eli. We went to school together. And I was concerned about Arnold. He was a fragile kind of person.'

Janice jumped. The mare twitched her ears backwards and shifted her feet nervously. Janice's hand tightened convulsively on the reins. 'You mean you don't think Arnold killed Nicole.' Her eyes widened, and for a moment Gillian saw naked fear in them.

'He might have. But if he didn't, he's paid a terrible price for being a misfit.'

'He did it,' Janice said fiercely. 'He must have.' She kicked her heels into the mare's ribs. The mare shot off, moving at a quick trot. A low stone wall ran parallel to the road; behind it was an empty pasture fringed by brilliant maples. Janice bent forward, and the mare lightly leapt the wall, then raced away across the grass. Janice didn't look back.

'She's frightened,' Edward said, watching horse and rider recede into the distance. 'I wonder why.'

'Because if it isn't Arnold, then the killer's still free? That's a good enough reason,' Gillian said thoughtfully. Somehow she didn't think that was all that was on Janice's mind.

'Tell me, why would you apologize for telling the investigating officer something he ought to know?'

'I didn't apologize for telling him, I apologized for taking her information and passing it on without telling her, or offering her the chance to tell him herself.'

'But you were doing the right thing.'

'From one point of view.'

'The one that counts. It's important that people pass on useful information. We couldn't function at all, otherwise. Suppose you'd left it to her—how long would it have taken her to come forward?'

'Yes, but if *you* pull information out of people and use it as you see fit, that's your job. It's not mine. I treated her the way her parents do.'

'It's her friend who was murdered—she must want to know who did it.'

'That's not the point.'

'I thought it was.'

'You sound just like a policeman.' Gillian flung her hands in the air.

'Your mother flings her hands up just like that.'

'Your mother wears army boots. Whatever that means,' she added.

They laughed.

Next, Gillian drove Edward to Stanton, to see the campus. The college was quiet; they could hear the thwack thwack of a tennis game beyond the half-empty parking lot. Delamar House stood dreaming in the cool sunshine.

The central hall gave Gillian pleasure whenever she went in. At this hour the entire space glowed. A river of light spilled down the stairs from the window over the landing. They stopped to look at the big Delamar. It was the only large painting in the house; Olympe had sold the rest. The sun's rays didn't touch it directly, but light gilded the air, and the painting bloomed. It wasn't a landscape, like most of his work, but a portrait of a young girl, though there was landscape in it, too. She was perhaps twelve, wearing a long dress and petticoats, leaning back in a swing that hung from the branches of a huge, gnarled tree. A complex bower of foliage hung all about the upper space of the picture, the sky visible behind. The swing rose high in the air, and Olympe's dress flew up, showing a froth of petticoat beneath. She was laughing with glee and kicking off her shoe, alone with the leaves and sky.

'It's the painter's daughter,' Gillian said. 'Olympe Delamar. She founded the college.'

'It looks familiar.'

'Like the Fragonard.'

'The one in the Wallace Collection. Yes.'

'It's Delamar's rebuttal, I think. He takes Fragonard's idea and turns it around. Here, the girl on the swing is an image of American freedom and innocence instead of old-world vice. I wonder if that's why Olympe kept it.'

'A suitable subject for the college?'

'Yes. But maybe she just couldn't bear to part with it. I couldn't. Edith Wharton admired it, too; she said so in one of her letters.'

They went outdoors again, to look at Nicole's dormitory window and the woods behind. They followed the path to the bank of the Hudson and watched the river's calmly moving surface. Leaves fluttered from the trees along the cliff and drifted down and away, flickering as they tumbled past, swooping and sinking and dwindling out of sight.

'The girl in that picture is so light-hearted,' Gillian said. 'I haven't felt like that in a long, long time.'

On the way to the Hornbecks', they passed the entrance to Arnold's driveway and came to Dee's Pond. They rattled slowly over the bridge.

Gillian pointed. 'That's where they found her.'

'Was it where she was killed?'

'I don't know. The police haven't said.'

'And have they found her bicycle?'

'Edward! That's what's been bothering me, especially since you asked about the bicycle last night. When I drove down here that evening, I saw a reflector. It flashed at me as I went by. It wasn't at the bridge, it was higher up, along here. I knew there was something, but I couldn't remember what it was. I suppose I ought to tell Eli.' She made a face.

'Why don't you trust him?'

Gillian was silent for a moment, searching for a concrete example. They hadn't had much interest in discussing Eli last night. She couldn't claim he was mishandling the case, because she wasn't privy to most of his activities. Eli was vain, egotistical, moody, and something of a bully. He had a chip on his shoulder and she was pretty sure he didn't like women.

Those qualities made her wary of him, but they didn't mean he couldn't do his job—or if they did, then most of the detective heroes in crime fiction couldn't do theirs either.

'He's too anxious to convict Arnold,' she said.

'If you have a theory, you chase it.'

'Ye-es, but—'

'There's always pressure to close the case. If you have a suspect, you keep after him.'

'But surely you have to follow up other possibilities. You can't have tunnel vision.'

'How many murder cases has he worked on?'

'I don't know. He might have seen some domestic murders. Probably nothing like this before.'

'He's probably being run ragged. Stanton College must have some local heavyweights on its board.'

'It does.'

They turned on to Beacon.

'But something still bothers you,' Edward said. 'What?'

'Bad vibes.'

When they arrived at the Hornbecks' to collect Estelle's car, Gordon and Martha were both outside. They were standing at the top of their drive where it joined Beacon, conferring with Alice Nelson, who had her dog with her. Gordon and Martha were both short, but she was stout and perky, while he was spindly and reticent. Alice was taller and stood very erect, and she was in the midst of a pronouncement.

'I always thought *Juicer* was a piece of trash,' she was saying. 'Simon Steele should have had his mouth washed out with soap, instead of being published. And now I suppose it will be a bestseller.'

'What's happened?' Gillian asked.

'Didn't Estelle tell you? The police were all over Simon's property yesterday, looking for something. They came back this morning—they're still there.'

'We don't know what they want,' Martha Hornbeck struck in, 'but yesterday they asked us where he was.'

'It *was* Nicole Bishop I saw going down his driveway. I knew it,' Alice said. 'His poor wife. Roberta's such a sweet person.'

'Not always,' Martha said. 'The way sound carries here is very tricky—you don't hear what goes on at Simon's, but we do, if it's loud, and the breeze is right. She wasn't always sweet. She could yell like anything. She has a terrible temper.'

'And the language,' Gordon Hornbeck added. 'Worse than the navy.'

'Really?' Alice said, doubting any assessment that wasn't her own. 'Well, I suppose anyone married to Simon would have been driven to it. His grandfather was such a fine man. Poor Ben. He must be turning in his grave.' The dog sniffed the air and tugged at her leash. 'All right, Coco, we'll be on our way.'

'I don't suppose you heard any noise the night Nicole was killed?' Gillian asked Martha.

'Not a thing. We don't, usually. Gordon heard a car start when he was putting out the garbage, at around eight o'clock, that's all.'

'Simon's car?'

Gordon shook his head. 'The police asked me that. I couldn't be sure. I know bird calls, but cars all sound the same to me.'

'Do you know any owl calls?' Gillian said. 'I know what barn owls sound like, because we have them, but that's all.'

'I know a few—the screech owl, and the great horned owl. That one really hoots—sends the shivers down your spine. There aren't many left around here, though. Farmers don't like them. They can acquire an insatiable appetite for chickens. What the farmers forget is, they also eat rodents. A great horned is big enough to kill a woodchuck.'

'I don't think Gillian needs to hear a lecture on owls, dear,' Martha interjected.

'But I'm interested. I like owls. Gordon, you didn't ever talk to Arnold Mitchell about them, did you?'

Gordon looked startled.

'He couldn't have,' Martha said. 'We don't ever see Arnold.'

'How did you know?' asked Gordon.

Martha stared. 'You did talk to him? When?'

'It was a few months ago. In the summer. I was out bird-watching, down by the marsh. Just looking to see what was there. I go down there most days. Arnold came along with his camera. I showed him a bittern—they're very hard to see.' Gordon thrust his meagre chin skyward. 'They stand with their bills sticking straight up in the air, and the stripes on their throats blend in with the reeds. He asked me about the bird population, and I got to talking about the birds I don't see so often any more. Including the great horned owl.'

'You never told me that, Gordon,' Martha objected.

'It didn't seem like something that would interest you,' he answered mildly.

Gillian heard a clumping sound along the road and turned to look. Carrie Pilgrim was coming towards them, stumping down the middle of Beacon in her thick-bottomed laced shoes. Gillian hadn't seen her in several years. She was rather alarming looking, tall and pale and bent, like an old grey house leaning on its foundations. Her hair had thinned, and the skull showed through it. The planes of her face were sharp under rice-paper skin freckled with brown spots. Still, she stumped unstoppably along the road, planting her stout cane with a firm hand, and her nose stuck out, bold as a Medici's.

'Carrie!' Gillian said, extremely pleased.

'Yes, I'm still alive. Isn't it remarkable?'

'The police are back,' Martha remarked.

'So I see.' Carrie turned to Gillian. 'How's Estelle? Martha told me she injured her ankle.'

'Puffy. She's keeping off it today,' Gillian said. 'This is Edward Gisborne.'

'Your Englishman.' Carrie looked him over. 'Estelle's talked about you,' she said to him. 'I haven't been to England in twenty years. It's a different country, these days, I'm told.'

'Oh yes,' said Edward gravely. 'We've got central heating now.'

'They've added the Turner wing at the Tate since I was last there.'

'It's very good. Turner should be delighted.'

'He's always been a particular favourite of mine. But I don't travel now. I like the view from my own windows.'

Carrie laughed, a wheezing caw. Her long yellow teeth showed.

'Would you travel as far as Salt Hill Road?' Gillian asked. 'I'd love to see you, and so would Estelle, but I think she won't be mobile for a while.'

'I could come for tea. Lily will drive me. Afternoon tea. I don't go out in the mornings; sometimes I still have enough energy to paint. And I fall asleep when it gets dark.'

'Tea, then. It's Lily Regan who works for you, isn't it?'

'Yes. I'm lucky to have her. She's smart, and she's got a good strong body—which I don't any more. Lovely to look at, too. Like a Renoir.'

Torchie had once been pretty in just that way, Gillian remembered, with milky skin and hair just the colour Renoir gave his redheads. She glanced down the road. Alice Nelson was standing at the head of Simon's driveway, watching something. The dog was watching too, her whole body alert.

'You're a detective, aren't you?' Martha said to Edward. 'Has Gillian told you about the student who was murdered just down the road?'

'Yes. It's a pity.'

'Estelle said you'd put lots of murderers behind bars. I wish you were working on this case. I don't think Eli Pink is going to solve it.'

'Why not?' asked Gillian.

'Well, he hasn't done anything about our burglary, has he? We all know that Pat McElroy is no good; I'll bet if Eli looked under his bed he'd find a heap of stolen property. But he never seems to get anywhere with it, he just tells us it takes time to collect enough evidence.'

'A friend of mine taught him in high school,' Gordon said. 'He said Eli Pink was obnoxious.'

Alice was coming back with the dog, and with Eli Pink. Eli was carrying something in a clear plastic bag. When he arrived, he showed it to them. It was a scarf, a narrow scarf with a tangled fringe, in a distinctive silky blue-green hue, threaded with thin yellow stripes. It was stained and dirty, but obviously beautiful, even seen through the folds of plastic.

'Anyone seen this before?' Eli asked.

Everyone stared at it. Gordon shook his head.

'I've no idea.'

Martha and Alice reluctantly concurred. They didn't remember it.

Gillian and Edward said nothing.

Carrie kept looking at it. 'I remember that scarf,' she said. 'I remember it quite well. Now where did I see it?' She shut her eyes. Eli watched her. All of them watched, their eyes darting curiously to the scarf and back again to Carrie's face.

'Mmmhmm,' said Carrie at last. 'Simon wore that to a New Year's Eve party you gave, Alice, it must have been last year.'

'Goodness, Carrie! How can you remember that?'

'I noticed the colours.'

'You know, you're right. How amazing. Now that you remind me, he came back the next day to look for it. He said he'd lost it at the party. We looked all over, but we never found it. He wasn't very nice—he hinted that someone at the party must have stolen it. Good heavens, we'd known everyone there for years.'

'Are you sure?' Eli said to Alice. 'He complained about losing that scarf?'

'Positive,' Alice said firmly. 'He was so cross I offered to buy him another one, but he told me it was handmade—he couldn't get another like it. It was very expensive, but I thought he was rude and silly. Typical of Simon. I remember saying to my husband that if we had another party I wouldn't invite him.'

'Where did you find it?' Martha asked Eli.

'Buried under a few stones in the woods by the driveway. It hasn't been there long. Not anything like a year.' He turned back to Alice. 'I'd like a guest list for that party.'

'Good Lord,' said Alice.

'We were there,' Martha said. 'So was your mother, Gillian.'

'Anyone seen this scarf since then?' Eli asked.

Silence. No one had, or could remember if they had.

'How much did he pay for it?'

'Something ridiculous. Over a hundred dollars.' Alice looked at it. 'Now, why -?' she began.

'I have a feeling,' Gillian said, 'that Simon is wearing a scarf in the book jacket photo of *Juicer*. It's a black and white photo, and I'm not sure it's that scarf, but if it is, then you'd know he had it and when.'

'I have *Juicer* in the house,' Martha said eagerly. 'You could look at it.'

'He's got several copies in his study,' Eli replied shortly. He looked at Edward. 'Friend of yours?' he asked Gillian.

She introduced them.

'Gillian didn't tell me you were coming.'

'It was a last-minute decision.'

'Staying long?'

'A few days.'

Eli grunted. 'Well, don't let me interrupt your holiday.' He looked at his watch. 'I'll be back for that list,' he said to Alice. Then he turned and started up the road towards Simon's driveway.

'Do you have a minute?' Gillian asked.

'A minute on the way to my car.'

'Excuse me,' Gillian said to the little group, and hurried after him. She didn't know what Edward would do; he could look after himself.

'Eli,' she said, catching up, 'I've finally remembered something about driving down the road that night. I saw a red bicycle reflector.'

He stopped. 'Where?'

'On Dykeman's, between Beacon and the bridge, the right-hand side.'

'What time?'

'Twenty past eight, maybe twenty-five past.'

She was conscious of the neighbours watching, Martha's jaw gaping, Alice faintly indignant.

Eli began to walk again. 'What exactly did you see?'

'I just saw the shine of the reflector, and possibly a glimpse of wheel. I know I thought "bicycle". It was in the trees. Could it have been Nicole's?'

'That's where we found her bike.' He glanced back up the road. 'Martha Hornbeck. What a pain. She thinks I've got nothing to do but look for her portable TV.'

Gillian decided not to mention that Gordon had talked to Arnold about owls. Eli would only scoff.

They reached Simon's sloping driveway. Gillian looked at the pretty house, its complex interplay of roof planes, the cars parked in front. Roberta should be on her way back with Simon. Did they know the police were here?

Eli's beeper went off. He looked at it irritably and yanked it off his belt. 'Everybody's on my ass.' Then he was moving down the drive towards the cars. She walked back towards the neighbourhood committee gathered in front of the Hornbecks'. Invitation lists from last year. A partially buried scarf. Nicole Pierre.

Edward came to meet her. 'Well?' he said.

She threw her hands up. 'What's trump?'

CHAPTER 21

They drove back to the farm in convoy, Gillian in front in the Buick, Edward following in Estelle's Saab. She made the turn on to Salt Hill, towards home. Her spirits lifted. The road curved and bumped over the stony land, the thin, cracked asphalt grey with age. She drove without thinking, the map printed behind her eyes. She knew every dip and rise, every pothole and frost-heave. The road was the same as always. The same. What did that mean? That she had traveled this narrow country way a thousand times, and each time she'd seen a different play of light on leaves, unique shapes of winter snow. Only by knowing these differences could the sameness—the sameness that was home—be recognized. Image was laid over image until the many layers of memory fused, became a knowledge that was in the body. She knew this road. The knowledge worked without thought, beating steadily, like her heart.

Though it was Saturday, when weekend visitors cruised the back roads, there was little traffic. The few houses, all but one or two, were the same ones she had ridden past on her bicycle when she was ten. At night, the deep country dark still lay between the trees, though the clouded sky turned smoky orange, burning with the reflected glow of nearby cities. Deer still crossed the road, and she'd seen a fox only a few weeks back.

She hit a stretch where the road was more gravel than asphalt and dropped to twenty-five as she passed the Brewsters' house. She wasn't especially interested in the Brewsters, but the sight of their pond from the road triggered a memory. Something delicious. She slowed even more, gazing at the placid oval flecked with yellow birch leaves. She'd been driving home alone, a long time ago, before she went away to college. A summer night so bright, so still, that she'd stopped to marvel at the round moon mirrored in the pond. It was August, and the air was heavy with the heat of the day. The Brewsters were away; the house was dark. She'd left the car, walked through the cool grass to the pond's rim, listening to the crickets. The moon's rays made a path across the water. Entranced, she'd stripped off her dress, her sandals, everything, and waded naked into the pool—a moment of solitary bliss, arrowing across the stillness, the dark and silver ripples sliding past her thighs like a silk slip falling, the round moon splitting into shivering ribbons.

She'd come to a complete stop. She glanced into the mirror; Edward sat in the Saab behind her, a quizzical look on his face. She would tell him later why she'd stopped, about her midnight swim, the feeling of delight—the delight that Delamar had captured in his painting. She drove the last half mile in a trance of memory. Then the white gables of her own house came into view. What next? She and Franklin needed to have a quiet chat, but she didn't feel up to it. She had to talk to Edward without nephews and mothers and brothers and half the county joining in. There was a lot she wanted to say.

When they got back, calm had settled over the household. The two boys were outside, marching Jasper's Lego figures into a fort built of sticks. Rumpole was stretched on the sunny bench nearby, watching a late hollyhock blossom that trembled at the top of a long stalk. A single bee, excited by the warmth, buzzed in the heart of the flower. Inside, Estelle dozed on the sofa, while Audrey read by the window where she could look up and see what Jasper was doing. Franklin had gone for a walk.

Gillian and Edward went upstairs. There were five bedrooms—her parents' room, which was now her study, her own bedroom with the single bed, Franklin's old room, the guest room, and a tiny room cluttered with suitcases and a rocking horse and the electric fans that cooled the bedrooms in the summer. They went into her study and lay down on the old four-poster bed they'd slept in the night before. The bed was too high for Estelle to climb in and out of and had stayed where it was when she moved downstairs.

'I'm knackered,' Edward said. He lay with his hands clasped behind his head, his eyes shut.

'What do you think?'

'About what?'

'Anything. My mother; Eli; who killed Nicole; will it rain tomorrow?' She rolled over and wrapped her arms around him. 'Never mind. Don't think.'

'In England, I'd be thinking about the case. I'd be running through the details with you again, wondering what Eli Pink knows that I don't, crawling under the bridge where the body was found in case he'd missed something. But I don't have to do that here. It's peculiar. I feel like a helium balloon—and somebody's let go of my string.'

'That weightless, disembodied feeling? I get that every time I fly to England. Don't worry, all of you will be here soon.'

'By that time, I'll be back in England. Or half of me.'

She could feel his heart beating. The warmth seeped into her, and she thought about her narrow bed across the hall, and the chilly sheets on the double bed in her own house, where she slept alone. Jo's image of the Inuit, snuggled under their heaps of blankets in the same big tent, floated into her mind. This was her parents' bed. They'd been married for forty years. Half of Estelle's life. Then Nathaniel had died quite suddenly of heart failure, before his seventieth birthday.

Seventy had seemed a long way off then, when Gillian was still in her thirties, but now her mind could span the distance.

She sighed.

'What are you thinking about?' Edward asked.

'Something my mother said to me. She said her mind didn't want to die but her body needed to, so her mind was coming to terms with it.'

'Is yours?'

'One day I think so, and the next I'm a basket case again.'

'I was pretty ripped up when my father died.'

'I know, but you didn't let on for months.'

'I didn't know how I felt. We never got on. Perhaps my job had an effect—I filed him under natural causes. I'm practised at shutting off feelings about death.'

'Well, I'm not. I look into my mother's eyes when she's frightened and I see into my own grave, too.'

'You're not going to die tomorrow,' he said gently.

'Maybe not, in the one-day-at-a-time way we usually see things. But life is so short compared to death. Aren't there insects that only live for a few hours? Days, maybe. Whatever. I feel like one of them—a hundred years of life is a flash—a blink—here and gone. That's all. Then the void.'

'There's not a lot we can do about it.'

'Listen. Except for my sabbaticals in London with you, I've lived alone since I grew up. Until now, until these months with my mother. They haven't been easy, but I found out I could do it. And that I wanted to. Such a brief time, I can almost count the minutes going by. She brings home day lilies for me to plant, she looks at catalogues and orders bulbs that will come up in the spring, but she doesn't know whether she'll see them bloom or not, and neither do I.

'One thing I've realized, when I haven't been hiding under the blankets and whimpering, is that I can't keep putting things off. So I've made a decision.' She stopped. To say it out loud made it seem real. 'I've decided to quit my job.'

Edward looked startled. 'Are you joking?'

'Not at all.'

'But you've never wanted to do that. When I asked you to come to London you said you wouldn't find a suitable job there.'

She pushed a stray lock of hair out of her eyes and leaned on her elbow to face him.

'I've changed my mind. You know, I've been working for too damn long. Counting my schooldays, I've been an academic since I was *five*.'

He laughed.

'OK, it's funny, but I want to live a different life. I want to finish my book, and I'll never do it if I keep teaching, even if I'm not department head any more. The administration just keeps piling more crap on. When I'm done with the book, I'll look around and see. Do you still want me to come and live in London with you?'

'I thought I'd been moderately obvious.'

'Not lately.'

'Lately you didn't seem inclined to come at all.'

'I had to be here. Don't you see that?'

'I didn't. Now that I've seen Estelle, it's easier to accept your point of view.'

'Everything's changed. It's not just that I've realized life is short. Or that I don't want to keep commuting for another decade.'

'To your office?'

'To London, you twit. When I used to think about quitting my job, moving to England, all that, I panicked. I liked my job, which I don't so much now, but I was also afraid of being financially dependent. I couldn't live on your salary, the way Audrey lives on Franklin's, it would go against the grain.'

'You think she's wrong?'

'No, she's not me. And she has a small child. Audrey's perfectly aware of the issues and capable of making her own bargains. What I'm trying to tell you is that being here has let me—or forced me—to see things from a new perspective.

And real estate has gone crazy in Vancouver. I can sell my house for a big pile of money.'

'Enough to quit?'

'I could manage. And eventually, when Estelle dies, I'll have more. It feels immoral to talk about it, though.'

'Won't you miss the social life? The colleagues, the office, feeling part of something?'

'Yes. What will I do without the buzz of the hive? Teaching at Stanton keeps me from going stir-crazy. But another thing I've noticed is that it's heaven only having to go in two or three days a week instead of six. I'll find out what I need, how much structure, but I know I don't want to recreate my full-time treadmill. I really don't.'

'If you feel like that about it, then quit. I'll buy the champagne.'

'Good. Buy a case.'

'A case? I thought we had only a few precious hours of life left. Is there time to drink twelve bottles?' Edward laughed quietly. 'It's bloody ironic. I was pissed off when you told me you weren't coming to London this summer, but it's turned out to be a *Good Thing*.'

'You've been reading *1066 and All That* again.'

'Why not? It's still the funniest book I know. If I can take it to my grave, I'll laugh there.'

'Very disconcerting for your grief-stricken visitors.'

She moved closer, feeling his arms close around her, hers around him, encircling. The warm density of bone and muscle, the sweetness of skin, held her, like gravity, as the earth spun in the void.

'It was seeing you that did me in. I stopped being used to *not* seeing you.'

A while later, she didn't know how long they'd been lying there, she heard the sound of a car driving up.

She sat up. 'Damn.'

'What's that?' Edward said drowsily.

'Roberta.'

'That woman? I'm not going to second-guess Pink & Co for her.'

Gillian slipped downstairs and went outside. Roberta was still sitting in her car. Josh, absorbed in his game, hadn't noticed.

Gillian walked across the driveway.

Roberta looked up. 'Simon's been arrested.'

'Good God.'

'He says he didn't do it.'

'Mom,' Josh called out. 'We made a fort.'

'That's great, honey.'

'Come and see.'

'In a minute.'

'Do you believe him?' Gillian said.

Roberta shifted in her seat, nervously kneading a leather driving glove in one hand. 'He met Nicole last spring. They started, you know…' She halted and then said, 'having sex,' as if she were spitting out a dead bug. 'That was after she came back to Stanton this fall. He said she was crazy about him, and I believe that part…He can be so charming when he wants to.'

'He told you this at the hospital?'

'Before the police came.' She jerked the glove between her hands. 'She's been to the house every week. The silly girl. She spilled out her life story to him. What really gets me is that it all started because of his horrible book. She thought he was so sensitive! She must have thought I was some kind of monster.'

'If she thought about you at all.'

'She told him about Ecstasy Escorts, and all sorts of other things, like where she grew up, and why she ran away from home. He said he was fascinated, he'd never known anybody like her. She made him swear he wouldn't tell anybody— nobody knew but him. She didn't want her father to find her—she said she hated him.'

'She knew he was alive!'

'Her mother buried money in the garden so her father wouldn't get it, and Nicole took it. She was afraid he'd try to contact her if he found out. She'd never told anybody.'

'But she told Simon.'

'And you know what Simon did? He *taped* her. After the first time she started to tell him things, he plugged in his little voice-activated recorder whenever she was there. Without telling her.'

'Why?'

'He wanted to use her in a *book*.'

'Mom!' Josh called. 'Come on.'

'My hands are like ice,' Roberta said.

'No wonder. Is that why she broke in? To get the tapes?'

'They had a fight on the phone. About his drinking, what else? She was supposed to see him, and he broke the date. She got mad and told him she wasn't going to see him any more. And he told her that was fine with him, he had the tapes.'

'That's cold-blooded.'

'He says if Truman Capote could use his friends, so can he.'

'What friends?' Gillian muttered. 'But why did he tell Nicole?'

'He was angry, I guess. Hitting back.'

'Did she find them?'

'She must have. Simon said they weren't in the house. He looked all weekend.'

'But he says he wasn't the one who killed her. Who does he think did it, then?'

'Arnold Mitchell.'

'Arnold! Why?'

'I don't know. Because of the photos, I guess. And Arnold lives right down the road. He told me he was just trying to lie low—hoping the police could prove it was Arnold and would never find out that he knew Nicole. But then Eli Pink came to see him a second time, and he got scared. He knew that once the police started looking they'd find something, even though he'd cleaned up.'

Roberta didn't look crisp any more. Her lipstick had worn off and her hair was untidy. She squeezed her gloves into a ball.

'Why did he tell you all this?' Gillian said.

'Simple.' Roberta gave a harsh little laugh. 'I brought a bottle of Wild Turkey. I gave him one little drink and then wouldn't pour any more unless he kept talking. It's a good thing none of the nurses walked in.'

Gillian heard the crunch of gravel under running feet. Roberta was going to have to look at Josh's fort.

'I told him the police asked me where he was,' Roberta added. 'He knew they'd arrest him when they found the Mustang. There's blood in it.'

'Nicole's blood?'

'He says he found her in the car. She was already dead.'

Josh skidded to a stop beside Gillian. 'Mom!!!'

'And that's all I can tell you,' Gillian said to Edward later. 'Josh came hurtling over, and I didn't find out the rest—if Simon actually told her anything more. He found Nicole in his car! He must have been the one who dropped her over the bridge. He didn't put much distance between himself and the body.'

'How far would you like to drive with a corpse in the car?' Edward said.

'Not an inch. And he'd been drinking, too. He would have to worry about how well he could drive. Imagine being stopped for erratic driving!'

'I've known killers to be caught as a result of traffic violations. But not with the corpse in the boot.'

'Do you think he killed her?'

'It bloody well looks like it. That kind of halfway confession is sometimes a prelude to telling the rest. Your friend Pink should have a go at him.'

'Yes.' Gillian picked up her copy of *Juicer* and studied Simon's face on the back. He didn't look like a killer. He looked like a drinker. Dissipated, but not deranged. But what did killers look like?

'Too bad Nicole told him all her secrets,' Edward said. 'Perhaps if she hadn't none of this would have happened. Why do you think she did that?'

'He was her lover. There's a deep wish to tell everything to your lover. If you hide what you're ashamed of, you feel like a fake. You can't feel loved for who you really are.'

'Mm. But no one can tell everything. I don't know everything about you. Knowledge is always partial, so why the dire confessionals about ancient history? I can see that the escort work would be on her mind, but to tell him about her family, the money? Why, when she'd told nobody else?'

'To ease the pain?' Gillian felt sad. 'To be forgiven?'

'I suppose.' A glint of humour showed in his eyes. 'Well, you don't have to tell me about your terrible past. I forgive you all your secret sins.'

'That's good. But what about the ones I'm going to commit in the future?' She was still holding Simon's book. 'They must have had a fight when she broke in. I wonder if he didn't really mean to kill her.'

'Got carried away? His legal counsel will try that on, but hiding the body won't look good.'

'And what a botched job of covering it up. I know he was pickled, but it just goes to show that theory and practice are miles apart.'

'Theory?'

'He wrote thrillers with more dead bodies than Bosnia.' She studied Simon's photograph again. 'Look. It's that scarf we saw. He's wearing it. The stripes look just the same.'

Edward reached for the book. 'When was the picture taken?' He wore a perplexed frown. 'And why should we give a damn?'

❧

After dinner, Franklin volunteered to do the dishes, and Gillian stayed in the kitchen to talk to him. She described the surgery Lewis had suggested for Estelle. Franklin lit up.

'It sounds like a godsend. Have you talked to her about it?'

'No. I rather think Lewis has.'

'Then why aren't things moving? She should see the specialist.'

'I asked her about surgery once, and she swatted the question away.'

'But that's crazy. She wouldn't be so tired; she wouldn't be at risk the way she is now.'

'Franklin, try to put yourself in her shoes. She can't do any of the things she enjoys any more. And it's not just her heart. Everything else is breaking down. She's in pain all the time, or drugged. Even the new operation would be hard to recover from, aside from the risks of going into the hospital. She's still got all her wits; she's done her own cost-benefit analysis. And there are a lot of nasty ways to die. A heart attack is relatively kind. What would *you* do?'

'I'd try it, goddammit. It might give her another year. She could see Jasper when he's eight, maybe even nine.'

There were tears in his eyes. Gillian noticed she was crying, too. 'Then you talk to her about it. I've tried.'

CHAPTER 22

Gillian and Edward slept late on Sunday, and when Gillian went downstairs in search of coffee, she found the rest of the family already up and about, including Estelle, who looked more alert. She was doing the *Times* crossword. Audrey was making pancakes, and Jasper playing with Rumpole, dragging a string along the carpet. Franklin was reading the editorial page. The scene reminded Gillian of the old days, the long-ago summers on the farm that memory made perfect. She tousled Franklin's hair.

'You all look like a poster for a family-values campaign.'

Franklin looked up at her through his reading glasses. 'Pancakes on Sunday morning are the foundation of family values. Audrey knows this. That's why I chose her to bear my child.'

Audrey hooted, spooning batter on to the griddle.

'What's "bear my child"?' Jasper asked, ears pricked.

'It means to give birth, to have a baby,' Estelle said, keeping her face straight.

Jasper looked bored. 'Oh, that.'

'I gave birth to your father, you know,' she added, pointing at Franklin.

Jasper looked at his father, and then at Estelle. This was a new idea. Puzzled, he wrinkled his nose, and for a fleeting instant, he looked like Estelle.

'That's why I'm your grandmother, dear,' she finished up.

'Oh,' he said, losing interest. He jerked the end of the string and Rumpole pounced. 'When are the pancakes going to be ready?'

After breakfast, Gillian asked Estelle where she wanted the day lilies to grow and went outside to plant them. As Gillian scooped holes in the cold, crumbly dirt and separated the fleshy roots, Estelle watched through the window. Then Franklin appeared beside her. He began to talk; Gillian could see his gestures. He was a persuasive talker when he chose to be. She went on digging.

Jim Whitlock's Jeepwagon came along the road and stopped at the bottom of the driveway. He got out, and she saw that he was wearing a jacket and tie. Church, she thought.

'I haven't seen you since that night at Arnold's house,' he said as he came up. 'How are you bearing up? You've got a crowd here this weekend.'

'We do. And it's exactly what we need. How are you doing?'

'I just came from church. Lots of people there.'

'Was everyone gossiping about Simon Steele?'

'Oh, so you know he's been arrested. Everybody's pretty shocked. They all thought Arnold was the one. Poor Arnold— he really got the short end.'

Gillian smoothed the earth over the lilies and stood up to press it down with her feet.

'It was Pat McElroy who threw all that paint on Arnold's truck,' Jim said. 'He bragged about it to a couple of his friends at school.'

'It got around?'

'Things have a way of doing that. My son heard about it; he was the one who told the police.'

'Good for Brian.'

'He was disgusted.' Jim shifted from foot to foot.

'It's colder than yesterday,' Gillian said. She wished the weather would stay warm. She liked the smell of the dry grass, Estelle's roses, the feel of the soft dirt, the sun on her arms. She picked up the watering can and began to sprinkle the packed earth.

'Yesterday was almost like summer again. It couldn't last. I want to ask you about something.' Jim sounded uneasy.

She set down the can and looked at him.

'It's about the night we were at Arnold's house, when we were in the darkroom, and the police suddenly arrived, remember?'

She nodded.

'I was putting a binder back on the shelf. A strip of negatives fell out. I was going to put it back, but then Eli started yelling. I got distracted, and I forgot. I forgot all about them. This morning, I found the negatives in my pocket.'

'Can you tell what they're pictures of?'

'Yeah. Girls running. There's a great shot of Nicole.'

Gillian felt lost. 'Nicole. Another picture of her?'

'Yup.'

'Oh God. What—?' Then she stopped. 'But if Simon killed Nicole, it doesn't matter.'

'Exactly. What I wanted to ask you was, what should I do with it?'

'Let me see it.'

He pulled an envelope from his coat pocket and opened it. 'I feel like putting it back—I shouldn't even have it. But I can't take it to Arnold's house now.'

'No.' She stripped off her gardening gloves and grasped the negative strip carefully by the edges. Her fingers were clumsy after digging. She held it up to the light.

Jim felt in another pocket and fished out a magnifying glass. 'Here. Look through this.'

She held the negative up to the bright sky and positioned the glass. It was Nicole, no two ways about it. She wore shorts and a sweatshirt and a Stanton cap; her legs were extended in a long stride, her hair bouncing up from her shoulders.

'Nice shot, you're right. I wonder when he took it.'

'No idea. It probably wasn't anywhere obvious when the police were looking, or they would have found it.'

'How weird.'

'What?'

'He took it, and she disappeared.'

'Yeah.' Jim looked uncomfortable. 'What should I do with it?'

'You'd better give it to Eli. He won't care about it if he's got the case against Simon all tied up, but if there's any room for doubt, you'd be in a peck of trouble for keeping it.'

'That's what I figured. I just wanted to show it to you first.' He took the negatives back and slid them into the envelope.

'What do you think about Simon?'

'He must have been out of his mind. How could he do such a thing? And there was blood all over his car. He loves that Mustang—Brian told me.'

'Is it special?'

'Sort of a collector's item.' A breeze blew a few dead leaves around the garden. 'Time to put the storm windows up,' Jim said.

'Franklin and I can do it.'

'I'll come over next week. You know I like to. Your mother won't take any money for the pasture.'

'Come and have a drink afterwards. You can meet Edward,' Gillian suggested.

'I'd like that. Oh, didn't you tell me you'd seen the semi that turned over last week?'

'That's right. I had to detour to get home.'

'A nurse who works in intensive care at the hospital was at church today. The driver's regained consciousness.'

'I heard from Jean that he was going to be all right. That's good news.'

'He's been talking about a little red sports car—it came out of nowhere, right under his wheels. He swerved, trying to avoid it, and that's when he flipped over.'

'And the car just drove away?'

'It must have. It was nowhere around when the police got there. He thought it was a Miata.'

'Does anyone around here own a car like that?'

'I'm not sure. Brian might know.'

She put her tools away and went back inside to warm up. Edward was upstairs, making calls. Estelle was sitting on the sofa, stroking Rumpole and staring into space. The others were getting ready to go biking. Gillian found Franklin in the hall.

'You talked to her?'

He nodded, frowning hard at a stuck zipper.

'Well?'

'She won't do it,' he said briefly. 'Damn. There's a thread tangled in the teeth.'

'Let me.' Gillian tugged at it. Franklin stood still, like a child being dressed. 'Was she angry?'

'No. She asked me if Lewis had contacted me, though. You were right, he's been pushing her. I thought I would push, but I couldn't. I started to talk about Jasper, and she said don't.' His voice quavered.

The thread pulled free. 'Do you still want to talk about where else she could live?'

'Not today.' He zipped his jacket closed, as Jasper and Audrey came down the stairs, ready to go. 'At Thanksgiving, if you want. I'll take a long weekend.'

Gillian walked into the living room. Rumpole was gone, but Estelle hadn't moved.

'I hope those day lilies will be all right,' Gillian said, sitting down beside her.

'Oh, they'll survive. They're tough,' Estelle said.

'So are you.'

Estelle spread her fingers, bent and swollen at the joints. 'My hands are as knobbly as those roots. I tried to do some gardening last week. I was looking out, and the part that you'd weeded and raked looked so nice, I thought, I'll just go out and do a little deadheading—nothing difficult. I would have liked to weed, but I can't get down low enough. So I went out with my secateurs, and I put on Nat's old boots, and I tried. But I couldn't squeeze the secateurs properly. My hands were too stiff. I just stood there, feeling helpless.'

'Oh.' Gillian flinched, imagining Estelle toppling over, lying in the dirt until Gillian got home, probably hours later. She wouldn't wear an emergency call button.

'I couldn't do anything. I couldn't even keep my balance very well, because the dirt was so soft and Nat's boots are too big for me. They have to be; I need to step into them without bending over. So I went back to the shed to take them off again, and I had a hard time even with that.'

'I thought you weren't going to try that sort of thing when I wasn't here.'

'Well, I did. But I can assure you I won't try again.'

Rumpole appeared in the doorway. He trotted across the room and deposited something on the carpet at Estelle's feet.

'It's not a bird, is it?' she said. 'He's such a blunderpuss he can't usually catch them.'

Gillian bent over and picked up a tiny Lego figure, bright blue and red. She laid it in Estelle's palm. Rumpole jumped up, settling on the sofa cushions with a self-satisfied purr.

'Funny little beast,' Estelle said, her fingers closing over Jasper's toy.

Gillian went away to find Edward. He'd hung up the phone and was stretched on the thick carpet in the bedroom, doing sit-ups.

'At least one mystery is solved,' she said. 'My poor mother. She didn't tell me she'd been adventuring in the garden while I was out. It's not how it would have turned out in Nancy Drew, but Nancy didn't have a mother.'

Edward looked at her blankly, his breath hissing between his teeth as he lifted his shoulders off the floor.

'The footprints in the garden.'

He completed his set and then relaxed. 'Oh, of course. I'd forgotten. Good job it wasn't Pat McElroy, doing a little reconnoitre.'

'I've been meaning to talk to Estelle about locking the doors when she's out. But going out on her own doesn't seem to be in the picture, not for a while. Come downstairs and make a fire, why don't you? It's cold.'

She reached a hand to him, to help him up, but he grasped it and pulled her downward, into the square of sunshine on the rug. 'I'm not cold,' he said smugly. He wasn't. He was warm with exercise, but also with a vital force that burned at a higher temperature than hers. He locked an arm around her and rolled, and she was under him, flattened between the carpet and the weight of his body. She looked into his face, inches from hers, the familiar line of cheekbone, the tiny flecks of light in the brown eyes, crinkles at the corners, the marks of humour and fatigue etched deep. His hands moved under her clothes, and her skin shivered with pleasure, like the pond shivering the moon to ribbons.

'A fire,' he murmured. 'Let's see if I can remember how it's done. Use plenty of kindling, isn't that the trick?'

The phone rang. They ignored it.

'Jo phoned,' Estelle said when they came downstairs. 'I called you but you didn't hear me. She wants to meet you at the Dutch House for a drink. I said you'd call back.'

'Maybe she has news,' Gillian said.

They decided to go before lunch, while the others were still out bicycling.

'What are those chain links?' Edward asked, as they drove into the Dutch House parking lot.

'During the Revolution, we chained off the Hudson, to keep you Brits from sailing up it.'

'Did it work?'

'I believe it was never tested. We built the first submarine, too, to blow your ships out of New York Harbour.'

'And did you?'

'No. It was a one-person sub, and it worked, but attaching the mines to the ships didn't.'

'If the chain wasn't used and the mines didn't work, then how did you contrive to win the war?'

She laughed. 'When I was in school we used to joke that we won because you guys had to wear red coats and march in straight lines. Those chain links are probably fakes, by the way. The ones at West Point are bigger. Remember Bannerman's Island, with the dilapidated castle on it? Bannerman made a bundle of money selling fake links that were part of an old anchor chain. He was in cahoots with a junk dealer who called himself Westminster Abbey.'

'Sounds like *1776 and All That*.'

There weren't many people in the Dutch House yet, but Jo was already sitting in a chair near the fire. At the front, near the door and the draughty windows, the room was cold, but in the back it was cosy. The four-foot logs were throwing off plenty of heat. Frankie was polishing the glasses, watching football on a miniature television behind the bar. Gillian saw the bright screen when they ordered their hot rums, but the sound was off.

'What's the news?' Gillian asked Jo. 'Or would you rather not talk about it?'

'I do want to. That's why I phoned you. The police have found Nicole's father.'

'So he *is* alive.'

'Alive. She didn't lie about her mother, though. Her mother's dead. The police told Margaret she died in a cigarette fire ten years ago. Nicole ran away from home a month later. Her father says he hasn't seen her since.' Jo watched the flames flickering among the logs. 'It's a sad story.'

'Why did she run away?'

'Because she didn't want to be with her father. It was his cigarette that started the fire that killed her mother. Or she thought so.'

'Where was Nicole at the time?' Edward asked.

'Sleeping in the basement. She didn't know a thing until the firemen came and hauled her out. The fire was upstairs.' Jo looked depressed. 'Her father's an alcoholic.'

'Ten years ago. How old was Nicole?'

'Thirteen, as she said.'

Gillian was silent. She'd lost Nat before it seemed fair, but not while she was still a child, not when the loss would shape her whole life. Her story wasn't tragic, Nicole's was. Nicole had lost her mother—and her father, too, since she apparently saw him as a murderer, or the next thing to it. Eli must have gotten that from the tapes; surely Nicole's father wouldn't have told the police why she ran away. It was even possible that he didn't know. On the other hand, Nicole, at thirteen, might well have accused him to his face, if she hated him. Maybe that was why he'd never seen her when she was staying with her aunt. Had he tried? Had he cared?

'He never saw her again? Her own father?'

'She refused. And her father and her aunt—her mother's sister—weren't on speaking terms. She thought he was a loser and her sister never should have married him. She told Nicole that.'

'Still,' Gillian said, 'he couldn't have tried hard, or he would have found some way to see Nicole and talk to her.'

'He told her when she was eight that he didn't want children but her mother had her anyway.'

The fire snapped, and a red coal landed on the apron of stones near their feet.

'I feel so bad,' Jo said. 'Like such a failure. I thought I knew Nicole, and I didn't know anything. I thought I cared about her, but I didn't care enough.'

The bar was slowly filling up. The buzz of conversation in the room was louder, but Jo was speaking in a half whisper. They had to lean forward to hear her.

'Don't feel so guilty,' Gillian said. 'It's not your fault she's dead.'

'But why did she die? And why Simon Steele?' Jo answered miserably. 'Why, why, why?'

'You know he's been arrested?' Gillian said.

'Roberta thought Margaret should know right away. She phoned. She's not coming in tomorrow. Simon's her husband—it must be awful for her.' Jo turned to Edward. 'But did he actually do that to Nicole? And why would he? What do you think?'

He shook his head. 'It's not my case. I'd want a lot of information I don't have before I could answer your questions.' He smiled to soften his refusal. 'If I *were* on the case, I'd be reluctant to answer for other reasons. But I've never even seen Simon. What kind of drunk was he, for example? Did Roberta ever come to work bruised?'

'I never saw any bruises. I don't think she's the kind of woman to take that.' Jo halted. 'But we don't know, do we?' she added uncertainly. 'Lots of women are beaten and are too ashamed to tell anyone. And the clever men hit them where it doesn't show.'

'What's going to happen to Nicole's body?' Gillian asked.

'Her father's coming down to make the arrangements,' Jo said grimly. 'Margaret will have to see him. The college will do what it can to help.'

'Will he want her things?'

'I don't know. He's sure to want the money—whatever's left in the bank.'

'If he doesn't want the things in her room, let me know. Leslie Lang will.'

CHAPTER 23

'You were very circumspect,' Gillian said to Edward as they were driving home.

'I don't mind speculating with you, but other people might take my wild guesses seriously. Remember what you said yesterday about people knowing that using information is my job? I can't make conjectures in public; people will always think there's some authority behind them. Leaving aside my own reputation, think of the harm I might do to innocent suspects.'

'OK, I see your point. But no one can hear us now, unless the car's been bugged. Eli must have found the tapes.'

'Obviously. That would explain how he knew so much about Nicole all of a sudden. Simon's voice will be on them too, and his name. It's inconceivable that she wouldn't have spoken his name.'

'No wonder they were searching Simon's house. But where did they find the tapes?'

'On Nicole, don't you think?'

'But they've had her body for over a week,' Gillian protested.

'And it was soaking in muddy water all night. Those tapes would have needed a lot of lab work if they were going to yield up anything useful.'

'That's true,' Gillian said slowly, 'but surely if Simon killed her, he would have pocketed those tapes. Destroyed them, too. If he didn't, he was out of his mind.'

'You wouldn't believe the cack-handedness of killers. The amateurs, that is. They make the most astounding errors when they lose control. I had a case once in which the perp left his wallet at the scene of the crime because he changed his coat in a hurry. And Simon was three sheets to the wind.'

'But Roberta said he looked for the tapes all weekend. How do you explain that?'

'He might not have been certain that Nicole found them. Suppose he only woke up after she'd got them, and *then* they had their row. If he was drunk, and he killed her and then became desperate to get rid of the body, he could have dumped her in the car and driven straight to the bridge.'

'You mean without thinking of the tapes until afterwards?'

'Yes. Would he dare go back to the body? Besides, if he's like most people, he'd wonder whether he'd put them away in the wrong place. Suppose she ransacked his study; he'd have had a job trying to find them. How would he be sure they were gone?'

Gillian tried to picture this. Nicole frantically hunting in the bedroom—the study?—emptying drawers, with Simon sprawled on the sofa in the next room, or perhaps even snoring on the bed while she searched the night-table beside it. Nicole hurrying, her heart pounding. Maybe she knocked something over. He woke suddenly, saw her ransacking the room, jumped up, tried to grab her and missed ... If Nicole had been hit over the head with a bottle, or cracked her skull on a coffee table, the elements of the story would hang together. It was harder to believe that Simon had picked up a knife and used it. Unless Nicole had tried to fend him off and it had gone wrong. But surely they must have fought about the tapes?

'Think about the bicycle,' Edward said. 'He forgot that, too, or it would have been under the bridge with the body.

He only saw it when he returned, and he had to get rid of it. So he did the simplest possible thing—wheeled it a little way down the road and left it.'

'And where does the scarf come in?'

'The scarf doesn't fit. But why does it have to come in? It may have nothing to do with the case.'

'But if it does, then the problem looks different. And I'm worried about his car. If he didn't kill her in the car, why did he let it get bloody? If he was *compos* enough to get rid of the body he must have known it would be stupid to get blood on the car.'

Edward shrugged. 'He was in a hurry, and he wasn't sober. Besides, how else would he get rid of her? He wouldn't throw her over his shoulder and walk down the road.'

'And another thing. Roberta fed him whisky to get him talking, and he'd had a concussion. Do you really think that in his condition he'd be able to make up a story to fit the facts? It seems possible to me that he told the truth, or some of it.'

'That he found Nicole dead?' Edward raised an eyebrow. 'You're the one who didn't want Arnold to be guilty. If you reject the case against Simon, don't we go back to Arnold?'

'Not necessarily, though I suppose he can't be ruled out,' she said, thinking of the negatives Jim had found. 'The killer could be someone who hated Simon Steele. If Simon didn't kill Nicole, then maybe whoever did it tried to frame Simon for the murder.'

'"Do not on any account attempt to write on both sides of the paper at once,"' Edward murmured.

'I'm serious. If he told the truth about finding her, then one reason she could have been in his car was that someone wanted her found there. Simon was on a binge; everyone knows his pattern; with any luck he wouldn't have discovered her body for another day, even two. There would already have been a hue and cry, a search for her.'

'All right, it's a hypothesis,' Edward said. 'Then whoever hated Simon followed Nicole to the house and watched her break in, saw that Simon was out cold, and seized the opportunity?'

'Yes, but this person already knew Nicole was seeing Simon—that was why they followed her.'

'Who, another lover?'

'I have to admit, I wish one would come out of the woodwork. Unless one of her clients was more than a client, there's only one person I can think of who has violent feelings about Simon and would hate Nicole for having an affair with him.'

'You mean Simon's wife, don't you? Roberta.'

'I'm afraid so. I wish I didn't.' Gillian's voice was troubled.

'She's a friend of yours.'

'Well, I haven't known her long. Not like Peggy or Jo. But I liked her right away. She's a wonderful person at work—energetic, competent, always taking trouble for people, always patient. It may have been a very different story at home, but it's a real shock to think that she might be capable of lethal violence.'

'And deception.'

'Yes, she would have been manipulating me all along. It would be less hateful to think that Simon did it.'

'What makes you suspect her?'

'I don't exactly suspect her. I just—'

'Just what?'

'I can't prove anything.'

'I shouldn't worry about that,' Edward said. 'She can't hear you and neither can Eli. Nobody but me will know you're out on a limb.'

'All right. It's a lot of little things. Her recent behaviour hasn't been in character. I thought she was feeling rocky because she's so torn about her divorce, but what if there's another interpretation? Why did she take me with her when she went to get the cheque? That was odd. What if the form she wanted me to sign was a pretext to bring me to her office at the right time? She never mixed up that sort of detail. It's possible that Roberta wanted a witness. I remember thinking she was pressing Simon's buttons—at the time I put it down to sheer animosity. But she pointed out the mended window to me first; she didn't have to do that. And she asked him about the car, too. This was a week after the murder, and the police were showing no interest in Simon—if she was waiting for him to be arrested, it would have been driving her up the wall.'

'And why did she want you along?'

'For protection, if he suspected her, I suppose—she was dubious about his motives for inviting her to come and pick up the cheque. And I would be useful as a witness who could testify to the broken window and to Simon's reactions. The Mustang was hidden in the garage, but she taunted him about it, almost as if she wanted to make sure I noticed that.'

'So you think she could have followed Nicole to the house?'

'If she did, and she got there, and found Nicole in the house and Simon blotto, then she might have confronted Nicole. Sexual jealousy makes people do crazy things, and Roberta's outbursts of temper at home have been pretty spectacular. If things escalated, and Roberta killed her, then letting Simon look like the murderer -' she trailed off.

'Would kill two birds with one stone?' Edward supplied. 'Perhaps. But why assume they had an argument? If Roberta knew Nicole and Simon were having an affair, and she was bent on revenge, she could have gone to the house with the intention of killing Nicole and making Simon look like the guilty party.'

'I guess it's possible. It seems so calculating. But I'll tell you what's been puzzling me: Nicole was tall and strong, even if she was thin, and she had street smarts. She wouldn't have been that easy to kill, unless she was taken by surprise. How could Simon have done that? She would have kept an eye on him. But if Roberta planned to kill her and waited for her outside—in the dark—if she attacked from behind, Nicole wouldn't have had much of a chance.'

'And do you have ideas about the scarf?'

'If Eli's interested in the scarf because it played a part in the crime, then I don't see how Simon can be the killer. He lost that scarf, and if he found it again and used it, he wouldn't bury it by his own driveway. He'd burn it or dispose of it somewhere else. I bet someone buried that scarf so it would be found—hoping it would be identified as Simon's.'

'Rather a stretch, after a year.'

'It was very distinctive. He'd also made a fuss about it.'

'And someone had to keep it all that time. You don't have to fit the scarf into your theory just because Eli Pink put it in a bag with a label.' Edward grinned. 'There's no accounting for what the police find interesting. We have to sniff at every lamppost.'

'OK, forget the scarf. Think about Roberta: she's furious about his book. It humiliated her. She feels he painted a false picture of her and destroyed her character. But she certainly hasn't detached herself emotionally—if she did find out about Nicole, she would have been madly jealous. She knew his drinking pattern better than anybody. Jim told me Simon adored his car. Roberta would have known that as well. Leaving the body in the Mustang looks like revenge to me.'

'Could she do all that without falling apart afterwards?'

'You saw her in an unusual state—if it was real. She's known for her organizational skills and her ironclad composure. She also goes to a gym regularly—she's very fit.' Gillian took her eyes off the road briefly to look at Edward. It was a relief to talk to him, to someone with his experience, who would make no hysterical claims for A's innocence or B's guilt, someone who understood her, to whom she would trust her life. His face wore the half-frown of concentration that she'd seen in her mind when Peggy asked what he looked like.

'Let's look at this from another angle,' he said. 'What's helpful about your theory is that it puts the action outside, and the evidence you've been told about—the blood in the car, the scarf, if you like—doesn't take us inside the house. At most, it takes us to the front door, where we have the broken glass. If you really want to review alternatives to Simon, then the field extends beyond Roberta. Why shouldn't the villain be Arnold? Suppose he was obsessed with Nicole.'

'I find it hard to suppose that,' Gillian said. 'He was a gentle oddball, not one of those loonies who slice up prostitutes.' She heard the tension in her own voice and stopped. She was doing exactly what she was grateful to Edward for not doing—getting upset about a theory. 'And I believe he went to the woods at Stanton to look for owls,' she said in a more neutral tone, 'because Gordon Hornbeck talked to him about them.'

'Is there any evidence he took pictures of owls?'

'Not that I know of. But, Edward, I've only just thought, after he took that picture of Nicole, he would hardly have started popping off flash bulbs in the woods behind the dorm.'

'All right, perhaps not, and perhaps he didn't know about the dorm until he got there. Just bear with me. He might have had a side you never glimpsed. He saw Nicole naked in a window. It does happen occasionally—a man becomes erotically fixated on a woman he's never met. Didn't you tell me Eli said she looks like you, when you were Nicole's age, and that Arnold didn't want to talk about you? Maybe that's got something to do with it.'

'Jesus, Edward, I don't want to hear that.'

'You think I like the idea?'

'Anyhow, she doesn't look much like me. Eli could have said we were the same type just to needle me.'

'Fine, set aside whatever Eli said. Arnold sees Nicole naked. He sees her passing on Dykeman's Pond Road, with the running team. He takes more photographs. He also sees her go by on her bicycle, alone, and he follows her to Simon's. He peeps through the windows, perhaps he even sees them have sex. Suppose he does this several times. He's torturing himself, but he can't stop spying on her. He broods. This time, he watches for her, and follows her, and when she comes out of Simon's house, he's waiting. He attacks her. Perhaps his intentions are confused, but in the event, he kills her. He knows nothing about the tapes, and he doesn't look in her pockets.'

'Why does he put her in the car?'

'Perhaps he didn't. She may have tried to get into the car and lock it, to get away from him. Without the lab reports, we can only guess.'

'And the scarf? How did he get hold of Simon's scarf? He couldn't have been at that party. He wouldn't have gone, even if he'd been invited.'

'Suppose Simon dropped it after the party, and Arnold found it on the road early in the morning. He seems to have been the sort who wanders about at odd hours.'

'Would he have known it was Simon's?'

'Buggeration!' Edward sounded suddenly exasperated. 'We don't have enough information. We're reading tea leaves.'

Gillian chuckled. 'You coppers are spoilt rotten—you get all those lab reports, and postmortems, and witnesses telling you things, you don't 'ardly have to rub two brain cells together, do you? The cases solve themselves.'

Edward reached over and mussed her hair. 'Don't tell anybody, but all we do is write reports.'

Gillian drove for a couple of minutes in silent thought. They were nearly home. 'I wish I could steal Eli's notes. We do need more information. If Roberta or Arnold stabbed Nicole, what did they stab her with? Would either of them be carrying a weapon? Arnold would have seen her going by on her bike, and Roberta could have seen her leaving the campus, but neither of them could have been sure she was going to Simon's. This killing seems opportunistic to me, like theft from a house with an open window. Even if Roberta wanted her revenge, I can't picture her packing a knife in her purse, waiting for the chance.'

'The same problem arises in Simon's case, unless he happened to be boning a chicken when they had their fight.'

Gillian turned off the road into the gravel driveway, but stopped at the bottom. 'Edward! The window! Simon's broken window! The glass! Shards of glass!'

'As the weapon? The killer would have cut his hand to ribbons on it.'

'Not if his—or her—hand was wrapped in a scarf. *Simon's* scarf.'

Edward looked dubious. 'It would be harder to manage than a knife with a handle.'

'But it would do the job.'

'I'd have to see the pathologist's report. A narrow piece could have been driven into her throat, with force behind the blow. It wouldn't have to go very deep for her to lose a lot of blood. But it would be a nasty bit of work to hold it and a struggling victim.'

'And the hole might look messier than a knife wound.'

'Very likely.'

Gillian touched her foot to the pedal and the car rumbled gently up the driveway to her usual parking spot. 'What did you think of Eli, by the way?'

'I wouldn't want him on my team.'

'Why not?'

'He'd be an irritant. And who'd tell him anything useful? He antagonizes people.'

'Ah! The penetrating eye of Detective Chief Inspector Gisborne! Do you know what they say at the Yard?'

'What?' Edward asked warily.

'They say: DCI Gisborne writes his reports with a sharp pencil.'

'I use a computer.'

'What is the world coming to? Computers, central heating—your soldiers probably don't even march in straight lines any more.'

Lunch, a haphazard array of delicatessen favourites, was delicious, but Gillian had a hard time paying attention.

'Beam her down, Edward,' Franklin said at one point. 'I've asked her for the bread twice.'

'What? Sorry,' Gillian said. 'I was thinking.'

'When you were little,' Estelle said, 'you sometimes stopped still with your fork in midair, like playing statues. I've got a picture of you in one of the albums.'

'I'll bet it wasn't when she was eating dessert,' Franklin said.

'No, I think it was broccoli.'

'I don't like broccoli,' Jasper announced.

'But it looks so pretty,' said Estelle. 'Like little trees.'

'People don't eat trees,' Jasper said witheringly.

'Hah,' Estelle replied. 'And who had pancakes with maple syrup this morning?'

Nimbly, he changed targets. 'Your paper towels are white,' he said accusingly to Gillian. 'You should get the brown ones.'

She was caught off guard. 'They're hard to find around here.'

'*We* have brown ones. Brown ones don't use bleach.'

Gillian's eyes met Edward's across the table. He was looking amused. 'You're awfully quiet,' she said.

'I was sharpening my pencil.'

In the late afternoon, Franklin and Audrey loaded the bicycles on the roof of their car and drove away, Jasper waving through the rear window until they were out of sight.

Estelle said, 'I think I need a little sherry.'

Edward put down the Sunday *Times* and stood up. 'I'll get it.'

Estelle, in search of further consolation, sifted through her stacks of flower catalogues. 'We should plant some more roses,' she said, half to herself. 'Parson's Pink China, I wouldn't mind another one of those. They still bloom when the rest fade.'

Gillian was curled in the window seat, looking out at the dimming light of the afternoon, the trees etched against a charcoal sky. Eli had told her Nicole was stabbed, but he hadn't revealed anything about the big bruises Maya and Lynn said they saw on her neck. No one heard Nicole scream, though the Hornbecks had often heard Roberta shouting at Simon. The scarf was connected to the crime. If the scarf was used to choke Nicole unconscious, then the glass could have been an afterthought. It would have been easy to use, if Nicole had already stopped fighting. Maybe Roberta—or Arnold, or Simon—thought Nicole was dead, and then she started to revive. Any one of them might have panicked at that, but only Roberta might have wanted to spoil the car. A Mustang was the kind of car men identified with when they wanted to pretend they were young. A Freudian theory of the crime would discuss the bloodied Mustang as an act of symbolic castration. And would be of no earthly use to anybody.

Simon was the prime suspect. He had to be, given the evidence. Nevertheless, he might be innocent. If the disturbance roused him, then what? He'd see the broken glass, just as he told Roberta, and lurch out to investigate, perhaps just after the killer left. He'd find Nicole's body. In his car. A shock of that magnitude can produce an illusion of sobriety, Gillian reflected, and the power to act. He could have chosen to call the police. But he probably touched her and got blood on his hands, possibly his clothes. He might even have wondered whether he'd killed her. In that case, he would have been terrified of calling the police.

'I talked to TZ Brewster this morning, while you were out,' Estelle said, breaking in on Gillian's thoughts. 'She called to see how my ankle was—Alice told her I'd had a fall.'

'Nice of her to call,' Gillian said inattentively. Edward brought her a glass of sherry.

'Yes, but that's not why I mentioned it,' Estelle said. 'TZ told me something interesting, but I didn't want to talk about it earlier. *Pas devant les enfants.*'

'Yes, Jasper's got sharp little ears. What did TZ tell you?'

'It's about Arnold. I was rather upset when you told me that the sad business about Tommy Mitchell had been dragged up—remember you said Alice had mentioned it?'

'So did Eli.'

'Well, I asked TZ about it, and she told me there was no doubt that Arnold was at home when Tommy was out hunting and got killed. There was no question of it having anything to do with Arnold.'

'How does she know?'

'Marsh told Beau, at the time. Marsh knew, because he was a judge, you see,' Estelle explained to Edward, 'and he and Beau Brewster were very close. Virginia—that's Arnold's mother—was away, visiting her own mother, I think, or maybe her sister was having a baby. Anyhow, Booter brought a woman home with him the night before it happened.'

'A woman!' Gillian said. 'You mean a -'

'Exactly. He was the kind of man who would do a thing like that. Bring home floozies.'

'Where is Booter now?' interrupted Edward.

'Dead,' Gillian said. 'Natural causes, if you call galloping cirrhosis natural. It's amazing that nobody murdered *him*. What about this woman, Mother?'

'She was still there the next day, even after Booter left, TZ said. She was drinking coffee in the kitchen in a pink robe with lace trim. That's what the doctor said. So Arnold wasn't home alone when the accident happened. But they told Arnold not to mention her, and nothing was said about the woman at the inquest, because the death *was* an accident, and nobody wanted to hurt Virginia any worse than she'd been hurt already.'

'They kept it quiet?'

'Virginia had just lost her son, for heaven's sake. And the doctor said it was an accident, it was clear as day.'

'So poor Arnold was left to be haunted by vague rumours.'

'Nobody believed them.'

'Not until Eli Pink starts investigating another case thirty years later and thinks Arnold's a killer who never got caught. Poor Arnold. The furies seem to have been after him since the day he was born.'

Gillian swallowed the last of her sherry and stared out at the countryside. It was getting dark fast.

'What puzzles me,' Estelle said a few minutes later, 'is how TZ can remember all that when she never can remember what's trump.' She twisted sideways with difficulty and switched on a lamp beside the sofa.

'Have you told Estelle about the scarf?' Edward asked.

'No, why don't you tell her? You were there.'

He did. Gillian listened, still in a black mood about Arnold.

'The scarf belonged to Simon Steele, according to Carrie Pilgrim,' Edward finished up, 'but he lost it, a year ago, at a New Year's Eve party given by Alice Nelson.'

'What a good memory for names you have,' Estelle said.

'Does Alice give a party every year?'

'Oh, no, not any more. The previous one she gave must have been four or five years ago. I always go. I nearly didn't, this year, because the roads were icy, but Lewis and Kitty brought me. Kitty's very thoughtful.'

'Who was at the party?'

'Everyone, I suppose. It's hard to remember. Simon and Roberta, the Hornbecks, TZ. Not Beau, he was dead by then. A lot of neighbours from Dykeman's Pond Road. Carrie was there, she wore an ostrich feather boa she'd found in a trunk.'

'Your memory's better than mine,' Edward laughed.

'It's got a mind of its own,' Estelle said darkly.

'Do you know anyone who has a red Miata?' Gillian asked, from her perch on the window seat.

Estelle peered at her. 'I can't see you, dear. It's too dark over there. What's a Miata?'

CHAPTER 24

On Monday morning, the frost was white on the shed roof, and the water in the bird bath was filmed with ice. The last hollyhock bloom had withered.

'Winter's coming,' Estelle said. 'I hate winter. I'm always cold. Do you suppose Paula's mended any of those sweaters yet?'

'I can go and see,' Gillian offered. 'Edward's got to prepare for his conference this morning; I'll go while he's working. Do you want anything from Jean's?'

'Batteries,' Estelle said. 'My flashlight is getting terribly dim. And could you check the emergency candles? I always like to have a box, in case the power goes in an ice storm.'

'Should I go moose hunting while I'm at it? Lay in a meat supply? Jim's coming over to put up the storm windows this week. I'm sure he can butcher a moose.'

The road was slithery in spots, but would be dry later in the morning. Frost shadows lay on the lawns, tracing the shapes of barns and trees. The puddles in Jean's parking lot had dried up.

'Estelle says winter's coming,' Gillian announced when she saw Jean.

'I could have told you that last summer,' Jean retorted. She ripped open a carton of Winstons and filled one of the wooden slots on the wall behind the counter. The shop was empty of customers. 'I've got a special on Prestologs this week.'

'Jim splits our firewood for us.'

'That's right, I forgot. Here, come and see what I've got.' She moved to the end of the counter near the window display. On the floor, open but unpacked, was a big cardboard box. 'Gaggia,' Gillian read.

She looked at Jean, dumbstruck.

'It's a cappuccino machine,' Jean said.

'I know.'

'I got it second-hand, but the owners only had it for a couple of months. Then their building was sold; they lost their lease. As soon as I install it, they're going to give me lessons.'

'Jean, that's wonderful. It's revolutionary. But please, promise me one thing. Don't take the Christmas lights out of your window or I won't recognize the place.'

'Don't worry.' Jean laughed. 'Those lights aren't moving until I do. And I'm not leaving anytime soon. The thing is, I need more help these days. If I've got to have somebody in anyway, then I can have one of these machines. Never could before; they take too much time if you're running the shop by yourself. Fancy coffee will bring some of the new people in. At least I think so—and you've got to gamble a little in life, right?'

'Sounds like a sure bet.'

'That's the only kind I like.' Jean glanced at the old coffee machine; the last drops were drizzling into a fresh pot. She poured two cups. 'Did you hear the news this morning? About that truck accident? The semi?'

'Not another one!'

'No, no. The one that happened a couple of weeks ago.'

'The last I heard the driver was going to be OK.'

'Yes, he's awake—out of the coma. And he's been talking. Looks like he crashed because he was trying not to hit another car. Janice Grogan's little sports car.'

'Janice Grogan? What kind of car does she have? All I've heard is something about a Miata.'

'Miata. That's the name. I couldn't think of it. Janice Grogan has a red Miata. Looks like a toy. The truck driver started blabbing about a little red sports car as soon as he woke up. It drove straight on to the highway, practically under his wheels. That kid's lucky to be alive. Little car like that would have been squashed flat if the truck hadn't swerved. She wouldn't have had a chance. The driver said he just about had a heart attack when he saw the car go straight through the stop sign. Accident squad's been checking it out. Asked everybody up and down the highway whether they saw the sports car go by. Ray's wife was just leaving the store—she goes home around seven-thirty or eight, except at Christmas when they're too busy.'

'The liquor store.'

'That's right; it's not even a mile down the Post Road from where the accident happened. She was outside, and she saw Janice Grogan go by. She was looking up the road because she'd heard some kind of a noise. She thinks it was probably the truck's brakes. Janice was going way too fast, she said.'

'She told the police that?'

'Yup. So then they went and had a look at the car.'

'And?'

'And it had a brand new fender.'

'You're kidding.'

'I swear to God.'

'That doesn't sound good.'

'No. And that's not the whole story. They've already found the old fender.'

'Where?'

'A body shop in Poughkeepsie. Janice Grogan might be charged. Reckless driving and leaving the scene of an accident.'

'The police must have some proof, then. Red paint on the truck, probably.'

'Y'know, that truck driver could have died.'

'Janice must have panicked.'

'Yeah, OK, but the guy's been in the hospital for over a week. She's had time to think twice. And so have her parents. But Kitty went with her when she took the car to the body shop.'

'Oh. You think Kitty tried to protect her? But maybe she didn't tell her mother about the truck. Maybe she said she got dented in a parking lot.'

'Nah.' Jean picked up a damp cloth and swabbed the counter. 'Nobody heard a thing about that little Miata until the truck driver woke up. And we would've. Parents don't pay for their kids' car repairs without bitching. It's the kind of thing people talk about. Nope, the Grogans were keeping it quiet.'

'The cops must have put in some overtime finding the body shop.'

'A lot of phone calls. But those cars—Miatas—aren't that common around here.'

'They're certain it was Janice driving it?'

'Who else? Ann knows the car; it wouldn't have been Kitty behind the wheel.'

'No, but why would Janice be driving so recklessly?'

Jean shrugged. 'If I had a dollar for every accident around here that was caused by kids driving like lunatics, I could retire.'

Was that why Janice had seemed so desperate when Gillian and Edward had seen her—because she'd heard that the truck driver had said something about a little red car? Gillian finished her coffee, bought batteries, candles and matches, and promised to come in and sample Jean's cappuccino as soon as the machine was up and running. Nothing stays the same, she thought, with entirely mixed feelings, as she drove away.

She decided to stop in at Stanton and see how Roberta was doing. It was confusing to like her and feel sorry for her and at the same time to wonder whether one was being a complete fool. Gillian could mention Janice's accident, see how Roberta reacted. Last night, when she'd asked Estelle if she knew anyone with a Miata, she'd been wondering if there could be a connection between the Miata and Nicole's murder, and whether Eli was working on this possibility. The timing was right. And if the truck driver said the Miata 'came out of nowhere,' then the only place that it could have come from was the bottom of Dykeman's Pond Road. Nothing else joined the Post Road at that point, not even a driveway. It was a T-junction, there was a stop sign at the bottom, and there was no problem with limited vision; anything coming up or down the main road was obvious. She knew the intersection well enough; she passed it every time she drove north on the Post Road from Salt Hill.

What could Janice have been doing on Dykeman's Pond Road that had upset her so much that she'd ploughed straight on to the highway under the wheels—and presumably the lights—of an oncoming semi? Had she been in a rage? Jo said Janice followed Nicole around like a puppy. Maybe it wasn't Roberta who was jealous. What if Janice had been in love with Nicole, with secret hopes that were smashed when she found out about Nicole and Simon? She would have felt betrayed, especially if she'd built her fantasies on some friendly gestures from Nicole. Rumour said Janice had once tried to set fire to her parents' house. Was she capable of violence? Gillian considered Janice's mutinous silences, her sudden shifts of tone, her awkward intensity, her surprising skill on horseback. There was certainly a turbulent personality living in that muscular little body.

Roberta was in her office. She looked tired.

'I didn't get a lot of sleep last night,' she said. 'I was thinking about Simon. If he hadn't written that stupid book, none of this would have happened. He would never have met Nicole.'

'You think he's guilty, then?'

'I can't believe it. But I don't want to. You know what's funny? When everybody thought I was the biggest bitch in New York because of what Simon wrote, I wanted them to know what a prick he was. Now everybody thinks he's a murderer, and I feel worse than when they thought I was a bitch. I don't want to be married to a murderer.'

'Does Josh know his father's been arrested?'

'Not yet. I took him to stay with his grandparents for a few days. I was afraid some idiot at school might say something to him. But he'll have to know soon, unless the police find out that someone else did it.'

'I was just at Jean's. She told me Janice Grogan's in trouble over the accident on the highway that happened the night of the murder.'

'Jean always knows what's going on. Kitty was here this morning. She's pulled Janice out of school for a couple of weeks. She hardly said a word to us—just that Janice had to come home while they straightened things out.'

'I wonder what Janice was doing on Dykeman's Pond Road. It's not the shortest route from the college to the Post Road—or anywhere else.'

'Maybe she was looking for her father.'

'Looking for Lewis? Why would she look for him up there?'

'He uses a cottage on Dykeman's. A doctor friend of his bought it two or three years ago, but he lives in Ohio and only comes once in a while. Lewis uses it as a getaway.'

'A getaway from what?'

Roberta shrugged. 'Who knows? The immaculate Kitty, maybe. I steer clear of Lewis. He made a major pass at me last year. I couldn't believe it at first, and then I wondered if I would have to quit my job. He's not the kind to take a subtle hint, and I had a feeling he could be a mean son-of-a-bitch if I was too blunt and dented his ego.'

Gillian was thinking of how it would feel to be the object of Lewis Grogan's desire. Her face showed it.

'Yeah, ugh,' Roberta said. 'I kept thinking, "Why me?"'

'You're still here, though. You must have handled it well.'

'I had to be pretty direct, but when I was, he took it like a gentleman. He's not such a bad guy. It started with him asking me to do some extra work for him. That's how I know about the cottage—because he said I should come there, it would be easier than driving over to his house. It seemed sensible—it was before I left Simon, and I could nip out briefly and leave Josh at home. But then Lewis started offering me a glass of wine when I got there, and saying he knew it couldn't be easy being married to Simon. I fell into the trap—I was mad at Simon, and I yakked about it too much. Things just kept drifting in the wrong direction. So I stopped meeting him at the cottage. Then he started showing up more often at Stanton, making excuses to come into the office, and he was always touching me, you know? Finally, I said, "Look, you've got a wrong number. I don't care if you fire me, but I'm *never* going to bed with you." He pretended it was all in my imagination, but I know it wasn't. Anyway, he let it drop. He hasn't bothered me since then. At least, I think he hasn't.'

'What do you mean?'

Roberta looked uneasy. 'I thought I saw him once, in the trees behind our house. But I'm not sure. I could have imagined it—or, who knows, it could have been Arnold. Lewis is not the kind of man to stand in the dark waiting for a glimpse of me in my underwear.'

Gillian agreed. Lewis wasn't that kind.

'I never told Simon,' Roberta added. 'I was sure he'd say something nasty.'

'Not as nasty as Kitty, if she found out.'

Roberta laughed faintly. 'You may be right.'

Gillian stayed to chat for a few more minutes, then left the college and headed for the cleaners, her mind busy with Roberta's story. Could she have made it up? Not the part about the cottage, but Lewis's sexual interest in her. Gillian couldn't see what Roberta would gain by inventing such a tale. And her reactions had seemed genuine. So, suppose it was true. What did it matter? Communities were so complicated. Wherever you looked under the surface, there was a lot more going on than was obvious. The story probably had nothing to do with the murder, unless Roberta was deliberately creating confusion—inventing tales of Peeping Toms, or worse. She'd told Gillian a lot about Simon; maybe she thought now that she should have been more reticent. It was impossible to be sure.

What about Janice and her car? If she'd followed Nicole to Simon's and seen something happen there, she would have told the police. It wasn't credible that the accident would make her conceal such a thing. But she'd said nothing. Ergo, she'd seen nothing. On the other hand, if she herself had killed Nicole, she'd have a very powerful reason for keeping quiet about the accident. The news that the truck driver had remembered her car would have been devastating. Was it possible? What role had Lewis and Kitty played? Did they suspect? Did Janice kill Nicole and then go rushing home? Or to the cottage for help? She might resent her parents, but they'd protected her before. She would have a pretty shrewd idea of how they'd react and what their powers were. Did Lewis take charge, tell her to clean up and drive home? Cover up the crime, the way Kitty covered up Janice's role in the accident? Gillian jumped. That could be *why* they'd tried to conceal the Miata's damaged fender. They didn't want anyone asking questions about what Janice was doing on Dykeman's Pond Road that night. Somebody ought to have a look around Lewis's little getaway, Gillian thought. If Janice went to see him the night of the murder, Lewis would have removed any obvious traces, but some tiny clue might be left—it was hard to sterilize a scene, once it was contaminated with evidence.

Her next stop was the cleaners. On the way, she indulged in some unkind thoughts about Lewis Grogan. Lewis, who was arrogant and liked to bully people and tell them what they ought to do. How would he like being exposed as a man who would conceal evidence implicating his daughter in a crime? How many boards of governors would find him a desirable member then? Well, maybe most of them, Gillian conceded. The courts might not prove that he and Kitty knew the truth. He would deny it. And there was Kitty's money.

Gillian felt sorrier for Kitty. If Janice had killed Nicole in a violent fit of anger or jealousy, it was a tragedy, and whatever wrong Kitty had done, Gillian was pretty sure she'd never recover from the blow. Lewis wouldn't suffer in the same way. He was too convinced of his own singular value.

At the cleaners, Gillian asked for Paula, who was in the back. While she waited, she watched the automated rack running the clothes in their shiny bags around a track attached to the high ceiling. The clerk punched in a number, and the bags traveled along the track until the correctly numbered bag arrived at the front counter, where it stopped, like a train at a station. The space below the track was used for ironing and mending and folding, and the high ceiling let the heat rise. It was an efficient design, she thought, though the air was still hot and dry and smelled of cleaning fluids and the scorched odour of ironing. The women she could see working were dressed for the heat in thin shirts with short sleeves. She knew their faces and some of their names—Marie, Paula, Sandra. They'd been working here for years.

Paula appeared, her stooped shoulders more bent than usual. She had a worried, apologetic expression on her face.

'Please tell Estelle I'm sorry, the sweaters aren't ready yet. I thought I'd have two of them fixed, maybe all of them, today or tomorrow. They're cleaned, but I haven't been able to do any mending.' She held out her right hand, the fingers spread, the skin on the knuckles dry and chapped. The forefinger was swollen and red. 'It's getting better now, but it was just terrible for a couple of days. I couldn't hardly use my hand. It was too sore.'

'A cut?'

'A splinter. Not wood, though. A great big silver of glass. Sharp as a needle. It went right in under my nail. Hurt like dammit, I can tell you. I couldn't get it out. Couldn't even wiggle it.' Paula inspected her finger and shuddered, remembering the pain.

'What did you do?'

'I went to the emergency room. May had to drive me, it was touching a nerve; I was almost crazy with it. They took it out, but it broke, and it wasn't easy to get it all. They gave me some stuff to put on it. One good thing, I was worried about the bill they'd send me, but insurance will cover it, because I got injured on the job.'

'How did it happen?'

Paula's round, good-natured face flushed with indignation. 'Stuck my hand in a pocket, checking for tissues, you know, anything left there, and jammed my finger right on to the splinter. The things people leave in their pockets! The doctor was going to throw it away, but I saved it, because I'm going to show it to Kitty Grogan next time she comes in. What's Dr. Grogan doing sending things to the cleaners with broken glass in the pockets? He should know better. Isn't that right?' She looked around for confirmation at the other women within hearing distance. They chorused their agreement. The subject had been thoroughly discussed.

'Kitty brought the jacket in to be cleaned, and she wanted me to sew a new button on it; he'd lost a button off one sleeve. She brought another button in; he gets his tweed jackets from some fancy tailor in London, and they give them a bag of extra buttons, Kitty says. They're horn buttons, not plastic.'

'Broken glass. Was that last week? I saw Kitty here when I brought the sweaters in. She showed me a button you sewed on.'

'That was it,' Paula said. 'I sewed the button on before I went through the pockets, so the job got done. She picked the things up last week, but I didn't say anything because the boss was here. Kitty's a big customer; I knew if I had to stand there with him trying to keep me quiet and telling her it was nothing, I'd go nuts. I don't want to be fired, I just want to show her the size of that splinter and give her a piece of my mind.'

'When did Kitty bring the jacket in?'

'The Friday before. I wouldn't forget—everybody was talking about that murder over on Dykeman's Pond Road. They found the poor dead girl the day before.' Paula shook her head. 'Anyways, I've got to get back to work. Tell Estelle I'm sorry about the sweaters not being done. Maybe Wednesday.'

Gillian reeled out of the cleaners and flopped down in the driver's seat of her car.

'What the hell can it mean?' she muttered. Could the glass be glass from Simon's broken window? What was it doing in Lewis's jacket? Had he found it? What had he planned to do with it? Kitty had brought the jacket to the cleaners; she hadn't known the glass was in the pocket. She couldn't have had any worries connected to the jacket, or she wouldn't have shown it to Gillian. Could Janice have been wearing it? How much had she told her parents? Would they have an inkling of the truth if she hadn't told them? They might believe that Simon was the killer, and the accident and the murder were separate events that merely happened to occur on the same night. Had Janice gone to Lewis's cottage? That would be worth knowing. Bugger, Gillian thought. Edward was right about the tea leaves.

Now what? She had to tell Eli about the splinter of glass, like it or not. He was the detective on the case, he had access to the police lab where they could prove whether the splinter came from Simon's front door and matched anything they'd found on Nicole's body.

She started the car, and drove south on the Post Road until she came to the Dykeman's Pond turn-off. She took it. Roberta had told her where the driveway to the cottage was; she wanted to look at it.

CHAPTER 25

She cruised past Beacon, wondering if the police had finished searching Simon's house. There were no signs of unusual activity today. Then she slowed. The second driveway on the right, Roberta had said. The first one was short; the house was near the road. No cars were parked there. She drove another fifty yards, to the next opening. She peered through the trees. The cottage was further back, the end of the drive invisible from the road. She had almost come to a halt when she saw Lewis's Mercedes bumping through the woods, coming from the cottage towards the road. Hurriedly, she stepped on the gas, following the road downhill to Dee's Pond and the bridge where Nicole's body had been discovered. She climbed the next rise, passing Arnold's driveway. A moment later, she saw the Mercedes in her mirror. Lewis drove fast, and his car could handle the curves. For a couple of minutes he rode her tail, and she cursed his impatience. Then, at the junction with Croft, he turned right and sped away, probably towards the college, she supposed.

She should go home. She should go home and phone Eli. Instead, she turned the car around and drove back up the way she had come. This was an opportunity too good to miss. She parked on Beacon. She didn't want to leave the Buick in the cottage driveway. The road was empty, the residents hidden in their private, forested domains. She slipped out of the seat unobserved and walked back down Dykeman's until she came to the cottage driveway. She looked up and down the road. There was no traffic coming. She turned quickly and walked at a smart pace down the hard-packed gravel. The drive curved to the right, and then she saw the cottage.

It was a pleasant little place, very new, about the size of one of the guesthouses on the large estates. There was no view of the river, but if seclusion was what you wanted, there was plenty. She walked up to the front windows and peered in. It looked perfectly ordinary. A nice kitchen, with sliding glass doors, a living room with a stone fireplace. She walked around to the back and found a bedroom. The blinds were down to keep the sun out, but she could see around the edges. The bed was made; the bureau and tabletops were bare. If Lewis worked at the cottage, he left few traces. But perhaps the study was upstairs where the computer and the fax couldn't be seen from outside. The house had an alarm system, so she wasn't going to get in.

She scanned the driveway briefly; she didn't expect to find anything, and she wasn't disappointed. Her watch said 11:20; it was time she was getting back. How far was it from here to Simon's, she wondered, and walked to the edge of the clearing. She stared through the trees in the direction of Beacon. She couldn't see Simon's house, or the Hornbecks', but they might not be far. Lewis might have heard something from here—if he'd been here. There was a faint depression in the fallen leaves, a bare suggestion of an opening among the saplings and twiggy thickets that grew in the shade of the taller trees. A deer path. She knew what they were like. Yes, there were some deer droppings. She followed it, to see if it led her towards Beacon. The ground was rocky and uneven, but the deer path skirted the boulders and treacherous hollows under the drift of dry twigs and dead leaves, offering easy footing. Suddenly the light brightened, and she was at the end of the trees. And there was Simon's house.

She stood still, surprised at how close it was. The empty lawn sloped steeply up to the terrace. The living room and the study were uncurtained, open to the view of the river, the house as quiet as if it had been closed for the winter. If Lewis had found the deer path, he could have spied on Roberta quite easily. But she and Roberta agreed he wasn't the type. Roberta hadn't mentioned the deer path. That was interesting, but Roberta was hardly the woodland nymph; she wore expensive little Italian shoes and wouldn't go scuffing through deer droppings and dead branches when the road was available. She probably didn't know how short the walk through the trees was.

Gillian turned around and started back. She could have walked up through Simon's garden to Beacon, but she didn't want to chance being seen there. There were too many neighbours, and Eli would have forty thousand fits if he thought she was poking around Simon's property.

In less than five minutes, she was back at the cottage. The clearing was still empty. Relieved, she strode quickly across it and headed back down the curving driveway. Too late, as she rounded the bend, she saw him. The Mercedes was parked halfway along the drive, and Lewis was leaning against it, waiting for her. She flushed, then paled, feeling trapped. She had a crazy impulse to turn and run the other way. She was trespassing, and he'd caught her. What was she going to say? She kept walking towards him, and towards Dykeman's Pond Road, visible a hundred or more feet beyond him.

'I thought you'd be here,' he said. 'I saw you stop at the end of the driveway a little while ago.' He moved a little, blocking the narrow space beside the car. 'So I decided to come back.'

She was only a few paces from him now. She stopped.

'I wanted to ask you how Estelle is,' he said in a casual tone. 'Did you talk to her about the procedure I explained?'

The question caught her off guard. She'd expected Lewis to be angry.

'Franklin did,' she answered shortly.

'Good. I'm glad to hear it. As I told you, I can recommend a surgeon.'

'She doesn't want it.'

'That's nonsense. You could persuade her. You should.'

'She has her own doctor,' Gillian said. What was he up to? Why had he come back? He didn't know what she knew, or why she was there. But he had such a compelling need to know that he'd come back to confront her. Alarm bells went off loudly in her head. He was still fencing, half pretending an interest in Estelle, but he was blocking her way. 'Look, I'm expected at home, and I'm already late,' she said.

'What are you doing here?' he said, not moving.

'Roberta mentioned the cottage to me. I was curious about it.'

'Curious? About what?'

'It's new. I take an interest in what's built around here.'

'This is private property. It's customary to ask.'

'Well, yes,' she said, 'but she said the owner didn't come very often. An interest in architecture isn't a crime.'

'There isn't any architecture in the woods back there.' He nodded towards the edge of the clearing to the right of the cottage.

He knew she'd found the deer path. For the first time, she noticed the binoculars on the dashboard of the Mercedes.

'I thought there was a path, but it's just a deer trail. They usually peter out in the middle of nowhere,' she said.

'Simon Steele's house is up there. Where he killed the Bishop girl. It seems a funny place for you to be walking by yourself.'

Was he trying to warn her off? 'The killer's in custody, isn't he?' she said, her voice a shade tart. 'There should be nothing to worry about.'

He looked at her narrowly. 'It was my daughter Janice who told the police he knew Nicole. She told you, too, didn't she?'

He was definitely worried. The police had Simon, everything was going to be all right for Janice. But he was still worried that Gillian was snooping around. Maybe worried about what Janice had told her, or what she'd found at the cottage. She could tell him that—nothing.

'Poor Janice,' he said. 'She's feeling terrible about that truck accident. She stopped at the stop sign, you know. The truck driver was going way too fast. She misjudged his speed, but it was dark, and she's only been driving for a couple of years.'

'I thought the driver said she'd run the stop sign.'

'That's his story. It won't hold up in court.'

It probably won't even get to court, Gillian thought, the Grogans would see to that. The truck might have been speeding, that was possible; the highway patrol should be able to tell by the skid marks. And Janice might be less culpable than gossip would have it, but she'd driven away without a scratch on her skin and only a dented fender, while the truck driver had trashed his truck trying not to kill her and had spent ten days in the hospital. Lewis hadn't even acknowledged that. 'Whoever was at fault, Janice shouldn't have driven away.'

'She was upset,' Lewis said. 'I'm not sure she realized what had happened.'

So that was going to be the story.

'She'd had a quarrel with Kitty,' he added.

'Which upset her so much she didn't notice her fender getting scraped? Or look in her mirror and see the truck turn over?' Gillian said sceptically. 'What was she doing on Dykeman's Pond Road, anyhow?' He seemed to want to tell her about Janice.

'Just driving around. She didn't want to go back to the dorm.'

'Didn't she come to see you?' As she asked, she saw his body tense, and his eyes flicker. She almost stepped backwards, reacting instinctively to the bunching of his muscles. Then he smiled, as if to contradict his body language. 'No,' he replied smoothly. 'She knows better than that. Kitty puts up with her childish temper, but I don't.' He looked at his watch. 'I mustn't keep you.'

Suddenly, he could hardly wait to be rid of her. She could have told him the feeling was mutual, but she knew he knew it already. She walked down the driveway, her back stiff with the effort not to look back. Lewis slammed the door of the Mercedes. When she reached the end of the drive, she heard the engine start.

She almost ran up Dykeman's to Beacon; she didn't want to be walking on the edge of the road when the Mercedes burst out of the driveway. She got into the Buick, made a U-turn and then went north, taking the short route to the Post Road, where Dykeman's came out near the Dutch House. She had better stay far away from Lewis Grogan, she thought. He would turn south on Dykeman's, if he were going home or to the college.

On the Post Road, she realized she hadn't fastened her seatbelt. She hauled it across and clicked it into place, slowing slightly as she did so. She glanced in the rearview mirror. The Mercedes was following. Lewis must have waited for her to leave and then taken the same route. The Mercedes was coming up fast. She sped up to increase the distance between them, but he stayed close. The Benz was faster than the Buick, she couldn't leave him behind if he wanted to tailgate. She tried slowing down, to see whether he would pass. He stayed right behind her, so close she thought she could see him glaring.

He'd been driving right up her back side on Dykeman's earlier, but this was worse. He was furious, now. He wanted to scare her, wanted her to know how much he'd like to run her over. She took a deep breath. She just had to drive down the road, and not let him rattle her.

She could stamp on the brake, that would settle him. But she didn't want to be in a crash. She might get hurt. What a fool she'd feel. And who would look after Estelle? She passed the Dutch House on her left. He was still right behind her, only inches away. A driver going the other way gave them a startled look. The lower end of Dykeman's raced towards her. This was where the accident had happened. Her eyes flicked irresistibly to the mirror, to the silhouette of his head and shoulders hunched over the wheel. Then she forced herself to watch the road ahead.

Now the turn to Salt Hill. It wasn't the logical route for him to take if he was going home; he would go on down the Post Road. Surely he'd made his point, he wouldn't pursue her all the way home. She slowed down and turned left, letting out her breath. After a few yards she looked back over her shoulder. He was still following.

Jesus, she thought. She sped up. It was awful having him right on her tail. He dropped back a little, and the gap widened to a couple of car lengths. What was he doing, following her home? He'd come close to violence at the cottage, when she'd asked if Janice had come to see him there, but he'd restrained himself. What kind of confrontation did he want now?

He was still fifteen or twenty feet behind, but they were driving faster than she normally drove on this road. They were going up and downhill, the Buick bouncing too much, but this part of the road was fairly straight. The question about the cottage couldn't affect the accident, Gillian thought, Janice had gone down the Post Road after the crash. The question must bear on the murder.

Now the road twisted, winding through a patch of woods and high rocky outcroppings. He closed the gap and then nosed almost alongside her rear fender. He was frighteningly close to hitting her. She edged over, to let him pass, but he stayed close, moving into the blind spot on the passenger side. She couldn't see him in her rearview mirror, and there was no wing mirror on the passenger side. She didn't dare turn her head; she had to watch the potholes. She sped up once more. It was intolerable not to be able to see him. He came into view behind her and then slid into the blind spot again, quicker than before. She couldn't nudge any closer to the shoulder or she'd be off the road. That's what he was trying to do, she realized with a jolt of fear, force her off the road. He'd frightened her on purpose, and then he'd waited until they got to the most dangerous stretch of Salt Hill, and now he was going to engineer an accident. A lethal one, if she hit the big rocks. She could try slowing down, but she didn't know what he might do then. Every instinct said flee.

She stepped on the gas and pulled ahead once more, and moved to the left, towards the crown of the road. There was no other traffic, and she prayed no one would come suddenly around a curve. She was driving faster than she should, but what if he pulled abreast? He could squeeze her off the narrow pavement.

The Mercedes handled well—a lot better than the Buick. It was a bloody good thing she knew the road like the back of her hand. Every bump, every pothole, the arc of every curve. The Buick wasn't built for sinuous roads; it wallowed. A skid on the dirt and she'd be toast.

The car lurched. He'd butted her back bumper. A Mercedes could wreck the bumper of another car and not show a dent in its own. She gripped the wheel as if she were drowning and someone had thrown her a rope. She was sweating and breathing hard. Her heart hammered. She came to the gravelly part and felt the car fishtail a little but kept going, past the Brewsters', past the blurred trees and silent fields, the great upthrusts of hard rock that could crumple the car like foil. There was only one thought left in her mind. If she could just get home, just get there, this madness would have to stop.

The road straightened out again. She could see the house in the distance, the hill, the mailbox, the rose bushes, here came the driveway. She hit the brake and turned hard left, off the bumpy tarmac and on to the gravel. The Buick slopped like water in a bucket. A grey blur crossed the mirror—the Mercedes flying past at a strange angle. She hit the mailbox with a deafening crunch.

'Oh no,' she groaned. The world spun for a moment. Then it was still. She thumped the wheel with her fist. 'Goddammit to bloody hell. No fucking steering.'

She was all right, she thought. She couldn't feel any pain. What a shock. She shut her eyes. Then she heard the latch click and the car door swung wide. Her eyes flew open. Lewis bent over her. The adrenaline flooded, hot and stinging; she unbuckled her seatbelt and slid away to the passenger side. Her hand was on the door, she got it open, but then Lewis straightened. He stepped back. Through the windshield, she saw Edward belting down the driveway.

She sat still.

'I saw the accident and thought I'd better stop,' she heard Lewis say.

Edward leaned into the car. 'Are you all right?' he demanded.

'F-fine.'

'Are you sure you're not hurt?'

'I think I'm OK. Really.'

'What happened? I heard one hell of a crunch.'

'She must have taken the turn too fast,' Lewis said. 'It's a rough road. Well, if there's nothing I can do, I'll be on my way.'

'I think we're all right,' Edward said. She thought he mumbled a polite word or two. Then he slid into the front seat next to her. 'What happened?'

She didn't look around. 'Is he gone?'

Edward twisted around to check. 'He's getting into his car. Why?'

'He didn't hit anything?'

'He just pulled over. Why?'

'That's Lewis.'

'Who in bloody hell is Lewis?'

'Lewis Grogan. He's the killer. I think he is. I'm almost sure.'

'The doctor chap?'

'Yes, him! The one who used to be a surgeon. I told you about him.'

'And why—Never mind, bugger Lewis. For the third time, what happened to you?'

'He tried to run me off the road.'

'*What?*'

Her body quivered with the aftershock. Edward put his arms around her and held her tightly.

'Tell me,' he insisted.

She leaned against him. The tilted mailbox made the world look wrong. For a moment, the car seemed to slide, like a boat heeling over in rough water. 'He followed me all the way from Dykeman's. I went to a cottage there. Lewis uses it; it's right behind Simon's house. Lewis found me there. He got mad, and he chased me in the car. I thought at first he was just bullying me, but I'm sure he was trying to force me off the road—make me crash. If I didn't kill myself, he'd finish the job and it would look like an accident. I was doing all right, because I know the road so well, but I forgot about the soft tyre when I turned. I just had to get away from him.'

'I heard the most awful bang. I shot over to the window and looked out and saw you. I don't think I've ever run as fast in my life.'

'Oh God, I hope Estelle didn't hear it.'

'I think not. She's resting. Why do you think Lewis was after you?'

'Because I was nosing around the cottage, and because he gave himself away. I asked him a question, and he reacted, and he knew I saw it. He looked as if he could kill me. He didn't dare, or he thought an accident would be a lot easier to get away with. Who would ever believe it wasn't one? The main thing is, he had to get rid of me immediately, before I had a chance to talk to anybody else.'

'Are you certain?' Edward was suddenly angry. 'Why in the name of God did you go to his cottage without me?'

'I didn't expect any danger. I'd just found out about Janice's car—I hadn't had time to think. I saw Lewis leave the cottage, and I'd never even thought about him as the killer.'

'Then what makes you so certain now?'

'At first I thought he was protecting his daughter. I'd just heard from Jean that Janice's Miata was on Dykeman's the night Nicole was killed, and I thought Lewis didn't want anyone to connect her to the cottage because she'd gone there after the murder. Where else could she go if she was a mess? Not the dorm. Then there was the broken glass.' Gillian was aware that she was gabbling. She slowed down and explained.

'Hmm,' Edward said. 'Highly suggestive, but not conclusive. Enough to get the full attention of anyone in homicide, though. Why Lewis and not Janice? Because he chased you?'

'Yes, he took that risk for himself, not Janice. But not only that. The scarf—he had the opportunity to take it at the party. The glass was in the pocket of his jacket, not hers. Roberta thought she saw him in the woods. And the way he looked at me.'

'But why would he kill Nicole?'

'I haven't any idea. But there's the glass. That's evidence.'

'Yes—*if* it's part of Simon's windowpane. You'd better report it as soon as you can. I wish we hadn't let him get away.' Edward was angry again. 'I'd like to wrap his Mercedes around his neck.'

He looked at her carefully and ran his hand gently over her shoulders, checking for damage. 'Are you sure you're all right?'

'Yes.' She was still wound tight, her eyes wide, all the warning signals flashing. His other hand was cupped around her knee. She was suddenly hot all over, as if all her blood vessels had dilated. 'I'm fine. Just in shock.' She twisted around to face him. 'I'll be OK if my heart doesn't break my ribs.'

He laid his hand lightly against the bones under her breast. She felt her heart thudding against it, the blood tingling in her palms. The next sensation rose, an erotic rush sweeping across the fear like a riptide. She almost laughed in surprise and half collapsed against him, pinning him to the back of the seat. Then she pulled back a little to look at him. 'I'm perfectly all right, except for being out of my mind.' Her eyes, she thought, must look like blazing electronic highway signs. He was reading the message. The anxiety left his face, replaced by a glint of amusement and then something else she knew, a permeability, as if one of the protective layers around the self dissolved. Through it gleamed the diamond core of the impersonal, the glitter mirrored in her own gaze. She moved closer. His hand brushed her thigh, slid upward.

A few minutes later, she remembered she was in the car and drew away. She started to laugh again. 'I feel like a teenager.'

'I didn't have a car when I was that age. Don't we do this in the back seat?'

'That's where things get serious.' She pushed her skirt down. 'But not in broad daylight in the parental driveway.'

'And not directly after pranging the parental Buick?'

'Oh God, I haven't even thought about the car yet.'

'It doesn't look too bad. Just the wing and the headlamp, and your left front bumper's crumpled.' He rolled down the window, reached out and opened the end of the box. A catalogue slid into his hand. 'You know, there are better ways of disposing of your junk mail than driving over it.'

She laughed again. Her blood was full of champagne bubbles. 'Darling. Would you be kind enough—if this hunk of metal still moves—to park it for me in the conventional way? I don't want to right now.'

He moved into the driver's seat and bumped the car backwards to the road.

It's the most remarkable thing, she thought. I feel different. Something's happened since I've come home. It's as if a door that's been closed isn't any more. It's partly being in the valley again, being back here in this landscape. I'm me, in this place. And it's partly making up my damn mind about what I want. I've been divided for so long. I must have been shutting myself off so as not to feel too much.

The big car glided serenely up to the house.

How amazing. To get sensuality back. It was like losing your eyesight so slowly you didn't notice it going until someone handed you a pair of glasses and you could see again.

'I should phone Eli right now,' she said, hurrying up the stairs. There were papers scattered on the floor where Edward had been working; they must have fallen when he rushed downstairs. She took the phone from the desk and dialed Eli's pager. She left an urgent message for him to call her back.

Edward gathered up his papers and tossed them on the desk. He looked a question.

'They'll beep him,' she answered. The blood was still racing in her veins. 'Now, where were we?'

'In the back seat.'

She glanced dubiously at the phone. Maybe Eli would be busy for a while.

Edward moved towards her.

She patted the bed post. 'Can I interest you in this old four-poster, sir? It's got some mileage on it, but there's plenty of room in the back.'

Edward inspected the bed. 'I was thinking of something with four-wheel drive. But I'll take it out for a spin.'

He reached for her, and then the phone rang. It was Eli. She could hear noise in the background—a jumble of voices, phones ringing.

'You called me,' he said. 'The message says it's urgent.'

Edward walked to the window and looked out. Gillian turned away so she could concentrate on the conversation. 'Yes. Look, Eli, you know that Lewis Grogan sometimes uses a cottage right behind Simon Steele's house?'

'Yes, what about it?'

'And he and Kitty have been keeping quiet about Janice's Miata and the accident.'

'I know.' Eli sounded irritated. 'What's this about?'

'I'm not quite sure. But Kitty took a jacket of Lewis's in for cleaning and repairs on Friday morning, the day after the body was found. A button had been torn off it, and—'

Eli interrupted her. 'A button?' he said sharply.

'A horn button.' She had his attention now, but why did he care about the button?

'Did you see the jacket? What colour is it?'

'A brown tweed, a sort of dull tobacco colour. From London—it's probably a tweed woven for his tailor.'

'Well, Jesus, what am I supposed to do with that?' Eli suddenly sounded angry. 'I can't mess about with a guy like Lewis Grogan because his jacket's missing a frigging button.'

'Let me finish. The point is, there was broken glass in the pocket. Paula cut her finger on it. She had to go to the hospital to get the splinter out.'

'Even so—'

'She wanted to show the glass to Kitty and complain. She saved the piece of glass.'

'She has it?'

'Yes.'

'Oh.' There was a silence. 'You know that Simon's under arrest, don't you?'

'Yes, I know.'

'Shit. I guess I'll have to have the goddam glass analysed. I had a feeling when I heard about that Miata that things were going to get complicated. But what would Lewis Grogan have to do with Simon Steele and Nicole Bishop?'

'I don't know. There'll be something. He nearly drove me off the road today after I asked him if Janice went to the cottage to see him that night. I think she did, and he wasn't there. That's what he doesn't want anyone to know. She went to the cottage while he was at Simon's.'

'If there's anything to this,' Eli began, then broke off. She waited. Then he said brusquely, 'You think Janice knows?'

'No, but she's frightened. She senses something wrong, maybe in the way Lewis reacted to her accident.' She heard yelling in the background and another phone ringing. 'Listen, Eli,' she added quickly, before he could hang up, 'call me when you know about the glass, will you?'

'When I get a minute. Thanks, I guess.'

She put down the phone. 'He didn't seem very happy,' she said to Edward.

He looked at her drolly. 'Happy? He has a man under arrest and you ring him up and tell him he's wrong, that you've got evidence that may implicate someone else; and this someone else isn't the village weirdo but an influential pillar of the establishment? And you think he's going to be happy? The poor bugger's probably wondering if he'll have a job next week.' Edward turned his head at a sound. He moved back towards the window. 'Who's that?'

She hurried across and looked out. 'It's Jim Whitlock, our neighbour. He's come to put up the storm windows. I'm afraid I'll have to go down. Why does everything have to happen at once?'

'Bloody hell.' Edward was looking fed up. She didn't blame him. 'I think I'd better try to finish the rest of these,' he said, picking up his papers again.

Jim was in the shed, fetching the aluminium ladder. He claimed he didn't need help, but in the end, he climbed up the clattering rungs and handed the screens down to Gillian, who stowed them in the shed and handed up the storm windows. It went quite fast, considering how many times they had to move the ladder. Gillian spotted Estelle at her bedroom window watching, and waved. She waved back and vanished, reappearing a few minutes later at one of the windows in the living room. She hated the ritual of the storm windows, Gillian knew. It signified the onset of winter. She was always elated when they came off in the spring.

Jim wouldn't stay after they were finished but promised to come over on the weekend. 'We got a little surprise today. Kind of sad,' he said. 'Arnold left a note. He wanted Brian to have his truck, so he could fix it up.'

'Didn't he say anything about his photographs?' Gillian asked.

'I don't know.'

'We should try to make sure they're not thrown away— that one of the historical societies gets them. It's odd that he didn't say anything about them.'

Jim scratched his head. 'He knew Brian loved that truck. Maybe it was the only thing he had he thought anyone cared about.'

'Did you give the negatives to Eli?'

'Not yet. Haven't had time. I still wonder if they mean something.'

'Well, I don't think Arnold was deranged,' Gillian replied, 'so maybe he just liked looking at her.'

Carrie Pilgrim came for afternoon tea.

Gillian went out to meet her and found Lily Regan already helping Carrie extract herself from the passenger seat. Lily had presence. She was big and boldly coloured, her thick frizzed red hair like the burning bush caught in a ribbon. Her skin was white, without freckles; Torchie must have been fanatical about sun protection, Gillian thought, probably because she'd burnt like a newborn baby herself. Lily had penciled black eyebrows and brilliant lipstick. Carrie had said Renoir, but for the moment Lily had decided to be a Toulouse-Lautrec. Her yellow quilted jacket was covered with embroidery and beads, and she wore black tights, a long black sweater and blazing yellow ankle warmers.

'Will you come in?' Gillian asked.

Lily shook her head, smiling. 'I'm meeting somebody.'

'Lily's deprived,' Carrie said. 'She needs to go listen to some deafening music. I won't let her play it loudly enough. I can turn off my hearing aid, but I still hear it if she plays it the way she likes it. Awful stuff—what is it, Lily, the Six Inch Spikes?'

'Nine Inch Nails. It's not music for brilliant old artists. It's music for brilliant young artists.' She got back into the car, laughed and waved and drove away.

'You get on well,' Gillian said to Carrie.

'That's to Lily's credit. I'm a cantankerous old despot.'

In the house, Carrie settled in an armchair near the fire. Gillian brought in the tea tray. For once, there were cookies she'd made herself. Thin, crisp, lemony cookies, and a big pot of Earl Grey tea. She'd even polished the spoons; that is, Edward had.

'I had no idea you could bake these things,' Edward said, as the first batch came out of the oven.

'You never gave a hoot whether I could or not. That's one of your many attractions.'

'And what are the others?'

'I'll make a list for you when I come to London. There will be world enough and time.'

Then they talked more about Lewis, while she rolled out another sheet of chilled cookie dough and he sat at the kitchen table with the tarnished teaspoons. She didn't want to say much to anyone else, not until her conjectures were supported by some lab results, or some other concrete proof.

'It's interesting that he tried to seduce Roberta, of all people. Simon's wife. I wonder if he was really attracted to her,' Gillian mused.

Gillian had got out the best china cups and a silver tray. Estelle bit into a cookie with a bright look of contentment.

Inevitably, the conversation turned to Simon's arrest.

'Gillian told me you remembered the scarf Simon wore at Alice's party,' Estelle said to Carrie. 'That was remarkable.'

'I don't forget colours,' Carrie said. 'But my eyes aren't what they used to be. I can't see a thing in the damned museums any more—the rooms are so dark.'

'What did he want to know about the scarf for? Gillian said that Eli Pink wanted a guest list for the party. Wasn't that strange?' Estelle remarked to Edward.

'Not if the scarf was connected to the murder and the party was the last place anyone had seen it,' he answered.

'Simon Steele has never been worth two cents,' Carrie observed.

'Do you think he could have done the murder?' Edward said.

'He nearly killed eight people once, a long time ago, but it wasn't murder.'

'What do you mean?' Gillian asked.

Carrie sat hunched in her chair, a teacup in one gnarled hand, her old eyes hooded, her thin white hair a halo in the firelight.

'Simon was spoilt rotten,' she said. 'And his father was a damned fool. He gave Simon a sports car to bribe him to finish college. Of course, he crashed it. Ben knew he would, told me it would happen. Told me he asked Simon not to bring the car up here when he visited. Ben didn't want the accident to happen here.

'It was useless to ask Simon not to do anything he wanted to do; he did what he pleased, and nobody could ever say no to him. He drove up here after a party, with some girl in the car, and another boy crowded into the back behind the seats. He wanted to show them the house, he said. It was winter. There was a lot of ice on the roads, though not on the highway; it had been salted. Simon had been drinking, of course. He hit another vehicle, another carload of teenagers, on the highway. It was a bad crash. There were five college kids in the other car, and almost all of them were injured. Two went through the windshield. Every ambulance in the county was there.'

'Was anyone killed?' Gillian asked. She'd heard a version of this story before, but not in detail.

'No, no one died. But two boys were in the hospital for weeks. I'll say one thing for Simon, he stopped drinking and driving after that. I don't think he ever did it again. And that was over twenty years ago.'

'Roberta taunted him about drinking and driving, I remember that,' Gillian said. 'He was livid. He said he hadn't done it in twenty-five years.'

'She knows Simon's tender spots,' Carrie said.

Twenty-five years ago, Gillian was thinking. When was that? I was in Cambridge, wasn't I? And the farm was closed all winter.

'You're sure no one was killed?' she asked again.

'Quite sure,' Carrie answered. 'Why?'

'I was just thinking. If he'd killed one of those college kids, then there might be somebody around who still hates him, who'd want to kill him, or ruin his life.'

'Now?' said Estelle.

'I know it's been a long time, but sometimes rage comes back—something makes it flare up again, after everyone else has forgotten the old story.'

'When you're my age,' Carrie observed, 'hatred seems to be beside the point. Or so I feel.'

'Rather a waste of time,' said Estelle.

'Exactly. But then, we're old. Very old.' Carrie rasped out a chuckle. Then she looked at Gillian. 'There were a lot of accidents that night. It snowed and melted and then froze. The back roads were appalling.'

Gillian had been about to get up and pass the cookies around again, but she sat still. When Carrie told stories, you listened.

'As it happened,' Carrie went on, 'I was out that same evening, at a dinner party over in Connecticut. I shouldn't have gone, with the roads the way they were, but I did. There were several people there who'd bought some of my work. I was driving home, and I was late, because the roads were so bad. I saw a car in a ditch, and I stopped. It was Lewis. Lewis Grogan. He'd spun off the road and hit a tree, and he was trapped in the car. I couldn't pull him out. He was conscious, but he couldn't move. All he could say was, "Get an ambulance. My hand, my hand."'

Lewis! Gillian thought. She glanced quickly at Edward. He'd forgotten his tea. Estelle, sitting on the sofa opposite, looked puzzled and uneasy.

'So I left him there,' Carrie continued, 'though I didn't want to, and went to phone for an ambulance. I found a pay phone at a gas station and called, and then I went right back. I had a blanket in the trunk of the car; I sometimes used it for wrapping my canvases. I put it over him and waited. And waited. It took the ambulance about forty minutes to get to him. It seemed like forty years. He was dreadfully agitated about his hand, you see. When the ambulance finally got there, Lewis tore their heads off for taking so long. The driver said there were accidents all over, too many to handle. But he said that the big problem was the crash on the highway— a drunk college boy had put half a dozen kids in the hospital. Lewis asked who the college boy was, and the driver said he didn't know. And then Lewis said he was going to find out if it was the last thing he did. He said that if he couldn't operate again, that boy would be sorry he was born.'

Estelle looked bewildered. 'You mean Lewis blamed Simon for his accident? But Simon wasn't there.'

'He blamed Simon for the delay—for having to wait so long. All he cared about was his hand—was being able to operate again. He knew already that he might not. If the ambulance had gotten there sooner, there could have been a chance, I suppose. At least, that's what Lewis believed.'

'Good Lord,' said Gillian. 'Does that mean he's had it in for Simon all this time?'

Carrie sighed. 'I don't know, of course.'

'Lewis isn't a forgiving man,' Estelle said unhappily.

Carrie nodded. 'He's an angry God,' she said, her face sombre. 'Never enough sacrifices at the altar.'

'If Lewis hated Simon, would Simon have known about it?' Edward asked.

'I don't think he'd have any idea. Lewis hoped for a long time that with enough therapy, he could work again. And you know, Simon didn't move to Ben's house until a few years ago. If Ben hadn't left him the house, he probably wouldn't have moved up here. I doubt that Lewis thought about Simon very much before he came back.'

Gillian started. 'And, my God, not only did Simon settle here, but then he wrote that book about being a drunk. It turned him into a local celebrity. Gall and wormwood for Lewis.'

'Goodness, Carrie,' Estelle went on, 'you might have told me this before. Kitty said once that you found Lewis in the ditch, but she never said a word about blaming Ben's grandson.'

'Lewis was lucky not to freeze to death. He was lucky I came along when I did. I thought he'd realize that, when he'd had time to recover.' Carrie held out her cup for more tea.

CHAPTER 26

'Too bad my conference isn't in New York instead of Washington,' Edward said.

Gillian looked north again. The track was empty. 'It would be handy. I could meet you at the station every evening, like a fifties wife. What time do you finish on Friday?'

'Noon.'

'Good. You'll be back for dinner. I wish you weren't leaving, though, you just got here.'

'I'll call you from the hotel. I want daily updates.'

'Carrie's remarkable, don't you think?'

'She's a sibyl.'

'I've been realizing what her story means. It means Lewis just used Nicole to get Simon. He must have started brooding about Simon after he turned up again, and gotten angrier and angrier. That's why he was after Roberta—to get at Simon. And then *Juicer* came out and he found that intolerable. He used the cottage to spy on Simon, and then he used Nicole when she fell in love. It's monstrous. He didn't care who she was.'

'If you've got it right. I'd like to know what the lab says about the glass.'

A point of light appeared far up the track. Newspapers were folded, and the scatter of waiting passengers condensed.

'I didn't realize this weekend would be such a circus,' Gillian said. 'I'm sorry.'

'I wasn't expecting to have you to myself—though I didn't know it was going to be like Victoria Station. Perhaps it's just as well—it's given me an idea of what it's like for you when you land in the middle of *my* life.'

The train was nearly in.

Edward picked up his suitcase. 'I'm not used to being idle.'

'I know. You withstood three days of it admirably. I'll put you to work Saturday—you can fix the mailbox.'

'Just don't change your mind about London while I'm away,' Edward said.

'Not a chance.'

Gillian kissed him goodbye and then stood on the chilly platform, her collar up and her hands jammed in her coat pockets, until he found a seat and looked through the window. She waved as the train pulled out. The three days until Friday seemed long, much longer than the same exact number of days that had just passed. Then on Sunday he would go back to London.

In the meantime, she admonished herself, in the meantime, she had work to do. It was hard to take an interest in the fact, but this afternoon she had to stand in front of a class again, and try to focus their attention on academic pursuits. Not to mention her own wayward attention. And she had to mark papers.

Somehow, the day went by. She went through the motions and waited for news. She fled the campus as soon as her class was over. Estelle was creaking around the house, moving erratically, as if her batteries were low. She leaned heavily on her cane and gasped a little at each step. The evening dragged by, interminable. Gillian stared at the phone, willing it to ring. How long would it take them to analyse the glass fragments? How long until she knew? After Estelle went to bed, she put on some Haydn quartets and sat marking the papers her students had handed in. The telephone was obstinately silent. She poured herself a drink and stood looking out at the night, her heart beating absurdly hard when she saw a pair of headlights skimming the nearest rise. Later, in bed, she caught herself listening to the hall clock and counting the ticks.

Wednesday morning started early and threatened to last until Doomsday.

'You're awfully restless,' Estelle said, as Gillian fidgeted with a leaning tower of *New Yorkers*.

'Some of these are four years old, Mother.'

'There are articles in them I want to read. Go and clean up something else; you're making me nervous.'

Gillian drifted to the window and then to the bookshelves. The family photograph albums were stacked there, layered like sedimentary deposits, memory strata going back to Estelle's girlhood and beyond. The oldest leather bindings were starting to crumble at the corners. She should do something about restoring them before they turned to dust. Put it on the list, she thought, a little wearily.

She pulled out a familiar album from her own childhood. There she was, her hair in two tight braids, the shorter ends escaping and rising everywhere in a defiant fuzz. She and Peggy, inseparable, a tangle of legs in the hammock. The two of them again, in their nightgowns, and in bathing suits, splashing each other in the Brewsters' pond. There was the class picture from fifth grade; at ten, Peggy was already pretty, Gillian was long and thin-legged, like a water bird. Two rows back, Eli was clowning, scratching himself under one arm. His mouth was open in an O; he was probably making monkey noises. Torch Regan, who'd hated being so big, was in the back row with the tallest boys. And there was Arnold, at the end of Eli's row, visible space between him and the next boy, though the rest of the class was bunched together. His eyes looked unfocused, as if he'd forgotten where he was.

Gillian turned the page. A party. Peggy's parents, the Brewsters, Carrie Pilgrim looking formidable, like a caryatid on the lawn. Franklin, in his pyjamas, being carried up to bed by Nat. And Estelle, standing by the fireplace, wearing a little black dress with a scoop neck, a cigarette in one hand, a martini glass in the other, her face tilted back, just on the verge of a laugh.

'Gillian?' her mother said from the sofa.

'Mmm?' She came back across the room, still holding the album. She held it out to Estelle. 'I love this picture. It's you exactly. And you look so happy.'

'I'm sure I was. It was a very good party. Gillian, why did you ask Carrie about people who might hate Simon? And talk about rage coming back and Lewis being bitter about Simon Steele's success? Has someone done something to Simon? I thought it was Simon who'd been arrested for killing Nicole.'

'He has. But it's possible that he didn't do it. There's room for doubt.'

'You can't possibly think that Lewis is responsible! I know you've never liked him.'

'I'm afraid I do think so. What's missing is the proof. But I know I'm right.'

'Lewis! I hope you're wrong. You must be. Think of Kitty! They've been such good friends to me.'

'Except when Lewis bullies you about medical treatment.'

'I was cross about that, too. But I believe he meant well. Lewis is concerned. He doesn't know how to show it any other way. He's used to telling people what to do.'

'He expects the world to dance to his tune. And it does, almost always—but not when he went off the road and mangled his hand.'

'That was very bad. He hasn't been easy to live with, I know that. Kitty never says a word, but I can see.' Estelle sighed. 'He might have been different, I suppose, if his career hadn't been cut short. I don't have the energy to argue with you, dear, but it's been so long since he had to give up surgery. Do you really think he's so angry about it now?'

'I think he must have been angry about it always, but he wouldn't have tried to destroy Simon if Simon hadn't come back and then started to be a success. You told me Simon was famous—at least around here. Lewis would have been famous—a celebrated surgeon. I'm sure he thinks so. Instead, he lives off his wife's money and gets prizes for roses. It's not the destiny he thought was rightfully his.'

'What does Edward think?'

'Edward says he doesn't have enough information, but he doesn't know the people. And he hasn't suggested that I've got it all wrong.'

'Poor Kitty. I don't know how she'll live through it, if it's true. She's a proud woman.'

'And Janice. She's Lewis's daughter, and Nicole was her friend.'

After lunch, Estelle retired to her room to rest.

'Come and watch a movie with me if you want to distract yourself,' she said. 'I think I'll put on *Roman Holiday*.'

Gillian decided to phone Eli instead. She could stand the suspense no longer. She left a message asking for news. She paced up and down, and then turned on the radio. Callas's voice filled the room, and Gillian forgot everything for two minutes and listened until the aria was over. Then the programme ended; news was next. Gillian muttered and switched it off again and looked through her pile of unmarked essays. The phone rang a few minutes later and she jumped for it, but it was Edward. She wanted to talk to him, but she was reluctant to tie up the phone. If Eli called, and the line was busy, he might not try again. She kept the conversation short.

'I'll call you as soon as there's anything new,' she said at the end. 'I turned on the radio and heard Callas singing *Tosca*. Lewis would have made a perfect Scarpia.' Then she hung up and waited some more.

In the middle of the afternoon, Gillian heard the sound of a car. She looked up from the essay in which she had just marked a paragraph that appeared twice, and saw a rusted light-blue sedan, with a taped-up crack in one window. As it came to an abrupt stop, she recognized Eli in the driver's seat. She hurried to the door.

He was already coming up the walk. He wore a fleece-lined bomber jacket and jeans and dark glasses, instead of the coat and tie which had made him seem so unfamiliar when he'd visited her at Stanton. 'I was passing,' he said. 'I haven't got much time.' He took his glasses off as he stepped inside. His eyes were bloodshot.

'Time for coffee?' Gillian said. 'You look as if you could use some.'

'Well, if it's quick.'

He followed her to the kitchen. He unzipped his jacket but kept it on, pulling out a chair and straddling it, leaning his arms on the back. Gillian put the kettle on, got out the sugar and cream.

'Well?' she said.

He scratched at his unshaven jaw. 'I'll tell you something. I don't like my job. Your boyfriend, does he like his?'

'Yes.'

'Maybe it's different where he works. Maybe he doesn't work for a bunch of bureaucrats and politicians. I'm being put through a meat grinder already, and it's just starting. This Lewis Grogan thing, it's trouble.'

'The glass? Have you got the results?'

'Yeah. The glass is a match for the old glass in Simon's door.'

'Then it was Lewis.' Her voice was shaking. 'Thank God it's over.'

'Over? Maybe if it was Arnold Mitchell it would be over. Who in the county would give a shit if Arnold Mitchell was arrested for murder? But Dr. Grogan—that's another story. Do you have any idea how complicated my life is going to be? Do you have any idea how many millions Kitty Grogan has?'

'Don't you have enough evidence?'

'I don't know. Can you ever have enough with the defence a guy like that can afford? There was glass in his pocket. There were matching glass fragments in the wound. It ought to be enough, but who knows?'

'So he did actually use a piece of glass. He can't have planned that. What did he plan to do? He must have had that scarf with him.'

'I don't know about plans. I can tell you this: Nicole was choked first, before she was stabbed. The body tells us that much. She was choked with the scarf you saw. What happened next is guesswork, because Steele destroyed most of the evidence. But there's still enough blood in the car to suggest that she bled to death in the passenger seat. The guy knew just where to cut.'

'Wouldn't some of the blood have gotten on him? On his clothes?'

'Maybe a little, not much. He was skilled; she was unconscious. She was laid face down and he chose a vein, not an artery. The blood would have flowed, not spurted out.'

'And she was just left there, in the Mustang.'

'Then he went part way up the driveway and shoved the scarf under a couple of stones. My guess is, he had a knife, or he planned to take one of Simon's, but the glass looked like a better idea. He wanted her to bleed, or he could have just strangled her and let it go at that.'

'And then he walked back to the cottage and cleaned up. Have you found anything there?'

'That's today's job. One of the many.'

'Why were you interested when I told you Kitty had had a button sewed on the jacket? Did you find one?'

'I found a button on Steele's driveway. A horn button, like the kind Paula sewed on Grogan's jacket. I found that the first, no, the second time I went to see Simon. The first time, I saw the broken glass; by the second time he'd mended the window. I couldn't match the button to any of Simon's jackets—but then I thought he might have gotten rid of the clothes he wore that night.'

'But surely Lewis didn't put the piece of glass he used on Nicole into his pocket afterwards?'

'No, it was a smaller piece. He must have picked up a couple of shards, in case one snapped. Maybe stuck one in his pocket. No nurses to hand him things in the Mustang. A sliver probably broke off and caught in the wool, and he never noticed it. If he'd been luckier, it would have been thrown away.'

'He took an awful risk.'

'He's arrogant. Guys like Grogan think they can walk on water.'

'Have you let Simon go?'

'For now. I don't know what we're going to do about him. He did his damnedest to dick us around.'

'Lewis might have watched him go to jail for murder.'

'Maybe. But Steele made a sweet frigging mess of the case, moving the body and cleaning up the car. We'll never know what we would have found if he'd left things alone.'

'And there's no connection between Lewis and Nicole?'

'That's one of the other problems. We can't find anything. He knew Steele all right; he must have hated his guts. The whole picture doesn't make sense, otherwise. He had to be setting Simon up. Not because of the girl. But why? The highway patrol's got some old story about Grogan's crooked thumb and a night when there were a lot of kids in an accident, but nobody knows what it's about.'

'Carrie Pilgrim does. She was there. And there's an ambulance driver who'll remember. Lewis had it in for Simon. Talk to Carrie.'

'Carrie. Are you sure?'

'She told me about it. And before Nicole came along, he tried to score off Simon by screwing his wife.'

'So what you're saying is, Grogan was looking for an opportunity. Nicole was it.'

The phrase echoed in her head. 'Nicole was it,' Gillian said, half to herself. That was the worst thing.

The kettle whistled. Coffee. She'd offered Eli coffee.

'You found the tapes Simon made of Nicole, didn't you?' she asked, getting up.

'How did you know about those?'

'Roberta told me.'

'Oh yeah. That Roberta, she gave Simon a real working-over before we got to him. If I were married to her, I'd be a drunk, too.'

Gillian poured boiling water into the coffee pot. 'And what would you be if you were married to Simon?'

He looked at her mockingly. 'Queer. Between the two, I'd probably rather be a drunk, but since I don't want to be either, it's lucky I'm single.'

'You don't like people much, do you?'

'No. Not much. How about that coffee?'

She brought it to him. 'Didn't you feel sorry for Nicole? She had a pretty harsh life, and now she's dead at twenty-two.'

'I saw her father. He's a pathetic old fart. Skinny, wears shiny pants. He didn't even know about the money.'

'What money? The money Nicole told Simon she took?'

'Yeah. It was over fifteen hundred dollars. You want to know my guess, her mother was planning to take a walk. Her father said Nicole was a wild kid. He used to strap her but it didn't do any good.' He spooned sugar into the coffee.

Gillian wanted to shake him. 'Did she tell Simon on those tapes how she got into the escort business?'

'Oh yeah. She met Leslie Lang, who was already into it, big-time. Nicole told him she couldn't believe how much money she could make. For nothing, she said.'

'Nothing! She didn't place a very high value on herself, did she?'

'Five hundred bucks is high. I wouldn't pay anybody that much.'

'Eli! You know what I mean.'

He'd been stirring his coffee, round and round. He put the spoon down. 'Yeah, well, she wanted the money. It was a way out. I think maybe after she got here, she had some different feelings about it. She told Steele she wasn't going to go back to the agency. That's an old song, though.'

'You're too cynical, Eli.'

'Realistic.'

'Cynics always think that.' Arguing was pointless. 'You never traced her aunt?'

'Nope. She's someplace, I guess, but we haven't found her.'

Gillian poured him another cup of coffee.

'Thanks.' He reached for the sugar. 'I owe you.'

They sat in silence for a minute. Then Eli glanced at his watch. 'I've got to get moving. Can I use your phone?'

Gillian brought him the cordless, and he hit the buttons. 'I guess Stanton College better start looking for a new trustee,' he said over his shoulder as she left the room.

She'd heard stirrings from the direction of Estelle's room. She walked through the living room. Rumpole appeared in the doorway and scooted across the floor, then Estelle lurched unsteadily into view. She felt for the door, then rested against the jamb.

'Dear.' She paused for breath. 'I don't feel very well.' Her skin was colourless. She was sweating.

'I'll call Dr. Brinker. You'd better sit down.' Gillian grabbed the nearest little chair and Estelle sank into it, gasping. 'Have you got your pills? Have you taken one?' Gillian asked.

'I took one.'

Gillian ran to the kitchen. Eli was still on the phone. He saw her, said, 'I'll call you back,' and hung up.

'It's my mother,' she said, grabbing the phone and dialing. 'I think she's in trouble.' She was put through to Dr. Brinker. Eli stood up. Don't go, she wanted to say to him, but Dr. Brinker was talking. Eli leaned against the wall, watching her.

'The doctor will be here in fifteen minutes,' Gillian said as soon as she hung up.

'Look, you want an ambulance,' Eli said. 'They'll get here faster.'

'No! Estelle doesn't want them. Dr. Brinker knows what she wants.'

He looked through the doorway to where Estelle sat white-faced on the chair. 'You should call an ambulance.'

'I'm doing what she said she wanted me to do.'

He hesitated, then shrugged. 'OK. She's your mother.'

'Help me. I'm supposed to put her in her bed. I can't lift her myself.'

They carried Estelle to the bed and set her with her back against the pillows. Gillian covered her with a light blanket. Estelle's eyes were closed; her breath wheezed in her chest. Gillian pulled a chair up and sat holding her hand; the fingers were cold. Eli stood by the window, looking out.

Estelle opened her eyes. She saw Eli, and a puzzled look crossed her face. Her gaze shifted back to Gillian. 'Lewis,' she said with difficulty.

'Yes.'

'He gave me one of my best roses. The Bourbon Queen.' Her eyes closed again.

The minutes dragged by. Hurry, Gillian thought. Hurry.

Estelle's lips moved, her eyes still shut. Gillian leaned closer. 'Nat loved that black dress,' she murmured. Gillian's mind scrabbled frantically. Black dress, black dress. Oh, the photograph at the party.

Estelle's eyes opened, wider this time. She looked frightened. Her hand clutched at her chest. 'It hurts,' she whispered.

'Car,' Eli said. 'Looks like the doctor's here. I'll let her in.'

The next half hour passed in a blur. The doctor came in and Gillian went out of Estelle's room. Eli said he had to go. She thanked him for staying until the doctor came.

'That's OK,' he said. 'I hope she'll be all right.' He patted her shoulder with awkward sympathy and left. There's still a human being in there somewhere, Gillian thought. Then she forgot him. She went back to Estelle's room.

Dr. Brinker said, 'She's more comfortable now. I've given her some morphine.'

'Is it her heart?'

Estelle lay very still. She looked waxy, but Gillian could see that she was breathing.

Dr. Brinker moved away from the bedside. 'Congestive heart failure. The left side. Her heart can't handle the load. I've given her some drugs to reduce the pressure and the fluid in her lungs. A diuretic and ACE inhibitors. Remember, we talked about them at the office? They dilate the blood vessels. Her heart won't have to work as hard.'

'Is she going to be all right?'

'She's stable right now. This was bound to happen sometime soon. The drugs may give her quite a lot of relief. She could do pretty well for a few months. But there's no certainty. We'll have to see how it goes tonight, first.'

'I'll call my brother.'

'Yes, that's probably a good idea. I'll come back in a few hours—sooner, if you need me.'

Dr. Brinker went briskly, kindly, away, and Gillian stood in the doorway of Estelle's room, listening to her breathe. Then she picked up the telephone. She called Franklin and left a message with his secretary; she called Audrey and spoke to the answering machine; she called Edward's hotel and got his voice mail. When she hung up the house was filled with silence. She went back to the bedroom and looked at Estelle again.

Gillian poured herself a small glass of whisky. She sat down to wait.